EVERGOLD

EVERGOLD

Matt Boatman

JONES MEDIA
PUBLISHING

Disclaimer:

While all attempts have been made to verify information provided in this publication, the Author and the Publisher assume no responsibility and are not liable for errors, omissions, or contrary interpretation of the subject matter herein. The Author and Publisher hereby disclaim any liability, loss or damage incurred as a result of the application and utilization, whether directly or indirectly, of any information, suggestion, advice, or procedure in this book. Any perceived slights of specific persons, peoples, or organizations are unintentional.

Printed in the United States of America

ISBN: 978-1-948382-18-2 paperback
JMP2021.2

CONTENTS

CHAPTER ONE

There's something not right about this place. In so many ways it's like Earth, yet, the presence of darkness is heavy. Far heavier than Earth. He must be the cause of it all.

From the Journal of JahKub, champion of three trials

I GASP FOR AIR. SWEAT runs down matted hair into my eyes. I sit up and move fingers across my face and neck, body heat rising. Looking around, I try to ascertain my situation. The world is a blur of grey, white, and green.

In and out my vision focuses and de-focuses with my pulsing heartbeat. My mouth opens, but no sound comes out. Where am I? Where is my car? This doesn't look at all like Dakota. I should be in my car on the way home. I reach for my cell phone to call Drew, my mom, anyone, but it's not in my pocket. It must still be in my car, wherever that is.

I notice a flickering orange haze out of the corner of my eye. As I stand and begin to stagger toward the blur of orange, my head pulsates, vision becoming more clear.

Suddenly and without warning, the wind is knocked out of me. I'm tackled to the ground, back driven into the dirt by a heavy chest. My eyes bulge and I begin to panic as I fight against my assailant. "HELP!" I sharply scream, suddenly able to speak again. "HELP!" My words are dampened by the struggle.

I claw at the assailant's neck, trying to pry his hand from my mouth. He simultaneously holds my face into the ground with his left hand, while punching me with his right. I bite his left hand as he lands a heavy blow to my temple, nearly knocking me out. I'm losing my vision again. I struggle to breathe. Then I see his eyes.

One is pure ice—eerily like mine. So light blue it could be mistaken for white. The other is black. All black. Not just his pupil or his cornea. The entire eyeball is darker than the night sky above his head. He covers my mouth, which is now leaking blood into the sleeve of his robe. A cloth is wrapped tightly around his mouth, covering everything below his nose, strapped to his face by a loose, metal chain, which connects to more chains on his chest. He holds a finger to his covered lips, eyes never leaving mine.

Over his shoulder I see a tall, pallid man with sucked in cheeks and midnight hair. Next to him is a girl nervously biting her lip and looking around. The wind kicks up the skeleton of a desiccated leaf between us.

"You need to come with us," says the tall dark-haired man, nodding his head once. Slowly, the chained man lifts his dirt-crusted palm from my mouth. He keeps it close, ready to shut it if needed. He straddles me, right hand now pinning down my left arm.

I'm not about to go with these strangers. "The hell makes you think I would do that?" I ask.

The girl speaks up, quaver in her voice. "Look, I get it. We don't know what's going on either, but this robed guy has been protecting the two of us since we woke up like you a couple of days ago." I look around at them, trying to figure out all of the information from that one sentence.

"Wait. S-s-say that again please?"

"Listen, dude, you don't want to get caught out in these woods. Something ain't right about 'em. Tried to warn the last guy we found, but he wouldn't have it. Took off up that hillside not twenty minutes ago."

The chained man slowly gets off of me, ever ready to shut me up again. He looks at the dark-haired man and puts his finger to his mouth once more. The chained man flicks his head to the left and begins to walk through the long grass. The other man follows and the girl urges for me to come. I watch them walk until I can barely see their heads over the tall grass.

Below me on the declining hillside, I can see the orange glow clearly now. It isn't my wrecked car. It's a campfire kicking up sparks in a valley between two hills. In the background are silhouettes of much larger mountains. I think I can see that they are snowcapped but I'm not certain.

My hands get clammy as cold terror grips me. I hear a scream from the hills to my left. "NO, NO, NO, NO—PLEASE, NO—HELP! SOMEONE HE—" The snapping of something strong and organic echoes through the pines. Then complete silence, save the flickering sparks.

I change my mind, jump up, and run to the trail the trio had just forged. I catch up to the girl. She looks left over her shoulder and nods in approval as we leave the tall grass and enter the hills to the right of the field.

* * *

We walk in silence for hours. The road is a long, windy dirt path bordering fields and forest where lifeless people half-heartedly labor over the land. The eyes of these people watch us move carefully, quietly, slowly. Their movements are frail, their efforts even more so. Are they overworked or just malnourished? Either way, there's something not right about the way they stare at us through those dark, sunken sockets. It's almost as if something has sucked the life out of their souls. Every few miles we run into a group of them, and every time the reaction is the same—stop working, slowly bring their gaze to us, then watch us without any expression or indication of what they are thinking.

Then there are the dead. After hours of traveling, we pass by cold, lifeless bodies lie across low-hanging branches. No burial for loved ones out here, apparently. Not having much experience with the dead, my stomach begins to knot up and panic sets in. Water wells at the back of my nose and bile rises under my Adam's apple. My thoughts aren't crisp. My brain feels jumbled and logic is hard to find. I feel as though I am being run by the emotional component of my mind. I wonder for the thousandth time— where am I? I pray this is a joke, or an elaborately schemed reality TV show, otherwise I cannot fathom what I am seeing. This cannot be real.

We press on through the night. More than once I try to ask questions of the group, and more than once I am instantly shushed. I fear if I try again the chained man will not be so gentle about quieting me. Once day breaks the chained man permits us to talk more freely and rest intermittently. We still aren't allowed to sleep, but my nerves would have kept me awake anyway. It's been nearly twenty-four hours now, and I am thirsty.

"Fresh kicks," the dark-haired man says to me. I glance up at him. It feels like such an out of place thing to say in a situation like this.

"Thanks," I reply, not sure if he is being sarcastic or not

"What kind are yours?" the girl asks. He looks down at his feet.

"I dunno. Some off-brand I had before I went to prison."

"Is your prison around here?" I ask. They both laugh. The dark-haired man rests his hands on his kneecaps, apparently enjoying my stupidity. The girl isn't doing any better, although she is trying harder.

"I wish," he says.

"Was it you guys who pulled me from that wreck?"

"I wish," the girl says.

"What do you mean, 'you wish?' Am I on a show?"

"If by 'show' you mean a television show, then no, I'm afraid not." The girl's tone is serious again. "This place is evil. There's something unsettling about this forest. It feels alive. Like it gives life and takes life from whom it chooses. The things we have seen so far have been concerning, to say the least," she says, looking at the dark-haired man anxiously.

The chained man, who has been listening to our conversation, snaps his fingers at us and motions for us to follow. "Why are you following this guy anyway?" I ask the two.

The dark-haired man shrugs. "Did you not hear what happened to the last guy who ignored him?"

True. And what other option do I have? No food. No water. Not the remotest idea where I am. Soulless laborers watching our every movement. Some guy killed in the hills barely a hundred yards from me. Dead people across tree branches. At least these two seem semi-normal, although the dark-haired man worries me. I look back at the trail behind us. A desolate road with no landing place.

On the other hand, I assess continuing with the group. A dark-haired man who is apparently a convict, a girl who seems nice enough, and a strong man in chains—chains that someone else had to have put on him, right? I can follow them, or, I can bet on myself to make it out of here. But where is here? Where on Earth do people tear at the ground without purpose and leave their dead loved ones strewn across tree branches? Is it possible I am not in Dakota? Is this a dream?

I don't have a real reason to follow them, except that they seem to have a better grip on the situation than I do. But, I've been in bad situations before. I just need to find a water source in the next day and then I will be okay.

As I try to decide what to do, the group gets further and further away. Time is of the essence if I want to continue with them. Now out of sight, I close my eyes and take in a deep breath, thinking about the time I got lost on a hunting trip in bear country, where I survived three weeks with nothing but my knife. It was hard but that trip helped me become the man I am today. I think about all the things I did then to survive. I could do this alone.

Just as I make up my mind to survive on my own, one of those lifeless workers lifts a greyish purple finger at me from the forest, crossing over the threshold and onto the road for the first time. I hurry to catch up to the group.

* * *

After another stretch of ceaseless walking we reach a camp in thick forest at dusk. Around a mighty fire are twelve perfectly round, creamy white orbs that look like they're made of glass. The fire burns small logs with ferocity that a splash of gas would normally give it, but constantly. The flames attempt to lick the ten-foot high branches nearby, reaching the same ceiling every time the ebb returns. To the right are three feebly made cabins. The roofs are thatched with leafed branches from the forest. The doors are made of uneven sticks that prevent it from shutting flush.

To the left of the fire are three trees with chains dangling from their branches. The chains look like they are meant to hang a person, crucifix-style, but instead of nails, there's a metal platform to stand on, five feet off the ground. The dark-haired man asks the chained man, "These too?" The chained man nods. I wonder what this means. The chained man taps me on the shoulder and points to the chains on the tree furthest to the left. I shake my head. When I don't move, he nudges me toward it. I clench my jaw and tighten my fists. My heart beats at my eardrums.

The girl looks to the dark-haired man in desperation. "I can't believe we have to keep doing this. Why must we suffer more, Ranger? And look at that flame. It's not that big, but after a while, we just might burn."

What is going on? "Not that big?" I ask, incredulous. "That thing will burn me alive, not to mention all that metal will melt my skin. There's no way I am going to be chained up there willingly."

The dark-haired man, apparently named Ranger, walks near it. "As crazy as this sounds, it's not producing heat."

This is getting weirder and weirder. "You're lying."

"Come feel it." I walk over, keeping a weathered eye on Ranger as I approach. He isn't lying. The fire produces no heat. I wave my hand through it and then even leave it in for a few seconds. Nothing. No damage, no burnt skin, no fried hairs—nothing. I look back at the group hoping someone will give me more information.

The chained man stares at me with narrow eyes. The blue and black is unsettling. Again, he motions for me to get onto the metal platform.

He's got to be kidding. "I won't go up there."

"Just do it, man. Ranger tried to fight him in the beginning and almost died. And you heard—someone else *did* die. Just go," the girl pleads.

I shake my head in disbelief. This cannot be happening, but I see no way out. The chained man is much stronger than I and who knows what is in the forest. I walk up to the platform and turn around. Quickly, the chained man circles me, strapping me in and adjusting and moving my locks. He makes me stretch my arms out the full length of my wingspan.

Once I've been secured, he puts Ranger and the girl in the same position, with the girl between Ranger and me. A cool breeze licks the pine trees and teases the heatless fire. The girl shivers. The chained man disappears into one of the cabins dividing our fire from the forest.

Seconds later, he walks out with three poorly crafted jars made of brown clay. Ranger and the girl immediately protest. I wonder what awful substance could be in the jars to make them react like that.

"Nooo. Not again. Please don't make us drink this again," the girl pleads.

"Dammit," Ranger says, shaking his head in defeat while looking at the ground.

"What? What is it?" My pulse starts racing.

"Just drink it and pray the night moves quickly," Ranger answers. The chained man tips the jar toward Ranger who gags as he drinks its contents. He gags some more and spits out what looks like flakes of clay. A rich, earthy substance oozes out of his mouth and over his bottom lip. He stops moving for seconds. Then he begins to hyperventilate. Then he screams. The sound echoes through the night sky and drives birds out of nearby trees.

The girl begins to cry as the chained man moves toward her. He has remnants of clay stuck to his finger tips and palms as he tips the jar toward her lips. She also gags and nearly gurgles up the liquid, then drops her head. Her hair hangs over her face, like a prisoner in the stocks.

The chained man tosses the empty jar and approaches me. I have no idea what to expect. He motions for me to tilt my head back. Ranger is screaming now. The girl is whimpering. The wind is blowing hard. It blows my hair back into the tree. The chained man's robe flies at me. I don't want to do this. I struggle against the chains. I look down at my hands. Is this really happening? He closes on me. I pinch my eyes shut to protect them from dust. The chained man opens my mouth with little effort, forcing the contents of the jar down my throat. I drink the substance. It tastes like thick chalk water and pine needles.

I feel my chest immediately get tight. Tears stream down my face. My hands fight to clutch my chest. I want to hide.

My vision becomes fuzzy, then clear, as if a giant magnifying glass was being moved close then far away from my face. I can see small branches with intricate detail on trees one hundred yards away, then, as a visual seesaw, I cannot discern anything and everything seems far away.

In one of my moments of clarity, I see that the chained man is carefully watching me, hunched over, scientific. He pinches the fat on my ribs then under my biceps, then stares into my eyes. The girl continues to whimper. Suddenly, Ranger screams, "OH NO, HERE IT COMES AGAIN, ATIA."

Atia. That must be the girl's name. I need to do something to distract myself from whatever it is that's coming. I begin to count sheep. I try to count out loud but my words are slurred. I can't speak. My legs struggle to hold my body up. I fear my arms will rip out of their sockets. It's as if my mind and my body are not my own. Anything I try to hold in my mind's eye quickly evaporates. I'm losing control.

Someone asks me a question. I can barely hear between the sound of wind passing by my ears and Ranger's screaming. Another question. I can tell it's coming from Atia, but I still can't hear her.

"What did you say?" I scream to her. Finally I can speak.

"What. Is. Your. Name?" with the last part, she runs out of breath.

"Nirue," I tell her. The chained man runs back into the cabin, leaving us alone.

Then, the visions begin.

A woman with frizzy hair sits alone at a dimly lit table in a dark room. A bar. A bar in an inn. Men pass her by and each time they do, she sprays herself with perfume. Then more perfume. Then so much perfume the people around her begin to choke, then they all die. Then the barkeep flips her a coin and she stands up, revealing a pregnant stomach. She steps on the faces of the men as she leaves the inn.

Next I see a man swimming for his life from a dark shadow. It's me. I am swimming and looking behind me as bubbles escape my lips.

I see three sheep and a shepherd sitting on a green field in day. Then it's night. Then it is morning. It's a time-lapse view of the same thing over the course of four days.

I can't escape. I feel like I'm drowning. It is the feeling of trying to wake up but some outside force keeps me from doing so. An out of body experience. I can't breathe and I can't think. I can just observe, but nothing more. I am in a dark cave. I am running. I carry a torch as I run. Whatever is chasing me is getting close. It extinguishes my torch. I fall down. It grabs me by the throat and squeezes tight.

I feel completely alone. I wonder if people at home even notice I am gone. Where am I?

Lucidity. The wind is so fierce it is hard to shut my own eyelids. A creature with long claws and a tail with a triangle at its tip watches me from a high perch from a tree on the other side of the fire, just left of the last cabin. The creature is blue with black stripes. It has giant oval eyes that are all black, and it smiles at me with long sharp black teeth.

The creature bounds down from its high perch onto the roof of the nearby buildings, then down and gracefully around the fire. It stands directly behind the fire, revealing all of its horrific features, then, it violently bounds at me. In moments it reaches me, its claw touching my stomach. It looks at me with black, lifeless eyes.

I try to scream but I can't. I can't even move. I am paralyzed. Tears of fear stream down my cheeks, but I can't blink. It traces a claw across my stomach, drawing blood from the lightest pressure possible. Standing at eye level, the creature holds up a long golden nail in its hand. It slams the nail into the tree above my head. In my mind I flinched.

Next, it pulls a golden bow from somewhere behind me and hooks it to the nail. Without moving its lips the creature speaks. "Evergold" is what I hear. Its eyes tell me it knows I heard it, though I don't know what it could mean. A bow. Memories come flooding into my head. Practicing on my parent's ranch for the Olympic qualifiers. The Olympic qualifiers. Hunting. Driving home from the qualifiers. Talking to my mom. Talking to Drew. The feeling of a sturdy arm and the surgical precision of my shot. The feeling of holding the bowstring perfectly taut. My memories quickly evaporate as I return to the present.

The creature moves on to Ranger and Atia. It takes one last look at me, then my vision fades again. I fight to see what the creature is doing. Will it kill Atia and Ranger?

Then another creature appears on the same perch. It looks somehow different. This creature is black with red markings. My vision is blurry, then magnified again. The new creature grins, revealing white razors. Its body language tells me it doesn't intend anything good. The chained man emerges from the cabin. He looks at the creature, then noticeably swallows with raised eyebrows. He's scared of this thing, whatever it is.

He rushes back into the cabin, leaving the door open. This new creature crawls down the tree face first, leaving me alone. It bounds toward the cabin and inside, then back at me. Again, it smiles. My vision goes blurry. I hear a muffled scream and see a flash of blue. It grows bigger. I pass out.

CHAPTER TWO

He tricked me. Like a schoolkid falling into the not-so obvious pit, my demise has become somewhat certain.

Daltoor, the night before he died

I WAKE TO THE SMELL of food. Ranger and Atia are already eating around the still blazing fire. The chained man notices I am awake and sets me free. I crane my neck in circles and rub my wrists. They are red and tender to touch.

A plate with food steams on a log. There are four logs total, and all are claimed save the one with the food. I sit down and begin eating. Ranger tells me its pork sausage, over easy eggs and bammy—a type of flatbread made by mixing the cassava root with salt in coconut oil. I look at him blankly.

"How was your night?" He asks me while flipping a pocket dagger up and down, always catching the grip. He seems to do that a lot.

I wipe pork grease from my lips and say, "Fine. Yours?"

He smiles and shakes his head. "Good."

"And you?"

Atia shakes her head and doesn't respond. She opens her mouth and motions her hand as if she is about to say something, then decides to eat instead. I shrug and finish my food.

The chained man jumps up as if he had forgotten something. He quickly runs over to my tree and removes the bow, and a note under the golden nail. I notice Atia's nail is blue and Ranger's black. He throws the bow down and quickly reads the note. He looks at me, then back at the note, then me, then the note, then drops his hands in disbelief. He looks to the sky, raises open palms upward then over his heart. Then, the lock over the chain on his mouth clicks open. He lets it slide off of his body.

He then carefully picks up the bow and begins to study it, carefully, the way he examined me last night. His chains rattle as he adjusts clothing under his robe.

"This is the first time the creature came down from the tree" Ranger offers.

"So you saw that thing too? What did he say?"

"*Darkwater*. Thing sounded like a snake."

"Did he talk to you, Atia?"

"Yeah. He said, '*Dicers*'." My curiosity takes over, so I walk to the chained man and grab the note he left on the ground. It reads:

"*Use these weapons of old to kill King Maji in Rizcarth.*"

"What does it say?" Atia asks. I read her the note. She rubs her forehead, as if working the answer out of her head. Ranger rips the note from my hands, as if he doesn't trust what I said. Atia peers over his shoulder. I decide to forget them and examine my bow.

It is perfect. Long and strong and gilded with depictions of epic battles from history. Zeus versus the titans. Leonidas and the 300. I notice one that doesn't make sense. I bring it closer to my face to investigate. It's a picture of a man sharpening the claws of a huge beast. The man is tethered to the beast. The beast stares out while the man looks down, busy working.

Then I am handed a grey axe with green runes carved up the edge of the blade. Focused on the present, the chained man claps, sending a miniature sonic boom through the trees. I see a visible pulse wave begin near the fire and grow into the forest, like a drop of water on a still pond.

"Time to go," Atia says.

"Go where?" I ask.

"Just follow him and don't ask questions."

We walk ten miles to the northwest of our camp. I know how far because I counted. The chained man stops us at gazebo looking structure made of weathered greystone. Leading to the gazebo is a stone path made up of twenty steps. Moss has infested the pillars over the roof of the gazebo. Before the steps are three chests. One green, one blue, one black.

"It's time you understand what is going on. My name is Bertram. I am your Sherpa. You, my friends, were all in terrible accidents. Accidents that by all rights should have taken your life. You are in a coma." I shake my head. Atia's arms slowly drop to her sides. Ranger's jaw is slack. He continues.

"You see, there are three universal laws that can never be broken. The first is you can never go faster than the speed of light. Even if traveling on a vehicle at the speed of light, you could not propel yourself outward to then go faster than the speed at which the vehicle is traveling. The second is that cause always comes before affect. I cannot break your shin with a swift kick before I deliver the swift kick. My action of kicking you must come before the reaction of your shin breaking." Ranger's shin bone snaps. Then, Bertram kicks it. I almost lose sight of what's going on due to Ranger's howling. Bertram claps his hands. Ranger rubs his shin bone, which is now completely healed.

"THE HELL WAS THAT FOR?" Bertram ignores him and continues.

"The third, and most applicable here is that the Universe cannot accept a soul until death has completely conquered it. Once a person enters a comatose state they are sent to another habitable planet. There are literally thousands. You were lucky enough to land here. Now, where was I?" He scratches his chin.

Atia says, "We are in a coma."

"Right! Thank you. Now, you aren't dead but you aren't alive either. It's a glitch in the system if you will. This is your last chance to cheat death. It is the Universe's way of figuring out what to do with you. Of *testing* you. This place is reminiscent of Earth, but very different at the same time. Creatures are fiercer. Adventures are more bold. The rules are skewed, slightly. Physics doesn't apply as soundly as earth. You are able to push the limits if you can figure out how. Each and every one of you are here for different reasons. Each one of you have trials you must complete. Four in all. Some you must do together, others you must do alone. If you complete your trials without dying, you are given a second chance on earth. If you die here . . . well, you know."

No one speaks. The wind blows through the empty pines. In the distance, a grey corpse staggers north of us with no direction or purpose. The funneling air moving through the pines reminds me how alone I really am now. Ranger breaks my daze.

"I think it's quite obvious who these chests are for," he says with an air of certainty. "Atia gets the blue because of *Dicers*. I get black because of *Darkwater* and you get green by process of elimination."

Bertram gives a nod of approval. I had that thought but also reasoned with other qualifications. Ranger was the non-player in my eyes. His weapon and hair color only qualify him for black. Atia and I were toss-ups. She has ombre brown and light blue hair and I have icy blue eyes. It could have gone either way, but Ranger was right. Curses for looking at every angle.

I move to open my chest and am grabbed from behind by Bertram. He wags a finger at me and points me up the steps. We proceed up the stairs. Ranger first, then Atia, then me. Bertram holds his hands inside his robes kimono-style. The mid-day sun shines between two pillars directly onto his face. He looks older than before, and worried. He pulls a golden staff from a nearby pillar and enters it into a small hole in the floor. Our world speeds up.

In an instant, we land at the top of a sand dune with the accuracy and speed of a hummingbird—controlled and concise. Dust and sand fly three stories high. It's devilishly hot, and we're still in the clothes we woke up in. My boots are filled with sand. Ranger tilts his head parallel with the ground and starts hitting it with a fist, like a swimmer does to drain water from an ear. Atia's skinny hands canopy her eyes.

We travel down the dune creating large holes with each step until we reach flat ground that has the appearance of a road. It certainly has the wear and tear of travel. Bertram points down the road. "Finish in no longer than two days." He vanishes.

"So now what?" Atia asks.

"Figure out a way home is my vote," I offer. Ranger shakes his head.

"It won't work. Did you not hear what Bertram said? We have to do these things to get out alive."

"So what, you think we should just show up, unannounced, get a meet and greet with some King, *kill him*, then mosey on back to this spot?"

"You got a better idea, smart guy?"

"Yeah. Ditch you two scramps and get the hell home."

"Yeah I've tried that too. Bertram found me and chained me to him until Atia woke up. And what about the blue creature, huh, 'scramp'? What about the fact you were sitting there, wherever the hell you're from, now you're here? Explain that to me, Nyrew."

"It's Nirue, bro." As mad as I am, he has a point. None of this makes sense. I have a golden bow and quiver across my back, after being teleported from a forest to a sand dune with two strangers. They are my best chance for survival.

"Sorry, man. Sun is getting to me. Much hotter than where I'm from! Let's start by picking a direction. Which way should we go?" From down the road, Atia points and says, "We head that way." I look at Ranger, who dares me to challenge him with his posture. I shrug and begin to walk. It's my best chance to make it out alive, and at this point, that's the only thing I care about.

* * *

We hit the road with a good pace. Nobody talks for a few minutes, then Atia speaks up. "What do you guys think about this task? I mean, how are we supposed to *kill* a *King*?

I don't say anything. Ranger answers with confidence, "I'll walk right up to the bloody bastard and cut his throat open." I smile because I know that if he's the one that will put himself out there, that means I'll have a better chance of making it out alive.

"Okay great. If it's that easy I'll just poke around the local seamstress while you slay the dragon," Atia says sarcastically.

"Sounds great 'Tia. Pick out somethin' sexy for me. I think somethin' black would look great with your brown and blue hair."

"Don't call me that you buffoon," Atia exclaims amidst Ranger's laughter.

The road stretches for hours. The sun is sweltering hot. I've always enjoyed a good sweat. It clears the mind and rids the body of toxins. I don't enjoy a sweat like this. "Much more of this and we will be in trouble," I say. "We need to get water."

Ranger stops and pretends to fix something in his boot. "Don't look up," he says calmly. "There are two people watching us about three-hundred tics away." Atia and I freeze.

"How do you know they're watching us?" she asks.

"At first I didn't think they were. That's when there were five o' them. I haven't seen the other three for a while now. They keep veering off path and takin' high vantage points. Get ready." We walk another mile to a fork in the road. There are two signs loosely nailed to a wooden stake. One pointing right, one left. Dark red paint crosses out what had previously been written in white. The sign to the left now reads "Death." The sign to the right reads "Rizcarth."

Atia says, "We should follow the signs."

Ranger agrees. I shake my head. "Where did you see the group of men watching us?" I ask. "Just up there." Ranger points *Darkwater* left of the fork toward some palm trees.

"Then we go left."

They exchange narrowed side-eyes. "We have to go to Rizcarth, right? Assuming it is a city, it would make sense there is more travel to and from it. It would make more sense that a group of thieves would hide out on the road to the city than the one less traveled. They would go where there is more traffic, right? Besides, the original signs were carved and filled with white paint. They have a more professional look to them."

Ranger and Atia aren't convinced. I glare because the post mid-day sun is directly in my eyes. "Look. We don't have much time before nightfall and we have a group of men watching us. I'm thirsty and just want to get a better grip on the situation. I'm going left." Ranger and Atia argue for a few minutes then decide to follow me.

We walk another hour before the road suddenly stops in front of a dune roughly twenty oxen wide and forty tall. Ranger starts to say something smart when an arrow whizzes by my head. Ranger unsheathes *Darkwater* and I immediately load *Evergold*. Two men approach us from a dune on the right. "Put down your weapons, *assassins*," one of them yells.

I respond, "Not a chance, you put down yours."

They look at each other, never dropping their aim or weapons. At the same time, thirty or so men appear from behind surrounding dunes and descend upon us, arrows pointed at our heads. I tell Ranger and Atia to put down their weapons. In seconds, we are completely circled.

CHAPTER THREE

Terrible circumstances are what brought you here. But don't you realize, the only way out is by believing? Faith is what this world would ask of you.

Siam, journal entry number forty-eight

WHAT BUSINESS DO YOU HAVE in Rizcarth?" The fat one asks.

I look at Ranger, then back at him. "We are just travelers passing through."

"So . . . You're not an assassin?"

"No?"

"Excuse me, then! Sorry, so sorry! We thought you were part of King Maji's men!" A fat bald man with white around the ears runs over to us. He is wearing sandals and a white robe with a blue stripe running from the top to the bottom. The rest of the men relax their weapons.

"You will have to excuse my friend. Sykel over here is a little string-happy. He's a shoot first and ask questions later type of guy. We thought you were assassins going to the city. Our mistake. You have to understand. Look at the way you're dressed! Anywho, the name is Davn." He extends a hand. I take it. He draws loose circles with his left index finger in the direction of the man that shot the arrow. "Sykel over here is my brother."

Sykel speaks. "We are a militia group killing every would-be assassin that attempts to go to Rizcarth. Did you see our sign?"

I shoot an "I told you so" look at Ranger and Atia. "That explains a lot. So you don't like this Maji guy?"

The group laughs through cloth covered mouths. "First of all, its pronounced, Mah-gee and no, we don't like him. You serious?" Davn asks.

I look around and then decide to puff. "Well, we aren't from around here but we have been hired by a wealthy and respected man to take care of this Maji, as you say. But to be honest we just got here and are not up to speed on the situation."

"Are you now?" Davn says spryly while rubbing his chin. Some men continue laughing, which causes Ranger to grit his teeth. Davn catches Ranger's frustration and offers two open palms to me, "Don't mind them. Do you know what you're up against? It will be quite the task to even find him, let alone get to him. Come." He motions for us to follow.

It's getting later in the day. Beneath us in the distance is a magnificent city with a huge river flowing through it. The entire city sits in a basin which slopes down in elevation from all angles—like an exaggerated valley of sorts. It's a good thing this place doesn't rain much.

A thick and vast forest of palm trees surrounds the city itself. There are four entrances into the city, with walls of trees acting as a funnel to each one. In the middle of the city is a rock with a building carved into it. Not quite a mountain but also not a hill. Its steps lead down into the city square.

Davn points to the structure in the rock. "Just in there is your prize. The citizens that now grace those streets were the most ruthless killers imprisoned for hundreds of miles around. Rapists. Murderers. The cruelest of the cruel. Maji freed them all, one by one from all the surrounding cities that trade with the capitol here, until he had a big enough group to overthrow the capitol itself. Maji's guards are the finest of the lot. The worst in moral and the best in fighting. The most extreme on both spectrums.

Anyone who attempts to kill King Maji will die. It is axiomatic." He lets out a low, long sigh.

I begin to say something but Atia cuts me off, "We have no choice. It's hard to explain. But we gotta try."

Davn looks at Sykel. "Well, if you must, you must. Sykel – garb them with appropriate attire so they may enter. Tonight is as good a night as any."

We spend the next ten minutes changing into new clothes. Head to toe we get a makeover. On our feet are boots of animal hide that are light and good for moving in the sand. We don tanned tunics and white cowhide shorts. Red sashes are tied across our foreheads with knots in the back. I add a rawhide belt and a few smaller red sashes across my biceps. He gives us each a Niqab. "Now you look the like a Maji assassin," Davn says.

"You said this was as good a night as any. Why?" I ask as I tighten one of my bicep sashes.

"Tonight is a celebration. Tonight is a night where the assassins drink the blood of animals. It's a pagan ritual and, if you ask me, an odd one even for the bloodthirsty. They follow animal blood with wine. *Strong wine.* They believe the wine mixes with the animal blood and replenishes all the blood they have ever shed in battle. They say, '*New blood, new energy, new life.*'"

The King will surely be among the many. You might find your opportunity to achieve your task. *If you can find him.*" Davn purposely makes eye contact with this last statement. Ranger and Atia don't notice but I do. "Best of luck to you. From the people of Golon, from the Senators, for mankind all around this desert, we wish you blessings."

"Thank you," Atia says to Davn. The men exchange forearm grips. After a few miles walk we enter the forest of palm trees. It's much more dense than I expected, yet visibility is excellent due to the thin nature of the palm-trunk. Colorful snakes and scorpions bury themselves in the sand as we approach. Atia spots a black scorpion scuttling up a tree trunk. She stabs it with one of her *Dicers* and uses the other to extract poison. Her *Dicer* leaves a blue glow in the trunk. Ranger and I think it smart and collect poison ourselves. We spend nearly twenty minutes doing it.

It takes us another forty minutes to get from the edge of the palm forest to the row of trees leading to the city gate, not counting the time we spent collecting poison. We approach the west gate and pull the Niqab's across our face, so only our eyes are visible.

"I feel frozen when I look at you," Atia jests. I smile.

"What's the plan?" Ranger asks.

A plan. Of course they want a plan. The only problem is I haven't thought of one yet. I have had to spend so much mental thinking on my situation that I haven't thought about what I would do once we got into the city. It's not like I have any experience in these things.

"First let's figure out who the King is. After that we will *improvise*." Ranger appears hesitant as he stares into the city. He looks at Atia, who shakes her head and gets behind him. "Well, ain't like we got a choice," he says, putting one foot in front of the other.

Getting into the city is easy. We get a few weird looks but nothing *too* alarming. The clothing Davn gave us helps us blend in. By now, the sun has tucked behind the curvature of the horizon, although the city is lit well enough for us to see.

It is magnificent. Smooth tan and red marble buildings loom over grey cobblestone streets. Establishments, trade stations and living quarters are untarnished and without blemish. The river we saw from the dune runs through the middle of the city, for the entirety of the city and beyond. It divides the city into two halves. A large bridge made of smooth grey and tan stone spans the river.

We walk up the bridge. Three men are arguing over a game of dice. Other than that, there aren't many people traversing. I take a deep breath. I look up and notice that I can see every star in the universe. This is much more than I have ever seen. It's as if the atmosphere has been lifted and the heavens revealed. It looks somehow different than the sky I remember in rural Dakota, though, I can't figure out why.

At the apex of the bridge I look down at the river. There is a hint of algal bloom illuminating the bottom with a light neon-green hue. A massive creature swimming in the river cascades shadows off of the walls of the stone canal. Something as big as an elephant. No. This would dwarf an elephant. This creature disperses water like a grown man in a bathtub. It is hundreds of yards away, but closing quick. It dives and is gone. Atia and Ranger look at each other quizzically.

I maintain focus. I have always been good at that. Ten seconds. Twenty seconds. I find the shadow. The creature is beneath us. As it goes under the bridge it disturbs the algae, producing a neon-green silhouette of the creature. I catch the end of it and run to the other side to see more.

A whale. A massive, full-grown whale is swimming in a river in the middle of the desert. I suppose I should stop acting so surprised. The drunkards that had once been arguing begin to cheer. Almost at once, everyone on the bridge and banks of the river let out a roar. We partake in the cheering to maintain our disguise, though awkwardly. I look back up into the sky half expecting a dinosaur to fly down. In the distance, I can hear music coming from the square just on the other side of the bridge. The festival has begun, and so has our first trial.

CHAPTER FOUR

There is something special about life-or-death scenarios with those similarly situated. It can feel like a game that isn't all that bad to be a part of. That is, unless you lose.

Tharamir, the Voice of the City

WE CROSS THE BRIDGE AND head into the square. "What a macabre scene," Ranger says under his breath. Crossing a single bridge was all it took for the beauty of the city to disappear. Bodies hang from nooses on almost every balcony. Some of the victims are women and children. Apparently these killers didn't discriminate. Toward the center of the town square is a three story bonfire. Rising from the center of it is a statue of a whip intertwined with a scroll.

There are other smaller fires scattered about the main square. Twenty yards to the right of the biggest fire, two men duel. The sharpness of their blades cut the cool desert air. The sounds of the blades are crisp, as if the wind is sharpening the already razor fine edges.

Four musicians come down from one of the many hills in the city. They play make-shift lutes and Zurnas. Further north of the fire, dogs are eating the remains of a man. We find a vendor selling questionable meat and flasks of water. I put my axe to the man's throat.

"We'll take three legs and four flasks of water." I don't show any emotion, but underneath my garb, I am sweating. My red headband keeps it from entering my eyes. I stare my icy blues into his browns. I figure in a city of thieves, murderers and rapists, you have to take what you want. Offering this man a few shams and negotiating a fair agreement would make us stand out. Ranger follows my lead. He walks behind the vendor and presses *Darkwater* into the small of his back. The vendor never turns around. He displays a rotten yellow and brown mouth in a sinister fashion.

"It would be my pleasure . . . I didn't catch your name. Matter of fact, I haven't seen you around these parts."

"Don't worry about me," I say with an authoritative posture. "I'm right in front of you. Worry about me when I'm out of sight. When you sleep at night. Worry when you walk alone among the palms. THEN, you worry. For now, give me my damn food and water." He lifts his hands up, palms toward me in surrender. He gestures toward his supply cart nearby. I flick my head toward it. He moves slowly and in plain sight. Ranger keeps close watch. The vendor fills a couple of bags and walks over. He shoves them into my stomach and walks away, cursing at me in a foreign language. A crowd of people nearby see this and whisper under their breath. The vendor yells something up one of the sloped hills in a language I have never heard.

"What are you thinking?" Atia asks me with an open mouth, tongue displayed slightly forward in disgust.

"*Fitting in.*"

"Well you sure know how to draw a crowd," Ranger says, looking up the same alley the vendor just yelled at. Five men stare at us from the top. One of them yells something and points.

I don't know what it means but I know it's bad. Dice games stop. The subtle pluck of a lute alerts me that the music has also stopped. People from all around the square gravitate toward the scene. A slight breeze kicks up a miniature dust devil. For a moment, all that is heard is the spinning dust. The group descends from the alley, walking through filth and over rotting corpses without breaking eye contact with us.

"Which one of you robbed my brother?" No response.

"Speak up, coward."

Before I could step up Ranger unsheathes *Darkwater.* "I did. What of it?" It's now I realize how truly massive Ranger is—a specimen of physical health and prowess. Truth be told, I wouldn't want to fight him one on one. I'm glad he's on my side, for now, and I'm even happier he's engaging in the one-on-one combat and not me.

"Good. The bigger they are, the more food for my dogs." Ranger doesn't flinch. "Shooting a man through the back. Where is your honor? Why does he have your bow?" He points to me. A murderer talking of honor. I totally misjudged the situation.

Ranger doesn't answer. Rather, he stares at his opponent, eyes tight like a door barely cracked open. His red headband blows in the wind. People form a circle. Atia whispers to me, "I didn't see everyone getting worked up when those men were dueling earlier. Why the big deal now?"

"I don't know. Maybe this guy is someone important." Ranger enters the circle to meet this challenger. There is no formal meeting of the blades or cordial bow. Just fighting. The man uses two short scimitars. He flings them around with skill, grace and speed. He dances around the ring in a taunting manner. Ranger stays calm and focused. The man urges the crowd to get animated. They do. The second the fighting begins, I feel sick to my stomach. What was I thinking being glad someone else decided to fight for me? What kind of man am I? I feel the urge to knock an arrow but resist as I see the challenger's posse watching me. You've got to change, Nirue.

The attacker jumps and tries to land an overhand aerial attack on Ranger. Ranger greets the attack with *Darkwater* and deflects the blow. He lands an uppercut-punch right into the stomach of the challenger. The crowd collectively gasps. Ranger goes on the offensive. His attacks are wild but strong. Three overhand hacks then two side swings.

He looks tired. Two scimitars cut through the air and nearly hit Ranger as he ducks. They cut off the back of his headband. Ranger gets more focused. He holds *Darkwater* out in front of him to keep the assailant at distance. The man laughs and continues to taunt Ranger and the crowd. "*Arrogant piss*," Ranger says under his breath.

With wide eyes and a bulging neck he sprints at his challenger. Screaming wildly and spilling drool from his lips, he jumps and brings *Darkwater* down with all of the force in his body. The challenger tries to deflect but neither his body strength nor the strength of his scimitars is a match for Ranger or his blade. *Darkwater* slices right through and cuts deep into the head of the challenger, all the way to the jaw. Blood rushes down his neck the way a river flows down a steep mountain in heavy rain. When Ranger removes his blade, brains spill out on the cobblestone. The crowd erupts.

Atia and I scream for Ranger, adrenaline coursing through our veins. Ranger stumbles backward, lips parted. His knees wobble together. He smiles at us. Something's wrong. He looks at us again and clutches his chest. Ranger falls to one knee.

CHAPTER FIVE

Is time always on your side? Is it always against you?
Is it real?

Reflections, verses 5–6, Tao Lin

WE RACE OVER TO RANGER.

"Are you okay?" Atia asks touching his neck, his shoulders then opening his eyelids. He brushes her hand away.

"I'm fine. Whole thing just drained me is all. Never seen someone's brains before." I press a palm to my heart and look upward. I walk closer and offer him a trembling hand to get up. I'm so glad it wasn't anything worse.

When everything settles down we find a small fire unattended and take some time to eat around it. The meat, albeit stringy and tough, fills our bellies. A man gives us a bowl of soup in honor of Rangers dominance. It tastes like bark but we eat it anyways. We don't have utensils so our hands suffice for the time being.

"You did great out there," Atia says quietly. "What was going through your head?" Ranger pauses and stares at a family strung from a low hanging balcony.

"Nothing, really. I just sort of swelled up with anger. I had good distance on him with *Darkwater* and didn't want to let him get close."

"You know you didn't have to do that for me. I can fight my own battles," I say.

"I know. But I've always been that way. Always figured the biggest man has to represent the group, even if it ain't his gripe. Seems to always get me worse off than I started, though."

I feel differently about Ranger now. Blood will do that to a man. I trust him. What he did shows he really is in this with me and not against me. Here I am, glad he enters the fight for me, and this dude lays his life on the line for someone he hardly knows. Never again will I doubt the big man.

"Alright then. But next time, I fight my own battles. Deal?"

Ranger smiles and nods in approval. "Deal."

A voice speaks up from the shadows. "You guys aren't from around here are you?" The man's face is shrouded in darkness beneath a black cloak and niqab. He hits a pipe that swirls green smoke through the air like an uncoiling snake, momentarily illuminating his dark eyebrows. "What makes you say that, stranger?" I ask.

"Those weapons you bare—they aren't familiar, and I am familiar with weapons. And the way you handled that merchant . . . It wasn't custom. Since Maji established the code, we buy from merchants. Otherwise, how could we eat?" I'm not sure what to say. He is right and I was wrong. I thought I was fitting in. Instead, I was standing out.

"You're lucky your friend over here handled your dirty work. That man was one of the ten." Ranger follows my lead and pretends to know what they are talking about. Atia doesn't pick up on it. "The ten?"

The man chuckles and steps into the light. He offers his pipe to me, stem first, and has a seat in between Ranger and Atia. I wave a decline. "King Maji picked the ten deadliest assassins in Rizcarth to protect him. Fortunately for him, they do. They bear loyalty to the King. He released them from prison. He gave them a new life. With that came a city with few rules. Protect the King and live by the code."

"Who are you?" Ranger asks.

"I am Zajic. I am the son of a prominent Senator who used to rule this city. I am under-cover, doing a reconnaissance of sorts. We intend to take this city back. If we fell the King we can take back control. Strike the shepherd and the sheep will scatter, they say. These people will jump at each other's throat and the city will implode. Everyone will want to rule once Maji is dead. The hard part is getting to him."

"We intend to kill him," I tell Zajic. He laughs.

"Keep your voice down! Look . . .you should stay away. If an assassination attempt goes bad he will double down and hide out in his fortress. We can't have that. We *need* him comfortable and trusting of his people. That way our men can take him out. You will just spook the roost."

I clench my jaw. He doesn't understand. There's no point in trying to explain, so I change direction. "You're probably right. What is this festival anyway?"

He laughs again. "This is their biggest holiday of the year. A day dedicated to celebrating the sack of Rizcarth. You see that whip and scroll?" He gestures toward the top of the big fire. I nod.

"That was how the Senators used to rule the people of Golon. They would conquer a city and give their people the choice between slavery and death. Not much of a choice, but a choice nonetheless. The whip represents the disengaged nature of my people. We were just as heartless as these assassins. But what else was there to do? If you attack a city, the city must fight back. If you win, you cannot thank them for the fight and leave. No. You must either kill their people or enslave them. There is no other way around it."

"What about forcing peace? Like telling them that if they attack again you will kill them, thereby giving the survivors a second chance for the time being?" Atia asks. Zajic shakes his head. "It doesn't work like that. If you leave them be, they will lick their wounds and regroup. After a while, the realization that we killed their loved ones will set in and with enough time, we will have a whole other uprising. They will formulate a new leader and next thing you know, we're in another war. We couldn't risk that happening. Then we lose more of *our* men, for what? So that we feel good about ourselves? I'll tell you what feels good. Looking across the table and seeing my family and not having to look over my shoulder everywhere I go."

He bows his head as if remembering something terrible. "I suppose you don't know how the festival works, eh?"

"We know the basics," Ranger puffs.

He absently rubs at his arms and shakes his head, as if he cannot believe how pathetic we are. "Here is how tonight will go. They will have celebrations and partake in customs from all over Golon. At the end of the night there is a contest. Whatever you do, *do not enter the contest.*"

"What contest?" I ask.

"Rizcarth has spent the last two weeks choosing the prettiest woman out of all their slaves to be King Maji's Queen. Every year he does this, and every year he grows tired of having a woman around shortly after marrying her. For the game, you must try to convince the woman to bed you. She will be with King Maji's mother. The Queen and Maji's mom have been getting acquainted ever since she was chosen. You get a few sentences to pitch yourself, and that's it. If she doesn't like you, you die. If you say something the King doesn't like, you die. If she chooses to sleep with you, you live. So, yeah, I suppose it's not all bad, but still, don't enter."

"Sounds like a set up. Won't the King kill you for trying to sleep with his wife?"

"Yes and no. The King is no babe to perversions. He wouldn't think of his Queen any different for bedding another man because she will be dead in a few weeks anyway. She is of no more value than the rotting corpses littering these grounds. But it is merely an excuse for him to kill the innocent. Trust me, if you don't win you are certain to die, and he does the executions himself."

"I'll do my best to stay away," I say while looking at Ranger.

We finish eating and grab our things. Camels draw eight carriages near the city square. They are more like wagons than carriages as the roofs have been cut off. Each one is full of barrels. As the camels get closer to the main fire, it becomes apparent that the barrels are different colors. The first four wagons carry barrels with a russet shade to them while the second four are black. The blood. I had forgotten. "I suppose we will be drinking some blood tonight," I say to the group.

"You don't *have* to," Zajic says. "You could practice your bartering skills again," he says with a mocking smile.

I shoot him a stern look. "No times for jokes goodman. I could have gotten us killed."

"*Relax.* What did you say your name was again?"

"I'm Nirue. This is Atia and the big fella over there is Ranger." Ranger does a curtsey. Atia rolls her eyes.

"So how does this work?" She asks.

"How does what work?"

"I mean this whole notion of drinking blood. Do we just go up and get a cup?"

"Basically, little flower," Zajic says while scratching his chin, eyes in the sky. I break his chain of thought.

"What do you mean, 'basically?'"

"The blood you will drink has been harvested since the process of selecting the Queen. They finished yesterday, which means the older barrels may be poisonous by now." He starts going into more detail but it is too late. A trumpet blows in the square.

People begin walk toward the now-tapped barrels. Men push and shove to get to the front. "Everyone wants to be first to tap the newer barrels," I whisper to Ranger and Atia.   "Could be. Could also be that they are barbaric and being first is instinctual," Ranger suggests. I shrug.

By the time we get our drinks filled, the first three barrels had been tapped. Then he comes. King Maji descends down the long steps from the fortress in the rock. His clothing is outstanding. He dons a sun-yellow tunic and matching shorts. The furs used for his boots are a lighter shade of yellow and more course and fine than any fur I have seen.

"Lion hair," Atia says to me. "I'll never be able to forget the look of it."

"He must have stolen it on a raid. I can't imagine having lions out here. Then again, they did have a whale swim under a bridge." She laughs at that.

Surrounding the King are nine assassins garbed in all black.

"Citizens," he says with a booming voice. "Today marks the anniversary of the day we took back our lives!" He raises a fist. The crowd yells of approval. "Too many years we had to lurk in the shadows to get what we wanted. A brotherhood of *killers and thieves*. Killers and thieves they called us! *Assassins* . . ." He stops and looks in the eyes of his followers. No one speaks or moves. They are subordinately reactive to his every action.

"Do you remember your lives citizens? Do you remember being deprived of your women and children? Do you remember seeing your children thrown to a pit of starving crocodiles? I do. My life was bereft of anything good. But it made me *stronger*. It made us *stronger*! Now we are a group of men who do not hesitate to slit the throat of fortune! Today is not just a time of remembering. It is a time of discipline. A time to reflect on everything we have gained and everything we have to do to maintain it."

One of the nine hand him a cup of blood. He tastes it before handing it to Maji. "Let us drink the blood of the slain beasts we have stolen from the city across the dunes! This blood will replace all that we lost while taking back our city, and will renew our spirit to fight! Oh . . . I almost forgot citizens. Your King has a present for you! While you were all busy raiding Senators, I have collected the sons and daughters of *The Royals*." He says these last words with a serpentine accent.

Zajic leans over. "The Royals have ruled Rizcarth for the last two centuries." I keep my eyes on Maji. "Tomorrow, after we have celebrated, I will dismember their bodies for all to see, and we shall feast on their flesh!"

"*Feast on their flesh?*" Atia says with spit coming out of her mouth. Ranger hesitantly raises his palms at me.

"Come brothers. Let us drink to our fortunes!" The crowd screams and then chugs. Atia and Ranger look at me. I start to chug. If you have ever had blood you would understand what it tastes like. The texture is thick; milky like. It has a hint of metal, like drinking old well water from a copper mug. Atia struggles to hold it down. I see her pour most out in nearby shrubbery.

A second horn blows. We stand around and make small talk waiting to fill our cups with wine. An older man without his niqab ushers camels carrying the black barrels. It appears everybody left their niqabs off after drinking blood; everybody except the nine. My stomach feels woozy. We make our way to the line and fill up, only to return to where we were standing before. King Maji makes his rounds talking to people he is familiar with. Six men cart out a massive tan woven-basket from one of the hills surrounding the square. It looks like something you would keep a cobra in, but there is no snake in the world that would need a basket that big. The men bring it near the fire and begin to dance around it with their tongues out.

Ranger seems to be focused on the men with the basket. I attempt to pick his brain. "What do you suppose that's for?"

He shrugs. "At this point I don't know. I don't know anything anymore Nirue. This is all so much to take in. One day I'm in Ireland fishing with my dad, the next thing I know I'm spilling the brains of a guy I don't know in a city full of assassins."

"*Citizens, Ranger,*" I say facetiously.

He cracks an unwanted smile. "I suppose you're right, Nirue. But don't you think this is all a little strange? I keep hoping I'll wake up and this nightmare will be over." I pause for a moment, then offer encouragement.

"A man has not lived until he has looked death in the eyes and overcame it. Some people may see our journey as an affliction—something to be avoided at all costs. I say the real affliction is a man who spends his whole life in the comfort of mediocrity and protection. Better to have faced the greatest fears the world has to offer than to have never lived."

He takes a few moments to respond. "Aren't you scared? I mean none of this makes sense, and I know it's not a dream. We can feel *pain* here Nirue. If I took out *Darkwater* and cut you open, you would bleed and you would hurt. Doesn't that scare you?"

"Of course. But that's the fun part," I say with a smile. Ranger tilts his head to the side and purses his lips. Then he shakes his head. As he's about to respond, Atia says, "Sorry to break up your little love fest but the Queen just showed up." She gracefully descends the stairs in a white dress. Her hair is dark and her skin tanned. It's hard to get a good look at her from where I'm standing. She proceeds to stand by Maji who is now back on the steps that leads to the fortress. His mother follows her down and takes a place next to the Queen.

"Citizens. Welcome the Lady of Rizcarth!" The men howl and whistle at her. A few make provocative comments. "One of you will be fortunate enough to bed her tonight! Indeed, if you win her heart you may lay with her in one of the finest beds in the palace!" This results in another cheer from the crowd. "No use in wasting time. Let us begin! Good luck." A third trumpet sounds.

A few bold men form a line in front of the procession. Maji stands in the center of the nine, the Queen to the left of him and his mother to the left of her. He takes a seat on the steps and the nine follow suit. There are four men in line. Others hesitate to compete. "I guess people figured out the futility of Maji's game," Atia snarls.

Maji stands up after a few minutes. "Surely you would like to sleep with her! Come, and see what you may have." His lack of patience is becoming more apparent. Still, no one comes. He takes a blade from his boot and slashes an opening down the left side of the Queen's dress, exposing her long slender leg. She shudders but does well to hide it. Her skin is beautiful. I begin feeling the urge to join but I hesitate.

"Where's Zajic?" Ranger asks. I look at Atia. She points to the large basket. He has his tongue out and is dancing around with the others.

"Wonderful," Ranger sneers. "Too much wine," he says. "I saw him go back for thirds not too long ago."

Maji is now in the crowd choosing people to participate. He makes his way around the left side of the big fire. We sneak to the other side of the basket to avoid being chosen. We lose sight of him.

"What should we do?" Atia asks. "Are any of you droops good with women?" Neither of us answer. Ranger volunteering for me earlier makes me feel obligated to do something. But this is a different game than fighting. There are too many factors out of my control.

"What about you volunteer, Atia?"

"Huh?"

"It's actually genius. She probably doesn't want to 'bed' any of these guys. So maybe, if a girl enters—" Atia's eyes widen, bottom lip quivering. I feel a hand on my shoulder from behind. I look at Ranger who has turned white. I see yellow out of the corner of my eye. *Maji.*

CHAPTER SIX

*No one has ever seen him. No one has laid eyes
upon that which is the cause of it all. I hope to, someday,
so that I am the last to do so*

*From the Journal of Yazmif,
day one after entering camp*

"GOOD FRIEND, I DON'T THINK we have met. Why don't you join my game? Maybe if you win we can get to know each other." He slaps my back and walks around to my front. I feel eyes on me. "We could even be *brothers* of sorts," he winks at me and walks away. I have no choice. One of the nine comes over and tells me to leave *Evergold* and my axe with my friends. Pretending to be clumsy, I sneak one of Atia's daggers into one of my boots. I turn back to Atia and Ranger, give them a look of reverence and start walking. Here goes nothing.

I make my way to the line. Focus. I am about three fourths of the way back. Not a terrible position. I need to be able to hear what people were saying in front of me. But, I can't be last otherwise I risk someone winning before I get my shot, which is certain death. Everyone has their niqabs off now. A man behind me leans over my shoulder and whispers, "Fancy your chances do ya?" His breath smells like he went for thirds from the blood barrel. I don't acknowledge him.

What am I going to say? What happens if I win? If I lose . . . I cannot hear what the men at the front of the line are saying. All I hear is Maji's laughter.

One thing I have learned about women is that it is important to exude confidence. If a woman can sense any sign of weakness in your game, you're cooked. In this case it becomes more literal than I like. Every time a man is dismissed he is bound and thrown in the bonfire. The square becomes smoky and smells of human flesh.

I'm getting closer to the front. My mouth feels dry. I hold my breath, swallowing air to stay quiet. You have to exude confidence, Nirue. Focus. Only eight men left in front of me. I can now hear a bit of the conversation, but not enough to discern any real words. The man two spots ahead of me pisses himself. A scream is drowned out by the sound of breaking logs from behind. Seven left. The next guy up begins to sing a song.

The sailor's song is all but lost and heroes come and go,
Here on my shield I bare the crest of tales for young and old,
My lady if you'll hear my wo-

Maji holds up a hand. He walks over and locks eyes with the man. The man noticeably swallows. "A *song* my friend?"

"Yes sir. I-I-I didn't know it would offend you, I didn't mean ta' boil your blood."

"You should have thought your words wiser. No Queen of mine will be moved by some *Senator's nonsense*. Save this one for me. He gets the same treatment *The Royals* do tomorrow. Now, BACK TO THE CONTEST."

Six left. I can't figure out why that song offended him so much, I just know that I won't be singing. I'm finally close enough to see the Queen. She is out of my league, no matter what world I am in. She's tall with black hair, olive skin and a small aquiline nose between two large Peridot colored eyes.

Back to the game. Focus, Nirue. The guy in front of me gives me angst. He has the confidence and swagger of a man who has rarely been turned down by a woman, if ever. I measure the rest of the people in line. Two are old and fat. She won't pick them. Another one is much too young to win the Queen's heart. Two others are twins that have noses the size of the dagger in my boot. One of the fat men approaches her and starts telling war-stories.

"I killed three-hundred o' em that day I did. I tell ya what lassie, I'll keep ya nice and safe, I will, even if it's just for one night." He reverse cups the side of his mouth. "And I have been blessed with a member a horse y' be jealous of," and offers her a wink. She doesn't respond. Maji's mother rolls her eyes. He looks around for something to save him. He knows time is running out. Maji is laughing so hard he slaps his knee. While curling down his laughter he dismisses the man. Five left, but only one in front of me. It's going to be between this guy and myself. Maji assumes a relaxed position among the granite steps.

The self-proclaimed, huge-membered man is trying to argue his way out of the ropes. The guy in front of me leans back, "You should get out now. This game is over. Start thinking of a way to escape, man. If you hear some howling tonight, just know it ain't the coyotes, it will be Signy here."

"NEXT," Maji screams. The man in front of me graces me a smirk before heading up.

His first move is aggressive. He walks right up to the Queen and starts whispering in her ear. She giggles. Not good. He whispers sweet-nothings and backs away to see her reaction. He does this a few times in a row.

Keep the faith. He hasn't got her to talk yet. Matter of fact, no one has. He puts his hand on her lower back and begins rubbing ever so lightly. It's a great move and he's pulling it off perfectly. Not too far down as to touch her offensively, but just high enough with the perfect amount of contact to let her get acquainted with his hand. They say it is important for a woman to associate good feelings with your touch. Then, a stroke of fortune.

SLAP

She pushes him away and points him down the stairs. Yes. She doesn't say anything, but her eyes do the talking. Whatever he said pissed her off.

While prince-charming walks down the stairs, I see his eyes well up with tears. I actually feel bad for the guy, arrogant or not.

"NEXT."

Curses. I spent the whole time analyzing everyone else that I didn't think of what I was going to say. What am I going to say? I look over and see King Maji reclined on the stairs to my right. He points and gestures his left hand across his body, ushering me to the area.

I walk slowly to gather my thoughts and my breathing. The only thing that comes to mind is an old trick I read when I was pretending to be studying abroad. It was from a book called *A Pander's Guide to Savviness: How to Bed the Woman of Your Dreams*. The book was written by a 17th century monk who gave up the church and went on a lifelong journey to bed as many women as he could. He wrote about all the tricks he learned along the way.

For some reason, one trick stands out in my head. *"Don't pick the lock with the Gate Keeper around. Charm the Keeper, charm the lock."* I never knew what he meant until just now. I walk up to mother Maji. Here goes nothing.

"It must be quite a pleasure to see your son doing such *incredible* things. You must be *so proud*. I smile at her. She nods her head and smiles back.

"I bet you have ... What? One hundred suitors at your door every day? Tell me, how does your son manage to keep them away?"

She blushes and replies, "Well it's not like that ... I mean I ... I haven't really thought about men in a while and wasn't really expecting your question. What did you say your name was?"

"Name is Nirue m'lady. You're even more beautiful when you smile."

I grin ear to ear. Maji is bordering between rage and confusion, not knowing which emotion to run with. He is tense and ready to pounce.

"All I'm saying is that you must have something really special about you to produce such a wonderful man like Maji over here." I extend my hand toward the King.

"This one really is a charmer," mother Maji says. Maji relaxes.

"Excuse me, good sir, but isn't the point to charm me?" Yes! I got her to talk.

"Yes, my Queen, I suppose it is. I'll get to you in a second." Her eyes sparkle in the moonlight.

"In a second? You're supposed to charm me, not the King's mother." Mother Maji twiddles her fingers at me flirt-fully.

"Well, the truth is Signy . . . I'm just not sure you are my type. That's all." Where once there was chattering and commotion there is now silence. I can hear the crackling of the main fire behind me.

"Wha-what do you *mean* I'm not your type?"

"You see—and, please, don't be offended, but I'm not looking for the type to love me and leave me. That already happened to me once, when the Senators took my wife . . ." I pretend to fight back tears. "It's just easier if I don't get involved."

I see her sympathize with me. I hate playing the sympathy card. "Why are you here then?"

"Same reason you are. I have to be."

"Do you not want to win? Say I choose you, would you not bed me?"

"No. I would bed you. Though, if there was a snake devouring a rat near us, I am not sure who would finish first," I say through a grin. This causes laughter among the crowd. Even Maji gets a kick out of my joke.

"If you don't choose this one, I'm claiming him for my own!" Mother Maji says. "I haven't seen a man with proper charm in ages!" The Queen smiles at her. I can tell she wants her approval. Smart.

"Ladies, ladies. No need to fight over me. There's pleeeenty of Nirue to go around, and the night is young." I offer the Queen a wink. She giggles at that.

"Well, what's it going to be Signy?" Maji asks. The Queen peers around me at who's left in line, then stares into my icy blue eyes.

"I have made my decision. I choose Nirue."

The crowd erupts. For the first time, I am glad. Then Maji holds a hand up to the crowd. He stares at me with hand in the air.

"Unfortunately, that cannot happen. Citizens" He looks back at the crowd, "We have a traitor in our midst."

CHAPTER SEVEN

*I read that one day here is like a few
minutes on Earth. But that's just a guess,
for no one really knows with certainty.*

Arismoren, Scientist of the Fallen Citadel

MY HEART DRUMS AT MY head. It's hard to swallow. Maji nods at
the nine. Two run up the stairs in my direction. I brace myself for what's to
come. The assassins walk past me and grab Signy by either arm. She kicks
at them and at the air, trying to squirm away. They bring her next to Maji.
He rips her head back by her hair. She extends her lower jaw, snarling at
him.

Maji addresses the crowd, "We have discovered your so-called Queen
has been working with a group of Senators on a plot to take their city back.
Citizens, do you know what we do with *traitors?*"

Shouts of "Hang her!" and "Burn her alive!" are two suggestions
I could hear through the many. Maji nods his head at a few, and seems
inspired by a suggestion to feed her to his dogs.

"I'll take care of her," I say with more authority in my voice than I actually feel. Maji looks at me. Then he asks the crowd, "What do you think, Citizens? Should we let Nirue kill the traitor?"

"No!"

"She is an enemy of the group, not just him!"

"Let me kill her."

The nine stand firm. Signy spits at me. I wipe my face and look at Maji. He shakes his head and begins to respond. But before he could get a word out, his mother says, "He won the contest, Maji. He won the contest and he gets the night with her. Tradition is one of the many tools we must emphasize if we wish to *sustain*." His posture goes stiff. He has a hard distinctive jawline and pinched lips. He flashes a cold, insincere smile at me.

Through gritted teeth he says, "Certainly. You have until dawn." With that, he dismisses us with a wave. The crowd becomes restless and challenges Maji. At the front is Ranger and Atia. "Look for the blue," I say to them before walking over to Maji. Signy rips her arms free and fixes her hair. She lifts her chin and dusts off her dress.

Three of the nine escort us up the stairs into the palace. Hanging over the entrance is a large balcony. Supporting it are white Corinthian columns with stories written into the stone. We enter through the columns into the foyer. The foyer has two sets of stairs hugging the right and left walls that lead up to the second floor. The place is poorly lit, making it hard to see.

We are lead led up the left staircase to the second floor, then through twisting hallways to the left. I see the big room with the balcony. The guard makes a right and escorts us into a smaller room with a smaller balcony that faces opposite the city square.

"Since I am the winner, I would like to bed her in the room with the larger balcony. I think it would be nice for the men to be able to view the Queen occasionally."

I stand behind her, kiss her neck and caress her exposed leg. She elbows me in the mouth. I crane my neck and rub my jaw, "I think Maji will appreciate it." He stares at her leg the same way a scavenger watches a predator eat its prey.

"Like he said—you have till dawn." I nod.

I see one of the nine leave and two others stand guard outside my door. They aren't typical guards who sit straight faced with thousand-yard-stares. They move among the shadows, keeping careful but surreptitious watch. I shut the door.

Signy immediately runs to the other side of the room. She grabs a book and holds it out in front of her like a shield, eyes focused. I ignore her and begin looking for anything I can use as a rope. There is a kings-sized bed with sheets draping down on all sides. A gold chest sits neatly in front of it. There isn't much else except for drapes that cover the entrance of the giant balcony. They are tied off with ropes. I unravel one to determine its length.

Signy frowns and her posture loosens. I continue on my task. I go to the other drape and gather its rope. I hold off the curtains with some extra linen I find lying around. I walk out to the balcony and take in my view. Straight ahead of me is the square with the big fire and basket. I can't believe those people are still dancing. I see the carts and the dead bodies but no sign of Atia and Ranger. The stars illuminate the palm forest in the distance. I look for a moon but cannot find one.

I walk back into the room. "What are you *doing*?" she asks me.

"Just messing around. I have never been royalty so it's fun for me to see all the fine things."

"Play me straight, Nirue. I am no snake in a basket. You cannot charm your way out of everything." I look down and then back into her light green eyes. They remind me of a vine snake. "What do you think I'm doing?" She pauses.

"I think you are plotting an escape. But why? You should not be harmed. You won the contest."

I don't respond. "Unless you plan on doing something, I don't know, noble?" She grins, then quickly hides her smile. I smile back, to reassure her—communication without speaking. "What makes you think a nice guy like me would be plotting something noble now, hmm?" She paces the room. "The way you said, '*I have to be*' when I asked why you were here. I sensed some resentment."

Again, I don't respond. She comes and sits next to me on an outdoor sofa. "I just want to know if you are going to do something to Maji, and, if you are, then I want to be a part of it. He killed my family right in front of me. My little brother . . ." She begins to cry.

I rest my hand on her thigh and wipe the tears from her eyes. "For so many reasons I have to do this—far too many for me to explain, or understand myself, really. But, rest assured—I am either killing Maji or he is killing me. There's no way around that."

She looks up at me with teary eyes. "Thank you, Nirue. Thank you, thank you, thank you. You must promise me one thing though."

"Sure."

"Let me help you kill him. I promise to not get in the way. Just let me do *something* so I feel like I have avenged my family."

I sigh. "Okay. But you have to do exactly as I say. Okay?"

"Okay." She wipes the tears from her eyes and smiles in satisfaction. I know that her opportunity will likely never come, but I pretend nonetheless.

We don't speak for minutes. I stare at the bonfire, contemplating a way to get to Maji.

By far the most underrated aspect of the mind is the automatic response to human speech. Without prompt, the mind flashes and focuses with great detail on the speaker the moment their voice utters a syllable. I notice that as Signy interrupts my daydreaming with a question. I forget what she asked me so I change the subject.

We spend the next few hours on the balcony talking of abstract things. Signy points out that Maji looks pretty drunk. Good. I'll wait till he goes to bed and kill him in his sleep. But what of the nine? I saw how hard one of them was to kill.

Maji gets up and falls flat on his face. Two of the nine carry him up the long set of stairs. Still no sign of Ranger or Atia. When Maji and his men are safely under the balcony I take the *Dicer* I had hidden in my boot and tie it to a rope. I tie the rope to the sofa Signy and I had been sharing. I let it hang down so that it can be clearly seen. A knock at the door.

A strong man with a pronounced jaw stares at me when I open it. "Maji wanted me to see how you two were faring." His voice is deep, like he's talking into a barrel.

"Just fine until you came in." I stare back at him.

He smirks. "Just remember, you have until dawn." Behind him I see Maji being carried into one of the rooms. I nod and shut the door on him. She looks at me desperately. "Please Nirue, *please*. You have to do something fast. I've been trying to keep my mind away from what he will do to me. *Please*." Her eyes make me want to crumble. How could anyone hurt such beauty?

I don't speak for a few minutes. I play scenarios out, trying to think of something that will work. My stomach drops.

"What?" she asks me.

I motion her to the balcony. It's a few hours past midnight. I suspect dawn will be here soon.

"That man today . . . That wasn't Maji."

"What do you mean?"

"I mean that wasn't Maji. Why would an assassin King willingly drink himself to a stupor and carouse with the likes of us? Think of the definition of assassin. To be the best assassin you have to see all angles and always expect the unexpected. Think about what that entails. You must be ready for *every evil* the shadows hide. You must be the shadows. The whole time I knew something was amiss, I just couldn't figure out what. The fake Maji was impressive, but he didn't strike me as a man who could lead the worst of the worst killers, what, taking orders from his mom and such."

"What makes you think that man today wasn't him?"

"I figured it out when that guard came to check on us. He didn't know that I saw the fake Maji being brought up the stairs. He told me that Maji wanted to know how we were doing. Fake Maji was lifeless being carried into a bedroom. It was bad timing for him. The real one is still out there." She shudders at that. Her voice drops to a whisper. "What do we do?"

I shake my head and look out at the square.

At the same time, I hear the crash of swords and the struggle of two men in heated combat. Ranger.

CHAPTER EIGHT

Life comes at you quick. It makes a hard turn and you suddenly find yourself scrambling to plug the next hole. Out here? Nah. Out here is post-apocalyptic. I've been dying for this reality.

Steel, a true believer

I RUSH AND GRAB THE *Dicer* dangling from the balcony. We run through the hallway into the large common area. An arrow takes out a guard sprinting at us. I look down and Atia waves at me. "You guys having fun yet?" she muses. I throw her the *Dicer* and she tosses me up *Evergold* and my quiver.

Two of the nine lay dead which leaves only seven, plus Maji. "We gotta find Maji," Ranger says as he runs up the stairs. "I saw him being carried in here. Luckily, being a killer doesn't make you a great fighter. I already took out two more guards."

Before I could explain what I figured out, a knife comes from an unknown location and sticks into the wall behind Rangers head. "Down! Down to the first floor!" I yell. We rush down the stairs. I motion them back into the shadows.

"Play the shadows to our advantage. These assassins won't fight us in the light." They all nod in agreement. "You and Atia take the right wing. I'll take her and flank the left." Ranger hands me my axe. We move quietly. Soft steps staccato off the rock walls, though I cannot determine from where they originate. I ready *Evergold* and give Signy my short axe.

Our hallway leads to a chest shaped room full of scrolls. Lit torches along the walls play tricks on my beating heart. Atia and Ranger meet me from the other entrance. I point to my eye to ask them, "You see anybody?" Ranger shrugs and shakes his head.

The middle of the room is the darkest. We group up and walk into the belly of the beast. Two assassins jump down from parapets swinging scimitars. Another two jump down and run away from us.

I nod at Ranger, who takes off toward our assailants. His massive size draws their attention away long enough for me to pick one off. I get him through the eye. Ranger kills the other quickly. Atia's daggers give away our position like a beacon during a cloudy night at sea. I motion for her to sheath them.

At the end of the room is an altar in front of a wall of scrolls. There, tied up in a chair is the fake Maji. Atia looks at me quizzically. It's a trap. She heads toward him. I grab her by the shirt and yank her back.

"That's not the real Maji. I figured it out when I was in the room." She stares at me blankly. We move toward him slowly. When we get closer we see his throat has been slit and his hands are nailed to the wooden chair he is propped up in. It wasn't a clean slice wherein the carotid artery was allowed to bleed out. This man's neck has been sawed. Signy slowly backs away from the body. A voice comes from a parapet above us.

"Thought you could kill me so *easy*, did you?" hisses Zajic.

Ranger tightens his grip on *Darkwater*. "I knew we should have never trusted that miserable piss."

Maji laughs. "You think the assassin king would expose himself like that?" He points to the fake Maji. "You think a man like that could lead the worst killers to walk the earth? Fools. I spotted you the instant you walked into my city."

He hops down from the parapet and lands on two feet and one hand. As he stands he draws two short swords. The tips are covered by a piece of leather. The big man that knocked on my door appears from a hallway I didn't know existed. Two others come in support. Maji laughs and walks backward into darkness. The others follow suit.

I grab my axe from Signy and give chase. "Take this bow and shoot anyone who chases after me!"

It's now or never. As I run after him, I feel hot air rise into my lungs. I am tired but the adrenaline of the moment powers me through. The hallway twists and turns steadily downhill.

Maji turns down a hallway made of red brick that ends with a tri-fork. He goes straight. His two guards go right and left. "Ranger, you follow the big guy. Atia, take Signy and go after the other. Leave Maji for me."

The middle route leads down to an underground wine cellar that is cold and smells of dirt. Maji knocks over empty barrels that were blocking a hallway leading further down. He moves fast. I can barely keep up. I see a flash of his tunic just in time to choose the right path, as these hallways have many options. A perfect keep for assassins. If I lose him now, I will lose him for good. I run with everything I have.

I eventually find him in a drain-out where the river meets the main sewage canal from the city.

"For a crap assassin, I give you the crap house." He bows and motions toward the canal. I hold my axe in front of me and stare him in the eyes. The sun is coming up. A loud bell sounds in the distance.

"Ahh. Just in time. Isn't it beautiful?" He flicks his index finger matching every stroke of the bell. "Looks like your big guy couldn't catch mine. You see, that is our 'distress signal' if you will. Quite a wonderful design, actually. The Senators designed it so that anyone in the city could hear it clearly—no matter where they were. In moments you will have the best killers in Rizcarth upon you." He grins and plays with his hands like a greedy man scheming over a pile of gold.

"You know, after you told me of your little 'plan' I was wondering when you were going to make your move. I waited around with the tongue-dancers, hoping you would show your hand. Then, a blue dagger hangs from the balcony." He inhales deeply then exhales slowly before laughing.

"I was so thankful you were stupid enough to hang that dagger. Now, I will use your body as a reminder to all would-be usurpers. I will hang your limbs from the parapets. Your head will sit atop the scroll and whip. Your eyes will be my new necklace."

He moves clockwise around me. We have some distance between the canal but not enough to feel comfortable. I twirl my axe around. He removes the leather from his blades.

"I took my time with these, just for you. It's called *Necropoison*. It's unique in that it keeps you alive while it kills you. Just one poke and within minutes, you won't be able move your limbs. The good news is your nervous system works perfectly fine. So while your lungs collapse and bleed out into your other vital organs, you are awake! You just can't move. It's supposed to feel like drowning." He smirks at that last comment.

I'm tired of this. I'm either going to die or I'm not. I have to at least try. I lung at him and he deflects me with ease. He laughs. I cut at his legs and he jumps. "Not very good at fighting, are we Nirue?" He laughs again. This guy is toying with me and I don't really know how to fight like this. I decide to try Ranger's tactic—constant aggression.

I grit my teeth, lunge, and roll under his swipe before returning another leg attack. I land it this time and tear open his right calf. He screams and evaluates his wound from a distance. Lucky. He underestimated me. He must be waiting for a crowd to showcase his skills.

His eyes widen. He rears his head back and howls. He moves forward with a series of lunges. Down left, down right, down left, uppercut. Hack after hack he swipes at me from all angles. I continue backing up. I'm sloppily deflecting his hits now. But, I do have one advantage. Without one of his legs I can keep good distance. I near a wall. He pushes me against a wall and closes.

He brings his swords down in a crossed formation at my head. Our blades connect. He drives into me, knives still crossed. He's getting close. While trying to bring the blades to my neck he grunts and blows spit into my face. His rage turns carnal and I see the madness in his eyes. I'm losing the strength contest and those swords are beginning to point inwards toward my throat. I can see veins pulsing in his white fingers. My muscles are quickly losing stamina.

I look down and notice that he is solely pushing off his left leg. There's only one way I win this fight, and it isn't a straight-up sword fight.

I press my head as hard as I can into the stone behind me, causing it to bleed. He regrips his hands on his swords and in that moment I take my left leg and prop it against the wall. I then lift my right heel and smash the side of his good knee. A loud pop echoes through the drainage room. I blew out every tendon, tendril and bone in his knee. He screams and buckles to the ground. The shock makes him lose grip on his weapons.

I pick up his swords and he spits at my feet. He starts to talk, clearly trying to buy time. I take a long look at his poisoned sword. I walk over to him and stick it deep into his left thigh while staring into his eyes. His mouth hangs open, frozen.

Aware of my limited time, I rush back to the tri-fork. "ATIA. RANGER. SIGNY!" I hear a distant call. After a few minutes, they find me at the fork.

"Did you kill him?" Ranger asks me, hands on his knees.

I nod. "How did you guys fare?"

"Signy almost saw the block, but we killed two of his guards." Ranger smiles.

"Let's go. This place is swarming with assassins."

They follow me down the hall through the cellar and into the drain-out. Maji lays still with his eyes and mouth open. His body went from pale to snow white in the short time I was gone.

"Maji sounded the alarm. These guys know the palace and city way better than we do. I think we take this river out."

"Nirue, you saw what was in there! I'll take my chances with the assassins. At least we are on land," Atia begs.

"I think we should listen to Nirue." Signy says. Ranger agreeably shrugs at Atia, who rolls her eyes.

I strap *Evergold* to my back, secure my short-axe and turn around. A distant shout comes from the tri-fork. "We don't have time to discuss this. I don't know about you, but I'm jumping in."

Atia reluctantly agrees. "Alright. Let me go first though." She jumps in and is immediately swept away by the current. Signy jumps in next. "After you, Ranger." He looks down the hallway toward the screaming assassins. I flick my head as to say "get on with it." He dives face first with his hand straight in front of his body. I turn around and see shadows forming in the hallway. I take a deep breath and dive in.

The current is fast moving. It's hard to stay above water. We are all moving the same speed. I can see Ranger and Signy but not Atia. The river dips well below ground level so that excess rains can runoff into it. This makes it is easier to hide. We pass through the mountain and out the back of Rizcarth safely into a delta where the river separates into two different streams.

Waiting for us is Bertram, although, there's something different about him. I try to think of what as I shake out my wet hair.

"Congratulations Nirue, Ranger and Atia."

That's what is different—he has less chains on, most notably around his body. And his robe is a softer blue instead of black now.

"I never thought I would say this, but I am happy to see you," Atia says while chuckling. She has been the consistent positive thinker in this group. Ranger is obliviously ringing out his headband. Signy looks out over the dunes, sand peppered over her glistening olive skin.

"Bertram, this is the Lady of Rizcar—" I begin to say before he cuts me off.

"I know who she is. Mighty fine to meet you." He smiles and she returns the gesture. He turns to us, "I think we should get back as soon as possible. There is still much to be done."

I don't really want to leave just yet, but I highly doubt I have much of a say. Ranger and Atia are playfully rubbing and grabbing at each other. I keep my head down, pretending to not see anything. Signy turns to me.

"Thank you for everything, Nirue. You have saved me from the shackles of slavery and shown me that there are yet good people in this world. I will never be able to repay you."

I unsuccessfully try to not smile. "It was nothing, really."

"I hope, in the aftermath of all this, my people may reclaim their city as the rightful owners of Rizcarth." I nod somberly. Then she walks over to me and grabs me softly by the jaw. "I will never forget you, Nirue." We embrace for a long hug. Dammit. It would have been nice to have stolen a kiss from the Queen while undergoing this miserable journey. I can't wait to get this over with.

"I will surely never forget you, Lady of Rizcarth. I wish there was more I could do to help."

She smiles and looks at me with her beautiful greens. "Do not worry about me. My people are hiding in a place nearby. I will tell them what happened here today. Go. Do what you must." With a half smile, I nod.

Bertram points for me to take position between Ranger and Atia. I look one last time at Signy. In a flash of green we are gone and back on the jumpkey in the mossy forest. Three orbs change from white to sandy brown around the heatless fire. In the strangest of ways, I feel at home. First trial down, three more to go.

INTERLUDE I

AN AFTERNOON PHONE RING INTERRUPTS Celia's daydreaming. She is sweeping with yellow dishwasher gloves on. Children are wrestling over a toy truck in the next room over.

"Mrs. Nyles?"

"This is she," Celia replies as she shakes a child off her leg.

"My name is deputy Cardiff. I'm sorry to tell you there has been a terrible accident. It's your son." She gasps as her hand flies toward her chest in disbelief, broom clattering to the floor.

She shakes her head, voicing denial, "Oh no. No no no no. Which one?" She asks knowing the answer already. She only has one son left who is a thrill seeker.

"We aren't sure . . . He's carrying two IDs—Nathan and Andrew."

"It's Nathan . . . Andrew was killed years ago."

"Ma'am, Nathan was just air-evacuated to Lincoln hospital on Filmore. I hate being this person Mrs. Nyles, I really do, but things are looking grim. I would head over as soon as possible." She drops the phone, nearly falling over but bracing herself against the wall and the refrigerator.

"What's wrong?" Kylie asks.

"Everyone in the car. It's your brother. They say he's hurt bad."

Four children and their mother pile into a van. Celia calls her husband. "Hey wife!"

"*Honey,*" Celia says sobbing. "*It's our boy. Our baby boy. Nirue is hurt bad. He has been helicoptered to Lincoln hospital.*" Dennis flinches. His world gets blurry. He grabs at his stomach. With tears in his eyes he sprints out of the office. He prays while driving double the speed limit.

The children and Celia race into the hospital. Celia leaves her car running outside of the entrance to the emergency room. Dennis had just beat them there.

"We're looking for Nirue Nyles. Where is he?" Dennis asks.

"You mean Nathan? I presume you to be the father?"

He nods. "Yes, Nathan!"

"I'm sorry but you won't be able to see him for a while. His situation was so critical the doctors had to take him immediately into surgery. Once he is out of surgery you may see your son." The family holds onto each other, sobbing, clutching at articles of clothing.

Thirteen tortuous hours later a short man with a hair-knit comes out from behind an "employees only" door. He walks slowly, head down, hands held in front of his body. Celia squeezes a blanket so tight her knuckles become discolored.

"Mr. and Mrs. Nyles?" he asks. They both nod. Celia's chin trembles as she squeezes Dennis' hand. He barely notices. News about their son is moments away.

"My name is Dr. Skelton. Your son was in a terrible accident. From talking to highway patrol, it appears your son was on the I-40 heading east. He was behind a big rig and tried to make a blind pass. As he came up over a hill he was one hundred feet from a tractor trailer coming the opposite way. It appears he flipped a number of times." Dennis grips Celia. "Your son was not killed in the accident, but he shouldn't be alive. He broke nearly every bone in his body, and his brain . . .Well, we performed an emergency craniotomy for multiple subdural hematomas." Dennis pinches his eyes shut.

"There's no easy way to put this. Your son's brain was bleeding and we had to open his skull to evacuate the blood."

"Is he *okay now*?" Celia asks, hyperventilating.

"Come with me." He walks them through the twists and turns of a busy hospital. People on stretchers are being run by. Red and yellow lights flashing. Doctors are being paged to different departments. They eventually arrive at a room behind a large door. The fact that their son wasn't behind a curtain made Dennis feel uneasy. These are the long-term rooms.

The sight in front of Dennis and Celia is, at best, a living nightmare. Celia collapses, saliva stringing between her lips, not able to inhale. Dennis pinches the top of his nose and begins to sob.

Their son has been intubated through the trachea. He has matching tubes coming out of his nose and his elbows. His eyes are black and swollen shut. His lips are so swollen that his skin has cracked and split. Skin can only be stretched so far. The top of his head is shaved, leaving a wide scar moving from his ear to the apex of his skull. He has cross-stitching along the scar to prevent splitting. Remnants of orange antibacterial stain his face and hair.

"Your son is in a coma. We don't know when or if he will come out," says Dr. Skelton. Celia inhales and cries out, "My *baaby my baaaby*," she moans with tears running down her face, "*what ever happened to my baaby. My poor poor baby. Why does this have to happen to him? My baaaby. This can't be happening*," she says as she grabs the sides of his bed, trying to drag herself to her son.

CHAPTER NINE

If I could summarize everything I have learned in one word, it would be hope. It is the one thing they lose. Out here on some distant planet, light-years away from family, friends and comfort, their will to live will be tested. They may even question the purpose of their life, or life itself. You must be their beacon of hope. They must believe that there is a light at the end of the tunnel, if they are to make it home and you are to be granted access to our Kingdom, broken of your chains.

Letter from Alanai,
Successful Sherpa after 2,474 years of attempts

WE WALK TEN MILES BACK to camp in near silence. Only a few words are said. None of them important.

Bertram ushers us to a nearby river and provides us with fresh clothes. We take turns bathing. It feels good to wash the dirt and blood off of my body. I was covered in sand.

I slip on a loose-fitting hooded shirt that is made from a type of hemp. Not the itchy kind—the kind that has been treated repeatedly to provide comfort. I notice Ranger and Atia are wearing the same thing. I'm glad we get something comfortable to wear. Hopefully we can adequately rest before our next trial.

We sit and eat a much-needed meal around the fire. Bertram provides us with beans, smoked venison and blueberries. The berries are a nice compliment to the tougher, more gamy tasting venison.

We shared a few glasses of mead and talk about our recent adventure. Ranger and I have a good laugh at the tongue dancers. "Maji did a good job blending in with them. For a moment I thought his tongue might fall out of his mouth," Ranger jokes. He nudges me with his elbow. "So, what happened when you were with Signy?"

His grin stretches from ear to ear. I notice Atia look up. I laugh. "Nothing. Honestly." I do my best not to smile.

"Uh huh. A man with that kind of charm doesn't let it go to waste. Nirue, you are a bloody liar."

"No! Honestly. I mean . . . We were flirting and what not but that was it." Atia shivers a little and gets up.

"You're a bad liar Nirue. I saw the way you held her before we left. You don't do that with someone you just flirted with." She fingers quotes for the last part, although, in a friendly way. Atia heads into her cabin. I can tell she is fighting a cold or something. Probably not used to whatever germs this place has.

"Forgive her, Nirue. I fear her sun is setting faster than both of yours," Bertram says.

"You know, I was thinking about that in Rizcarth. The way you told us to finish the task quickly. How long do we have to complete our tasks? How do we know someone won't pull the plug on us from the other side?" I ask.

"That is completely out of your hands. Your subconscious will hear things and interpret how long you have. But that is an estimate at best. You noticed the fire in the circle, yeah?"   "Yeah, I noticed. So?"

"All three of you see a different fire. The closer it gets to burning out, the closer outsiders are to terminating your life. Once off life support the game is over. Keep a watchful eye, for no flame burns at the same temperature."

The wind quietly blows through the highest point in the pines. Ranger breaks the silence. "And no sun sets at the same time?" Bertram nods, eyes never leaving the fire.

"Well let's get going then. What's next?" I ask, standing up and loading my weapons.

"Sit down, Nirue. Tomorrow you journey to the jungle of Hardrain. There your task is a bit different. I will explain in due time. But remember one thing: *Appearance is everything.*" He gets up and walks into Atia's cabin.

"I hate jungles," Ranger says. "I once took a visit to the Congo to check out an emerald quarry. I went with my dad. His friend wanted us to become gem runners instead of fishermen. Worst experience of my life." He kicks some outlying twigs into the fire.

"How come?"

"For starters I got bit by a spider the size of that orb." He spits. "Leg swelled up the size of these logs we're sitting on. Between the bugs, vegetation, rain, noises in the dark . . ." He trails off. "I just remember telling myself I will never go back to the jungle. What do ya know, here I am."

"The good news is we have our weapons. That should make getting through the growth easier. We will make it. Just like we did in Rizcarth," I say.

"I sure hope you're right."

Bertram comes back out with Atia. It's obvious she has been crying. We try to relax for a few hours before going to bed. The body language of the group is restless. The cold wind does the speaking for us. I decide to stay outside a bit longer than the group. I accidentally fall asleep against my log.

Bertram stirs me awake in the early morning while it's still dark. "It's time." We gather our things and head to the trail. Along the way I make an effort to strike up conversation with Atia. Her eyes are puffy. "Where are you headed once we get out of here?"

"South Africa."

"Is that where you were born?"

"No. I was born in Egypt but moved to South Africa when I was very young. I consider myself a native."

"So we have Ireland, South Africa and the place where they breed the best humans in the world. South Dakota." I grin at her.

She shoves me. "You are really something else."

Ranger and I laugh. "In all seriousness, what was it like growing up in South Africa?"

She kicks a rock while thinking of what to say. It reminds me of my dad. He used to tell me it's best to pause a few seconds before answering a question. That way, you say what you really mean and avoid impulsive responses.

"It was *normal* I guess?" Not a very thorough response for all that time. Ranger tells her to explain.

"To me it was normal. I can see why it may seem different to you, due to the amount of wildlife I grew up around. But to me, that was normal. The same way you probably thought you were living a normal life when you were a youth." Not me. I remember knowing I was different than everyone else. More bold. I had a thirst for adventure that couldn't be quenched by riding bikes and egging cars.

"That's true," I lie. The trek goes by fairly quick due to our conversation. I learned more about Ranger and Atia in that walk than I had in the last few days.

We finish the walk around the same time of day as our last journey. I'm still sore from Rizcarth. I hope this trial goes faster. We approach the stairs in front of the gazebo. The three chests are positioned neatly in a semi-circle. Bertram steps up and unlocks them one at a time. He uses three separate keys.

"This time you each get something from *Chests Vitale,*" Bertram states, bent over in the black chest.

Ranger gets a pot. He doesn't seem thrilled. Atia gets flint. I get a blanket that is impermeable to water. We all get packs. I think that means we're going to be there for a while. We wouldn't get survival tools for an overnight trip. Maybe that's why he didn't equip us at all before Rizcarth.

We start walking up the steps and into the circle. I make the blanket into a cape before we head off. Bertram looks at us, then a flash of green.

We land in a clearing with a circumference of thirty yards or so. Surrounding us is a jungle so thick that one cannot peer more than a few inches into it. It's mid-afternoon in Hardrain. Every creature imaginable is making noise in the sea of green.

We follow Bertram out of the frying pan and into the fire. Ranger leads the bush-whacking with *Darkwater*. Even with the mighty blade we make very little ground. It's not long until we see a snake the width of a human and the length of six oxen slithering over a fallen tree. Bertram calls it a Godboa. This place is not comforting. Everything in here is fighting something else for sunlight, like a hundred children simultaneously trying to get the teachers attention.

I walk with *Evergold* loaded the entire afternoon because I've never been in a place so alive, and I don't trust it.

Atia seems bothered with something in her boot. We constantly take breaks for her to sit and rub her heel. Ranger drips with sweat from all the hacking. It's hard to get a read on Bertram.

Birds sing in the trees. Bugs scream for a mate. Apes hoot and creatures unfamiliar to my ears cry. What worries me is what I can't hear.

We continue hacking. Half-eaten fruit litter the jungle floor. Ropy vines snake around trunks in suffocating loops. It seems as though every death is sustenance for life in this place. A swarm of ants cloak a fallen fruit. Downed trees have new plants growing on top of them. Atia screams as she accidentally steps through a rotten log revealing a refuge for larva.

Just before dark we make our way into another clearing. "I suggest we stay here for the night. At least we have room to fight, if necessary," Bertram suggests. Excited at the idea of rest, we collectively agree and get to making beds.

Bertram explains that we need to build them off the ground to avoid getting bit by crawlers. Ranger and I hack down some small trees with thick trunks to serve as the base. As we return them, Atia and Bertram use vine to tie them together.

Atia finds a nearby stream while collecting vine. She fills Ranger's pot and starts a fire to boil the water. When Ranger and I are done making the elevated beds, Atia has cold, clean water for us. She cooled our drinks with her daggers. It is much needed. We all drink a pot and lay down by the fire, save Ranger, who rolls his pocket dagger between his fingers, carefully watching Atia. He loves that dagger.

When I look to the sky, I notice the absence of stars. The opposite of Rizcarth, this sky only has one large purple moon with two smaller ones in its orbit. I rouse from my reflection to Bertram snapping his fingers at me. I sit up. As I hesitantly begin to ask a question, he snaps at me again, finger over his lips.

He rushes to the sleeping Ranger. He covers Ranger's mouth and whispers something in his ear. Ranger struggles for a moment, not realizing what is going on. Atia is already awake, wide-eyed and crouched, dicers ready, looking at the treeline.

CHAPTER TEN

*Read the forest. Read the leaves. Read the animals
and their reaction to you. Read what isn't there, for lack of
sound is often the loudest alarm you may get.*

*Posted on a wooden board
outside of the clearing in Hardrain*

FOCUSED ON THE FOREST, BERTRAM whispers, "Tempos. They could be our quick ticket."

I can't make out what he is looking at. I try to align my vision with Atia's. Then I see them. Massive elephants are clearing trees in the forest to our north. Black tusks rip trees from their roots. The upper half of their body is a fur hide that protects them from falling trees. Their eyes are much larger than any elephant I have ever seen.

"How do you expect us to capture one of those?" I whisper to Bertram.

"You have to give the patriarch food it has not eaten in a year. Something *rare*. Then it will trust you, and the rest will follow."

I nod and walk over to Ranger and Atia. "You hear all that?" I ask.

"Kind of," Atia says. "Something about food?"

"Yes. If we give the biggest tempo food it has not eaten in a year it will become subservient to our needs."

Ranger rips grass from the ground. "Where I'm from, everything four-legged eats this." He raises a fist of grass and heads toward the tempo. I laugh to myself. He never is one to think things through. He just goes. I remember Rizcarth and how Ranger saw the *Dicer* and immediately ran into the palace. I laugh again.

Atia and I catch up to Ranger. He slowly approaches the patriarch. The other tempos don't even notice my ant-sized comrade. The patriarch knows he is there, that's his job. He stands perpendicular to Ranger because his eyes are on the sides of his head.

Ranger has the grass in one hand and his other is directed in peace offering, palm toward the beast. He walks up and offers the grass. Seconds after it opens its mouth we smell its putrid breath. I can't imagine what it smells like to Ranger. He leans over and covers his mouth with the pit of his elbow to keep from vomiting.

The tempo eats all of the grass. Nothing. Bertram chuckles.

"And what the heaven is so funny, scramp?" Ranger asks pissed off.

"You thought *grass* was going to work?" Bertram slaps his leg in laughter. Ranger turns red. I can't tell if it's out of frustration or embarrassment. Probably both.

Now that we know the beast won't hurt us we start offering it everything we can. Lemons, bananas, leaves, apricots, bushels, vines, nuts, blackberries and kava root—all before the sun comes up. None of it works. Atia even tried a coconut.

"We've got to expand our search." I say. "Ranger, why don't you and Bertram head north and I'll take Atia south and meet back here in a few hours. Sound good?" Ranger and Bertram agree.

I use my axe to clear the way. The jungle is sticky. Water escapes out of me as quick as I can drink it. Thankfully Atia stocked up before everyone went to bed. We make good headway due to being in a particular part of the jungle that has tall canopy trees. They have been blocking sunlight from the ground plants for years now, so there isn't much to hack through.

Atia collects blue and purple flowers along the way. I kill a few large red beetles and wrap them in banana leaves to take back. "Can I ask you something, Atia?"

"Sure," she says while examining claw marks on a tree.

"What did your fire look like yesterday?"

She pauses. It looks as though she may turn around, but instead, she returns to fingering the claw marks. "It looked like a fire."

"Atia. I need to know, that way Ranger and I can speed things up if we have to."

She lets out a sigh and turns around. "It's about half of what it was before Rizcarth." She fights back tears. "It wasn't much to begin with."

I nod. "That's all I need to know." I give her a hug. "We're going to get through this. YOU'RE going to get through this, okay? Ranger and I will do everything in our power to make sure of that. You have my word."

She smiles and wipes her eyes. "It's just that, I don't feel as though I belong here and my fire confirms that."

"What do you mean? None of us belong here. Or, if you look at the other way, all of us belong here, for we all deserve a second chance."

She shakes her head. "I'm saying I'm not meant for this life. I can't catch a break. My life wasn't easy before this. Now I have to go through *this* to get back there? And to think, all I ever wanted to be was a housewife."

"There's no shame in that Atia."

"Well my mom would have disagreed. She used to tell me that I needed to stop settling and that I was just giving into misogynistic cultural views. But the truth is, I wasn't rebelling from my mother. I am just one of those girls that always wanted to be a mom, and now I never will." Tears well up in her eyes, causing her to look away.

"Atia, please don't cry. There's nothing wrong with wanting that. In fact, that's all my mother ever was, and I think my siblings and I are all the better for it. You know, for having her around."

"Really?"

"Really. And don't worry yourself over holding Ranger and I back. You're the only one that's been consistently positive so far. You're the only one who's shaped our perspective from dire straits to that of an adventure, solely with your energy. And, since we're being completely honest with each other, every single second I have spent on this planet, I have been scared out of my mind."

Saliva strings between her lips as she laughs and wipes her eyes. "You're just saying that."

"No, I'm really not. We all have problems that we hide. Our face is but a mask, and sometimes that mask is honest, and sometimes it isn't. Mine isn't. The truth is my real name isn't even Nirue. It's Nathan." Atia pauses, wanting to ask me something but doesn't.

"My twin brother and best friend was killed in a terrible train accident right in front of me. We were . . .inseparable. It was like half of me died when he did, and I've been searching for that other half ever since." I look up into the canopy, pretending to search for food.

"His name was Andrew. Andrew—now talk about someone brave. Andrew was brave. He never backed down to anyone or anything. Me? I'm really not all that brave, Atia."

"But you killed King Maji! That alone takes a lot of bravery."

"You kidding me? I nearly pissed myself when I had to fight him. Frankly I had no business killing him."

"Then what happened?"

I kick a rock toward an odd looking tree. "His arrogance and my luck. Got a lucky cut on one leg early and the way the fight developed, I was gifted an opportunity to blow out his other one. But I should be dead. Besides, that doesn't make me more confident. If anything, it makes me wonder how much more luck I have left. Besides, I ain't exactly excited to head back to my old life either."

"Why?"

"Just . . . It's hard to explain," I say looking away. "I had a twin brother— Andrew—he was, well . . . He was my best friend."

"It's good to know I'm not the only one feeling this way then. With no way out I mean."

"No, you aren't," I say, quickly turning the conversation toward a more positive note. "Plus, I have a feeling you're going to do something great. Something that will get us all home. I know you are meant for something miraculous, Atia. We all are, and we all have a certain genius about us. It's just most of the time, we impose our own self limitations and rob ourselves of our potential. Don't be one of those people."

"Thank you, Nirue," she says as she wraps her arms around me. I levitate my hands over her back, because I know Ranger would be upset. I can tell he likes her. But the truth is, we are just friends, and this is a friend-hug, nothing more.

After embracing for a moment, Atia moves her hands off my neck and points. "Look at that tree, Nirue." Atia points to willow that reaches only half way to the top of the canopies. Yet, it is in full bloom. Not a single branch is void of green. On top of that, there appears to be a hole at the base of the trunk. As we get closer to the tree Atia freezes. "There's something in it. I-in the tree. Look!"

I keep my eyes on her for a moment before looking up. High up in the tree is a person with different color leaves surrounding his face like a mane. It's a boy. I take one step and he vanishes. Three leaps from branch to branch and he is lost amidst the canopies. "What do you suppose that was Nirue?"

I shake my head. "I dunno. He looked like a boy. Did you see the way he bounded out of the tree?" I trail off. "We'll have to ask Bertram." She agrees. Around the tree Atia notices a reddish-orange flower that we had not seen yet. It has the petals of an orchid but the structure of a tulip—long and skinny. Atia grabs a handful. We had been traveling for about an hour so I suggest we head back. She agrees and we return to our trail, hopeful we have the right food.

It takes us a little over two hours to get back. Apparently I hadn't made obvious enough signals to track our way back. When we arrive Ranger and Bertram are already feeding the patriarch what they had found.

Ranger started with a type of climbing vine. Nothing. Bertram gives it a buttress root. Nothing. I try the beetles. Nothing. We give it everything in our packs. Atia tries blue flowers to no avail. "I'm starting to think big-fella over here has eaten his fair share of everything in the forest." I jest. Ranger shakes his head in disbelief.

"Oh! What about those reddish-orange flowers? Did I give those to you Nirue?"

I check. "No. I thought you had them?"

"Found them!"

"Where did you get those flowers?" Bertram asks.

"Near a small tree amidst bigger canopy trees" Atia explains. "Why?"

"No reason. Just curious." He avoids eye contact like he knows something. Atia shrugs and feeds it the flower. It stops moving and white appears in its giant black eyes. Not a lot, but enough to notice. It lets out a trumpet and tucks its front legs underneath him. The trunk rests on the ground for a makeshift ladder. The other tempo's come from deep in the forest and join the patriarch in its stance. We high-five each other.

Before we get on I suggest we make some sort of controlling device. Bertram agrees. We gather up the thickest vine we can grab from the surrounding area. Ranger cuts off strips of bark to use as bridles in the tempos' mouth. I fasten vine through the bark and insert it in the creature's mouth. I nearly vomit. Bertram has to make three different bridles due to picking the hungriest Tempo.

It is a delicate walk up the trunk to the head. I feel like I'm hurting it, but really I am the equivalent to a fly on my own head. Its back is comfortable. The thick wool provides for a good butt-cushion and the creature's rigid spine makes a nice saddle. Once everyone is fastened we set off following Bertram's lead.

The tempos are great trailblazers. On them we move ten times as fast as we would on foot. They also provide security. There are an endless number of creatures with even more places to hide. I'm glad we are twenty feet off the ground, but even this high we aren't a third of the way up the trees.

We trek until near dark before stopping and setting up camp. We tie up our tempos and begin the process of creating beds. Before long we are fast asleep.

We wake with the sun and quickly clean up. I rouse Ranger to pick up his pace a bit. He mumbles curse words at me.

We hop back on our tempos and set off. Miles ahead of us is a mesa that towers hundreds of feet over the trees.

"You would have to stack the tallest tree in Hardrain on top of itself forty times over to reach the top," Bertram declares. Waterfalls come off it at all angles. Sunlight cascades off the light blue rivers pouring down the mesa. "Beautiful," Atia says through a smile. It really is.

In another few minutes our view of the mesa is blocked, and we are back staring at a wall of trees. Bertram pauses his Tempo and looks at us, "Well, we are at a crossroads of sorts. We can take our Tempos directly at the mesa. That way is perilous. Or, we can circle toward the coast, which will add at least a day to our journey, but is much quieter. Keep in mind, you haven't entered the grounds yet."

Ranger opens his mouth, but before he says anything I cut him off, "I say we go straight through. Let's just get this done." Atia casts me a sideways glance then looks down at her hands. Ranger looks between us, figuring out what is going on.

"Makes no difference to me. This is still only your second trial," Bertram offers, non-sympathetically. "Ranger?"

"Atia?"

She bites the inside of her cheek and fiddles with the reins in her hand. "I guess whatever Nirue thinks." Ranger narrows his eyes, focusing on Atia. Keeping his eyes on her, he nods his head toward Bertram in agreement.

"So it's settled I say." Bertram shakes his head and adjusts himself in his saddle.

"So be it." He offers. He flicks the vines and kicks the sides of his Tempo. He mumbles under his breath. I think I hear him say, "Just when you think you have a good group, they go and do something like this."

"What'd you say?" I ask him. His eyes are wide, surprised I heard him.

He looks back at the trees as if nothing happened. "Be quiet in these parts. Please. For all of you. For all of us." I shake my head and spit onto the trail. This guy is up to something.

Four sweaty hours behind the butt of the patriarch Atia is riding we finally see the mesa walls. I pull my Tempo to the forest line on the right to collect new vine for my bridle. I hear a low-bellied growl. Atia screams. I see her tempo rear back on its hind legs and trumpet.

"JUST HOLD ON ATIA," Bertram yells. I can't see what is going on so I yank my tempo to back to the left.

Two giant black cats stand in front of Atia, baring teeth, drooling, veins pulsing from ripped legs. Two more jump out from either side and begin to circle us. They have long, serrated sabre-teeth. Their entire bodies are black except for half of their tail, which is light red. One of them snaps and jumps up at Atia, claws flashing. The patriarch instinctively turns to face it with his mighty black tusks. The remainder of the tempos try to form a circle. Instead, we end up forming the shape of a chicken's foot with my side being the most exposed.

The cats circle us. The biggest one has red in the fur down its nose. It stays still, evaluating every move we make. Their eyes are deep and black.

I load *Evergold* and wait. I can't get a clean shot with all of this movement. While we are in formation, Atia's tempo does its job to scare off the cats. But the more it fights them off, the more exposed it becomes.

"Atia," I yell, "try to keep close to us. I think they are purposely trying to bring you away from the group." She pulls on the vines with all of her strength but nothing happens. The tempo doesn't even feel her.

One by one the cats induce the patriarch into a charge and little by little they gain ground. Then they make their move. Two go underneath and bite at its hind legs. It screams and gets on its front feet to fling the assailants outward, like a bucking horse. When it dips down in front, the biggest cat jumps on its trunk and begins making its way up the head. Atia's *Dicers* tumble to the jungle floor, blue glowing through rotted leaves.

Her tempo tries desperately to shake the cat but its claws are too deep, its grip too tight. Atia slowly crawls backward on the spine of the patriarch, hands gripping the fur tight. The tempo is in full panic mode. It shakes and bucks and does everything it can to get rid this cat. If it gets to Atia, she will die.

I pat the side of my tempo. *"Stay still for me,"* I say to it while standing up. Bow in my left hand, I extend both arms out sideways to balance while my tempo moves around, trying to figure out how to help its patriarch. The big cat is now on the head of the patriarch and making ground on Atia. The tempo shakes hard and nearly loses the big cat, but the fur provides too good of grip for it to hang on to. Atia nearly slides off, but grabs a chunk of fur just in time. The cat is patiently moving toward Atia.

I go to my place and slow my breathing. I hear a few birds and the wind moving leaves. I feel the heartbeat of the massive creature below me. I can now feel my own heartbeat. I look up and have tunnel vision of Atia's situation. I load *Evergold* and wait for the tempo to stop moving. It flails like a beached fish gasping for air. It makes the shot nearly impossible.

I focus even harder. I begin to feel the tempo's movement below me like a wave. It is pattern like. I hear nothing but my own breathing now. I am sweating. A bead drops from my forehead into my right eye. I don't even blink. The creature gets closer to Atia.

It's just as focused as I am. Atia is holding on with two hands now, screaming for help. She looks to her right to see how close the cat is to her. Other cats are ready if she falls.

The big cat is three feet from Atia, but I still don't have a good shot. A smaller cat jumps up the side of her tempo, clinging to the wool. This diverts the main cat's attention just long enough for me to take my shot. High right. The big cat unbridles a deep moan. Atia screams and looks to me, then back to the cat. I balance against the movement of the tempo under me and aim a foot in front of the big cat. Last chance.

CHAPTER ELEVEN

*Focus is an ally. So is composure. For when one is both
focused and composed, there is a certain level of automation
that occurs and results in peak performance.*

Telanel, on training with sharp ends

EYES WATERING FROM NOT BLINKING, I loose another arrow.
Headshot. The big cat drops on impact. Even though it is dead, it dangles
from the tempo by its front right paw, claws stuck in the fur. The other
cats become nervous. Their formation is no longer clean. The tempos
sense this and begin to rush at them. They scream and claw at their trunks.
I nearly fall off of mine as it swipes a smaller cat into the tree line. The
remaining cats flee.

It takes us almost an hour to fully calm the tempos. It is only when
Atia offers the last of her special flowers that they stop jumping at every
cracked twig.

"I don't think I will ever be able to repay you," she says, face flushed. I
tip an imaginary hat toward her and smile. Ranger skins the big cat for me
and gives me all the claws. Each one is half the size of his forearm. Each one

sharp enough to cut skin with minimal pressure. He asks if he can take the fur and I let him. I wasn't going to do anything with it.

After three more hours of traveling Bertram yells for us to stop. We are forty yards from the base of the mesa, near one of the hundred waterfalls. I can feel the mist coming off of the bucketing water. It's refreshing.

"We need to set up camp here," Bertram says as he rubs the side of his tempo's ear and slides down the trunk to the ground. It's getting dark. I look to Ranger and Atia who, at this point, aren't going to argue with him. "I'll gather some wood for beds. Ranger, want to help?" He nods and grabs *Darkwater*.

We head into the forest, staying within earshot of each other. Ranger yells for me to come over. He holds the top part of a smaller tree steady while I hack at it with my axe. I notice the runes look brighter green than normal. It's probably the bark from this young tree.

We spend nearly an hour harvesting trees and head back to camp. Atia and Bertram have a fire going and are cooking a jungle stir-fry primarily made of vegetables. It feels good to sit around the fire. The tempos are tied up nearby, feeding on overgrown grass.

"Why did you want us to set up camp here?" Ranger asks pointedly. Bertram's body is slightly rocking back and forth. He seems on edge. Your journey begins through that waterfall. He points without looking at it. Once it begins, it will not stop.

"What's the trial?" I ask. Bertram pauses. "Survive."

He doesn't say anything more. I motion my hand clockwise and toward him, asking him to elaborate. "Well, I shouldn't say that's *all* you have to do. You must also wake *the Keeper*. But, the hardest part will be staying alive. Those cats were but an appetizer for what's to come. However, if you wake the Keeper in time, your odds will increase dramatically."

I've learned it's best to not ask questions in certain situations. Since I was a young man I loathed overly cautious people always asking questions, looking for security in every angle. It takes the fun out of it. The risk. Not me. I get the gist of a situation and go forward without looking back. In this situation, I'm going to do the same.

"Where is the Keeper?" Atia asks. I roll my eyes.

"Hidden. If I knew, I would tell you. Trust me." She cross grips her biceps anxiously. "Get some rest. You will need it."

When we wake up the next morning Bertram is gone. So are the tempos. We gather our things and make our way toward the waterfall. It doesn't take us long to reach the threshold. I have to yell so that Atia and Ranger can hear me over the torrent.

"Remember what Bertram said, once we enter there's no going back. Are you ready?" Ranger nods. Atia shrugs and jumps into the waterfall. Immediately after entering the cave behind the waterfall, the sound of a thousand birds springing from trees fills our ears. A drum beat staccatos off the walls of the cave.

Duh dun-dun-dun, Duh dun-dun-dun, Duh dun-dun-dun,
Duh dun-dun-dun.

We look around for the source of the sound but cannot find anything. We don't search for long because the cave leads straight up, void of any side channels. It takes us nearly five hours to climb to the top, although it was easier than I expected because a stairway had been carved out of the rock. At the top of the cave is a large opening that leads to the forest below. The area itself dips down in a concave shape, like a bowl.

The forest is thick. Thicker even than the forest that is now hundreds- if not thousands of feet below us. In the distance we see something massive moving through the forest. Whatever it is, it is headed right toward us. The drum gets louder.

Duh dun-dun-dun, Duh dun-dun-dun
Duh dun-dun-dun

"Do you think they are tempos?" I ask Atia.

"Maybe. But the tempo's we rode didn't move that fast. And they actually knocked down the trees, remember? Whatever that is just moves around them." She is right. It gets closer and the drum gets louder. We duck behind a rock at the top of the opening to conceal our presence. Atia gasps and covers her mouth. Ranger adjusts himself with noticeable unease. We all do our best to hold our breath. Time seems to slow down.

A hundred feet below us is an open field with hundreds of yards of space from its center. Colossal men crash through the trees to our right into a clearing directly below us. In a few bounds they are in the center of the field. They garb an assortment of bones in their ears, noses and lips. They are tanned and covered with tattoos. Their solo means of clothing is a loincloth.

Each carries a spear twice the length of Ranger—about half the length of their own bodies. It's hard to tell for sure because they are running at such a fast pace. In the opposite hand they don wooden shields with a symbol painted in white and red on the front. They appear to be on patrol rather than hunting something specific. The earth shakes when they run.

Ranger comes around the rock to get a better look at them. Two take off but one stays put, nose in the air, sniffing. It circles, looking for the scent of something. It screams. The other two stop in their tracks. It points in our direction. The other two scream and run toward the wall. I rip Ranger back behind the rock. A spear sticks into the rock wall above our head. Pieces of rock fly into our face. The wood part of the pole vibrates so fast it looks like it isn't moving.

"I think they are climbing the wall!" Atia says, clutching at our chests. A scream rings out through the cave.

CHAPTER TWELVE

Those creatures are beyond putrid. Filth drips from their rotting teeth. Stank reeks from their skin. But worst of all are those eyes—those cold, lifeless, instinct driven tar pits.

Sara, historian of the Jungle Valleys

THE DRUM BEATS LOUD. THE screams are getting closer, more frequent. I put the handle of the spear under my armpit and yank it out of the wall. I fall backward. The spear tumbles away. I try to grab it but the poles slides out of my reach. As I try to grab it I notice the giant men are occupied with something half way up the wall. I tell Ranger and Atia to be quiet. We peek over the edge.

The giant men are tearing something apart. All we can see is feathers flying and blood running down the tan wall. In a few minutes, they run back down the mountain, drum beat following them.

"Let's wait it out and see how long it takes for them to make another lap," Ranger suggests.

"Although, that only works if they take the same path." I offer. "I think we just go. We could be here forever. Besides, look how big this place is."

It's clear Ranger doesn't want to go down there. He adheres anyways. It's the right decision.

We make our way down the mountain, through the field and into the jungle fairly quickly. It's much more humid in the jungle atop the mesa. We are beleaguered by mosquitos.

"I bet there are over a thousand bugs per square foot in this place," Ranger says while swatting his neck. We get bit in every cleft of our bodies. I slip on some leaves and land in the mud. It has a smooth and milky texture. Atia points out the mosquitos don't bite me where the mud is. We cover our entire bodies in it.

It isn't long before we find out how this place got its name. Sporadic showers hit us the entire day. Raindrops are fruit sized and provide a sting whenever they land a direct hit. Hardrain. I look up as if to see if a higher being would smile at my recent enlightenment. For some reason the rain never collects in the forest. Ranger kept warning us about flash floods and the dangers they bring. However, the floods never come. We rarely ever see a puddle. Odd.

As a blessing and a curse, the rain does not cease. Rain means the bugs cannot bite us. It means we do not have to boil water and can collect it easily. It also means that bugs come back in larger numbers when it pauses. We have to reapply mud constantly. The mosquitos find the smallest deficiencies in Ranger's mud armor and proceed to expose it. It seems as though he has the sweetest blood.

At dusk we create a makeshift bed and use my cape as a roof. Ranger builds a fire with tinder from inside a dead log. He skins and cooks two snakes we caught on the way. One is overcooked and tastes like chalk. I don't eat it because it now lacks nutritional value.

It rains all through the night. My cape is long and stretched to provide a great roof. However, we are bereft of walls and the wind blows the rain in from the side. When we manage to relax in between spurts of rain, mosquitos make damn sure we don't take advantage of it. On top of that, thousands of eyes disconcertingly watch us from the forest.

I fully wake up when a mosquito tries pulling blood from my eyeball. I kill it for trying. I notice Atia had moved over and is now the smaller spoon against Ranger. He tenderly rubs her arm.

At dawn we waste no time searching for the Keeper. Even though he is dead tired, Ranger bush-wacks with animalistic drive. I have a lot of respect for him. After hours of traveling Atia happens upon three golden limestone bricks that appear to have been part of a path.

We cannot tell what direction we are moving in. Atia calls it "straight." However, the more "straight" we go, the more bricks we see, so we figure it's the right direction. Ranger finds one under the roots of a tree. Lots of trees in this area in particular have holes that seem to lead under their trunks and deep into the ground. It's not long before we are out of food and water. The denseness of the jungle is sucking the life out of us. We are hungry, thirsty and tired.

"I can't believe I'm saying this. I actually wish it would rain," Atia says while peeling dried skin from her lips. "It's crazy how quickly we gain then lose water."

"I wouldn't mind that either 'Tia," Ranger says.

I nod my head. "Let's press on, it will rain soon, we can be sure of that."

"Where are we even going Nirue? We don't have a plan and all we've found is a few measly bricks," Atia asks anxiously.

"The bricks are something at least. But, you're right, I don't have a plan. It makes sense to continue to try and find these bricks. If you have another suggestion, feel free to let me know. I'm all ears," I snap. She becomes noticeably upset by my reaction. I immediately regret my lack of self-control.

I feel bad because I know that my anger doesn't stem from the lack of sleep, or food, or constant mosquito bites. It's because I am sick of this twisted hand the universe has dealt me. I want to go home. I want to be with my family. I need to do whatever I can to secure a ticket back.

* * *

The bricks become more plentiful and easily detectable. The more bricks we see, the more confident we become. It hasn't rained all day. We are weary. Our once engaged conversations have turned to flippant repudiations of suggestions. Our once motivated speed has become a sloshing wade through the muck of malnutrition. We are exhausted.

We rest against a large tree with a sturdy base and minimal branches. While resting I notice a yellow brick structure and direct the group toward it. To my right is a wall that appears to be broken in half. I can tell because of the crumbled mortar and uneven shape. Below me are steps leading into a courtyard of limestone tiles. Canopy trees umbrella the square and block our view of the sun. At the end of the courtyard is a temple dilapidated from weather and time. A temple that, in its prime, must have been a sight to see. The brokenness of the temple suggests the structure would have pierced the canopy. I cannot prove that but my mind's eye tells me I'm right.

Atia and Ranger rush down the steps.

I walk slow, trance like. My right hand softly grazes the golden bricks with the gentleness one has when touching a piece of metal to see if it is too hot to grab. As I descend the steps, I feel the weight my emotions have placed on me. I feel anger and jealousy. I feel weariness and irritability. I feel anxiety and reluctance to go forward.

I try to relax. All this mud in my eyes and hair make it difficult to slip away into a day-dreamed stream of consciousness. These difficulties continue to pull me back. When I walk into the center of the square I have this urge to look up, so I do. I see a hint of grey but not much else because of the canopy. One, two, three raindrops fall on my face.

The rain starts slow and picks up quick, like a person who just hopped on a bike. A few hard pushes and it begins to pour. I close my eyes, take a deep breath and allow myself to let go. The water tastes so good as it fills my mouth. It breathes life into my soul. As I sit there, arms wide with rain pouring on me, I appreciate the significance of this lifeblood. The rain washes away my fear, anger and jealousy the same way it washes the dirt from my body. The water washes me inside and out. When I open my eyes amidst the rain I see Ranger delicately holding Atia in his arms. They are kissing.

I was wondering when this was going to happen. If asked ten minutes ago, I wouldn't have cared at all. Now, I am happy for them. Happy for my friends. Happy for the brief moments like this wherein we escape our fates of the unknown, where we deprive anxiety of exposing the flaw in our emotional mud armor. I have caught my second wind.

I walk over to them. It takes them a brief moment to recognize that I am standing there. They pull away from each other. Ranger's ears are red. Atia fiddles with her shirt.

It's pouring now, so I have to speak loud for them to hear me over the pattering.

"I think we should take shelter in there if nothing else." They nod and we hurry up the steps of the temple. Ranger uses his bag to cover Atia's head like a gentleman. Vines caress the open air of the doorway. There's a noticeable difference in temperature at the threshold. Moss has taken over most of the walls. Rain collects on the floors where the tile has given way to age and massive footsteps.

Because it's dark, we use 'Tia's daggers to light the way. We make our way through a vast hall that used to have vaulted ceilings. Now, trees have become the greater of forces and have found a way to grow through the tile and burst through the roof. Only parts of it are intact. It feels like we are outside even though we are not. The temple is not very big in size. It appears to only have one main room, save a small tunnel in the back that is lit by torches.

"Someone lit those torches," I say as I quietly avoid puddles. I motion for Atia to put away her daggers. We walk over to the tunnel and descend into a much smaller but brighter room. In the center of it hovers one of the giants. This one looks like the ones we saw traversing the forest yesterday but even bigger. His body is completely tattooed so that his skin appears to be a shade of green, save part of his face, which carries the red and black of the cats that attacked our party.

His jaw is pronounced and deathly strong. His eyes are closed. It feels like he is the one keeping himself hovering off the ground, but I know that's not true. A green aura surrounds his body like a force field. Shrunken heads hang from a low ceiling like beehives.

Along the sides of the wall are sentences in languages we cannot understand. We scour the walls for anything legible. Ranger finds one written in our native tongue. It reads:

"Here lies the Keeper. Hide your face from the darkness that masks the beasts. Light the wood to set him free."

We read it repeatedly to ourselves and achieve nothing more than slack expressions. None of this makes sense. We check every corner and crevasse for something to light. Ranger finds a piece of wood in a rotten chest in the corner and proceeds to light it on fire. Nothing happens. I take apart shrunken heads in the hope something will be inside. This leaves me with slimy fingers and gunky nails, but nothing else.

"Maybe we missed something outside," Ranger suggests. "I noticed some odd carvings in the stones near the path that leads down here."

"Worth a shot," I submit. "Let's do it."

We venture back outside and start turning over every stone possible, leaving none the absent. The pouring rain makes it hard to remember which ones we had looked under. Still, we have nothing to light.

"The hell are we supposed to light, huh?" 'Tia asks. "All of this wood is sopping wet, and it would take us years to light it all." Then comes the faint beat of a drum.

Duh dun-dun-dun, Duh dun-dun-dun
Duh dun-dun-dun

My back shivers. Ranger pauses mid-air. I run up the steps to see where it's coming from. The tune comes again, this time a smidge louder. I can see trees crashing in the distance behind the temple. They are moving fast.

"Quick!" I yell to them. "Into the temple!" Atia shakes her head and pulls out *Dicers*. "The hell are you doing 'Tia!" Ranger yells as he tries to pull her inside.

She shakes her head again and postures a battle ready stance. "They will find us in there. This is a better place to fight. I *have* to fight Ranger. My fire burns low." She says this last bit with tears in her eyes. Ranger's well up too. It's so much to take in with such little time to think. Ranger gives her one long look and pulls out *Darkwater*. He pretends to get ready to fight then grabs Atia by the shirt and drags her inside. She fights him like a cat avoiding water. *Duh dun-dun-dun, Duh dun-dun-dun.* The sound is deafening it is so close.

"DID YOU SEE HOW BIG THEY ARE, 'TIA? DID YOU?" He screams at her. I load *Evergold.* The sound of crashing trees means battle is imminent. The pouring rain does nothing to add confidence. Everything we have accomplished thus far will mean nothing if we can't make it out alive. I can hear Bertram now . . . "The hardest part will be surviving . . ."

Amidst the canopy the little boy with the mane of leaves hops into the square and stares at me. He is completely covered in mud. Frightened, he runs and dives into a hole at the base of a nearby tree. Then he is gone.

Atia and Ranger continue struggling. The rain gains momentum and comes down even harder. We hear a crash in the trees fifty yards beyond the temple. "FOLLOW ME!" I yell with my most commanding voice. They stop fighting and watch me dive into the hole underneath the tree. Ranger picks up Atia and throws her into the hole. I grab her and cover her mouth. Ranger dives in just in time to see the giants step into the courtyard.

They pause and sniff around like a bloodhound that has just lost its trail. Each one sniffing and smelling in circles. Their long hooked noses detect the faintest of scents as they re-create our every movement. This is the first time I have seen them up close and not running. They are ugly creatures, meant for something out of a nightmare. They smell rotten too. A lanky one crosses the threshold of the temple and lets out a scream so loud we cover our ears.

The little boy pats me on the shoulder and thumbs me to follow him. Atia, now wide-eyed and shaking, takes note and offers surrender. I lift my hand from her mouth. Ranger stares at the boy in confusion.

We are guided through a tunnel as black as a night with no moon and cloud cover. Tree roots and dirt make our cavernous trek that much more distasteful. The air is cool down here, like the runoff room in Rizcarth.

The little boy moves with haste as he twists through the wormholes. The venue is akin to an anthill, with endless routes to choose from. We make our way to the well-lit center of the human anthill. People young and old are donned in leaves of orange, green and brown around their faces like manes. They stare at us with curious eyes. The person I presume to be the chief sits on a chair made of wormwood. Once in the epicenter, I create a map of this place with my mind's eye. Guards approach us with dripping spears.

CHAPTER THIRTEEN

No man can be a sage in his hometown. Take him far away, where people aren't familiar with his past mistakes or shortcomings, and you allow him an entirely new reality.

Observations From On High, fourth stanza

THE CHIEF HOLDS UP A dirty hand. The guards circle us at a slow, watchful pace. "Who are these people and why have you lead them to our home, Sero?" The little boy sits cross-legged and keeps his hands folded in his lap. His eyes stay on the ground.

"I don't know who these people are, but I think they wish to wake the Keeper. I saw them collecting flowers for the Tempo near the tree of graces and noticed their strange appearance."

The chief scratches his chin with rotten nails that look as if he dug these tunnels with his own hands. "You speak of the prophecy, Sero?" The little boy nods his head.

A man with feathers in his headdress walks over and whispers in the chief's ear. He must be second in command. The chief looks up and takes in some air.

"You there. Let me see your bow." He motions for me to come over. I walk slowly through the guards and up wooden steps to the chief. I take *Evergold* off my back and hand it to him. He examines every crevasse of it as if he were a jewel maker, determining whether the raw block can be cut into a precious stone.

He whispers something into featherman's ear and the man nods. They talk for minutes about the depiction of the man chained to the beast. I cannot hear the rest of their conversation.

"Where did you get this bow?" the chief asks. I look to Atia and Ranger. How can I possibly explain it? A blue creature in a camp of which location, I still don't know? Even then, would that make a difference? This man cannot possibly know Bertram, or the blue creature. I give the only response that seems appropriate. "Home."

The chief's eyes change colors from brown to orange, like the leaves surrounding his face. Blood visibly pumps through his body. A vein in his shoulder becomes more pronounced. Was it something I said?

"IF you want to mock me, you WILL not leave here alive. My best advice to you, *stranger*, is to be forthcoming about your knowledge of these weapons." He takes a drink from a wooden goblet and his eyes change from orange to blue. I guess that means he relaxed again?

"What do you call this?" He holds up my weapon—my friend. "*Evergold*," I say, matching icy blues for icy blues. The chief's mouth slowly goes slack. He knocks the goblet off of the arm of his wormwood chair. His eyes go from blue to white—no pupils at all. Whispers and eyes fall upon me like I am the only light in a dark room.

The chief walks slowly down the stairs with demon-white eyes. His hands reach out in front of him as if the disappearance of his pupils have caused him to go blind. He makes his way to me and touches my face with both hands. They move around with curious precision, examining my features.

"So it is true." Whispers in the crowd. He motions for everyone to be quiet. "The prophecy is alive. You are here to save our people. To wake the Keeper, are you not?" I am hesitant to answer because I was never told that saving *natives* would be part of the task. I cannot afford, no, we cannot afford to spend any more time in this jungle than necessary.

"If saving your people is a secondary product of waking the Keeper, then yes." The chief grins and his eyes flash from white to brown again. He looks me up and down. "Then why don't we get started."

*   *   *

The chief fills our bellies with soup much better than anything our group put together thus far. It is rich and thick with nutrients needed to replenish our aching bodies. We enjoy fresh water and juices that give us a sugar boost. These people are colorful, and so are their drinks. I drink the spectrum of a rainbow in one sitting. Atia cuddles in Ranger's lap and kisses him with passion. Full, tired and dirty, I lay down on a cot made from stretched animal hide. I chat with some of the locals and they lend me answers to my various questions.

The reason water rarely collects on the jungle floor is because of their underground system. An old man with one tooth claims to be personally responsible for planting half of the mesa-forest. Younger generations roll their eyes and laugh the notion away.

An elderly woman with grey hiding behind her leaf-mane comes and sits at the end of my cot. She asks, "May I tell you a story young man?" I smile and nod my head. She reminds me of my grandmother, who used to tell me stories and scratch my back before bed as a boy.

She coughs and begins her tale. "Since the beginning of time, my people have lived in Hardrain. They hunted the woods and planted the ground, growing the land from a small orchard to a forest of unmatched diversity. We did so in peace, for our people were protected by the Keeper. It was a wonderful relationship." She smiles and looks up to the roof of the epicenter, as if remembering a memory long lost.

"He patrolled the jungles and fended off the Jboynei; those giant men you see running our forest. So long as our people gave him plenty of food to eat, he vowed to protect us. And so it was, for many generations.

Then a dark time fell upon the people of Hardrain. They became greedy and started murdering for simple acres of land and riparian privileges. Civil war lead to death and divisions among my people. This saddened the Keeper so. He tried to stop the fighting, talking to the leaders of the divided tribes. When this did not work, he began building a temple of golden bricks at the center of Hardrain. He told my people that if they did not stop their fighting by the time he finished the temple, he would fall into a deep slumber until awoken by a people deserving of his protection. This would leave them to fend for themselves, for he would not protect a people from death if they would willingly lay their own at its feet.

The Keeper spent months building this temple. Day and night and he worked. When he was near completion he sat on top of the temple that then scratched the skies, holding his last brick. He waited two weeks for the fighting to stop, but it never did. In fact, it only got worse. Greed, lust and corruption seeded deep into the heart of my people. Overcome with sadness, the Keeper began to cry. You could hear his moans from the farthest reach of our forest. He cried for days, and the weather matched his heart. Clouds covered the mesa and rain filled the jungle, bringing disease and death—never discriminating its victims. Without hope the Keeper placed his last brick down and closed his eyes. Our people began to die by the masses. A once vibrant culture diminished into scattered remnants of something beautiful. The rains never stopped."

She shakes her head and looks into her empty palms. "Jboynei moved in and killed off what disease did not. They hunt us down for sport. It has been this way for so long that we are now their main source of food. All they know is the hunt. My great-great-grandfather was one of the lucky ones to survive the Keeper's disappearance. Barely escaping death, he began burrowing underground. Other people joined in on the task and dug to hide from the Jboynei. My people were but a budding plant of what used to be a canopy tree. They spent years digging a vast underground network, wherein we could come up from under great trees, gather food, and duck away into our hole like vermin. My grandfather's brother said, 'the greatest luck to befall our people is the diversity of women to replenish our masses.' He was right. So our men and women arranged marriages and began raising children. Some women produced as many as thirty children. Our tunnels grew deeper and our canals much more coordinated. For years we battled flood from the rain, until we crafted divergents, which created the vast waterfalls you see spilling from the mesa."

"I had no idea that happened to your people. Greed is an insidious beast." She nods in approval, eyes far away.

"How do you wake him up?" "

"You must first visit his temple, which will explain much."

"I went to the temple and saw the writing on the wall."

"Ah. Good, very good. So you must think that a fire will wake him up, no?"

I sit up and adjust myself, slightly embarrassed at my apparent misconception of the riddle. "We didn't have much time to think about it before the Jboynei picked up our scent."

She dances a hand in front of her face. "Do not blame yourself. Half of my people do not understand the true meaning, for they dismiss our histories because of their trust in their own mind. What they can see, touch, feel, taste—that's what they believe in because that is what they can explain. You see, when people cannot explain something it is easier for them to trust in what they *can* explain. So, they build off what they can, and agree the rest must be provable by touch sign or reason."

"I don't understand."

"Think of it like this. The people can explain the rain as water evaporating into the clouds and returning to the ground. They know that from physically watching the raindrops return and fall, return and fall. They do not *believe* that it continues because of the Keeper legend, but rather because of a continual cycle that has been, and never will change. What they can't explain is a being that floats above the ground and seems to live forever. However, they do not believe the legend to explain the Keeper. Rather, they believe there must be some natural cycle to attribute it to—no divine intervention. Something that they can explain by touching, seeing, reasoning—you get the point. They would rather not believe that some questions simply don't have answers. But I believe different. There are two truths. Truths revealed and truths concealed."

I sit with my fists under my chin. I understand. It's easy for me to believe what she is saying. I came from a completely different world. A place where giants look like Ranger, and whales swim in the oceans, not rivers in the desert. I can understand why it is not so easy for these people to believe.

"So, if it is not a fire, how does one 'light the wood to set him free?'" She smiles at me with warmth that only true love can radiate. Not love like Ranger and Atia, who are now playing a game involving frogs and sticks with children. A love from a person who *values* life and understands the importance of virtue. A person who, when seeing such virtues in another person, falls in love with them because they are not like everyone else. They are *for* everyone else.

She points to the little boy who helped us escape the Jboynei. "You see Sero over here?" I nod. "You see the device he is playing?" I nod again and say, "It's an ocarina flute."

She agrees but lifts a finger to point out a difference while drinking some juice. "We call them wind-flutes." She pauses and continues.

"Hidden beneath a secret waterfall is a red wind flute. There will undoubtedly be Jboynei guarding it. That will also be your clue as to its whereabouts. I can tell you the general direction, but I cannot tell you its exact location." Sero walks up after eaves-dropping.

"I think I know where it is."

"Do you now?" The old woman smiles and lifts the boy to her lap. "If you are so brave and adventurous, where might this place be?" She asks, expecting him to say something silly, as any boy his age would.

"Past the darkness, just beyond the marshes I was chasing frogs. A green one with red and white dots hopped through a small waterfall entrance so I followed. Inside the cave was a sleeping Jboynei. The first time I ever seen one sleeping grandma!"

Her reaction is expectedly sour. This boy really knows where the wind-flute is.

"What do you think you're doing traveling that far outside the network, huh?!" She slaps him on the back of the head.

He squeezes his eyes shut and rubs the spot his grandmother just slapped. "But grandma I like to adventure. I would have never found these people by the grace tree if I hadn't left the protection of our network. Besides, the network is *stupid* anyway. It's cold and boring and full of worms." She scowls at him with the apparent aspiration to disintegrate him with her now fire colored eyes.

"If I might interject," I say as I tiptoe around the flame. Grandma's eyes change color from orange to black to pink. What emotion is that?

"If it wasn't for your grandson, we would have been dead. Our group was ready to take them on and if he wasn't there, we more than likely would have died."

Grandma takes a while staring into my eyes. Does she think I want to use the boy for my own purpose? Does she trust me? "Well, you most certainly would have died. You can injure the Jboynei, but you cannot kill them. Only the Keeper can. Their bodies heal within minutes of a wound." She looks the boy over. "Maybe you *are* as adventurous as I mocked you to be."

"Will you allow him to show us the way?" I learned it was always better to ask someone else's relative for such requests. If I allow the boy to ask, the answer will most certainly be no. Still, the answer is no, and it is unequivocal.

"If I cannot find the way, how will I save your people?" I ask her. She thinks long and hard. "A map," she says through gritted teeth "I will not allow this boy to come to harm. I won't. If the chief tells him to go, then that is another matter."

In that moment the chief rests a hand on my shoulder.

"Thought I heard my name being thrown about. What for?"

We take time explaining the situation and arguing for and against Sero joining the trip. Atia and Ranger are entirely unaware of the situation at hand. They are too lost in each other's eyes.

The chief hears both sides of the argument but denies Sero leave. He won't risk the life of a child—not for anything. Through gritted teeth I hold my tongue. Responding poorly won't help our cause, and these people are feeding us and providing shelter from the Jboynei.

In a few hours the tribe goes to sleep. Atia, Ranger and I are given cots in the epicenter. The children are in one wing and the adults in another. The chief has his own private tunnel. I explain our situation to Atia and Ranger. When I am sure everyone is asleep, I rouse my team. After a couple minutes of arguing with a cranky and groggy Ranger, I convince him to help me find Sero.

We quietly walk the tunnel of the children's wing, a single torch in my hand. Their beds have been dug into the walls of the tunnel. Bamboo sticks are elegantly stuck in the mud, spelling out each child's name in alphabetical order. When we get to Sero's bed we find it empty. Before I can suggest an alternative plan someone tugs at my tunic.

Sero, fully dressed with a small dagger and a travel pack motions for us to follow him. We climb roots up through the exit-hole and into the forest at midnight. Thinking on what the tribe will do once they realize we disobeyed their chief and are risking the life of a young boy in the process is worrisome. The sounds of the forest at night are even more cause for panic. I dust myself off once on level ground. Pitch black with no torch, we enter the dense forest, searching for the cave of the man-eating Jboynei.

CHAPTER FOURTEEN

Deny his whispers and his voice will be even softer.
Entertain the whispers, invite permanent house-guests.

Warlauffel: On Demons and Dark Things

SERO SAYS THE JBOYNEI AREN'T as active when the sun hides. The forest is alive. Birds, bugs and beasts illuminate the darkness with eyes and howls that would make the bravest warrior think twice about continuing. We follow Sero until daybreak, jumping with blades ready at the slightest of noises.

When dawn arrives we are noticeably tired. Ranger is worried, and rightfully so. Atia's health is declining at a rapid rate. I hadn't noticed it last night, probably because I have been so focused on waking the Keeper. During a break, Atia wanders off to pick bananas. Ranger uses this opportunity to speak with me in confidence.

"I'm worried 'bout 'Tia, Nirue . . ." his voice trails off while looking into the forest, making sure she cannot hear. "She feels cold. Her skin is becoming paler and she's walking funny."

Just reassure him. There's nothing else you can do.

I rest a hand on his shoulder. "She probably ate some bad jungle soup. Maybe caught some bacteria from unpurified water before we entered Hardrain. We will get through this and Bertram will nurse her back to health. Okay?"

He wants to believe me so he does. Truth is, I have no idea why her health is declining. It could be anything. I fear the worst but I have to keep his spirits up. He nods and smiles with the unrelenting will to think positive about the situation, as if it were him who was dying.

We get to the edge of the forest to a marshland with tall red reeds. Before we enter the reeds Sero directs us to a tree with bird nests on every branch. He tells us if we don't eat the eggs, we won't be attacked. At the top of the tree is the biggest nest, which Ranger could comfortably stand in. I don't want to piss off whatever lives there. Sero asks to use *Darkwater* from Ranger but isn't strong enough to wield it. He then takes one of Atia's daggers and makes deep cuts in the trunk.

He explains these types of trees harvest a sap that, when applied, hide one's smell from the Jboynei. Once we cut deep enough the sap trickles out like a small cut to the forearm. We spend an hour applying it to every part of our body and even our weapons. The sap hardens and makes us wax impressions of our former selves. We displace sunlight like syrup.

The marsh is the only area devoid of outlets. Standing water is collected in pockets, snaking their way through reeds, grass, and half submerged logs. Moldy decaying plants cause Atia to cover her nose with her tunic. Sero picks a spider from a glaring-web strung between grass stalks.

The wind howls at us like a beast warning off other predators from its kill. Reptiles furnish the land with watchful disdain for our presence. We are not wanted here.

Crossing the marshes takes more energy than I like. Between the sun beating down on our heads, the grass snagging and catching our pants, the sludge through the mud, and the mosquito bites, we wonder if the jungle isn't an easier trek. Eventually we make our way to the edge of the bowl.

Tucked behind mist is a rain-beaten rock spire that disappears upward into the clouds. A single raincloud pours down the spire feeding a constant waterfall. Frogs with red and white dots appear more frequently as we head toward it. "I think the rain cloud is a symbol of the Keeper's sadness," Sero offers. This boy carries the soul of a man much older than his body bespeaks.

We reach the edge of the spire and begin our trek up. Ranger carries all of Atia's supplies. She struggles to keep up with the group. I hope she can get better, but the prospects aren't promising. Sero, on the other hand, climbs the sun-dried rock with the ease of a spider on a curtain. The rock is tumultuous. The further we climb the more slippery it becomes. It is covered with holes, likely from weathering, which collect rain water and service breeding grounds for a variety of bugs. Sero grabs a centipede with white legs and eats it alive. He laughs as Atia holds her stomach, attempting not to wrench.

We find Sero's secret entrance. The boy looks like a golden statue as the sun reflects off his sappy skin. He points inside the waterfall, glancing at us to see what we think.

Whispering he says, "It's in there. Only two of us should go. Too many of us will certainly wake the beasts, and we need somebody keeping lookout." His eyes change from green to purple.

I assess the situation. The boy is the most nimble, Ranger the most strong, I with the best wits about. I look at Atia, who is a non-factor at this point, as she tries to harness vitamins from the hot sun. She looks like a ghoul trapped inside a transparent figurine of her once vibrant self.

I have to do this. Myself and Sero. He is the only one who knows how to play the wind-flute, and Ranger needs to be with Atia. There is no other choice. Ranger put himself in harm's way for me in Rizcarth. I'm up.

"I'll go." Ranger nods in approval and takes a seat next to Atia.

"Sero, do you think you can handle this?"

"Sure!" he says with excited ignorance. His eyes change from purple to blue. Ranger is noticeably unhappy that he has to sit this one out.

"Good luck brother," Ranger says as he grasps my forearm to his. As a man, I know Ranger wants to come. It's probably killing him that he can't. He feels like a scramp. But he has to pick the lesser of two evils. On one side of the coin he has to miss out on adventure and loses a direct hand in the outcome of this wretched game. On the other lies the possibility that Atia will die without saying goodbye.

I look at Sero and see nothing but excitement and confidence in his eyes. I, on the other hand, am scared. We can't kill these things and we can't wake them or we all die. That's a lot of pressure. Will they even be asleep?

"How do you know they will be sleeping? If they aren't active in the night, doesn't that mean they sleep during the night, and are active during the day?" I ask Sero. He shakes his head. "There is one fat one that does nothing but sleep. I think he just keeps guard. I have been in here more times than I told grandma, and every time he is sleeping. Problem is I can never steal the flute because he can smell me in his sleep. The waterfall washes off the sap." He points to the waterfall and shrugs.

"I can take care of that part," I say. How far inside do we have to go?" I was under the impression it was just on the other side of the fall.

Sero shrugs, "'Bout two, three minutes?" I take in the landscape for a moment. It really is a sight to see. Green marshland spotted with lakes full of activity, perfectly promulgating the circle of life, bordered by a forest unknown to anybody of my ancestry.

I take a deep breath and untie my cape. I put it over my head and let it fall over me like children who imitate ghosts with bed linens. I walk through the waterfall and throw it out to Sero, who appears through the waterfall with the cloak covering him with three feet to spare. We're in the belly of the beast.

CHAPTER FIFTEEN

I saw a man with a fatal wound. A tear through his chest, a wound he would not survive. There wasn't anything special about his last moments. No prophetic words of advice, no last heroic act. Just a realization in his eyes. It was actually happening. His time was up, and that was it.

Recorded statement from a soldier after the battle of Stourtin

THE PLACE IS DAMP AND dark and smells of excrements. We enter just far enough to escape the light beyond the waterfall, so that our eyes can adjust to the darkness. We should wait thirty minutes but adrenaline allows us only ten. Good enough.

We follow the cave deep into the mountain carved by the hands of the giant Jboynei. There are only two side routes that divert from the main tunnel.

My heart is pounding so hard it's physically moving my ribcage. I have to tell myself to breathe over and over until the mental fight begins to scare me. The fact that I cannot control my breathing makes me feel as though I am losing control. The reality is, my anxiety and instincts will continue to punish me until I relieve myself of the danger.

Back to the present. Fecal matter appears without any pattern I can deduce in my mind's eye, other than it being completely random. It seems these creatures don't care where they unload or where they eat.

At the end of the tunnel is a dimly lit room that I have to step back from momentarily. I stand spread-eagle against the wall, using my right hand to cover my mouth. Sero's eyes turn from red to pearl white. The smell is *too* bad. Dead bodies decorate the scene like something from a Shakespearean nightmare. Legs stick out of walls, arms hang from bone hooks on the celling, the heads of mighty black-cats sit one by one in a row of five.

Worst of all, there are *three* Jboynei sleeping around a stone platform. Not one that was made by any man, but one made from the Jboynei. It has been carved out of the rock with bones decorating its face, mortared together with guts and feces. Sero plugs his nose and points to the structure. Upon it lies a little red flute with a light green aura keeping it afloat. Words in a language I cannot understand are hurried across the wall behind it in blood.

Sero makes his move and I follow. My breath is hot. I risk the serious chance of catching a disease from these fowl creatures. At least if I had used my nose I could filter out some of it, but, under the circumstances, I breathe without my filter.

Like a deranged dog, the fat one lies in his own filth, right in front of the platform. To the right and left of the platform, two skinnier, yet equally filthy Jboynei sleep standing up. They keep their weight forward-balanced on bowed-spears like a high jumper in the moment before they release elastic energy.

I have a continual compulsion to look behind me. My skin is clammy; my muscles tense. Keeping quiet is much harder than I realized. Everything in my body wants to scream: my fingers, my toes, my hair, my eyes, my face. I want to leap out of my skin. It would be better if I were in the jungle and happened upon one of these beasts. At least then my fight instincts would kick in and I could have more confidence.

Not now. Now, I want to run. I want to be back sleeping in the comfort of the network and eating delicious fruits. I want to be with Bertram in camp, or even with Signy back among the comfy fixtures of royalty. I want to be home with my family in Dakota. But I'm not. I'm covered in sap in a cave with beasts that, with one false step, will not hesitate to use my spine as floss. Even worse, I'm not as brave as the little boy who does not even grow underarm hair.

He motions for me to go right of the fat one. He goes left. The fat one lies on his side with his legs scissor-like, open for the cut. My side has the legs. I carefully step over the first leg and avoid a chewed femur bone. It's a toothpick compared to the Jboynei's leg. I wonder if that's what it uses it for.

My breath is ceaseless. Instead of trying to control it, I hold it with each small movement. I can't hold it too long, or risk exhaling too much air, producing a noise. Some of my movements are involuntary. I am shaking.

I need to control myself. If I blow this, both of us could be killed. My eyes flash to Sero, who is already beyond the head of the fat Jboynei. I'm still in between its legs. I gather myself and go to my place. I now have tunnel vision, but at least I can control my body easier. With another step, I am past the first one.

Sero, with pure white eyes nods his head at me. I nod back.

Here comes the hardest part. The two spear-leaning Jbyonei stand inward, guarding the stairs leading to the platform. I have a guttural feeling telling me these creatures will be easier to wake than the fat one. It's natural. One sleeps deeper lying than standing.

My tunnel vision forces me to crane my neck to cover my surroundings. It's like looking through a spyglass. All peripherals are nonexistent.

Sero motions for me to wait at the bottom of the stairs. As carefully and quietly as I can, I grab *Evergold* and extract an arrow from my quiver, just in case. My eyes focus on Sero. He moves with grace, flawless like a diver entering the pool without a drop of splash. He gets to the top, noticeably holds his breath and plucks the wind-flute from its aura. I'm holding my breath as well. He looks to his right, nothing. He looks to his left, nothing. He turns around and looks at me with raised eyebrows like "We're almost there."

He begins what feels like the longest descent in human history, avoiding bones and flesh—anything that could cause a noise. Still the beasts sleep. Then he freezes.

Just below the fat one, a spider the size of my head crawls out of a skull. It emerges like death from a grave. We freeze and watch its every movement—every twiddle of its hairy legs. The spider is moving right toward the fat one. We hold our breath. I am sweating and salt fills my eyes, causing them to tear a little. I bite my lower lip. The spider stops right in front of the fat one's face as if to say its goodbyes. Not to the Jboynei, but *for* the Jboynei, to us. It scurries onto the cheek and then the nose. The Jboynei bellows and claws without concern of damage.

I turn and flash my eyes on the sleeping giant to the right of the platform. One eye is open, staring directly at me. Its eyes are black, just like the tempos, the cats and the creatures I saw at camp. In that moment the small end of the cave erupts in a terrifying frenzy.

The one that spotted me tilts its head to the ceiling and screams something out of a nightmare. I couldn't understand it and did not want to stick around and ask, but I know it was something communicative. In the same moment, it swings a spear in an arc-like fashion, breaking the pointed end against the back wall.

The other one wakes up, raises its head to the ceiling and lets out the same noise. The fat one is till attacking its own face as he searches for the spider. Sero is already gone. I run as fast as my legs can take me. The only thing I hear is ringing in my ears. I catch up to Sero in a matter of seconds, who's eyes are light yellow. We get to the area where two tunnels divert to the left and right. I go left, Sero goes right. I would prefer to have him with me but there is just no time to talk because the Jboynei are much faster than us.

My tunnel leads me to a dark pit of bones, blood and bodily excrements.

I know I won't have to face all three, because they were so close behind they had to have seen us split. Above me are three black cats in cages. Their ribs are showing. In a matter of seconds I throw them body parts, hoping to shut them up for the time being. There is a window that leads out of the cave and off the mesa. It is easily a thousand feet to the bottom. I tear my cloak and throw it out the window, hoping the Jboynei will think I jumped out. I take a deep breath and dive into the pit.

Moments later the creature pounds into the room. Its neck bulges as it screams, but all I hear is the ringing. I close my eyes and wait. The cats scratch and exchange swipes at each other. Only one Jboynei came in here I notice. I hope Sero made it.

It sniffs around, determined to find me. I can feel the room darken as it blocks the sunlight from the window. It whips his head around and scours the room. I close my eyes again, holding my breath.

Then, it jumps into the pit. It tears at the pit ceaselessly and sticks its nose into the newly-made hole like a dog burrowing for ground squirrels. It isn't long before he reaches me. He tears at the muck directly in front of me and, in the process, throws me up against the wall of the room. The cats scream and reach claws out at my presence. I smash my head against the wall. I am disoriented. Vision blurry. This is it—I am going to die. No more trials for Nirue. At least I won't be suffering any longer. I close my eyes and wait for it, but it doesn't come.

He hasn't noticed me.

In that moment something moves inside me. A surge of anger boils in me and explodes. While I slowly stand up I think:

I'm tired of being scared of these creatures. I'm tired of running and hiding. I'm tired of resorting to measures like lying in feces to hide. If I die, I die—so be it. But I damn sure won't die with my eyes closed like a coward. No. I'm going to fight. I'm going to fight until I die, because that's the type of person I am. I REFUSE to back down. It's now or never, Nirue.

I stand up and load *Evergold*. I focus and go to my place. My tunnel vision narrows even more. I put two arrows in its right foot. I put another two in its left. It screams. More ringing in the ears.

The creature is in pain but its wounds heal rapidly after it rips the arrows from its feet. I walk slowly backward through the room, eyes squinted like a man possessed. I don't even care to look behind me. The more it heals the faster it moves. Every fresh arrow leaves it more handicapped and unable to walk, until it heals.

I'm in the entrance of the tunnel and get an idea. I focus on the rope holding the cat cages to the ceiling. I notch and loose three arrows which drop all three cages of the black cats. The Jboynei doesn't even notice. Its right leg is almost completely healed so I put another one in for good measure. That slows it down a bit. The cats scream to be let free. They don't want to eat the rotten spoiled meat. They want it fresh. I continue backward, eyes never leaving the wounds on the Jboynei's feet. Every time a wound seals, I replace it with another from my quiver. I continue this and keep the Jboynei at a slow walk.

We take the side-tunnel all the way to the main one. It snaps and drools and grinds its teeth at me, frustrated from being slowed. It is as hungry as the cats are.

I continue leading it, shouting commands backward toward the waterfall which is now a hundred yards away. "ATIA! RANGER! . . . RUN! . . . IF YOU CAN HEAR ME . . . RUN! GET DOWN, NOW!"

I keep the creature at bay but I am running low on arrows. I have to allow it to get closer to me than I would like to continue this pattern. Then, the other two Jboynei appear from the side tunnel Sero chose. They sprint at me with snapping jaws. I put an arrow in each of their feet. They will heal soon. I barely register another noise above the ringing, originating from my old tunnel. Please be the cats.

Of course it's the cats.

They crash into the main area, moving so fast that they lose their footing and slide along the ground, slamming into the side wall. They leap back into the chase. In an instant they are on the back of the Jboynei that had been digging for me and tear at his neck and shoulders. They rip flesh from the bone and break its neck but still, the Jboynei won't die. It throws them off and sits down with its neck limp broken and without flesh. The cats move on to the other two. I put arrows into their feet and explode through the waterfall. No sign of Atia, Ranger or Sero.

CHAPTER SIXTEEN

The greatest relief I have ever felt? Has to be when a problem has been dealt with. There is no greater relaxation than when something that has kept me up at night is suddenly gone.

Kasis, the first Philosopher-Sherpa

DRIPPING WET, I RUN DOWN the mountain. Some of the wax washes off, but not all of it. The sun and body-heat take care of the rest. My lungs tire from the lack of long distance training. My eyes water from the burn. Still, I run.

My knees ache from having to constantly stop gravity from flipping me head over heel down the mountain. Still, I run. My ankle gets caught in a water pool and twists, tearing the tendons and muscles. Still, I run.

I run past the marshes and into the forest until I feel that I have gained ample distance between myself and the Jboynei. The problem is, I have lost the trail. I lost the trail and I lost my company. I am lost in Hardrain, and it won't be long before the Jboynei have picked up my scent. I need to find something. My company, or the network, and I need to find them fast.

I am deep in the jungle. All around me are all unfamiliar noises of evil. It's getting dark and I am far from home. I dare not yell out or else attract something unpleasant. Yet, for some reason, I don't *fear*.

Something changed inside of me in that cave. In an instant, I grew up. I made a statement that will forever change how I think and function.

I am Nirue Nyles, and I fear nothing.

After some time, the sun goes down, leaving me in the black, nothing for light besides the eyes upon me. They feel different, like they respect me. Like I did something for them. Maybe it is because I no longer fear them . . . I don't know. I can't keep my eyes open. I plop up against a large tree and shut my eyes for a moment.

* * *

I am moving fast. Much faster than I have moved in a long time. I feel as though I am flying. A white dot appears in the distance. Then another. They grow quickly. The light is blinding. They are moving too fast. I need to get out of their way. I need to move, now. I can't move. My hands begin to sweat. I brace for impact.

I wake up gasping for air. It was just a dream. I am starving, thirsty and smell like crap filled intestine. I walk at a slow pace, nursing my torn ankle. I don't know where I am going, I just look for yellow bricks.

I find nothing for hours. I think about Atia and Ranger and all that we have been through in such a short amount of time. I think about Ranger defending me in Rizcarth. I think about the three of us running through the darkness of a tunnel chasing an assassin king. I miss them. I am alone and against the clock. Not just the clock of the Jboynei chasing me, but the unpredictable clock of my basecamp fire. It could end me at any time. *I* could kill myself. I surely hope I have more time. I hope my fire is not burning out.

I walk for hours through the rain and torrent of bugs. Rain falls intermittently. I need a drink, so when the rain comes next, I find the biggest leaf I can and use it as a funnel. The water here is so pure.

I look up and see a bird with a wingspan that blots out the sun for two breaths. Impressive. I would love some of its eggs right about now.

Then it dawns on me and I track its every movement, watching it land gracefully in a tree 140 yards away.

Duh-dun-dun-dun Duh-dun-dun-dun Duh-dun-dun-dun

I pick up my pace and hobble to the tree as fast I can. The Jboynei are on my trail and I don't know how long I have until they reach me. It feels hotter than normal today. The mosquitos are out early but aren't as vicious as normal. It's never a good sign when creatures that suck blood for sustenance leave you alone.

I hobble through shrubbery, hacking away while putting all my weight on one foot as much as I can. I get to the tree of the big bird. It looks at me with inquisitive black eyes, beak darting—changing its view of me every half-second. The drum comes again, but I'm already cutting at the trunk. In a few minutes I am a speckled-golden image of myself. Other birds appear among the branches the same way a family of meerkats would—heads poking out from hidden nests on every branch.

I turn because I hear crashing in the trees behind me. The birds duck back into the protection of their nests. The largest one spreads its wings, as if it were going to fly, then folds and tucks them, merely adjusting itself. It readies for takeoff while staring into the distant forest. There is no hole under this tree, so I hide in some bushes behind it. I hold my breath as the Jboynei approach.

They push aside trees with the ease of a skipper wading through seaweed. They are more measured this time, for they must be—I came into their house, stole their precious item and escaped virtually unscathed. If they weren't immortal to anything but the Keeper, they would be dead. They can't afford to underestimate me anymore.

Despite my newfound feelings of confidence I make sure to stay well out of sight. I am in the deepest bush I can find, scentless to the Jboynei. Being scentless in my condition is counterintuitive to me. How can a man covered in the most vile of smells not smell like anything? I think of a quote from Cicero. "Does it not betray itself with its odor?" An omen.

Jboynei crash through the trees with force more worthy of a hurricane. They soon ease their hurry to a slow, lingering comb of my area. Blast, I think to myself as I duck behind the cumbrous tree. I feel like a melting lollipop against it. I press my back firmly against the trunk and tell myself: Relax. Slow your breathing. They can't smell you. You can't outrun them. You must be stealthy. No fear.

I feel the tree shake as the ox-sized bird flutters down and attacks the Jboynei. My breathing picks up, trying to decide whether to use this opportunity or remain hidden. The last time nature provided me a distraction it gave me a day to gain ground. It gave me a day to find my people. It gave me a chance to run. I remember an old Chinese proverb that holds the notion that one must know when to run in battle. This is one of those times. I stand up and duck between the fauna encircling the tree and head in the opposite direction of the monsters.

My first mistake was carelessly applying the wax. Albeit, I was in somewhat of a dash. When I applied the wax I forgot to put it on my weapons, behind my knees, and in the area where my forearm meets my bicep. Any one of these would have been enough to pick up my scent.

My second mistake was running against the wind. Again, time was no friend, but I had known the wind was blowing a certain direction for some time. I knew it when I followed the bird to its keep. Yet, in a moment of peril, I ran directly into it, essentially leaving a bread loaf trail for them to find me.

My third and final mistake was not fashioning extra arrows yesterday. I have one left.

My ankle is throbbing, swelling, and it's not long before a loud screeching sound pierces my ears, alleviating any hope I had left in the natural distraction. I pick up my pace despite the searing pain becoming more abrasive. I can actually feel my foot swelling up. I have no choice. I have no other options.

The beat of the drum draws strings at my heart like a mummer's puppet. What should I do now? I cannot kill them, so how can I distract them long enough to escape? Is the entrance to the network close? All of this reasoning occurs while I jump in and out of trunks protruding the soil like hands from a deadly grave.

Trees break behind me. I turn to see a Jboynei scream as he covers ten yards with every stride. I recognize this one. It's the same one that dug me from the hole. My heart picks up and so does my adrenaline as I go into full flight mode. I no longer contemplate the fight as I hack wildly through the thickness before me. In a matter of moments, the Jboynei will be upon me.

They catch me sooner than I anticipated. I feel my body unnaturally bend, as my head touches my heels when the Jboynei kicks me. I fly through the air like rock slung from a medieval catapult. My head smacks the side of a tree, sending me into a three-sixty spin. I bleed from my eyes, nose, ears and end. I have no doubt in my mind that internally, I am mush.

My eyes swell up with tears as I gather my bearings. No fear. I turn and loose my last arrow into the creature. I intended to hit his foot, but missed high and got it in the stomach. I crabwalk backward as it smiles and wipes the drool from its lips in soft approach. The kind of gait Jack the Ripper must have had when he cornered a whore in a dark alley without a soul in earshot. The evident certainty that, in moments, he would get his.

I will probably die out here.

It laughs as it plucks my last arrow from its belly the same way a botanist plucks a thorn from her finger. Tears now blind my vision. I am not crying because I *fear* death, but because I can feel it. I didn't feel it in the cave. Here, the clouds of another world descend upon me. I use a tree to help me stand up. In my mind I run through a thicket of bamboo, ducking and dodging each one with imminent precision. In reality, I am barely moving.

I try to run once more. I trip over a root and from the ground, half-turn around to see the creature's wound is nearly healed. I cannot tell if it is my heart or the congo drum beating in my ear. Either way, I hear nothing save a loud, rhythmic thump-thump, thump-thump, thump-thump.

More adrenaline as the Jboynei closes on me. I scramble out of the bamboo and hustle downward, toward a clearing in the inner bowl of the mesa. The Jboynei is already out of the bamboo and nearing approach. Another kick. I scream as I fly through the air.

This time my windpipe is compromised and I crack my canines. I can feel the bridge of my nose move when I shake my head, trying to clear my vision. I cannot breathe and my right eye is completely shut. I drool out chunks of my cheek as I turn to face my assailant. It's still walking toward me. The other two crush the remaining bamboo as they enter the clearing that now holds my near lifeless body. C'mon Nirue. Think your way out of this.

The Jboynei approaches and plucks *Evergold* into nearby tall grass. He picks me up by the chest and looks into my eyes. His head is massive. Holding me up, his chin comes to my knees. Rotten teeth centerpiece the tribal tattoos that surround its black, oily eyes. It smiles and exhales something that could be interpreted as relief. First, it searches my pockets, as if looking for something. My head droops down and blood leaks from every hole I have in my body.

It tires of trying to fit his coyote sized fingers into my pockets and tears off my clothes. My lifeless body is pale and covered in red, blue and black patches.

A few soft whistles echo out of the forest. Or was it a song?

The darkness in the Jboynei's eyes have a hint of gold in them. Small, then bigger; gaining momentum insidiously. Its eyebrows raise and jaw clenches. I can barely lift my head up. Every tree surrounding the clearing has golden light climbing up it, like a glowing gold vine. First the trunks, then the branches, then the tendrils, then the leaves. The inner workings of the trees are exposed through this process. *Light the wood to set him free.*

I am thrown aside as the beasts scream in unison. More ringing in my ears. A creature a half-body bigger than them crashes into the clearing. A green aura surrounds his massive tattooed frame. His eyes, however, aren't black. They are every color this jungle has to offer. Red, blue, green, pink, orange, yellow, purple. His teeth aren't rotten, they are white. His head isn't bald. He has a Mohawk cut close to his head. He bellows and smacks his spear hand into his chest three times and lets out a war cry to be heard outside of the grounds. He runs directly at the Jboynei. The Keeper.

The battle is over in a matter of moments. The one that had a particular fancy for me receives a javelin through the chest. The fat one, apparently angered by this, charges the Keeper unwisely and has its head ripped from his body. The Keeper then separates the spine from the head and extricates its brain from the skull. The last one starts running. Three full strides and a leap lands the Keeper on the back of the remaining Jboynei.

He jumps up and down and crushes the ribcage underneath him. Then the head. He collects the mess of bodies and strings them up from the trees. Whether it's for warning to other would-be intruders or food for the animals, I don't know. What I do know is that this guy is all business. Ranger, Atia and Sero come running to my aide. Atia gets there first.

"Nirue! What the hell happened to you?" She asks through a cough that sounds as if she's been smoking her entire life. "I . . . I . . ." Then all darkness.

CHAPTER SEVENTEEN

*The Fallen City is really something to behold. You can
tell it used to be majestic. It still is, in many ways, but it's
been ruined. And beauty ruined is cursed beauty.*

Stolintain, after completing his second trial

WHEN I COME TO, I am surrounded in a crowded room while people
with leaf manes stare at me, eyes ever changing color. The old woman is
forefront and smiles at me with love. Everyone is smiling.

I try to get up but the old woman rests a hand on my forehead and
eases me back into my cot. I'm covered in white bandages that appear and
feel to be made of spider-silk. "Rest, my good son. Soon our healer will
be back with the much needed ingredients. He will provide you with a
plant that sprouts once every ten years. It will heal your major wounds
completely, and your minor ones may linger a few weeks but will heal
faster than normal. We usually save it for our people and our people only.
Once, a boy who loved his pet cat wasted it on his stupid feline when—"

"Quit boring him with your stories Granny," Sero says as he jumps up
on her lap. She smiles at him.

"Right. Anyway, we took a vote whether to make you the first exception since the cat incident. Everyone in this room raised a hand in your favor. Save one."

"Who duthn't want me ta uthe it?" I say, causing blood to pool in my mouth. I hear Ranger laugh as he pushes his way to the front. "You, ya half-wit!" The room erupts in laughter. I laugh along and cough up blood in the process.

"Rest your eyes. We will see you when you wake," Granny says.

"Thee ya," I say as I close my eyes.

*   *   *

When I wake up the room has a much smaller audience than before, and I am no longer the focal point. Granny rests a soft hand against my cheek and raises a mug with the other. "Drink this," she urges. I use the palms of my hands to sit up. My ribs ache like they had been used as a straw man for archery practice. "Owwwwahh!" I say, pushing myself upward. My nose starts to bleed when I come to a full sitting position.

I wipe the blood away and take a sip of the drink, which, surprisingly, is quite sweet. It tastes of orange peels mixed with a mango cream that has been boiled with apples and bananas. I drink it in a few seconds and wipe my lips.

"Good. In a few hours you will feel back to normal. You should feel lucky, you get to miss out on all the *hard work*," she says sarcastically. I look around the room and notice what is different. There are fewer *things* in the room but not less people. Everything that once decorated the epicenter is now gone. Giant masks of war have been removed from the wall; the chief's chair is being broken down into smaller pieces; cots no longer edge the walls for rest. "Where isth everything Gran?"

She points up, smiles, and says one word, as if she had been waiting her entire life to say it, "Above." She then spends the next few minutes explaining everything that I had missed in my slumber, which was a lot more than I had imagined. Apparently I have been out near ten hours.

"So, Sero, in an effort to harmonize his adventurous reputation with his actions, escaped the Jboynei with ease. He jumped out of a window similarly situated to the room you were in and climbed his way around to Atia and Ranger. He explained the immediacy of their situation, wind-flute in hand, and the three of them ran down the mountain. Atia was draped over Ranger's back. They made their way across the marshlands to the temple. Atia wanted to wait for you but she was in no condition to fight, and they figured waking the Keeper would be the best thing to do."

"Well that'th all fine and dandy, but whatth tha heck tookth them tho long to wake him up? They could have thaved me a lot of pain!" Blood spills onto my chin.

"Well, once they got there they ran into a bit of a problem. Sero and his twin brother, Salin, are the only people in our village that know how to play the wind-flute. At first they tried simple songs like *Two Frogs and a Pear* and *Snake-River Flood* to no avail. Apparently there was a very particular song the Keeper wanted to hear before he woke up.

So, the boys spent all night and all morning thinking of what songs to play, trying this one and that one, taking suggestions from anyone who would offer it. Thankfully the Jboynei weren't there so the only thing that interfered with their ability was a lack of sleep. You did a great job distracting them!" I roll my eyes. She continues, "The whole tribe was able to think and offer suggestions. Eventually the tribe doctor suggested *Clouds of Vocation*, which neither of the boys could play.

It took roughly thirty minutes before Sero could play it clean. Between the old doctor trying to remember the tune, Sero translating it to the instrument, and then Sero playing it flawlessly, we became quite frustrated."

"Mmhmm," I say while drawing circles with my right big toe.

"I see someone is feeling better already!" She smiles and slaps me on the back. "Come, we're having a festival under the canopies for the first time in a century." She smiles.

I rest my eyes for a few more hours and when I wake, the room is empty save the cot that I lie on. They even took my blanket. At least they left me a torch, I think to myself, sitting up without pain for the first time in hours. I then test the different areas of my body. First I move my arms around as if I'm trying to draw circles on the wall with my elbows. Feels fine, nothing there.

Next I twist my upper body around, fists touching, knuckle to knuckle. That feels good too. I twist my neck—nothing. Fingers, toes, eyebrows—everything feels fine. Overly excited I jump out of the cot ready to run up the tunnel until I put weight on my right leg. "Yaaahhhrr!" My scream echoes off the empty walls surrounding my cot. This damned ankle.

I rub the crust from my eyes and journey up the western tunnel Sero took us through when he saved us from the Jboynei.

When I climb out of the tunnel I have to shield my eyes from the overly abundant amount of light emitting from the temple square. Torches made of bamboo and wormwood edge the center. Eleven elongated tables illuminate from smaller torches standing through holes that are symmetrically aligned every four feet.

Beneath the torches lay a host of food: Pig stuffed with snake meat is at every table. Eel stuffed rabbit topped with fried toucan eggs, fire-grazed duck in a chili-orange sauce and jungle bull-shoulder with baked cava root are other delicacies I spot.

Music fills my ears and gently lays there like a seashell slowly filling up with water, just before sinking to the depths. Young girls dance with young boys and sing songs that I have never heard. I see Sero and, I assume, Salin dancing around the prettiest girl, taking turns playing the wind-flute. Smoke rises into the canopies from large bonfires built neatly around the tables.

More pigs are being prepared by the bonfires. On this night the stars can be seen just above the temple, where the Keeper had burst out. The stars are beautiful and the moon is somewhat reminiscent of the Keepers' eyes—polychrome with various hues dancing off it like a kaleidoscope.

When my presence is known people stop eating and come to hug and thank me. The bigger warriors extend forearm-shakes rather than hugs. They are grateful but do not want to appear emotional. I get it. Ranger runs over to me and bids me to sit by him. After wading through the crowd I make my way to a wooden bench next to him. We sit across from Atia and Bertram.

"Hello Nirue," he says while swallowing a mouth full of food, less chained than the last time I saw him. "Hello Bertram. Atia, Ranger." I give them all a head nod. Not only is Bertram now less chained, I notice he is completely free of chains, and is wearing a beautifully intricate red robe with white laces. He seems to be in better spirits too.

"You have to try the eel Nirue, it's *divine*," Bertram says while pointing his wooden fork downward toward the food.

"Don't have the stomach at the moment. How are you feeling Atia?" She looks better with some food in her, but has still noticeably declined since the first day. A variety of animal furs, including the big cat that Ranger skinned drapes over her shoulders for warmth.

"Better," she says while covering her mouth, so as to hide the food inside. "I must have just caught the flu or something. We haven't been in the most sanitary environments lately."

"True."

"So, what exactly happened to you when you split from Sero?" Ranger asks while dipping some of his duck into the egg yolk with his pocket dagger.

I spend a good part of an hour explaining what happened to me in the caves past the marshes. Some scenes I was asked to physically act out, per request of the chief who has been drinking the local nightfire liquor. Ranger especially liked my idea of shooting the Jboynei in the feet.

When the fires get low and we have filled our bellies the chief jumps on top of a middle table, with no regard for the food or drinks he knocks over.

"Since I was a boy I have been hiding in those caves like a bug." He points toward the base of a large tree. "We couldn't hunt for our food freely, we couldn't harvest the ground, we couldn't even raise our children to run with the deer. Instead, we've had to *hide*."

A pregnant pause. "Until TODAY." If there was anybody still talking, their attention was now completely on the chief.

"TODAY we have become free. TODAY a young boy and three strangers have shown courage that the rest of us only wished we possessed. TODAY we have seen the reawakening of a legend, the realization of our *purpose* in this place. TODAY . . ." Tears run down his face. He takes one pointed finger and stops their progress on his cheeks. "WE ARE FREE."

The village breaks into cheers. The birds and beasts with eyes in the darkness seem to walk away.

"From this day forward we will have a celebration, on this day in this square. The day will be dedicated to honoring our three friends." He motions for Sero, who is picking leftovers off his brother's plate.

"For those of you who do not know this boy, this is Sero. From this day forward, he is your chief." Gasps and whispering fill the tables.

"Only a boy . . . No; only a *man* who had the courage to venture out of the network and *break the chains* like young Sero here should be the leader. Of course, I will provide as *very* persuasive council until he comes of the right age." Some of the older women laugh at this. The warriors seem pissed off. They shouldn't be.

The chief takes off his decorated leaf mane and puts it on Sero. It falls over his shoulders, more akin to a lei than a mane. Atia laughs and accidently snorts. Ranger teases her, causing her cheeks to turn red.

"Raise your glasses to Sero! Raise your glasses to Atia! Raise your glasses to Ranger! Raise your glasses to the Keeper! Raise your glasses to *NIRUE*! Most of all, RAISE YOUR GLASSES TO FREEDOM!"

Loud yells with tongue ululations follow chants and dances around the bonfires that have long out-glowed their torch counterparts.

We spend the next few hours drinking and dancing with the tribe. Eventually my lack of sobriety kicks in. In an attempt to take a break from drinking, I walk over to the steps of the temple, eyes up, looking at the stars. Sometimes I simply enjoy looking at the stars and all of their tales they seek to share. This feeling is especially so when I am without a woman and have been drinking. It's comforting for me.

I wander over to the steps near where the Keeper is standing watch. I keep my distance from him and lie on my back. I stare into the universe. It is a magnificent illuminant of things once gone and things to be had. Maybe I will go somewhere up there when this is over. After a few moments Sero comes over and lies next to me.

"Whatcha looking at?" I don't notice him until I turn my head. I had been lost in my thoughts looking at an especially close view of the Andromeda galaxy.

"Nothing in particular. Mostly waiting for this nightfire to lessen its stranglehold on my sobriety." He doesn't understand and doesn't say anything. "Where I'm from you cannot see that up there, just beyond the pink haze." I draw a circle three times so he can follow my fingers. "I take that back. You *can* see it, just not very good with the naked eye. It looks like a fuzzy star. Here, though, it shines how the Milky Way normally does. Where I'm from, you cannot see it this clear with a satellite or even a high powered telescope." He looks at me with sagging eyes and an open mouth.

"Oh, we call that the strawberry snake, because it's like a coiled up snake and its colored like a strawberry." I smile at him and act surprised.

We don't speak the next few minutes both in an unspoken agreement to enjoy space. It's a cool night, the wind blowing ever so lightly through the area. It changes the direction of the flames and scatters old leaves off the temple steps. It cools my body of a heat coming from within, probably due to the medicine I took earlier. I notice his breathing is much more rapid than mine, which makes perfect sense. His lungs are smaller and his heart beats faster.

After a few more minutes I close my eyes for a bit. The smell of old rain and forest fills my mind with memories of my parent's farm. I miss my family. I long to be home. This sucks. I seem to never be content. Why? Before the crash, I wasn't content unless I felt like my life was on the line. Now that it is virtually every waking moment, all I want is to get home. I must get home, no matter what. Sero breaks my chain of thought.

"Hey Nirue?"

"Yeah?"

"Can I ask you something?"

"Sure bud. Ask away." I intertwine my fingers and lay them on my chest.

"I'm not sure I will be a very good chief. I don't know what to do or how to fight. I just like to sneak around because it's fun. Do you think you can help me become a good one? I mean, I know it won't happen anytime soon, but after a few years, maybe I can become someone that people look up to. That's my hope at least."

I sit up and look at Sero. He is biting his lips and rubbing his hands together, anxiously waiting my response. Be positive, Nirue.

"People already respect you Sero, which is the hardest part about being a chief—not fighting or one-on-one combat. You've changed their lives forever. They will be in your debt until the day you die."

"But you and I *both* know that it was you who saved them, not me. You were the one who actually fought the Jboynei. You were the one that actually distracted them . . ." His voice trails off. "I just snuck out of a window."

"Sero, you have it all backward. YOU were the one that found the wind-flute. YOU were the one that had the balls to travel outside of the network. YOU were the one that woke the Keeper!"

"No that was my brother."

I shake my head, "Either way, none of this would have happened without you bud. Hell, I wouldn't even be *alive* if you didn't save me from the Jboynei."

"Yeah, I suppose you're right . . . I just don't *feel* like I saved everyone, you know?"

"Sero. Will you promise me one thing?" He nods.

"Never again doubt your role in today. Okay? I owe you my life. Not only have you saved lives by waking the Keeper, you have given them a new life; a reason to live! You are very young and this is a lot to take in. But, you are chief now, and you need to start thinking like one. Step one is remembering that you *deserve* to be here. Okay?"

He giggles. "Yeah, I suppose your right. And, with your help I can be a great one too!"

I pinch my mouth, biting the inside of my lip, looking into the forest, thinking on how to best let him down. "Well, unfortunately, I won't be around to see you flourish, which I know you will."

"Wha—What do you mean?"

"I have to go, Sero. I have to . . ." I can't possibly explain my situation to him. I have to let him down easy though. "I have other places to go. Other people need my help. There are a few things you will learn when you get older. One day I gave spare change to a beggar in a very, very poor town. When I gave him money, he grabbed me by the arm and would not let me go until I heard him out. He told me, 'Your soul is like a cup of water. If you spend your whole life living only for yourself, you will drain your cup of all the water and eventually, you will realize how empty you really are. But, if you live a life helping others, you will never run out of water, and when it's all said and done, nobody will be thirsty, least of all yourself.' Remember these words and remember this night. If you do, you will be a great chief."

He nods with baggy eyes. "But I don't want you to go Nirue." I remember my little brother saying the same thing to me before I left for college. I couldn't wait to get out of that madhouse, what with eleven younger siblings, some of whom were still in diapers. How I regret my eagerness to leave. I remember the laughter of the practical jokes, and the anger of the one being tricked. I remember how everyone would break out in song at the chagrin of my father, twelve kids singing at the top of their lungs. I remember the times when we would rally around each other when someone was suffering. We were crazy, but we loved each other. How could I have not been content with that life?

Man, I miss my family more than I realized. It's hard to fight back the tears in my eyes. "I have a little brother just like you at home. He is brave and tends to get caught up in the center of things more often than not."

"Is he brave like you?"

"Yes. But he is not as brave as you. No one is." I say this last bit with a grin and rub his head in a soft noogie. He laughs and swats my hand away.

"Let's go back to the party, I'm sure people will be worried where their new chief has wandered off to."

When we get back, the party has noticeably died. Torches have gone out, bonfires burn low, food is scattered around and men and women of all ages lie passed out on benches, tables and the jungle floor. Everyone except Ranger, Bertram and Atia.

"Let's go, Nirue. Time must not be underestimated," Bertram says, eyes to Atia then the jungle floor. I nod and hold up a finger to Bertram, then kneel down to Sero, meeting his eyes, which are a deep shade of jade green.

"I have to go now Sero. Take care of these people, they will surely need your bravery in the future. Thank you for taking me on your journey with you."

"Okay. Thank you Nirue, for trusting in me when no one else would." I nod my head. With that, we were off into the forest with a torch, following a red-cloaked Bertram, ready to start trial number three.

CHAPTER EIGHTEEN

Why are you disheartened, oh my soul? There is nothing you could have done for them. Every test has been not one of supernatural powers or cunning wit, or even marvelous strength, but of the heart. Though they were stronger, and though you thought the odds impossible, you never lost heart. Keep the faith, oh my soul. Fight the good fight. May the fire in your heart ignite the one at camp, for when you do not lose hope, everything falls together.

Final journal entry of Szell, champion of two trials, one day after his second teammate died

WE HEAD SOUTH. WE PASS under the ignominiously strung remnants of the Jboynei. Eventually we find the clearing where, just yesterday, I nearly died. Bertram whispers a few things under his breath and a jumpkey appears. Well, that's what we call it anyway.

Atia shivers and steps in. Then Ranger, then me, then Bertram. Three orbs spark into a fluorescent and jade green at camp. A flash of green and we were on our familiar platform. The scent of the dew covered moss and pine needles are a delicacy I have acquired a taste for. The night sky is a mosaic of patterned light emitted from the kindling of stars. Mist necklaces the tops of trees and the absence of eyes in the darkness below is another welcomed comfort. Tonight, I will sleep well.

On the way down the stairs Bertram orders us to return our stuff to the *Chest Vitales*. Of course, none of us has have anything left from what we had been given.

"The chests give only because *you* give. If you expect them to have something inside of it on your next quest, you must sacrifice," Bertram says with authority.

"What shall I give up? Certainly not *Darkwater*," Ranger protests. Atia slips her hands over the hilts of *Dicers* at the thought of losing them.

"No, no my dear Ranger—nothing that dramatic, not yet, at least. What can you give?"

Ranger shrugs and takes off a piece of leather he had wrapped around his wrist in our recent expedition. He throws it in the empty chest and closes it. Atia follows suit and offers a blanket she was using to keep warm. She shivers immediately after.

Lost in a daydream I soon become acutely aware of all of the eyes upon me. "Er, right. I suppose it's my turn now?" Bertram nods. "Well, you see . . . The thing is . . . I don't really have anything. I lost most all of it in Hardrain, save *Evergold* and my axe."

"How about these?" Ranger asks while throwing over a set of long black claws. "I pulled these when I skinned the cat. Bloody nightmare it was. Ya wudn't believe how deep these things were set. Anyway, 'Tia here wanted to make a necklace of em' for ya but she hasn't had the time. Why don't ya throw a couple in the box, call it square?

I smile gratefully. "Thanks, Ranger."

Nonchalantly, I open my chest and throw a few of the smaller claws in. No sound. "Hand me that torch Bertram." I take a closer look and notice the claws resting on a cloak, which I pull out of the chest. It's just like the night sky—dark, but peppered with white dots. Bertram anxiously scratches the back of his neck.

"What's wrong?"

"That's . . ." he points at it dumbfounded. "That's an obscurity cloak. I haven't seen one of those since my first group came through a thousand years ago."

"Why does that matter?"

"Because!" he says, clearly frustrated. "It means something dreadful is upon us."

"You got one thing right," a voice thunders from the forest. A hooded man emerges from the shadows. "I wouldn't do anything stupid. You're surrounded by my archers with necropoisoned tipped arrows. You are familiar with necropoison, aren't you?"

"We're familiar with its propensities," I say, gritting my teeth. "What the hell is this about huh?"

"Did I say you could bloody talk?" The man approaches me slowly. Every time I think he is about to stop, he doesn't; inching toward me not unlike a cat to a mouse in a trap.

"I thought it custom to reply with an answer, when asked a question. You *do know what a question is, don't you*?"

"You're reluctance to adhere to my authority will not engender a blissful outcome for you, Master Nyles."

How the heaven does he know my name? "The supererogation of your fancy words will not dissuade my intentions. Besides, how do we know you're not bluffing?"

He lets out a long sigh and motions a handless sleeve half-heartedly. Six arrows hit our chests and leak a black substance.

"Any more questions Master Nyles?"

"So you do know what a bloody question is." His hood cascades a shadow over his face like a mountain giving shadow to a valley; all I can see is the lower part of his nose and his cheekbones.

"You better learn to watch your tongue if you value its worth," he hisses.

I stare into the darkness where his eyes would be, clenching my jaw so hard I think I may break my molars. "Do you know what year it is, Master Nyles?" I continue staring, refusing to answer. "Ah. How quickly the intimidated learn. It is the 77th year since the prophets gathering. Which means, we roam the lands far and wide in search of people to participate in our tournament." His voice is deep like the yawn of a great lion. The old Nirue would have feared this man and this situation. Not anymore.

"The existence of your archers and the club tucked beneath your tunic indicates you are willing to fight if need be. Further, you wouldn't be prepared to fight unless you anticipated a fight coming. Which means, you came to either capture, or kill us. Had you not told us about your miserable tournament, I would have assumed the latter. My explanation in the last sentence lends credence to which way I am leaning now."

For the first time, his hands appear outside of his cloak. He begins a slow, prophetic clap. "A fantastic display of deductive reasoning Master Nyles. You will prove a worthy commander, if you are so chosen. Now, the choice is yours: come willingly or, the alternative. I imagine you can deduce what that means."

I pull my axe off my back and hold in front of my body. Ranger follows suit, as does Atia. Bertram has disappeared.

"I see. For a moment there, I was hoping you were going to make my life a bit easier. I should have known better of someone from the other side." In a flash he pulls a large club from his hood and strikes the ground, releasing a display of lightning energy across the ground like the aftershock of a nuclear bomb explosion. It blinds us temporarily and makes my body unimaginably hot. Atia's hair stands straight up. A few dozen archers close in on us, arms sturdy, eyes focused.

"Lower your bloody weapons," he says, not even checking to see if anyone listened. Atia, Ranger and I look at each other in unison. There's nothing we can do here. We are outnumbered and outmatched. We must wait for our time to attack. They are waiting for me to make a move. I am their leader, and they will follow me down whatever path I may choose. I cannot subject my friends to a certain death. Hold fast, Nirue.

Begrudgingly, I throw my weapons to the ground. "Ahh. *Evergold*," he says while examining my weapon. He pretends to pick up my axe when, in another flash, he lands a devastating uppercut with his club to the bottom of my chin. My eyes bulge and I experience an overwhelming sense of déjà vu. My world goes dark, and everything starts to spin. I blackout.

INTERLUDE 2

"A ZIPPO, A FOLDED UP newspaper clipping, two dimes and a wallet. That's all I went in with, and all I have now," Ranger said to his father. The view they shared would ordinarily engender a positive conversation. Not now. Now there is an invisible wall between the two. Too many things unsaid to be said.

"I'm sorry I never came to visit. With work and the prison being far away . . . Well, you know how your mother is."

"I understand," Ranger lied.

"Did you learn anything in there?"

"I learned that getting punished for doing what's right doesn't make doing right feel all that good." His father grimaced but did his best to hold his tongue.

"Don't worry, Dad. I know you'll never believe me or Mickey."

"It's not that we don't trust you, son. It's just the witnesses' stories were so compelling. And the prosecution's arguments seemed to make sense."

"I wasn't jealous of that guy dad and I would never hurt him because of some stupid girl. I was sticking up for Mickey. They—"

"I know, son, they were going to hurt him. And I know it's unfortunate that the boy you hit fell the way he did. Even his doctors testified that had his head not made contact with that broken concrete wall he wouldn't have suffered the brain injury."

"I was there. And don't believe for one second that I didn't feel horrible for what happened. But the way I see it, if you start something, you better be able to finish it. Was I supposed to let them just pick on Mickey? My brother? That's not how you raised me to act. Family—remember?"

"Let's not start your first day out like this. Help me on the boat today? Won't be long. Supposed to have a storm blow in early afternoon."

Ranger takes a long drag from the little bit that's left of his cigarette and ashes it under the bench. He looks out at the waves and inhales a deep breath of free air. Two years is a long time for a young man to be in an adult prison. After a few seconds he replied, "Sure."

His dad nods and begins his trek down the hill toward the marina. Ranger fights back tears for the fourth time in five minutes.

*   *   *

The waves make Ranger more uneasy than he ever remembered. Up, then down, then up, then just when he thinks he's caught the pattern, it fools him again. Ranger braces himself against a large crane to which the largest net is tethered.

"Pull up those lines, Ranger! The crane ain't workin' right," his dad yells through spray twice the height of the boat. Ranger notices worry on his father's face. The beads of sweat building on his forehead. Or maybe it's just the ocean spray, he can't tell for sure. But one thing is for sure—it's never a good sign when a seasoned fisherman looks worried at sea. His dad plays with a black joystick with a large red ball attached to the top, ever-looking over his left shoulder at the crane.

With one hand on the crane, Ranger stretches out the other to grasp the net. The sea is becoming unsettled. With his hand extended, the railing jumps up and smacks Ranger in the stomach, causing him to momentarily lose his breath. He closes his eyes. The pain wells up in his ribs. He feels a rush of blood and a certain pressure in his face.

"Ranger, what are you doing? PULL IN THE LINE!"

Ranger scowls over his left shoulder. He grits his teeth, reaches out again and begins to pull the overly filled net in. His arms are pulsing, bulging with veins. Blue rivers through sea ice.

The storm pushes in. Clouds merge, scattering lightning across the dark skies. Waves become bigger. Ranger groans as he pulls the net in. It is hard against his cold palms. The slime of fish make it harder to grip the hardened rope. He must be strong or lose his fingers. The rope digs into his flesh just below the middle knuckle. He realizes this net is too heavy for even him—the strongest man in all St. Anne's High School. That was a long time ago. Still, he cannot let his father down. Not after all he's already put his family through.

The boat moves up and down more slowly, as if to ready itself—calm, yet ready to burst. Waves begin to collect at skyscraper heights, undercurrent pulling surrounding water to feed the monsters. The storm is here. He wants to scream to his dad and tell him to cut the line but he doesn't, there is no time. How they have underestimated this storm. Fervently his father jiggles the joystick and hits buttons, desperate to get the line in and salvage the net. They can't afford to lose another expensive net.

The boat begins to dive. Ranger sees a swell building up behind the bow.

"DAAAAAD!" he yells through the pouring rain. His vision is getting increasingly blurry. "DAAAAAD!" he pleads. But his dad can't hear him. The momentum slows. Lightning flashes across the horizon, revealing a wall of deep, dark blue. Almost black.

Ranger tries one last time.

"DAAAAAAAAD!" he screams. He loses grip on the net. The boat climbs up, up, up. The boat is at 25 degrees. Then 30. They are losing speed. Another flash of lightning.

"HOLD ONTO SOMETHING RANGER," his dad screams. He realizes why. They are climbing a swell they cannot summit. Up, up, up they continue. Ranger's dad holds onto the gears of the crane. Ranger to the crane itself. 45 degrees now.

It's then that Ranger realizes how cold he is. How alone he is. How nothing in his life has ever amounted to anything. What happened to all of those hero stories where standing up for the weak one got you glory? A lie. Happy families are a LIE. Doing good is a LIE he thinks to himself.

Up, up, up the boat climbs. It now sits perpendicular to the ocean below it—a full 90 degrees. Ranger dangles from the crane like an ape on the branch. His father does the same. He notices his dad has his shirt wrapped around his hands for grip. He should have thought of it. Why do you always think of the stupid stuff, but never the smart stuff, Ranger?

All is still. Ranger feels sick. He looks down. The heavy net drips water toward the water below. His feet dangle. A shoe slides off into the ocean. It hits the bottom railing, bounces off the net and spins into the sea. Ranger cannot see the splash. His heart beats in the space between his eyes. He grits his teeth and adjusts his grip, but the weight of the net, and all of the fish in it pull the boat down, down, down.

"Hold on!" he thinks he hears his dad say. Thunder booms in his ears like the sound of smashing the backside of a steal drum. Lightning immediately follows the sound.

The nose of the boat leaves the water above and begins to tip toward Ranger. "No. No. Not this—not now," he pleads to God. The boat tips backward.

The weight of the wave and the boat pushes Ranger into a free-fall. His body slams into the crane, spinning out of control toward the water. It happens before he can even scream. He feels the cold, unforgiving weight of the sea blanket his body, cloud his vision and drive him toward the ocean floor.

CHAPTER NINETEEN

Madness is often hidden in creative obsession, yet celebrated as genius when understood by enough. A little support goes a long way for turning madness to self-acceptance.

Homeless man on the streets of Rizcarth

WHEN I WAKE UP I have a brown sack made of hemp around my head. I cannot tell which itches worse, the bag or the hemp rope tied firmly around my neck. Light reveals the small intricacies and frayed lines of the hemp sack. Other than that, I cannot see anything else. I am tied to a pole made of wood that leaves splinters in my body when I attempt to move. My arms are tied behind the pole, and other ropes secure my upper torso and legs, restricting any thought of movement whatsoever.

My body rocks up and down, as if I am traversing a hilly field. But the motions are too quick and constant. *Where am I?* The voices of men and women bustle around me like a crowded city market. Shouts of "Portside!" and "Untie the bends from the bollard!" ring my ears.

A woman yells, "Get that bloody cat from the edge! Can't have her going overboard." Overboard. Am I at sea? Who in heaven brings a cat on a ship?

I stay still for a while to intercept any information that may not be intended to land on my ears; although I may have showed my hand by my curiosity thus far.

"Look who *finally* woke from his little nap," a man says before bludgeoning me in my stomach. Dammit. I crane my neck and gasp for air. He hit me right in my air pocket. I let out the unwilling moans that accompany getting the wind knocked out of you.

"What a coward you must be," I say while accidently sucking in so much air that the hemp sack enters my mouth. "You are some warrior, friend. Hitting a man who is defenseless and BLIND!" Anger rises in my body as I try and break my ropes. The laughter of one hundred people fill my ears. Apparently I have the entire crew's attention. This is my chance.

I read once that seafarers are very superstitious people. I need to use that to my advantage. "Do you realize what you have done, coward?" Another smash to my stomach, this time a bit lower. My head drops in pain.

"Aye. I've made ya moan like a little lass have I." More laughter.

"Hit 'em again Caddis!"

"Shut your mouth Cuz before I make that head of yours me practice dummay!"

He comes up and puts his head right next to mine, resting his arm on the mast that I am tied to. "Any more questions, beautiful?" His breath smells of rum and lack of food. I pause for a moment and let out the most sinister laugh I can conjure up. Surprisingly, it comes more natural than I thought it would. Probably because I really do want to kill this man. I crave his head like a user craves the leaf. It's *unnatural*.

"What the hells he laughing at now?" A voice asks from the crowd.

"You have doomed us all. Everyone who has sailed these seas knows you don't hurt a prisoner unless he has his chance at reciprocity. We'll be lucky if we don't get thrown off course two-months' time. I imagine you didn't stock supplies for that long, did ya Caddis?"

He rips the bag off my head. The sunlight is blinding. I am tied to the mainmast of a ship that includes two other masts—the mizzen and foremast. Being as I am on the middle of the three, the main deck where the sailors do most of the hard work is front of me. Ropes and buckets lay about as does pools of sea water. The man and women are a disheveled lot, produced mostly of what appears to be pirates.

Tattoos and tanned skin promulgate their allegiances, and the flags flying high above the sails are no more comforting. Aboard are a couple monkeys and a black cat. No one wears anything resembling a functioning society. Their clothes are bereft of signs of a healthy civilization or hygiene. The white sun is high and bright in a sky aporetic of weather producing clouds.

"The hell you talkin' 'bout, eh?" He asks while spitting all over my face. I hate that. Had I free hands, I would wipe it off before answering.

"What I mean is, *un-bloody tie me before you curse us all to the depths you half-witted rotten toothed son of a—*" a quick knee to my stomach.

He walks around, arms half raised, gloating at his dominance over me. "You mean ta tell Caddis, the most fearless and savvy pirate the Sea of Pantine has ever seen ta cut you down and let ya dance? I think not me friend. Do ya take me for brains of clamshells do ya? The size of a sea-horse is it? I don't take kindly ta men makin' fun of me wits ya know. Just ask the depths of my intelligence." He retrieves a short zigzagged dagger from his red belt and taps his head, eyebrows raised.

"I didn't mean to tell Caddis his brain's the size of a seahorse." He grins with pride, not knowing that I am about to change course. "Forgive me for my nebulous description of your intellect, or lack thereof. After hearing you speak, I think a singular grain of sand will do comparable justice. A single, solitary *bloody piece of sand*." His eyes light up like a man who walked in on an adulterous wife. The crew goes silent. A monkey scrambles for a loose apple and hurries with it up the ropes. I can smell the salt of the sea and hear the waves lapping against the sides of the giant wooden ship.

Embarrassed and pissed off, he raises a dagger with yellow stained armpits and teeth to match. "YOU'LL PAY FOR THIS YA SORRY"

"THAT'S *ENOUGH*," a voice booms from helm. I can feel the sound waves coming from the hooded man. "Drop your weapon Caddis. This is one of our more prized captures."

"Did ya hear what he was sayin' boss? I should have his bloody head for this!"

"I am not concerned with the prick to your pride, Caddis. I pay you to deliver my captures safely to Pantine in one piece. I do not pay you to exact revenge on every man that hurts your feelings with words."

Hurt, he looks down and tucks his dagger away. He feigns walking away before landing another blow to my stomach. I feel air escape to the sides of my abdomen.

"Watch your tongue land-lubber. A man can only be pushed so far before he tosses good wits and coin to the side for blood."

"I don't think you could afford to toss your wits to the side, Caddis. You wouldn't have anything left." This time, he grins, and fire catches in his eyes like a small kindling in a damp forest.

"I'll be seein' ya soon lassy," he says as he pats his dagger.

The robed man walks up and removes a bag tied from another captive at the foremast. It's not Ranger or Atia. The man curses and struggles to get free but to no avail. He dons a white tunic and brown breeches with a brown belt. He is barefoot and is black as the cats in Hardrain.

The hooded mage walks over and stares at me without speaking. In daylight I can see he is older, but not too old. Crow's feet etch the outside of his eyes. Other than that he seems middle-aged. I place him about forty. His jaw is hardened like that of a man who is battle-tested.

"It seems you haven't learned from our earlier encounter Master Nyles. As a wise man, I would encourage you to realize your circumstances. One, you are in an isolated location with nothing but enemies around. That's right, your precious friends are not on this ship."

"What did you do to them" I hiss.

"Nothing. They are bound, just like you, on one of the many ships at our back. Oh, that's right, you cannot see behind you. Here, let me do you a favor." In three quick movements he pulls a dagger from a hidden pocket in his navy blue hooded-cloak, cuts the lines keeping me on the pole and catches me from falling on my face. His hands are strong and sturdy. He holds a firm grip on my shirt.

"Two, you do not have any weapons to defend yourself. Three, even if you did have weapons and friends, you could not overpower *me*, let alone all of these bloodlusts *and* me." He shows a hand to the crowd as if to display something on sale.

"I beg to differ. With my weapons and my crew, I would put us up against anyone."

"I applaud your bravery, Master Nyles. That being said, those who harbor the antithesis of wisdom are the first to fly the flag of carelessness."

"Who the hell are you huh?"

"In due time, Master Nyles. Until that time, keep your head down and your eyes about you. I don't give a spit where you sleep or what you eat, just make sure you do. We should make Pantine by tomorrow and gods willing, you will be alive. You can turn the tide in favor of my country this year at the tournament."

He wants me to help him.

"If you want some help you bloody well better give me some explanations." He lets out a drawn out sigh and motions for me to follow him around the deck.

"77 years ago a group of prophets met under a night sky as the biggest moon ever recorded in our skies appeared. There were six total prophets— three from the family that currently employs my services and three from another. For now, let's call these families 'us' and 'them.' The other was a neutral party. Each family was royalty in their own right in a country divided in half; our half and their half. Each family had chosen the greatest of their seers to attend a meeting and predict the future of our civilization. You see, the moon was causing quite a stir.

So they met, and, naturally, disagreed. Our seers saw the moon as a gift from the gods, while they saw it as a curse." He hands me a glass of dark liquid. I waft the top of the glass, recognizing the sweet sugary scent of rum. He takes a long sip and continues.

"The neutral party tried for days to get the seers to agree because it was in his best interest. If the families could agree on the interpretation of the newly acquired moon, they could live in peace, which meant trade between the divided nations would continue.

However, whilst they were all in the same room, any and all effort was fruitless. Do you know what to do when two parties cannot agree on what color the sky is Master Nyles?"

"You separate them." He nods in approval.

"Correct again. But do you know how to get them to agree?"

"You lie to them."

"In some senses. So, the neutral party commenced his plan. He went into our room and told our seers how bad the omen was. He explained that a moon so great and so vast must be interpreted as a sign to humble ourselves; an illustration of the power the gods hold over us. Then, he would go into the other room and tell them what a great blessing it was. He told them that because the moon did not destroy the tides (and so the ability to fish), it was a blessing from the gods that they approved of our lifestyle. The purpose of this was to persuade one side to see the other's point of view." He takes a long draw from his cup and tosses it aside. I take a drink from mine. It is bitter for rum.

"So he gets them to agree?"

"No, no Master Nyles. Quite the contrary. All he accomplished was a digging in of sorts. The more he tried to reason the more irrational each side became, and the more they found the others' arguments preposterous. In another attempt for harmony, he got both parties to decide on a contest of sorts to decide who was right. He convinced them that the gods would choose the winner and assist them in the game. Ergo, the gods would tell them who was right by the outcome of the contest."

"That seems ridiculous. Even if their gods would, for sake of argument, intervene, how would they know if the gods even agreed to partake in the contest? Isn't that a tad presumptuous?"

"It is Master Nyles. However, when under the express impression of divinity, men will throw reason to the wind."

"So, the parties agreed to hold a naval battle to determine the winner. However, our family was the naval giant of the time and made short work of their opponent. Infuriated, the other side called a meeting again and argued that the battle was rigged and not a fair representation of the gods' intentions. We laughably argued the opposite, but to what end? We needed *them* to agree to trade, and our domination only made them less inclined. They wouldn't agree and borders were reconstructed and trade took an indefinite hiatus. So, seven years later, the families agreed to a different game. Which you get to participate in," he says with a controlling smile.

"This has got to be the single most irrational and ridiculous example of an uneducated and deple—" another slug to my stomach. Apparently Caddis was listening in.

"The hell was that for sand brains?"

"For being alive ya bastard."

Without paying any sort of response to the situation, the hooded man continues. "Every year the games evolved. Every year they became a little more intricate—a little more dangerous. They evolved from a single contest to a multi-contest to a tournament, winner take all."

"For what? For some damned interpretation of a moon that reared its head 77 years ago?"

"You would be surprised at how important that is to some folk. Particularly, my employer. *Our* employer. Primarily it serves as a prosciutto, or crescendo to one's pride. The moon is long gone and therefore, no interpretation of its existence is particularly relevant. However, there are other things that make this tournament beneficial. For example, it churns a huge boost for the economy as you can imagine. People bet by the masses. The entire country centralizes to see the fights. Merchants come from the far corners of the seas like birds to a field of bugs. About the 5th . . ." he scratches his chin. "Or maybe it was the 4th?" His hands slowly fall in thoughts far away from here. "Anyway, some time ago we figured out the other family was recruiting warriors and naval captains to their team in an attempt to best us, so we decided to even the odds."

"What makes you think I would be so willing to aid your endeavor, Mister . . . uh . . . Whoever you are?"

"Because you have no choice. If you disagree I will simply kill you. You will be under watch day and night until you enter the tournament. Any sign that you or your friends are trying something cute, you get to watch your friends die before getting killed yourself. Besides," he waves a hand dismissively, "you will come to find that buying in will make your life much more comfortable for the time being. And, if you win, we will take you right back where we found you. The faster you win, the faster you get back to your tasks." How does he know?

"I'm no good at sailing though. I wouldn't know the first thing about a naval battle."

He shakes his head while finishing a fresh glass of rum. "No naval battle this year."

"Then what?"

"In due time. Until then, make some friends and try to fill your belly."

I lean over the rail and look out to the sea. Creatures like a water dragon slither between whitecaps. A shrill sound comes from a baby before being dragged down by a much larger one. Nirue . . . What have you gotten yourself into?

"So you got the lecture too huh?" To my left, the black man leans against the railing of the ship, looking at the snakes without the same shock I display.

"Sure did."

"Well then, it looks like we are to be teammates. Names Rustin." He extends a hand. "Pleasure, Rustin. Nirue. They call you Rustin because of your hair color?"

"Na. I colored it this way a long time ago. Used to be blonde but excessive sun exposure turned it this rust color. I decided to not change it. Seemed fitting."

I nod in agreement. "Where they catch you?"

"Rizport. It's ten miles due west of Rizcarth."

"I've ventured as far as Rizcarth. Haven't made it to the port."

"Yeah. I wish I had stayed in that miserable city. I may have been able to do something about what happened."

"What do you mean?" He clears his throat and hocks a loogie over the side railing before responding.

"Some bastard killed my family in Rizport because of some rumor tying them to some noble or something. Poisoned them in their sleep, that coward. He freed a terrible group of men; a group of murderers, mind you, that took me two years to get in chains."

"So you were city militants or something?"

"Yeah. Had been doing it for ten years. Worked my way up to murder hunter. Anyway, after he freed them, he convinced them to aid his efforts in sacking Rizcarth and then took the prettiest girl from our camp. Told everyone he was going to make her his 'Queen' or something. She was something else man." He smiles and rubs the back of his neck while stretching it out in circles. "She had the most beautiful eyes." Card face, Nirue. Card face.

"I imagine the prettiest woman from any town would be beautiful."

"Yeah. This one was something else though. Sheeuw," he says with a little whistle. My mind wanders to the night I spent with Signy. Her tanned skin was the perfect blend of brown and olive.

"Rumor has it the would-be king was killed and the girl escaped." His eyes light up.

"Oh yeah? You heard that? What happened?" Be careful, Nirue. Too much info he will think you a liar. Too little he will think you a liar. You need this guy on your side.

"Well I heard it from a traveling tink. You know, one of those guys that sell a bunch of useless junk?" He nods, hurrying me along.

"Sure, Sure. Who killed him?"

"Some foreigner. A man that could not be deceived by his tricks and who beat him at his own game. I heard he had an imposter stand in for him during some festival and then killed him while pretending to be tricked. Supposedly this guy had the wits and blade skills of a god. Not to mention he could shoot a fly out of the air."

"Wow. What a man he must be indeed. I saw this Maji. He may not have been the biggest of men but he was clever and quick with the blade!"

I smile, "Just what I heard." He leans back, looking at me with narrow eyes, trying to figure out if he'd been cheated. He spits again in the ocean. A snake with tendrils coming from its eyes and mouth eats it, and disappears into the depths. Its head was the size of my sternum. Note to self—don't get too close to the rail.

"ALL HANDS ON DECK!" A voice shouts from the stern.

"All hands on deck cap'n!" the crew repeats in unison.

"APPROACHING MADMAN'S STRAIT!"

"Approaching madman's strait cap'n!"

"KEEP HOLD OF SOMETHING STURDY AN' DON' LOOK IN HS EYES!"

"Aye cap'n, not in his eyes!"

"What's going on?" Rustin looks around quickly then shrugs wide-eyed.

"Never been this way have ya?" Cuz asks me.

"No, can't say that I have."

Cuz looks around, ensuring no one is in earshot. He flicks his head. "You need to follow me—Now!"

CHAPTER TWENTY

This place is crap. I don't like it and I want to go home.
I'm tired, hungry, and I want the luxuries of my old life.

Josayus, 38 seconds before his death

CUZ GRABS RUSTIN AND I, eyes focused on a slow approaching strait.

"Before the shallow reefs of Pantine lies the ghost of a captain gone mad." He spits over the rail. "Prollem is, capn's been dead for over three hundred years. Now his apparition appears every so often and tries to steal a few souls to man his ship. One o' these days he might get enough to sail again. Ha!" He slaps me on the back. "When we get close, DON' look in his *eyes*. Last guy that did lost all color in his eyeballs and never said another word again. Just tied knots in rope until Caddis cut his throat. Said he was cursed did he. You wouldn't wanna lose them perty blues now would ya?"

"I don't think we plan on losing anything on this voyage. Thanks for the insight," said Rustin. The man tips his feathered hat and offers a weathered smile.

A huge thicket of fog appears from nowhere just two hundred yards ahead of the ship. In nautical time, that's still a decent ways a way.

"What are you holding on to?" Rustin asks. I look around the ship. I notice the other ships in our fleet slowly making their way into a line. This passage must be narrow. Which means the captain will be close by.

"I think we should stay away from the railing, if at all possible." The problem is, the crew is way ahead of us. Any good place worth hanging onto is already taken.

"Seems as though we are doomed to the sides. So be it. I'm not a scramp," I offer to Rustin. He nods and takes a place up right behind me. I double wrap my hands in the rope as we enter the fog.

In a few minutes, a heavy mist falls over me, causing my heart to box at my chest. "WE'RE IN IT NOW BOYS. HANG ON, I SMELL TROUBLE IN THESE HERE WATERS!"

"Aye, cap'n, pirates ye be warned!"

In moments we are immersed in the fog so thick it blinds our left and our right. Lanterns shine off our starboard and our port. We are sailing between two canyon walls. No. We are sailing between two rows of rotten ships. The ships, like their captain, are apparitions of what once was. Ships made of once sturdy wood now rot with the grey-green of water and age. Shadows dance along their decks with unnatural grace. A type of grace that is not hindered by a flesh and bone.

"See that Rust?"

"Yeah. Eerie man. I suppose those are the ships this madman has laid claim to?"

"Your guess is as good as mine. Hang tight, I see a brighter light coming."

"NoooOOoooo. No No No. A man covers his ears and begins to kick and cry.

"Not my wife. Not her. Anybody but her."

"Don't listen!" Cuz yells at him. "Just the mad pirate playin' tricks on ye!"

Soon after more and more men tighten their grip and let out yells to drown out the sound. One bites his cheeks so hard that blood pours from his mouth. Two men jump overboard and begin to swim. "LET EM BE, THEY HAVE ALREADY GIVEN UP HOPE!" the captain yells.

"Aye, cap'n, hope be gone for them!" This time, the crew's response isn't so enthusiastic. Three other men chase the black cat up some ropes to the already overcrowded crow's nest. The mist floats chest high. My eyes begin to water.

A soft stringed instrument plays in my ears. Its melody is magical— literally. I feel drawn to it like the tales of the sirens, but this is real.

Then it comes. I figured sooner or later it would be my turn, and there he was. Dressed in red and black with long black dreadlocks, the mad-captain appears by the light of a blue lantern playing a lute. Just beyond him is my family.

"Holy spit Rust. My family is up there!" I say with a whisper-yell.

"I never knew my family but that's my favorite dog, man." The captain flicks his head back and forth among the crew, seeking to capture their eyeballs. Every second a new target, every flick a potential new soul. The violent changing of his gaze disturbs every parcel of my body. I want to be with my family again. I want this to be over. I want to wake up in a hospital room and start my recovery process. I want to feel whole once more. I won't ever ask for danger again if I get out of these trials alive.

Ever since I started this expedition I have felt a hole inside of me. Something not food nor drink nor good company can fill. I cannot say why it's there or when it will close, but when it does, I know I will cherish that moment, even if it is my last breath.

"You alright man?" Rustin asks. "You look like you're about to cry."

I shake my head like a dog removing water. "Yeah man. Sorry. Just feeling..." The music continues and gets louder each moment. I am now directly parallel with the captain. I can feel the flick of his head through invisible waves escaping his dreadlocks as they catch inertia. I want to look so bad.

A screech wakes me from my trance and the black cat falls lifeless at my feet. Its eyes are white and without color. Stiff as a board, it wakes up and starts a slow walk toward nothing in particular. Someone cuts his head off. Another yells something about the ultimate curse.

The music of the lute is charming; inviting. It prompts me to ask myself deep questions. Why should I want to go back? Why was I on earth in the first place? How do I know that Bertram wasn't lying, and I have teleported here or something? If I join the captain's ship, will I be immortal?

Rust loses grip and falls onto his face. I turn only to see the whites of his eyes.

"RUST!"

Caddis moves in quicker than a shark on a wounded seal. "You know what must be done," he says with a devilish grin. The wind picks up, rock every boat in the tormented waters, including the ones creating this ghastly channel.

"You stay away from him Caddis. I'll be damned if you are going to claim another life."

"The hell you talking 'bout boy? You think I took his life? You really want to live with this bastard tying knots in ropes the rest of his days? He's soulless and he's got to GO."

"Is he the soulless one, or are you? I would rather live a thousand days with an empty shell than one filled with the putrid sprite you call a soul. Stay away from him, less you want steel up your end."

At that moment Rust begins to kick and shake and foam at the mouth. Without thinking I grab a thick piece of rope and put it into his mouth. I grab his tongue and yank it under the rope so that he does not choke on it or bite it off. He lies in my arms convulsing as the tail end of our ship passes the mad captain. In the distance I hear screams and splashes of those gone and those to go. Caddis spits on the deck and wanders back to the stern.

When Rust wakes up he grabs his jaw the way a boxer would after a back alley fist fight. He loosens his neck and wiggles his arms and shoulders. While pulling thin pieces of rope from his teeth he nods at me, as if to say thank you.

"Thought we lost ya."

He shakes his head. "Na. Been inflicted with demon shakes ever since I was a kid. You did the right thing. Not many people know how to handle that situation. Many thanks."

I shrug. "Well I hate Caddis. And he was jumping at the opportunity to kill the friend of his back-talking enemy, so it seemed like the right thing to do." He looks over his shoulder, nodding in agreement, clearly tired from the demon shakes.

For a while, we don't talk. I don't talk. I need a little time to myself, so I head to the stern and sit down. The wind feels good on my hair, which has grown longer since this adventure started. My beard has grown in length as well. It shades my jaw, giving me the appearance of a hardened man, though, the truth is, I am hardened. My belly is now muscular and my arms are chorded. This trek has demanded a lot of me, and my body has responded wonderfully.

The wind urges my senses and spirit alive. I cannot help but notice a faint notion of peace. It floats above me as if I could tangibly grab it. Not peace of mind, a separate peace. The kind of peace you attain once or twice in your life.

The kind that allows you to truly live in the moment and understand the wonderfulness of it all. The kind that does not trigger past mistakes or future tasks. The lost peace that I dangerously searched for, yet have never found. There's something to be said about my adventure thus far, I think to myself as seawater splashes coolly onto my face. As much as this world has tried to kill me, it has been necessary to keep me alive. It isn't anything to be weary of. No. This is what I have longed for my entire life. This is the adventure I could never get on Earth. How could I have been so stupid? Why wasn't I content? Yet, while I endure these hardships, I shall not be ungrateful. Had I been content before, I wouldn't have ended up here. Now, I must make the best of my situation, and survive. But when I return, I won't undervalue another moment of my life.

It is midafternoon. The sun ducks behind a pair of clouds, cascading shadow and turning light blue water to dark blue. The smell of the sea and the recent loss of light awakens me from my meditation. Cuz walks up to me while cutting an apple with a knife.

"One more night and we be sleeping like babies in hammocks again," he says, offering small talk.

"We got another night at sea?

"Yeah," he says while popping a piece of apple into his mouth. "Prolly the easiest voyage you'll ever take to Pantine really. Lucky you were so close. Say, I've been meanin' ta ask ya . . ."

"Yeah?"

"All that talk about, well you know, doomin' us or what'eva . . . you know, when Caddis was givin' ya a hard time. That's just a fools tale like the city of Krakens, ain' it? We ain' really cursed is we?"

I take a moment to think of how to respond. I squint toward a horizon of mixed dark blue and light blue ocean, where sun rays break free intermittently seeking the approval of the water itself. Keep 'em scared.

"Well Cuz, I'm not sure how you want me to answer this. Would you prefer I be truthful or do you want to sleep well tonight?"

He stops carving, a worried look escaping large eyes. "I don't believe ya newcomer. I don't believe ya one bit. I've had many prisoners that were treated in worse conditions than you was and I'm still here ain' I?"

I feign a laugh. "Where I'm from, there isn't anything worse you could do than hit a blind and bound man. When at qualms with another, you either kill him or you let him go. You *never* limbo like that. If you do take him prisoner, then you at least give him the means to defend himself. Ain't nothing honorable about hurting a man who is defenseless."

I catch a snicker from Caddis on the main deck below. He quickly averts his eyes and pretends to be preoccupied with oiling the mizzen mast.

"I see what ya mean. Well, if it's any condolences mate . . . I didn' mean to rooster up Caddis to hit ya again. I was feelin' the itch for some blood. I get that way sometimes. You seem like an okay mate. I saw what ya did for your new friend back there. Ya got balls ya do."

I shrug. "I know you didn't mean any harm, and, just so you know, the curse doesn't apply to helpers."

"Ho! Good show then lad! I'll be seeing ya around then will I. Ya sure did lift my spirits. Had me spirits down in an eel hole did ya. Well, for any matter, come by later—I got some rum tucked away for a special occasion," he says while offering me a wink. I smile and look into the distant ocean that lies ahead.

As the sun sets, the clouds lose their dominion over its rays and the whole ocean sparkles like a mirage in the high desert of Rizcarth.

* * *

I wake up in the lower corridor of the bottom deck to the sensation of three small pieces of cold steel against my neck. No, just one zigzagged blade.

"Where's your mouth now boy?"

I struggle momentarily to see how good my chances are off throwing him off me. Not good. "You heard the man. You can't kill me. You really wanna piss that guy off?"

I struggle to get away but his large and mostly fat body sits on my chest. His left hand holds my throat while his right raises a dagger. In a flash he punctures the jagged dagger into my left side. I feel a coolness overcome my body as blood leaves the newly carved hole. He hits me again just above the spot he previously had. Blood leaks onto my face as my world gets smaller. Like a hole exponentially closing, I see Caddis and the primal nature of his eyes. In the distance I hear brief shouting. My breaths become smaller. I'm finding it hard to feel my body. The world is suddenly so cold.

CHAPTER TWENTY-ONE

Who do you invite into your home? Are not bad habits roommates? Do you not become who you spend the most time with?

Brother Thomsil

I WAKE UP IN A grand room with vaulted ceilings that come to point at a large marble beam above my bed. I'm in a bed with slippery silk sheets. White sheets drape the sides of my resting place and an early morning glow creeps into the two biretta shaped windows to my left, but not the ones to my right. The floors and ceiling and surrounding walls are all made of marble. A soft green cloth is wrapped around my waist wounds. This is the second time I have been almost killed in my already quasi-dead state.

It feels as though someone is prodding my wound when I breathe, and as though someone has pulled Caddis' knife from a furnace and placed it into my wound when I try to move. My eyes water a bit when I think of how lucky I am to still be alive. I can't figure out why I catch so many breaks, but I do. Slowly, a marble door slides open to my left. In comes a man with eyebrows like scorpion tails facing each other in attack. His face is fat and his white beard, beginning just under his bottom lip is long and skinny and tied with circular bands.

"How do you feel Nirue Nyles?"

"Who the heaven are you?"

He has a high-pitched voice and an even higher pitched laugh. He has a round belly and fingers that have not seen a day of work in their life, save picking up food from his plate. No callouses on his hands and his cuticles are perfectly groomed.

"I'm the reason you are alive. I'm the light at the end of the tunnel boy. Learning to respect my authority will save you much pain, my little treat," he says while twiddling his fingers at each other.

Mouth open, I stare at him. Did he really just call me his treat?

"Wha—uh . . . ah wha— err . . . who are you again?"

"Timbly!" he claps and half jumps with excitement. "Timbly is my name. I am the

dominus of this house. Tragic as it was, both of my parents were poisoned after the last tournament." He feigns sadness. "Which leaves me all of the property and rights and responsibilities . . ." his voice trails off, "and gold and authority to delegate duty . . ." He pauses and makes direct eye contact with me.

His eyes are like diamonds harnessing every evil emotion possible. Greed, envy, hate, jealousy, ego . . . I can tell he was given everything he ever wanted and then some. I have a good gut and, when I choose to follow it, I am always glad I did so. Like a mother's intuition. It's always the fear of failure or mischaracterization that places you in positions where you must decide if you are going to trust it, or not.

Right now, no such fear exists. "Who poisoned your parents?"

He giggles and spins around in a circle, hand pointing toward the ceiling.

"A tragedy, a tragedy it was! They never did find the killer. I was going to put all of the men in the city on a hunt, but then, as if hit over the head by the good news, I decided I didn't care all that much," he looks at me, daring me to say something.

I hold my tongue. I have an eerie feeling this guy has done some terrible things in his life and has gotten away with them because of his last name. That type of power and drive is dangerous. What could be worse than a person who feels entitled to things, even something as great as another person's life, and has the means to take it? It's a terrible combination, and I have to work for him. This is not good.

"So, are you going to play for me, or not?"

"Do I have any choice? AAAArrrrrghh!" He prods my wound with two fingers.

"What do you think?"

I glare at him like a mother bear who is chained to a tree would to a kidnapper dangling her cub above a fire.

"I could bring in my physikers, have them whip you up a concoction, and get you healthy by the start of the games."

"Sure. Why waste time, when we could be planning our strategy?" I respond. He jumps and points his toes then claps.

"Good! Good this is quite good! I will send my people for you shortly!"

Not even an hour later, a big man and a hunchbacked man come through the never closed door.

"Greetings, friend," the big man offers his hand. When I extend mine back, the man jerks me out of bed and into the air. I try to catch myself but a searing pain buckles my knees. The big man catches me before I completely fall and picks me up, cradling me like an overgrown baby. Out the door and down the hall we go, following the hunchbacked man with the crooked and pointy nose, down a damp hall lit by lanterns of a fire I have never seen.

I hear a whimpering. A soft familiar whimper, so soft and genuine it could calm a nervous deer. The noise is coming from a room guarded by another hunchbacked man, who quickly moves to block anyone's view of the inside. As I walk by I hear a muffled conversation, where I think that I hear someone say, "Never seen anything like this before."

After almost ten minutes walking we approach a long room full of man-sized bird cages hanging from the ceiling. This is a physiker's dream come true. Book cases line the wall. Knives, scalpels, rulers, empty notebooks and quills, jars filled with body parts of animals and humans in tainted water are some of the things I notice, while being brought to a bed toward the end of the hall.

An old man with a hunch so exaggerated he could see under the table pines over notes written in a language I have never seen before. Without turning around, he says, "Put him in the prophet's chamber." Then he turns around so swiftly his spectacles slide down to the edge of his nose.

The big man replied, "But Timbly wants this one for the games. He says we need him if we wanna win."

"His wounds won't heal by the time the games start, which is the week after next, by the way. It's the prophet's chambers or nothing. Tell Timbly to come talk to me if he has a problem with it."

The big man shrugs and walks me toward a painting of a knight. Everything about this painting is odd.

The knight is positioned on a Cliffside. He is covered in blood. It is a stormy night. The only source of illumination is a perfectly timed flash of lightning. His horse has its front legs raised in the air.

The knight has his helm flipped upward, so that you can see his face from his nose up. His face is painted like a clown, garnished in white, red and black to disguise his true features. A false mouth is painted on the helm. He has sharp yellow teeth, on an evil grin that stretches from ear to ear. He holds the barren remains of two murdered youths. In his left hand is the head of a female twin, in the right is the head of the male, eyes rolled into their skulls.

The big man offers me a sympathetic look, and whispers a word to the painting. The knight's grin increases, ever so slightly, and he tosses one of the heads into the air. The picture ripples and becomes permeable. Before I can protest, the big man throws me through. I turn around and find a block wall where the picture once stood.

CHAPTER TWENTY-TWO

*I love life. I LOVE being alive. As much as I complain,
I really am grateful for the opportunity for this breath. And
the next. If it's my time, I accept that, but I would be lyin' if
I said I wouldn't care for another.*

*Terabin, a farmer of the great Western Plains,
said with a big smile across his face*

I AM IN A NARROW hallway made of the same material of the castle I was just in. Knives protrude from the sides of the walls so that I must walk one foot in front of the other, carefully, to avoid being cut. I hit a dead end and see nothing but stone with cryptic ruins half painted and half carved. I feel around the inscriptions and wipe away some moss in the process.

SNAP!

I plunge downward into darkness on a stone slide. I drift down, faster and faster, ripping skin from my hands as I try to brace myself. My wound rips open but the pain hasn't hit me due to my adrenaline. I see a light below me and before I know it, I am in a free-fall. I land in a large snow bank. It immediately turns red from my open wound. I walk toward a circle of light.

Where I am is so strange one must open their mind to completely understand. Picture this: I stand in a circle surrounded by eight torches, all with a different colored flame. I am in the middle of a mountain valley with no sign of civilization for thousands of miles. I don't know that for sure, because it is pitch black, save for the illuminated circle I stand in. But I can see faint silhouettes of mountains that would take me hours to reach if healthy, and riding a horse.

Each torch leads to a different path. One path is green. I can see about five feet down its path because of the flickering green flame. One is purple, one is blue, one is platinum-white, one is yellow, one is pink, one red and the last is black. They all reveal a small section of their path. The way the black illuminates its small share of the path is hard to imagine, but it is happening— I'm looking right at it.

I hold my side. My teeth chatter as I decide what to do. It's cold and I am badly in need of medical attention. My favorite color is green, but favorite colors are no reason to choose a path. I am bleeding, so maybe I should pick the red path. Then again, that choice is not logical either.

I come to the realization that I, frankly, have no idea which path to choose. I must choose soon, or else die. Better to try than to not.

I choose the white one. White means light and light is always better than the dark, and, in a place of darkness, I could use some light. I pull the torch from the ground and begin to walk. Like the flame back at camp, the fire produces no heat whatsoever. I walk over to the other torches and put a hand near their flames. None of the other torches are producing heat, nor can I grab them from their respective holes.

The snow is bitter cold. The top of my neck hurts from hunching my chin so close to my chest. Numbness begins to take over my body.

The further I walk the colder I get. I imagine that from a bird's eye view, I must look like a star in the middle of a void in space.

As I walk I think on all of the things that have lead me to this place in my life. I begin to wonder if I had messed everything up. I wonder what it must be like to be another person looking at me. Every person sees themselves respective to their own fears, beliefs, wishes, and life experiences. Nobody ever sees himself for who they really are, because that doesn't exist.

There is no such thing as a true version of oneself. Rather, a being with consistent reactions to situations. One's true identity is always changing with the ebb and the flow of the world. But this is perfectly perfect, because if there were such a thing as a true identity it would be a robotic, repulsive existence of chemical reactions in a fixed environment.

People always said that all of your heartache and past mistakes make you into the person you were meant to be. But does anyone ever actually achieve that person? Or are we beings that, if we never died, would continue to grow?

My stomach rumbles with hunger. My body shakes and condenses into a more hunched position the further I walk. I am now completely out of sight of the circle I was once in. The only reason I can see my path is because of the flame. The wind kicks up snow into my legs, making my body quiver even more. It feels like someone hit me with a potato masher that has needles instead of metal lumps on the hammer face.

As I approach I see another silhouette of a mountain in front of me. White light protrudes from the base of it. I begin to run, but my legs give out on me. I am now face down in the snow feeling colder than I ever imagined someone could feel. I did not think anyone could possibly feel like this, as if they were being preserved for some future experiment.

I push myself to my feet feeling the dried blood of my wound crystallize on my side. I trek on but begin to feel loopy. A stag made of snow appears in front of me and runs toward the mountain entrance at an incredible speed. A man with the head of a bull and body of a man appears twenty feet in front of me and takes off in a dead sprint in my direction.

I am too weak to fight, too cold to run, and too hurt to do anything. I simply raise a forearm, turn my head and close my eyes.

POOF

It hits me and turns to snow at my feet. I continue onward.

I get to the base of a structure made of white marble buttressed by Corinthian columns. I see two giant fire pots at the entrance, just up the steps in front of me. I stumble up them and warm my body up. A shriek from behind comes and I turn around just in time to duck a bearded man riding a gryphon.

He lands inside the building and proceeds to light a fire in a large hearth without ever acknowledging me. He then sits underneath a picture of a knight standing in between two children and a dragon. He rubs his hands together and throws the gryphon a steak sized piece of meat.

"Get your end in here before you die."

I look around to make sure he's talking to me. He gives me a "Are you completely mad" type of look. I walk near the man. The gryphon yawns and stretches out its dagger sized claws. It eyes me the way any curious bird would, switching from one eye to the other with slight head jerks. "Come by the fire and drink this."

"What is it?"

"The only way that wound will heal before the games."

At this point, nothing surprises me. I down the green vial. It tastes like tobacco spit.

"Now, there are other certain matters that need to be addressed. First, why did you pick the white path?"

"I don't know really, it just . . . It just felt right at the time."

"Eeny-meeny-miney-mo?"

"Not quite, but sort of."

He raises his eyebrows inquisitively. "Either way, you made the right decision. Any other physiker would have drawn you out till you were near death and then miraculously saved you to make themselves look good. Especially that purple bastard. He's killed four people trying to do that."

"So any path I would have chosen, I would have gotten medical attention?"

"Sure, but you probably wouldn't have survived. This is the shortest most direct path to health. Take a look at your wound."

I pull up my shirt and watch as hands made of light go in and out of my flesh, stitching my wound up with light. Every stroke feels like a soft hand stroking a muscle after a long week's worth of work. Slowly, it disappears.

"Did Timbly ask you to do this?"

"Screw Timbly that sadistic boob. I have been in this role for over 4,000 years. I could never get a group through, so, here I am. Came really close a few times. I had one survivor make it to the final trial only to slip into the crack of a glacier and freeze to death! Can you believe that? But no, I don't work for Timbly. Timbly is one of the worst people I have ever seen hold his position up there. Never ever trust that man, you hear me?"

I nod. "Good. Next order of business. What if I told you that you could go home?"

I almost faint. Tears well in my eyes as I think about my brother begging me to not go to college.

"Wha—err . . . What do you mean?"

"Well I mean exactly what I asked, do you want to go home?"

"I mean, of course I do! I—I never thought this was possible, what with the orbs and camp and what Bertram had said."

"Ahh, so you were given Bertram. A wonderful man, that one. Before you get too excited, you must understand this offer comes with a price."

Always a catch. "What would that be?"

"Your friends will both be killed, and will never return to Earth."

I knew it was too good to be true. "Just say the words though, and you will wake up to be with your family in an instant. You are badly injured, yes. But, you will be back on Earth."

"You're going to kill them, then?"

He laughs. "Oh *heavens* no. They will die on their own time. I will show you—but understand, this is *only* if you choose to go."

He flicks the painting with a wand and it begins to ripple. I see Atia hung in a tree, the color of frozen water. He flicks it again and a movie begins to play out. Ranger is in a snow covered valley in the daytime underneath a ridge to his right. A knight wearing all black including an all-black cape dances toward him with sharp blades. Ranger raises *Darkwater* to meet him and an arrow strikes him through the neck. He drops Darkwater and reaches for his neck.

The man slows to a walk and puts the blade underneath Ranger's chin, so that Ranger stares into his eyes. The man smiles, says something inaudible and in one motion cuts his head off. Blood fountains from Ranger's head, his body in uncontrollable spasms. The man touches the painting again and it goes back to its original state.

"Sadly, this is the fate of your comrades should you choose to go. But, you will guarantee your own survival. Take some time to think about it."

"One question."

"Sure."

"If I don't go, are they guaranteed to live?"

"No. This could still very well happen with you there. But, without you there, they stand no chance in the games. With you there, they stand at least a chance to live."

"And will I remember them when I wake up?"

"No."

This sucks. I'm being tempted with the only thing I have wanted since I landed in this miserable place. If I choose not to go, who's not to say they won't die anyway? Aren't I being selfish to my family—the ones I am more loyal to if I *don't* go home?

I sit by the fire and ponder my decision. It would be selfish to go home and condemn my friends, but it would also be selfish to my family to not guarantee my safety. How much longer can I put my mom through this? What if I never come out of this alive? As I think, I look at the picture of the knight guarding the twins. They would certainly die from the dragon, if not for the knight. I think on the painting I saw before I entered this cold place, and the jester pretending to be the knight holding the severed heads.

INTERLUDE 3

ATIA QUIETLY ENTERS HER HOUSE after a long day in the library. With her books in one hand, she holds the knob open, slowly closing until the door is flush with the wall, then slowly releases the handle. Perfect, she thinks to herself.

She lets her heel touch the floor first, then smoothly transitions the rest of her shoe onto the floor, the same way a rocking horse moves. She does this with both feet, barely audible. When she moves for the handle to her bedroom, she hears a loud bang in the kitchen. She shudders at the sound. Her shoulders are tight near her ears.

"ATIAAA! Atia, is that yew?"

Reluctant to respond, she replies, "Yes, Uncle, but I've got a lot of homework and don't have time to catch up."

"Don't have time for the man who took you in, heh? You got time to clean up this damn mess you made, making all that noise and scaring the bottle out of my hand." She shakes her head, realizing that once again, she will have to study at the bus stop—the only semi-clean seat in close walking distance.

"I'm sorry, I really am, but I don't have time for this," she says, knowing it won't make a difference. Books fall off of the entry table. A mirror is knocked off the wall. Atia knows what is coming next. She puts her hair into a pony tail as quickly as possible and closes her eyes, arms braced against her sides.

Her uncle rips her off the floor and drags her to the kitchen. He grabs her head and shoves her inches from the broken bottle of whiskey.

"THIS MESS, ATIA—THIS MESS."

Crying, she replies, "Yes Uncle. I'm sorry Uncle." He pushes her head down, forehead making contact with the glass. She begins to bleed, but this upsets him. He rips her to her feet again. She squints as blood enters her eyes, left hand half-grabbing for her pony tail, a natural reaction.

"Did you just reserst me? Did you challenge meh?" he slurs.

"No, sir, I would never challenge you." She looks at him with sorrowful eyes. Oh what she would give to be away from him. Anywhere but here. One more month she keeps telling herself, not sure if she can really last that long.

They stare at each other. He struggles to stay up right, see-sawing this way and that, one eye looking at her, one rolling toward the ceiling. She doesn't know what to say, so she starts to clean. She gathers the big pieces of glass and dries up the liquor. She sweeps up the remaining pieces and puts them into the trash.

She ties the bag and heads to the balcony. She's gotten good at dropping their bags into the dumpster from their porch. No bother if she misses—the alley is so filled with junk, another trash bag would hardly be noticeable.

When she reaches the balcony she feels a presence behind her.

"Wherez my bottle?" Her uncle asks her.

"You just broke it, don't you rememb—" He slaps the bag from her hand.

"I JUST BROKE NUTHIN' YOU INGRATEFUL—"

"SHUT UP YOU STUPID DRUNK! I HAVEN'T DONE ANYTHING TO YOU. YOU'RE A WASTE OF LIFE. ALL YOU DO

IS DRINK AND BLAME YOUR PROBLEMS ON ME. I SHOULD HAVE NEVER LET YOU TAKE GUARDIANSHIP YOU ABUSIVE, MANIPULATIVE A—" with a closed fist, he strikes Atia in the face.

Backward she falls off the balcony. Four stories she tumbles, extended railings speeding her rotations as she makes contact with them until she hits the ground. Her body snaps and begins to swell. She knows this must be it, but she doesn't fight it. The hurt has accumulated such that she is ready to give up. She doesn't adjust her leg despite her shin bone showing through the skin. She doesn't try to lift her chest off of her hand that is making it hard to breathe.

A lifeless, beautiful girl lies among trash in the back alley of a bad neighborhood, bleeding from her eyes, praying that this is the last time she has to go to sleep.

CHAPTER TWENTY-THREE

*Try eating alone. Have some juice and hot caffeine of
your choosing. Smell your surroundings. Appreciate the
warmth of the sun and allow yourself to relax, if nothing
more than for a few moments.*

Beatrine's guide to present-mindedness

I WISH ALL MY DECISIONS were this easy. I spend the next few days
studying the past histories of the game and its victors. Baron the Great
once hid in the same spot for one week without sleep to ensure his team's
victory. Another man named Jon Thorn single handedly won a battle by
pretending to be dead and capturing the other side's leader when he got
close enough. The good news is, based on everything I have read, only one
person has died in the games, and by pure accident.

I am now fully healed, warm, and have been given an outfit of animal
furs made for a warrior. I say goodbye to the old man as I ascend a ladder
into the painting. I nod at the gryphon, nod to the old man and enter.
When I arrive, Ranger is on one knee with a hand ready to help me up. He
smirks, acting as though he is reluctant to help me up before ripping me to
my feet and giving me a big hug. "Good ta see ya again, Nirue."

"Good to see you, Ranger. Let's do this." With that, we walk back into the busyness that is the physikers room.

After some questions and a few introductions, Ranger and I are lead to the barracks to meet our team. The big man that had carried me into the physikers room turns out to be our Doctore, which, apparently, means the head trainer. There is just one, huge problem. Atia is gone.

Ranger looks around panicked before he asks Doctore, "Have ya seen a girl, with brown and light blue hair about, yay tall?" He gestures the height of a girl much shorter than he. He shakes his head.

"I have seen her, but she isn't with us anymore."

Ranger freezes. "What do you mean?"

"I know she was with you all before we got here. She was on my ship. She kept asking about you two. She was too sick to compete though, so we had to let her go."

I step in. "What do you mean, 'let her go'?" I ask, voice quavering. He shakes his head again.

"No. Timbly thought it better to trade her to the other side. Says the state she was in gives us a huge advantage. Said it would be good for gambling. It's almost as if they are down a man to start, even with those daggers. I tried to tell him it wouldn't be good for the morale of our team."

My heart drops as I consider the matter.

Ranger half curls his hands, flexing, neck veins bulging, and lets out a suppressed scream before storming out of the hall.

*   *   *

After Ranger is subdued seven different times for trying to find Atia, I convince him that we will steal her to our team once the games begin. It didn't help that Timbly didn't even give us an audience about getting Atia back. Ranger isn't happy about my idea but eventually agrees it's the only one that may actually work. He tells me they plan to get married once they wake from the coma, after the trials are complete. Apparently they have fallen for each other faster than I had realized. We are moved to a training barracks with the rest of our teammates.

We spend a few days honing our skills and training for the competition. Wooden dummies engulfed in straw serve as both archery targets and fighting dummies. They take our weapons and give us less than good practice ones.

Doctore is as ruthless as he needs to be. Our training regimen is gruesome, but I don't mind. We will be fighting with our lives on the line, and I need these people alive if we have any chance to win. There are ten of us total.

Every morning, just as the white sun peers over high mountains in the distance, a cymbal is struck with a sledgehammer. We run down into the foreyard of our living quarters in two parallel lines. I lead one, Ranger the other, with Rust right behind me.

We run for almost two hours, up and over hills in the rain. I am sore day two, and very sore by day three. By day four, my legs feel strong, and we run without stopping.

After running we are divided into our skill sets. I am clearly an archer, and Ranger a close ranged fighter. We hold trials to determine what everyone else should be. A skinny girl with freckles is decent with a sword but even better with katanas. Her name is Sabe, and she is as vicious as they come. She actually bit the head off of one of the dummies. Rust is an excellent fighter as well. His speed and agility are better suited for a close range fighting style, so he is given the short swords.

The other girls in our group are talented in their own regard, especially Faris with the bow. Doctore calls for a competition between us to see who is a better shot. The contest has a tree, a cage of hungry black crows, and strategically placed food for them to fly to. Three points for an in-flight kill, one point for a kill while the bird feeds. She beats me 13-12, and lets me hear about it. She is a boastful woman, and, frankly pisses me off, but her good looks make the loss and her bragging a bit more palatable.

The last of the women is a sweet and quiet soul named Tamra. She is caring, kind and dislikes battle. She grew up studying medicine and physics, so she has been designated as our healer. She has a unique ability to heal people one-thousand times faster than they otherwise would heal. If necessary, she can shoot a bow.

For the men aside from Ranger, Rust and myself, we have a surreptitious fellow who we call "Sly" because he is always disappearing and blending into the environment. Then we have Kam, and then the giant twins, Balk and Dalk. Sly is the quiet type and tends to keep to himself. I don't mind, because he weirds me out. Kam is a mage. He wields a long staff with a golden crystal attached to the top. His powers are elemental and include fire, wind, water and earth. However, using his power drains his body—the more powerful spell, the more drained he becomes.

Balk and Dalk are not the brightest, but they are huge. Not as big as a Jboynei, but much bigger than Ranger or Doctore. They both wield a massive sword and shield. They practice fighting on full grown spruce trees.

I train until my body screams for me to stop, and then I continue. I throw up, and continue. I pass out, and continue. I do everything in my power to set an example for the rest, who work almost as hard as I do. After our last day training, we sit in a circle while Doctore walks around us, hands held calmly behind his back. As we attempt to catch our breath, he says, "You are fine warriors, each equipped with unique abilities. Do not fall victim to certain strategies that expose your weaknesses. Think of your talents, and how to maximize them at all times. Understand your enemy, and use their weakness to your advantage. Never expose your weakness to them. Your training is complete, and you are now ready for the games. One last run, then dinner, then . . . War."

One last look and he takes off down the mountain. We briefly exchange glances, a few of the team rolling their eyes and snickering at the notion of "war." Sabe does her best, deep throated impression of Doctore, feigning a sword fight and saying, "I'm going to kill you."

No one immediately jumps up to run. Half of the team is still catching their breath, waiting for someone to be the first to be the first. I jump up and head down the hill.

* * *

The night before the games is upon us. We are called into a great hall with a long table for fourteen. At the head is Timbly, to the right is Doctore, and the rest of us pile in at random. Each of us is hungry and nervous for what is to come. I feel eyes on me and sense a need to exude confidence, so I do.

The table is golden and the plates are ivory. The forks and knives are polished silver, reflecting a warped version of the onlooker. Chandeliers hang thirty feet to rest nearly ten feet from our heads. They are filled with candles of the exact same burn, none are bigger than the other. The room has four great windows of the same shape as those in my bedroom.

There are two great cages on either side of the table. Each holds four of the biggest wolves I have ever seen. Timbly looks at us with accusing eyes, as if we have slighted him. Most of the table looks confused as to who he is. Maybe they haven't met him yet?

"You are no better than the beasts in these cages," he begins. "You are just as much under my control as they are. You are just pawns in a game that can be discarded at any moment. You are nothing but dung beneath my boots. No. Not even dung beneath my boots, because that would mean you are somehow attached to me, which is better than what you are. You are nothing, and will always be nothing. I don't care if you live or die. Just win. PERIOD!" he stands and slams his fists on the table. Plates and silverware rattle. Faris shifts uncomfortably, fanning her fingers out against her collarbone.

"Doctore, fetch me *one*." He nods and leaves the room. Timbly intentionally and obviously stares each one of us in the eyes. No one knows what to expect, and no one knows what to think. Tamra is trembling. The twins eye each other, as if to ask each other if they should do something.

Ranger has the soft, calm look of a man who wants to kill another. Not the burning, enflamed passionate hatred, but the sure hatred. Like it knows it's just a matter of time. I am worried if he presses to much Timbly's ego will kill him.

Doctore returns with a cat by the scruff. It looks annoyed, but fairly calm. Timbly rips it from his hands and holds it tight, so tight I can't help but think the cat is being choked. He walks over to a stool by the wolf cage straight ahead of me. He goes to the top and holds it above an opening. The wolves salivate and jump and snap at the cat. They bite at each other's necks to get closer to the opening. The cat shrieks and claws and flips to try and get away from Timbly's grasp. He looks at Tamra, who has tears in her eyes, feigning a smile.

He comes down from the ladder and stands directly behind me. I don't turn around. He grabs me by my face, "Too good to look are you Nirue? Too proud and *moral* to see these beasts eat? What do you think they feed on, grass? Are you as *blind* as you appear?" I hate this man too. He took Atia from us. He kidnapped us from our home and has delayed our trials, putting all of our lives at risk. I stare at him with the coldness of a glacier in a blizzard. He punches me in the jaw and shoves the cat into my chest in one motion. He still has a grasp on the cat. It scratches me and flips around.

"Feed them this, or I feed them you." I continue staring for what feels like an eternity. Doctore places a hand on my shoulder and whispers encouragement into my ear.

I grab the cat, walk up the stool and drop the cat in, all while looking at Timbly. A desperate feline shriek, then tearing. He grabs my face and screams, "LOOK! LOOK YOU DEFIANT LITTLE CUS, LOOOOK!"

I want to kill this man. Not with a knife or an arrow or a spear, but with my hands. I want to gouge his eyes out with my thumbs and feed it to his mouth full of broken teeth. I want to punch his head until his brains ooze out of the holes. I want to tear him apart, and my eyes give it away.

"I'LL HAVE YOUR HEAD FOR THIS YOU—"

"Timbly!" Doctore interjects. "He didn't mean it like that he just-"

"Oh yes I did!" I reply, now standing in my seat.

"You see HOW HE DEFIES ME!"

I continue staring while Doctore goes up behind Timbly and rubs his shoulders while whispering something in his ear. All I could make out was "most important piece . . .fame . . . fortune . . . respect of the world .

. ." Timbly nods his head and visibly cools down. "Yes . . . yes," he replies while rubbing his hands together. "Call for the chefs, let us eat," he says, exchanging glances with the others.

The air is thick as Timbly returns to his seat. The chefs serve us an array of gourmet foods. Cheese filled bread with mashed tomatoes is the first course. Next comes swordfish baked in butter and citrus, seasoned with parsley and nutmeg. For the main course, we have the freshest cut from Timbly's private stock of grass-fed steer, also draped in butter and accompanied with turtle soup served in the shell. The chefs insist we need vegetables, so they fine chop carrots and sprinkle it over crisp asparagus topped on a bed of lettuce with fresh-squeezed pomegranate.

Doctore stands and waits for everyone to acknowledge his presence. It takes only ten seconds before the last of the group notices the silence that has strangled the room. We weren't talking much before anyway. All eyes are on Doctore. "Allow me to explain to you the rules of the game."

He pauses and clears his throat. "There will be two bases, ours and theirs, ten people each team. The game is capture the flag." Whispers are exchanged around the table.

"This isn't your ordinary childhood game, or like any game you have heard about growing up. This year the rules are different. Timbly thought it would be better if there were more at stake. So, now, it is no longer elimination by capture." He rubs the back of his neck, avoiding eye contact with us—ashamed of what comes next. "This year, it is life or death." The dark room suddenly feels much darker.

CHAPTER TWENTY-FOUR

You need to learn the word "good." When you're in war, what're you gonna do when the enemy gets a leg up? What're you gonna do when your plan falls apart? You're gonna say "good," that's what, and you're gonna stare your problem in its eyes until you take its soul.

Tyr, second to champion all four trials

THE WIND BLOWS THROUGH THE hall, flapping flags and giving the already cold group shivers. Capture the flag? Life or death? Doctore continues.

"The bases will be very far apart from each other, with many obstacles in your path. The goal is to capture the other team's standard, bring it back to your base, then hold it there for one hour."

"How long do we have to capture it, Doctore?" I ask.

He shakes his head. "There is no time limit. This is only the third time this particular game has been played in the 77 year history, but the last two times it ended in about a week.

Now, you will be given plenty of supplies and food and water. Understand, however, that the landscape is not an ordinary setting. This game was intentionally built by the architects on what some would call "hallowed ground." I shoot a glance at Ranger, who doesn't notice me.

"Things are not as they seem, and *appearance is everything*." This time, Ranger feels my eyes. "You will need to be organized and disciplined if you want to win. The other side has not lost in a long time, and they have been unrelenting in their recruitment for these games. Some are calling them a 'team of gods.' I have to admit, I have seen their ranks and . . ." His voice trails off.

"I have always said that the underdogs have the upper edge when it comes to these things. Come together, follow your leader and take their standard. Be cunning! Be wise! Be strong . . . Be *TOGETHER*!" He raises a fist and we all cheer in unison. All except Ranger, who stairs out the windows.

"I have faith in all of you. After training you all in the limited time we had, I have chosen your leader for you. Trust my judgment, and know I only have your best interest in mind. Nirue, please come forward."

Timbly looks at me, fat leg crossed over the other, hands steepled, narrow eyes and a suspicious smirk. He seems *happy* that I have been chosen leader. Something doesn't feel right about this. Doctore hands me a green cloak that appears to be knitted reptilian scales. Its movement is fluid, its strength hard as a rock. He drapes it around my neck and connects it with a miniature golden bear paw. A perfect fit.

Doctore moves to his chair and takes a seat. Ranger doesn't seem to care what is happening. The rest of the room stares at me blankly. They want a speech? I clear my throat.

"Not all of us are as familiar with each other as we like." I pause. Even the wolves are silent. "Even if we had more time to become acquainted, I'm not sure we would all connect as friends outside of the confines of this place. The places we come from stretch from the farthest reaches of this planet, and then some." I pause again to gather my thoughts.

"I don't care if you have never been a team player before. I don't care if you have never been in a real battle. I don't care if the other side has a bloody dream team. All I care about is us. For the next week or month or year, I have your back. I will do everything in my power to make sure you are safe. I will literally die for you." I pause and look at everyone on my team. The big twins look eager, ready to jump out of their seat.

"This will not be a dictatorship, rather a democracy. I am open to suggestions and want us to round-table things, but if I make a decision, respect it. I will respect you, but if I do not take your suggestion, let it go. I will always do what I think is right for us, and I want for every single one of us to come out alive.

We were all *taken* from our homes, and forced over here. Now, we are being thrust into a game of life and death, where ALL WE HAVE IS EACH OTHER. There is no more *I* or *ME*, ONLY US. If one of us loses focus, for even one second, another could die. Each and every single one of us needs to realize how much we need each other. Take a look around. Meet the eyeballs of the ones who hold your life in their hands."

One last pause. "The truth is, not all of us *will* make it out alive. That's something we are going to have to understand. I ask one thing of you people. *FIGHT* for *each other*, not for yourself. Look deep within yourselves. Everything you need is already within you! You are BRAVE. You are POWERFUL. You are WISE. You are CLEVER. YOU ARE STRONG!"   The eyes of my teammates are widened with energy. I take a breath. "But, remember. Fear not this night, or the many to follow."

I wait for a response. Nothing. Did I not inspire them? I thought I had, yet, all I hear is the wind and flapping flags. I stay standing, waiting for *something*. It feels as though the room is inspecting every aspect of my body.

My angst is relieved when Ranger, with pinched lips and narrowed eyes stands and raises a fist. I nod to Ranger and raise my fist. Next, Kam stands, fist high and chin tucked. Then Rust. Soon the movement of chairs sliding backward fills the room, and my team unites silently, fists in the air.

* * *

Dinner goes quickly without speaking. It seems as though everyone has lost their appetite, both for food and conversation. Timbly is served all of his courses at once. He finishes them quickly, throws his napkin onto his plate and storms off toward the west wing. Conversation picks up after that. I have a nice chat with Tamra about the poisonous snakes on the rocky beaches just south of this city.

Spirits are lifted as a single glass of wine is poured for everyone. It feels like we are being given our last drink. We make solemn toasts to life and good fortune, and to memories lost and never forgotten. The big twins ask for more wine, but I had already given Doctore the discreet order to limit the wine to one glass per person. The night begins to cool as a breeze returns, sliding through the windows and licking the flames of the candles.

Eventually, we come to a place where we are full and tired. Sometime in between talking with the crew and finishing my wine, Sly had snuck off to bed. No one saw him leave. It's okay though, we needed someone to be the first to get to bed. Truth is, I'm dead tired and want to sleep, but I have to be the last to bed because I am their leader.

One by one they say their goodbyes and head to bed, except Ranger. I have the feeling that he wants to talk to me about something. He begins to say something, and then stops himself. He quickly looks away and tells me he is going to bed. I am curious, but happy that the last person is gone, so I can sleep.

I am the last person, save Doctore, to leave the dinner table. He nods and tells me he is heading to his room. I begin to head to my room when it hits me. I turn around and run into the shadowy hallway I had just watched Doctore step into. As I race down the long carpet through the dark hallway, I am grabbed from behind, knife on my throat.

"I was hoping you wouldn't try anything stupid."

With hands up I say, "Relax, Doctore. I just came to ask you for a few pointers."

"Why not do it before? At the table?"

"Didn't want my teammates to see. I want them to think I have all the answers, so they will believe in me more. There may be a time when I have to ask tall orders of them." Doctore waits for a moment, then releases his grip on me. "Follow me," he orders.

We walk to his personal quarters. He lights an oil lamp with a match, shakes out the match with his right hand and walks to a grand window. Below us is a beautiful town made of white pastel colored buildings with wooden support beams exposed at symmetrical angles. Lights from various lanterns look like a swarm of distant fireflies. Beyond the city below is the ocean. The cool, wet breeze fills my nostrils as I take a deep breath and pull my hair back. I've always wanted to live by the ocean.

"I almost killed you, you know. The enemy has eyes and ears all over this city, even in our midst."

"I think I know one, his name is Timbly," I suggest sarcastically. He doesn't smile.

"No time for jokes, you must listen to me. For every two people on a team that is killed, a 'special' is released into the grounds. These things range from animals to powerful relics to apparitions that serve their own purpose. My guess is that the other team will know this as well, so be careful how you go about engaging them."

"Like, always go in pairs?"

He shakes his head. "Like, be calculated in *everything* you do! From harvesting and hunting food, to scouting, to secret attacks or laying traps. You will need to anticipate the worst outcome at all times! Never allow yourself to be outmatched or outwitted, and do *NOT* underestimate the power of the specials! They are vital to your chances in this. Nirue, I am going to be straight with you. I have trained you and your lot, and a fine lot you are. But the other team is finer and more polished. They are warriors, warlocks and rogues from the finest institutions in the world. These people were bred for this competition. Their entire lives hinge on these games. Their leader is not one to bargain with, Nirue. He is an animal—cunning as he is vicious. You will never win a straight up battle with them, and trust me, they will certainly try to entice that. *Use* the land, *use* the specials and *use* your brain and work together. Then and only then will you have a chance. Your lot is unpredictable, which is one of the major advantages you have going for you. Keep it that way."

There is a silence. The wind flickers the flame in my lamp. "I don't know what to say, other than thank you. I will do my best to lead these people, and I will certainly remember these things you have told me."

He nods and looks me in the eyes before patting my shoulder.

"Oh, and Nirue . . ." I look up at him. "Don't feed the crows." With that, he ushers me to the hallway and closes the door behind me. My heart beats fast as I look down the dark hallway, thinking of everything I have been told, but particularly, that there are enemies in our midst. I blow out the lantern and head to my room. Best travel by dark.

I enter my room, check every possible hiding place for an assassin and go to bed. After only a couple of hours of sleep I wake to the ringing of a bell.

In between chimes I hear screaming and shouting in the streets below my room. I shuffle my way over to the window while rubbing the sleep from my eyes. Do they deceive me? I rub them even harder.

Men carrying torches run in unorganized lines, lighting torches off of one another and throwing them into the buildings, pluming smoke into the air and setting roofs on fire. I quickly put on my pants, tunic and cape. Before I get my socks on, my door flings open. Sly appears in the door, hands on his knees, panting.

"You've got to come, now!

CHAPTER TWENTY-FIVE

You've got to pretend! Pretend to them, pretend to us, but most of all, pretend to yourself. Rationalizing these games will leave you paralyzed while you analyze. It's a game—trudge ever onward.

Josephine Aldrunten, first female to successfully Sherpa a group through four trials

I RACE AFTER HIM AND almost slip trying to catch my footing. We hurry through a maze of hallways and stairs and end up in the dining hall where we ate last night. In the room is Doctore and the rest of my team. I am the only one not fully dressed.

"Nirue, there is no time to waste, riots broke out last night over the games. This is going to be the biggest games this world has ever seen." He pauses.

"How do you know that?"

Doctore shakes his head. "Because, every eve of the games, betting between us and them initiates. However, they determined that this year would be the be-all end-all. What I'm trying to say is, whoever wins these games, wins the rights to trade and essentially, a stranglehold on the economy forever. Riots are breaking out in anticipation, protest and excitement. We need to get you into the grounds before you are taken by the mob! Come! There is no time to waste!"

With that, he darts off down the main steps of the castle. Outside is a tempo-driven carriage, with room to fit us all. It is windowless. "What about my clothes, Doctore?"

"Won't need them. Everything you need will be at your base." Everyone files in with haste with me being the last to enter. Before I enter, Doctore grabs me and looks at me with unquestionable seriousness. "Nirue. Remember what I told you." With that, he runs back up the castle stairs and closes the giant doors. At the same time, I usher the last of us in the carriage.

* * *

The ride is bumpy and long. For hours nobody says a word, either because they are catching up on lost sleep, or because they have nothing to say. The silence is uncomfortable. I spend a few minutes trying to think of something to say but cannot. Finally, Faris breaks the silence in an unexpected way. She begins to laugh.

Tamra, who had been sleeping on her shoulder, wakes up a bit confused. Sly studies her with curiosity. Still, she continues laughing.

"What is it?" I ask.

Through her laughter, she says, "Imag—hehhe-—his face ha ha haha when he hahahe." It's a bit contagious, and I find myself smiling while trying to figure out what she said.

Gabe offers, "I think she's talking about Timbly?" She nods and attempts to control herself.

"Imagine that pathetic little tub-of-lard running around frantic as the city threatens to usurp him. He must have pissed himself! Hahahahahah." We all laugh. Even Ranger enjoys a good chuckle. I appreciate the humor, since it lightens our mood.

After Faris breaks the ice, people are more willing to open up. Some exchange hero stories while others give detailed background on where they are from. Everyone here is unique one way or another. Nobody is your average person, and better yet, everyone seems to get along.

The air in the cabin begins to cool dramatically as the road inclines. I figure the temperature has dropped at least thirty degrees. We aren't prepared for this type of weather coming from the coastal town of Pantine. Some become so cold that they have to snuggle up to their neighbor for body warmth. Kam conjures a small flame on the ground of the cabin that doesn't burn through the wood but yet provides warmth.

"Kam . . . We don't need you wasting all of your energy on such a silly thing as this," one of the twins offers. I can't tell which one since I haven't figured out how to tell them apart.

Kam chuckles, "No need to worry. Watch this." He creates another small fire at the other end of the long carriage, this time right in front of the twins so they can watch. He whispers something under his breath, eyes closed. A single flame appears first on his thumb. As his eyes glow brighter, the flame grows out over his palm then to both palms, allowing him to place it wherever he like. The flame is blue then red then orange. He drops the fire onto the floor, then rolls back his robe to show us his hand, which has the appearance of a dried fruit—as if he had left it in water the last few hours. He holds his pointer finger toward the big twins. After a minute or so, that finger changes from white and wrinkled to pink and youthful. The twins cover their mouths in unison, grabbing each other, amazed at what they had just seen. Kam smiles, shrugs, then warms his own hands by the fire. It becomes chillier as we continue to climb.

After a few more hours of traveling we reach our destination. Most of us were asleep when a loud knock startles everyone awake. We are greeted by a short but stout man covered in all black furs. He has a red beard and a no-nonsense demeanor. I look down the road we just traveled. Below me is a beautiful forest covered in snow that transcends into a deep mountain valley where the snow is not so heavy.

Before us is a large gate made of iron with spikes at the bottom of it. The red bearded man asks, "This all of ya?" I look around and nod. "Right then. Once ya enter this gate, there's no turning back. Any last words or requests?" I look around at my team who stands strong, yet cold. I do my best to contain my shivers. Before I can get a request out, the bearded man says, "I recommend you all get in there and put some warm clothes on before ya freeze. This be your base, where all your supplies are. The enemy's bases lies many miles in that direction, and even more around the bend." He points northeast and north with an exaggerated arm fluctuation.

"Right. Let's get going," I say while giving confident nods to the group. The bearded man cranks a lever with a glowing golden rod. He then inserts it into a pulley system that easily lifts the heavy gate which creaks as it rises into the ice mountain. The walls and floor are a matching ice blue—just what you want to see on a hot summer day. Not what you want to see when you are underdressed in the middle of winter. On the other side of the gate is a base made of stone. Rust is the first one through. The moment the last of us crosses the threshold, the gate slams shut, disappears, and turns into a grey stone wall to match our base. I feel the stone wall where a hole just was. The rest of the group seems to be getting acquainted with our base.

"Um. Guys?" Rust says, standing at the edge of our base, overlooking the arena below. I turn around, hand still on the stone.

A large horn blows in the distance. The games have begun.

CHAPTER TWENTY-SIX

Lies, Lies, LIES! IT'S ALL LIES!
He was CHOSEN!

Gumald, moments after insanity set in

JUST OUTSIDE OF OUR BASE is a woman that looks as though she hasn't had a meal in weeks. Skin hangs off of her bones, revealing the shape of each knuckle, of each joint. She is dressed in tattered tan clothing that is better suited for summer in Rizcarth. Hair covers her face, hanging down over her eyes, entering her mouth when she breathes. Steam rises from her body as if she has just walked out of a hot spring. With her head facing down, she holds up a single finger. Just like the gate that let us in, another keeps us from leaving our base.

"What the hell is that?" Kam asks, staring at the woman. Before anyone can answer, a bird flies near the woman, drawing her attention from the gate, causing it to drop a few feet from the slot in the stone ceiling. She shakes her head maniacally and returns her focus on the ground, the gate returning to its slot in the roof. I try to put my hand through the gaps in the gate but cannot. She has an invisible force field up.

"Rust, find us some warm clothes." Rust nods and runs downstairs. "Kam, how far can your powers work?"

"Depends. What element? What purpose?"

"Can you make me a moving distraction near the girl?" His eyes light up, realizing what I am getting at.

"Just let me know when." I nod, momentarily taking in my environment.

We stand in the main corridor of our castle-base. Our castle structure is simple. It is three stories with a basement, built into a sturdy mountain covered in snow. The top floor is roughly thirty feet above the ground floor.

The edge of the top story extends outside of the confines of our base and into the grounds. The top story is the sleeping quarters with a side for men and women. If you were outside looking into the base, the staircase winds on the left, reaching from the ground floor to the second story, filled intermittently with torches and windows. The base itself is made of grey stone with black mortar.

The ground floor is large in size and has all of the amenities needed for ten people to live. We have a place to cook, a place to eat and a large wood-burning stove to keep the place warm.

Below the ground floor is a basement of sorts. It is more of a storage unit than anything. There, Rust finds a variety of animal furs and warm clothing. We throw on the pelts of wolves, foxes, and even longsnouts, a ten-ton bear rumored to hunt the woods outside of the canyon walls. Balk and Dalk wear the brown longsnouts and Ranger wears a grey dire wolf tunic with his black cat cloak, a good fall camouflage to complement the girls' orange fox pelts. I fit into the only all-white wolf skin and my green cloak. I tie white pieces of cloth around my biceps like I did with the red cloth in Rizcarth. I feel warmer already. In the storage area we find plenty of dried food along with tools for farming and cooking.

Looking straight outward from our base, a thick forest with a frozen river running through it begins near the bend in the enormous canyon that makes up the grounds. In my mind's eye, the canyon is shaped like a horseshoe. I see shapes of people waving on the top wall on the left side of the canyon. I won't know if the canyon bends for sure until I check out the forest ahead of us.

To the right of us, a mountain path jets upward. It looks like there is a dense forest up on top of the mountain path as well. There is also a large hole in the ground-level of the mountain to our right, which appears to be the entrance to a cave. I call the group together.

"That woman seems to be keeping us trapped in our base. I'm not sure if the other side is dealing with the same problem, but we need to get into the arena before they do. Kam is going to make a distraction. Once the gate gets low enough to the ground, we attack the woman, then we scout."

"Who's going to attack her?" Faris asks, arms crossed.

"We all will, but I'll engage her first."

"Then what?" Sly asks.

"Sabe, Faris and Sly will check out the caves in the mountain to our right. Balk, Ranger and Kam will head out into the forest straight ahead, the one with the frozen river," I say as I point straight out of the base. "Rust, Dalk and myself will head up into the forest on top of the mountain to our right."

"What about me?" Tamra asks. I shake my head. "I'm sorry Tamra, we need you out of harm's way. You are the most important piece to our team. Without knowing exactly what is out there, I can't risk losing our only person with healing capabilities." She curls her lip and throws her hands down at her side before briskly turning and walking back into the base.

"Everyone stay downstairs with Kam. I'll be up here. Listen for the call."

The group heads down the winding staircase to the first floor. I place my hands on the gate, a knotted spiral of iron. I throw *Evergold* on my back and spit into my hands, in case I have to climb.

I slow my breathing and ready myself. "NOW!" I scream. Animals rise out of the snow and race toward the woman. Kam sends deer, tigers, longsnouts—anything he can think of takes shape and moves the way a real animal would. The first animal, a deer, hits her in the back. The gate drops a few feet, but is still too far for me to reach. As more animals approach, the woman starts to lose focus.

Clink

The gate rattles another rung down. I can hear the team screaming at her from the first floor. Another rung. After a few more animals the gate drops just below my chest. I immediately load *Evergold* and fire. My arrow hits the woman in her chest. Her hair flies back behind her face, revealing black sockets where eyes used to be. Black and green sludge leaks from her rotted mouth as she screams toward the sky. Up, up, up she turns and bounds into the air, reaching the height of one hundred men, high and far into the distant forest. Another jump. Now barely visible, we see her bound up and over the canyon wall.

Once gone, the gate completely drops. My team meets out in front of the bottom level. I urge them to move fast. "Men and women. Be careful out there. Don't do anything stupid or overly risky. Carefully watch for traps and natural hazards. Most importantly, don't engage the enemy if you see them. My guess is that they will be scouting as well, and we may run into them. Keep your distance and retreat if necessary. Be back by nightfall at the latest. Is that understood?" A collective head nod.

Rust points out stables on the other side of the base. We race to the stables and mount up. We break into our groups and head into the grounds.

After a few hundred-yard ride, Dalk, Rust and I come to a trailhead that leads up the side of the mountain. We climb the fairly straight path until we reach the area where the trail levels, a patch of frost covered dirt stretching out before the threshold of the forest. Tall trees rise out of the earth to brush the clouds. The trees creak and groan as they sway. Pine cones smother the floor near fallen branches covered in moss. The air is cold on my face, causing my nose to dry.

"Let's tie up the horses. I don't want to risk them breaking a leg in there," Rust offers.

"Agreed. Let's do it," I say.

We reach the edge of the forest and tie up the horses. Moss gets stuck under my fingernail as I climb over a log, dangling soft and wet in my hand as I enter the thicket of brown and green and a little bit of white. To my right, the grey jagged mountain thrusts its presence into the forest. To my left, daylight shines from above, exposing the nearby cliff edge. This forest is only about one hundred yards wide.

"Rust, remember that the forest is only about one hundred yards wide." No response. I turn around. "Rust?" He just looks at me. "Well say something man!" He points to his ear and holds open his palms to say "I can't hear you." It's then I notice I can't even hear myself.

I point to Rust and then my mouth as if to suggest, "You say something." Rust starts speaking and, based on the way his neck looks, even tries yelling. Dalk yells and slams his shield into a tree. Still, no sound. Matter of fact, this place is completely void of sound. No birds chirping, no boots walking. Emptiness.

I turn to them and give them a signal to follow me. Rust nods and Dalk gives me a thumbs-up. Above our heads, a creature bounds between the trees. This creature looks the same as the one from camp, except it has yellow eyes. It appears to be frightened by us.

I load my bow and head further in. The deeper we go, the darker it becomes. We get to a point where the world is so dark I can hardly see a few feet in front of me. Dalk and Rust nervously check our surroundings. I've got to show them I am not afraid. I turn and head further in. It is now pitch black, and we cannot see a thing, save a slit of light from the area we just came from.

I start to head back, but it is dark in all directions, and I do not know which way back is. A flame appears above our group. The blue creature laughs and looks at us from the heights of the pines.

"How long did it take you to figure out that sound doesn't carry in these woods?" With *Evergold* loaded, I look up at him and try to respond. Still, no sound. He laughs.

"You fool! You cannot speak to me with your voice! Only your mind." It flashes a mouth of yellow knives.

"We figured it out pretty quick."

"Not quick enough."

I pause and look at my teammates, who, apparently, have no idea what is going on. I don't know what to say and I am trying to not think strategically because the creature is reading my thoughts.

"You aren't the one I met at camp, are you?"

"Never-mind you that."

"What purpose do you serve?"

"What purpose does anyone serve? I am one of the many hands of the darkness. A poet if you will. I don't always listen to the hand that guides me. A hand that guides a hand!" It lifts its head toward the tops of the pines, letting out a rather unusual laugh.

"Be careful hunting these woods. There is plenty of game in here that will make your bellies warm. However, there may come a time where these woods are not safe—for anyone."

"When will I know?"

The creature smiles, "In due time Nirue." With that, the darkness leaves, and he is gone.

Rust and Dalk look at me curiously. The light returns to us like a blindfold lifted from the eyes. The darkness had grown insidiously to a choke, and the light returned in equal speed.

We press on. The further we go, the more this place is teeming with life. Birds, squirrels, foxes, deer—anything one could think of, save predators, and all in such a small setting, making the game easier to catch.

After an hour of traveling we reach the opposite edge of the forest on high. The sight below us is revealing. The grounds are indeed shaped like a horseshoe. As we follow the forest around the bend of the mountain, I hold up a hand to freeze my comrades. Below us, on a mirrored trail from the forest, is the enemy's base. I look at my teammates who are as surprised as we are. The enemy is hard at work, digging holes and setting up large defense walls and structures outside of their base. Before we are spotted, I duck behind a large boulder, just outside of the forest on high.

"Can you believe how small these grounds are?" Rust asks.

Dalk harrumphs. "We've only been traveling for an hour at most," I add.

"Can you guys see Atia?"

Rust peeks out and shakes his head. "They are too far to make out anyone for certain. Besides, I'm not sure I would recognize her. I only met her once I think."

I pop out and get a quick glance myself. A man in all black armor stands up in a chariot and points at the mountain toward us. As if a connected by a mental tether, their team freezes in whatever task they were doing and snap their heads toward us. We freeze. The man in all black whips the reigns and takes off toward up the mountain in his chariot. Four others hop on horses and quickly follow after him.

"Back into the forest! Follow me!" I command.

In a flash, we are long lost among the cold, dangerous forest with no sound.

CHAPTER TWENTY-SEVEN

The mountain was so high we could not breathe. So quiet we could not hear. The situation so dire, what else were we to do? Would you have starved to death?

Journal of the lost people of Jorinai, before the grounds came to be

THE FASTER WE RUN, THE more lost we become. I repeatedly stop to make sure that we aren't being followed, and that my teammates are still with me. We keep a good pace. My heart races as I run. A flood of thoughts and emotions overcome me. Doubt, fear, the need to lash out in a preemptive manner. Yes. I am losing more of my old self and becoming the new me with every passing moment.

In less than an hour we exit the forest to our trail. Panting, we pull up and catch our breath. "Anyone see if we were followed?" Rust asks with his hands on his knees. I look at Dalk. He shrugs. "I didn't see nuthin'. It's hard enough for me to run."

We laugh. "Well, I didn't see anything either, but that doesn't mean we weren't spotted. In any event, it doesn't matter if we were or weren't, just that we weren't killed or captured right out of the gates."

"Agreed" said Rust. "Did you notice all of the deer in the forest?"

"I did."

"What the spit was that blue thing?" Asks Dalk. I shake my head and gaze back into the forest.

"Not sure. Just know that it possesses magic and that it speaks to us telepathically."   "Tele-patha-kallay?"

"Through thoughts. He connects his mind to yours and speaks to you without moving his lips." I gesture my pointer finger from my head to his head.

"Oh. Okay." Something about that creature has Dalk on edge. I don't blame him.

"Well?" Dalk gestures.

"Well what?" I ask, not meaning to come off as defensive, but coming off as defensive.

"Aren't you going to tell us what it said?"

"In a minute. C'mon, let's get back to camp, the other team could be pursuing us." With that, we grab our horses and head down the mountain.

The sun is high in the sky behind a net of shapeless clouds in the distance. It's past noon but not quite sunset eve. The wind is cool as a breeze enters the hood of my green cloak. It dries the sweat covering my body from the run.

When we get back to camp, I ride up in angst because only Faris' group is back. I'm not surprised because we made such good time but still, the fact that Kam's group is not back is cause for worry. Without his spells we wouldn't match-up to their warlocks, and we are already at a disadvantage. Sly sits in a corner sharpening his blades, while Faris pops out of her seat to undoubtedly say something wise.

"You boys have a good time out in the woods? Find yourself a nice place to nap?"

"You know, Faris, if you wanted to nap with Nirue, all you have to do is ask him," Rust jests.

"Shove it, scramp," she says through a tomato colored face. "What did y'all find?"

"Good game and soil. Dangerous place, but quick route to the enemy base."

At that moment, I notice a group of crows perched on a nearby tree, peppering the orange, white and brown setting. Sly looks up long enough to notice the crows, before disappearing into a back room.

"Okay. Well, let's just avoid the forest until we absolutely need it, and set up traps should the enemy try and sneak attack. Sound good?"

We nod, collectively trying to hide our embarrassment that we had been thinking on something with such intensity that had a very easy solution.

"What did you find, Faris?"

She looks back at Sly who is gone, and then back at me. "It's a cave. But it's . . . different."

"How?"

"It's basically a maze. Most of it reflects, kind of like a mirror, but not exactly. It's just confusing. And we heard something howling deep within, so we left pretty early before we got lost."

I scratch my chin. "Any idea where it leads?"

She shakes her head. "No. But Sly thinks it leads to their base."

"A passage through the mountain? That would have to be even faster than the forest on high, don't you think?"

"What makes you say that?"

"Well, presumably, the grounds are shaped like a horseshoe, with one base at either point, and a mountain in the space between the two points. If you go straight and follow the river, that is the long way around, right? I guess we won't know for sure until Kam's group gets back. But, we do know for a fact that the trail over the mountain is a shortcut. So, maybe the mountain maze is a direct route, if we can figure out a way through."

Everyone shrugs in agreement. My excitement picks up, but I keep it under wraps, and say more pointedly, "We gotta map out that maze. Figure out where it leads and how. If we can get our hands on their flag, we may save a lot of time traveling through there. Let's make that an advantage to us."

"What if it's just a trap? What if there is nothing there?"

"Then we find a way to use that to our advantage too. I've got an idea."

I jump on my horse and head to the farm to the left of our base. It's only a two minute ride. I hop off and start looking around. I pick up rocks and toss them aside because they aren't good enough. It doesn't take long for someone to pipe up. "What's the deal boss?"

"You said the cave was a maze, right? Mirror like? I ran over some type of white flaky rock when I left this area, and it left a white mark on my horses hoof, see?" I say holding up its back leg. "We can use these to mark the walls so we never get lost."

Faris smiles. "Nice thinking." She and everyone else dig through the snow looking for the white rock. Luckily the snow has melted just enough in this area for us to find them. We each gather a couple handfuls and head back to base. As we ride up, Kam's group appears on the horizon. They are moving fast. As they get closer, they start pointing to the base. They better slow down or they will crash into us.

"Get into the base," screams Kam.

"What the heaven is going on?"

"It's bad, Nirue."

CHAPTER TWENTY-EIGHT

*We still aren't sure what happened to the people
of Jorinai. We know they had to survive in these
mountains through a harsh winter. The strangest
part is, their journals are mostly intact, including
their plans of survival and establishment. Yet here
is their camp, instructions followed to the last task,
and not a singular trace of one person.*

*Anthropologist and explorer, Shyll Baringer, two days
into excavating the Jorinai base camp*

"WHAT'S GOT YOU ALL WORKED up?"

"Get in the ever-loving base!" Balk wastes no time tying up his horse
and heading indoors. Neither does Kam. We follow suit and head to the
second story of the building. Sabe starts a fire. Something is strange about
their eyes. Ranger, Kam and Balk won't look at anyone.

"Don't go in that forest," Balk says with anxiety in his eyes.

Ranger and Kam look down and warm their hands by the fire. The sun
is going down out on the white horizon, the forest a glimmering orange
kindling.

I sit in silence waiting for someone to elaborate. Nothing.

"Speak, man!"

"It was really bad. It was . . ."

"Will someone use their words please?"

"I'll tell him," Balk finally says while standing up. He goes over to a wall near the mouth of the base. "It's my shirt, Nirue."

"Whaat?" I asked mouth open, crow's feet showing outside my eyes. Balk has his back to us. "It . . . ripped." He lifts up the back of his shirt to expose his butt cheeks. I see a grin sneak on his face. Kam and Sabe pinch their eyes trying to hold back laughter. Everyone else lets out a collective sigh of relief.

"You morons had me worried!" Faris says, storming out of the room. I can't help but laugh. A good hearty laugh that I haven't had in quite some time. "Nice one gents. You had me going too."

The three perpetrators are in tears. Balk, a rolling ball of hysteria, knocks over a shield decoration that was leaned against the wall.

"You should have seen your face! That was classic bahahahah," Kam says while wiping his eyes.

The mood lightens as food and drinks are served. We exchange stories as the sun goes down. I surreptitiously put a stop on a third round of drinks because I don't want to be a party killer, but I also don't want things to get out of hand. We enjoy each other's company and play cards that Tamra had found until everyone makes their way to bed.

*   *   *

The sun peers over the mountains of the chilly canyon. Wind rips through the valley, stirring up snow and fallen leaves. Of course, I am up much earlier than everyone else. I sleep less easy because of the burden I carry. The forest in the foreground is predominantly orange and white, with a frozen blue river serpenting its way far beyond the capability of my eyes. The wind is cold on my body. It feels as though I have been here before, and I don't know why. Just one day of exploration gave me the comfort of familiarity from an unknown origin. Soon, I smell food being cooked downstairs. Better head down and see what's going on.

The ground level is cozy. The furnace and fire pits keep it nice and warm, and the furniture is plenty comfortable. I enjoy the feeling of peace in the mornings. No more assassins, no more crazy jungle men, no more Timbly, for now. I see Faris cooking a pan of eggs.

My stomach grumbles and I offer her a smile before heading to the entrance. She smiles back and holds my gaze for a noticeable moment. Her brown hair cascades over her bony shoulders and collarbone, perfectly framing her large eyes and small, curved nose. She is in an oversized sleeping shirt that sags enough to reveal the true features of her upper body. Her legs are long and athletic. Her skin tanned like rawhide. She drops her gaze, and continues cooking. I hope my face didn't give away what I was thinking there.

I head back upstairs to the edge of our base. As I look into the canyon my mind races to memories long forgotten. I miss my family. I miss wrestling my little brothers and showing them how to catch bugs. I miss being a normal person where I don't have to worry about the lives of nine other people.

Do I really know what I'm doing? I've never been in a war, nor even played capture the flag. I've gotta figure out how to win. No. I'm going to figure out how to win.

"Still thinking about Balk's ripped shirt?" Faris asks while handing me a plate of eggs with toast. She has a seat next to me. We both dangle our legs off the edge. I look at her sideways.

"No. My family actually." She adjusts herself, obviously embarrassed that I did not flirt back.

"So what's the plan for today?"

"More scouting. I want to map out that cave and set up some traps on the known entry points to our base. We should also harvest." She nods her head while she chews, focusing on a point off in the distance. "You know, I'm not sure how we got here, but this whole thing is driving me nuts."

"What do you mean?" She puts her fork down on her plate, grasping for words that are just out of her reach. "I just think this whole thing is stupid. What kind of sick people put humans in a game of life or death, to no real end? I mean, what's the point of this?"

"I don't know, Faris. But I do know I will kill the people that are behind this, even if we all come out unscathed."

She gives me the same look she did while she was cooking. "You know, you don't have to act so tough all the time. I know you have a sweet side. A side of you that can be gentle. A woman doesn't always need a rough and tough front to get to her heart. I've seen the way you look at me, Nirue, it's okay." She places her hand on top of mine then intertwines our fingers. My heart skips and my eyes become watery. I feel something for her, but deep down I know I shouldn't get into this.

I know that I probably feel this way because I am a sucker for a beautiful face. I feel like it would be nice to have someone to keep me warm at night, especially someone as beautiful as Faris. But am I betraying something. Is it myself? Is it my team? I don't know, and in an instant, I pull my arm away, get up and move toward the staircase. "Time to scout," I say while heading down. I don't turn to see her reaction.

I get on a horse and ride to the orange forest with the frozen river. The river seems especially illuminate. I know I have another hour before everyone else wakes up and I want some time to myself. I ride hard. The sun is still coming up and the light is somewhat blinding. I pull a mask out.

I found it last night, patched into my cloak. I can pull it across my face and latch it either side of my cloak to cover my nose and my mouth. It helps against the cold. My horse is strong and fast. I can tell it enjoys the exercise. I need a name for this horse. I think I will call it Storm.

Before I know it, I reach the edge of the forest. I slow Storm to a trot while I breach the tree line. Parcels of sunlight dance between cool frost-tipped branches of dark trees. Sometimes, quiet can bring me peace. I tie Storm to a nearby tree and head to a dew covered log to sit down. For a moment, I close my eyes and take deep slow breaths, letting go of everything. The forest smells of pine and birch, grass, and cool, clean air.

It feels good to be alone. Even when I was in Dakota I used to venture off and find my alone time. It's my catharsis.

As I breathe deeply, I try to let go of my emotions. I let go of the anxiety of leading a group in a game of life and death. I let go of the feelings I have for Faris. I let go of the guilt I feel for falling for her so fast. I let go of missing my family and feel inspired to move on—to move forward with this endeavor.

A noise breaks my meditation. I hear a woman singing in the distance. It doesn't sound like it is coming from either camp, or anywhere in the canyon. It sounds like it is coming from outside of it. Her voice is soft and soothing. She sings single progressions of notes slowly, trance-like. I look to the tops of the canyon and see the shapes I had seen the other day from our base.

At the top of the canyon are three tall, anemic women with ragged clothes, much like the woman holding the gate up. It's hard to see them, as they are at least a hundred feet above me, even at the lowest dip in the canyon wall. But, even from here, I can tell they wear clothes that are much too meager for this cold. Their bodies are odd shades of pink and they wear bandanas over their eyes. Black circles from leaking ooze stain their bandanas. Trails of green slime trace their bodies. They wave their hands in un-rhythmic circles as if they are casting a spell over the grounds.

They must be magically telecasting the games to the crowds. Otherwise, how would the crowds stay updated? How would anyone know what is going on here for that matter? Nonetheless, that's not where the sound is coming from.

I gaze along the top of the rest of the canyon wall for the source of the sound. The beautiful, soft whispering in my ears. Storm noticeably relaxes. His beautiful stained-oak colored body shakes to rid fallen snow from his body. I smile. I go back to my log and close my eyes again. The voice enters my ears and my soul. I continue meditating, until a twig snaps and stirs me awake.

I jump and load *Evergold* in an instant. The girl's voice is slowly drowned out by thunderclouds approaching from the North. I get an idea. I jump on Storm and race back to camp before I forget or lose momentum.

When I get back everyone is up and about and ready to start the day. How long had I been gone for? I race into the building to find the big twins chowing on a leg of some kind of meat. It looks to be a large bird leg.

"Quickly, everyone grab their things and follow me." In a few minutes, we are riding headlong into the storm.

After a few minutes ride outside the castle I abruptly stop. The thunderclouds loom ominously in the distance, roaring warnings of what's to come. "This is the perfect time for a group espionage venture," I explain.

"With the looming storm and it being very early in the game, we need to spy on them and look for areas to set up traps. I don't want anyone in the cave in case it floods. Tamra, you stay behind with one of the twins, just in case they decide to try and raid us. Actually, I prefer if Balk stays behind since Dalk knows the forest up top. Since there isn't anything to hide behind once outside the bottom level forest, I don't want anyone leaving its cover. Ranger—you take Sabe and look for places to lay traps on the ground level forest."

"The one with the frozen river you mean?"

I nod. "The rest of you, come with me."

Everyone seems content with the plan, save the big twin. I don't care. We need his strength to protect Tamra should anything unexpected happen. On the ride up I explain the difficulty in communicating in a place where sound does not carry. We decide on a few hand signals and general strategy. The storm is now fully overhead. Dark clouds blot out the sun making the forest dark, damp and cold. I look up to the sky while tying up my horse. It's going to dump on us any minute now.

I look around and everyone appears ready. We head into the forest, which feels more like an arena than anything.

The quietness is maddening. I never realized how much comfort I gain from noise. The crunching of feet, the banter between my teammates, the sound an arrow makes when being pulled from its quiver all of those things act as a distraction. Now, all we have is our thoughts.

The fast moving clouds cause beams of light to appear intermittently, casting shadows among the trees, creating a feeling that at any minute, something is going to ambush us. After a few minutes it starts to rain *and* snow. We are getting soaked, but it is worth it. We need to gain intelligence on our foes, so, we press on. A buck and two does scamper away when they see us. After an hour or so of traveling, we reach the edge. I smile, so sure of myself and my plan. I move behind the big rock just outside of the forest and wait for everyone to get within a whisper-shot.

We gather around and I take a head count of my team. Faris, Dalk, Kam, Rust and myself. Something's wrong, we are missing someone. "Where's Sly?" Everyone looks around, but no one answers. "WHERE IS SLY?"

Faris says, "I . . .I don't know. He was right behind me most of the way, bringing up the rear. I stopped checking on him about half way through."

"You guys, this isn't good. Where could he have gone?" My mind races in a million different directions. Was it the blue creature? Did he get lost? Could he have gotten injured, and we just couldn't hear his cries for help?

"Hey, boss." Kam says on top of the rock, looking down at the enemy base. "You're going to want to see this." I hop on the rock and look down at their base. There's nothing there. No people running around, no fires burning in their castle—nothing.

CHAPTER TWENTY-NINE

When we found the second camp, we knew something was amiss. Why would anyone abandon their camp to go somewhere colder, less hospitable with less supplies in close proximity? What are they looking for?

Shyll Baringer

WITHOUT SAYING ANYTHING, I SPRINT back into the forest. The only people at our base are Balk and Tamra. We have to get back before they kill them and take our flag. We can't take theirs, for then we would have to fight them two men down with a special released in the arena. We *have* to get back.

I turn and motion for everyone to keep their eyes on each other, and to look for Sly. We spread ourselves out in a straight line and keep as fast of a pace as we can. No sign of Sly and no sign of the blue creature. The wind is cold, and all that was rain is now snow. It comes down more aggressively the longer we travel.

We push through the forest quickly and reach the end in record time. A loud, very low sounding horn booms through the arena, followed by a flash of white light. Sabe readies her weapon, Faris grabs the back of my shirt. The sound is deafening, and it's getting louder. Faris releases my shirt, collapsing to her knees while grabbing her ears. Rust closes his eyes shut as if that might help the pain in his ears. As soon as it comes, it leaves.

As everyone gathers themselves, a blood curdling scream emanates from below. The fact that I can still hear it sends chills down my spine. It's Tamra.

Another scream.

I hop on storm and head down the hill as fast as I can. The horse wants to slow down because of the slick conditions, but I ride him hard. I am the first off the trail, heart kicking at my chest the way I kicked at Storm. Red. Red everywhere.

Below me is the dead body of Balk. His body and shield are covered in arrows. His skin is burned, and a note is nailed into his chest. Blood from his massive body leaks down into the cave. Sweat trickles down my face as I read the note, despite the coldness of my surroundings. It says:

Nirue,

We have championed your champion. We could have stolen your relic and ended these games on the second day. But, what fun would that be?

I will slowly kill off every member of your team so that you know how miserably you failed. I will destroy all of your hope in every fiber of your being, before disgracing your very existence for the world to see. You are not worthy of the dirt you stand on while you read this. Do not ever think you can beat us, because you can't. Make your life easy, and kill yourselves.

The note slides out of my hand and falls into a pool of blood. My world begins to spin and my senses become dulled. I can barely see or hear. My vision is grey and blurry and my stomach is in my throat. Something stirs in the background—it must be Dalk. I need to get a hold of this situation before it takes control of me. They have gained a huge advantage over us morally and strategically. They're right, we have lost our champion. They came to our house and kicked us in the teeth. Maybe this was a doomed mission from the start.

Just like that, the world turned upside down. We probably just lost our best fighter and our second best fighter just lost his twin brother. Will my team quit? How can we overcome this? I suddenly feel the need to sit down.

"Do something!" Faris screams at Tamra. "Heal him! Don't just *stand* there!" Tamra starts to cry.

"There's nothing I can do! I—I . . ."

"You WHAT?" Dalk Bellows.

"Please don't be angry. He asked me to go get him some food and the next thing I know I come out here and he is like this. I tried everything I could but he was already gone. Kam, can one of your spells do something?"

He shakes his head somberly at Dalk, as if to say sorry. Dalk holds the bottom of his brother's head in his hands. Tears stream down his face. He breaks down into a sob for minutes, and then abruptly goes silent. After a few moments he grabs his shield and sword, and runs into the cave.

CHAPTER THIRTY

The unmarked graves should have been the first clue.
The rough, unperfected white orbs the second. But excusing
those signs, the note should have been it. Why didn't I push
Shyll harder? I will never forgive myself.

Bonda, assistant to Shyll Baringer

"CRAP," RUST SAYS, LOOKING AT the cave then me. I turn to Rust.

"We need to go after him. Rust, you and Ranger take over here. Kam, come with me." Kam grabs his staff and chases after him. I shoot Faris a quick look goodbye. Her eyes tell me to be safe. I can feel it.

In under a minute we are in the cave. No, more like a maze of mirrors. Though, they aren't quite mirrors, more like reflective rock. The tunnel leads straight for a few minutes before breaking into three paths. "Dalk?" Kam yells. "Dalk, where are you?" He looks at me with worried eyes, and asks, "What do we do?"

"Give me a second." I try to picture which way Dalk would choose. The more I think on it, the more I think he didn't think, and just ran.

"I don't know. Got any ideas?" Kam thinks for a moment. "Maybe. I think it's best we don't split up. Let's try the far left and see where it leads first."

"Okay. Go ahead, I'll lead up the rear." He nods and heads in. We travel for about ten minutes to a dead end. Etched in the stone wall of our dead end is the word "*Tomorrow*." Kam leans back, as if a further view would help him understand. We shrug and turn back to the tri-fork. We try the middle vein next. Large and distorted images of myself and Kam move all around us. In front, to the right, to the left, below and above, our bodies move in and out of existence among the tunnel. Even when we stop, our bodies continue to move along the walls, as if they have a life of their own. Kam clears his throat, breath becoming more rapid. I nod to him and we move forward. We hear a rumble in the darkness ahead, but press on—neither one daring to yell Dalk's name.

After running another ten minutes we find ourselves in a spherical room. "Little light Kam?" I whisper. He opens his palm to reveal a red flame. The tunnel leads us to an open area with sixteen different paths. Water drips from the ceiling into what appears to be a large stone birdbath. Stretching above three of the tunnel mouths is "*Kill Yourselves*" in blood.

"What now?" Kam asks. "Look at all these different passages? How did they know where to go?"

"Because they knew before they got here. They must have been tipped off by their Doctore."

"Did *we* get any tips?"

"Yeah."

"Well? Mind sharing?"

A low horn blows in the distance and a flash of light fills the tunnel, blowing our hair and cloaks backward as we shield our faces. The sound nearly bursts my ear drums. Oh no. Not this. Not already.

"Let's get out of here . . . quickly," I say.

"Aren't you going to tell me first?"

"You're about to find out," I tell him. He looks at me blankly. I take off down the tunnel toward our base. Kam chases after me, posing questions as we run. I don't have time to answer and just ignore him. My side is just beginning to ache when we reach the end of the tunnel.

When we get to the tri-fork, something is different. Instead of a grey tint to the walls, it is more coppery. We hustle toward the edge of the cave before Kam abruptly stops, causing me to crash into him. He holds a finger up to his mouth and frantically motions for me to move backward.

"Which way did we take?"

"The same way we took to get here, why?"

"We're at *their* base somehow."

"Wait, what?"

"Take a look," he points toward the mouth of the cave. I tip-toe so as to not make any noise, hugging the wall and easing my head around the corner to peer down the tunnel. I see their group somewhat in chaos. There are arms flailing and fingers pointing. The yelling and commotion seem to stem around something on the ground. I can't make out what it is, until their largest warrior bends over and picks it up. It looks like a dead body. It is a dead body. Whose? One of them is crying. It looks like a younger boy with short blonde hair. A man in all black smacks the dead boy across the face and takes a knee to talk to him. They have people that young on their team? An arm pulls me back into the darkness.

"See what I mean?"

"What, the dead body?"

"What? No. I mean, that's not our base."

"Oh. Right. Yeah that is definitely their base. How did we get here? Who was that dead person?"

"I didn't see it," Kam says. "Think Dalk got 'em after all?"

I shake my head. "I don't know. Let's just get out of here before we are made." Kam agrees, following me back to the center room.

As we run a flood of questions fill my mind. Who are these people? Does their team mimic ours? How did one of them die? How did we end up at their base?

I know the answer to exactly none of those questions. I stay close on Kam's heels until we reach the room with the oversized birdbath. A gryphon could bathe in this thing.

"Okay. So lemme get this straight. We went back the way we came, and ended up at their base?" He asks.

I shrug. "I mean, I think so? Is there a chance we could have taken the wrong path?" He shakes his head and wipes his brow in frustration. "No. I'm positive we went in the exact tunnel we came in earlier."

"Crap, man!" He thinks for a while. Once again, *"Kill Yourselves"* borders the top of the three tunnels straight ahead of us.

"This makes no sense."

"Agreed."

Neither of us say anything for a few minutes. "Look, it only takes us a few minutes to go through some of these. Let's just explore these two to the right and meet back in say, ten minutes?" Kam shakes his hands out and jumps up and down, as if to get the blood going.

He looks as though he is about to agree, then says, "I don't think splitting up is wise. Especially with their team lurking around. Let's just spend the extra time and go together."

"Done. Follow me."

I take off into the tunnel under *"Yourselves."* What we find at the end is startling. It's as if we are on another planet, or somewhere else on this one. A huge and desolate landscape lay before us. No snow. No sand. No bases and no mountains. Just flat, cracked dirt as far as the eye can see. Kam tries to say something but no words come out. We head back and into another one. This tunnel ends in a similar fashion, revealing a flat ice wasteland. Nothing but cold, hard, blue ice wind quickly picking up snowflakes and displacing them. We head back to the center.

"What gives man?" Kam throws his arms in the air. "How the heck are we going to get out of this room?"

"Relax, man. We've got to be missing *something* right? I mean the other team made it to our base, and back to theirs, right?"

This calms Kam down a bit. "True, true. Well what are we missing then?"

"Keep looking."

We search high and low for a clue—anything; something that will tell us the way home, or the order of paths. After fifteen minutes of turning over very small rocks, we finally sit down. "I give up man. I don't know what else to do." Kam suggests. At the same time Kam begins to quit, I realize how thirsty I am.

"I could use a drink." I go to get a drink from the fountain. However, I have to stand on the tip of my toes to reach it. When I look down, I yell for Kam to come over. Being about my height, Kam has to stretch to see as well. There, in the fountain as clear as day is a question in the water:

"When will you cease control?"

Befuddled, Kam and I stop straining to look and back away. He looks at me, and I back at him. "When will we cease to control?"

"Hopefully never? I don't know."

I got it. "I got it, Kam." Before he could ask any questions, I get up and look into the pool. "Tomorrow," I say to the water. The pool begins to ripple and drain. All of a sudden, a flash of wind and light race through a tunnel on the other side of the room. It's gone in an instant.

"C'mon, we need to get back to our team." Kam nods and takes off.

In a matter of minutes the all familiar grey reflective tunnel is behind us, as we exit the cave entrance. The blood covered snow looks like an oversized bullseye. The body is gone. Snow disrupts my vision as I look out into the canyon, searching for a sign of anything. The absence of my team from sight gives me anxiety. It creeps up on me and I obsess on my worries. I can't seem to chain together two positive thoughts and feel as though I am losing control. Kam feels my energy and his mood becomes dark as well. It's almost like we are trying to match the skies.

Everything is falling apart.

I've lost Balk, I'm losing Dalk and I don't know where Sly is. It's all my fault, too. I shouldn't have left my team so vulnerable. I shouldn't have—

Just before I could box myself up too bad, thunder booms directly overhead—loud enough to startle both Kam and I out of our own heads. "C'mon, let's find everyone." I grab Storm and head toward the base.

The snow is coming down hard, blurring images and soaking my clothes. I ride toward the base as fast as I can. It's getting dark fast. I pull up, not bothering to tie up Storm and head in. I see a small fire that's been reduced to coals and embers, staying alive with the ever present wind.

Kam comes down from upstairs and says, "No sign of anyone." Great. It's getting dark and no one from my team is around.

Then it happens again. A deafening horn blows and a light flashes across the canyon. We hold our forearms above our eyes while we look. In the distance a fire blazes near the frozen river. Echoes of cracking trees swirl through the canyon.

Curses.

"Should we go over there?" Kam asks.

"Do we have any other choice?" He turns his gaze from me to the canyon, then steps out of the base and into the storm. We ride out into the canyon at dusk, soaking wet with everything at stake.

CHAPTER THIRTY-ONE

*Your time is near. I sense the ripples across the
great pond—MY great pond. The same way a wave is
something the entire ocean is doing, I feel every one of your
movements. Your time is near.*

*Whispers heard at base camp during the second
search for the people of Jorinai*

THE WHITE SUN DIPPING BEHIND the white-walled canyon creates a hue of colors: Purple, orange, pink and blue all shine like welcome beacons for Kam and I to ride toward—a false comfort for what's to come. I can't help but notice the beautiful scene before me, despite the condition I am in. Internally, I worry because our base is left completely exposed, and the other team knows how to navigate the tunnels. But what is one person going to do against a bunch of them? Leaving Kam behind would be a death order with me as ultimate commander. I can't have any more blood on my hands.

Before we reach our destination, the forest of orange foliage detonates into complete chaos. What seems like a million crows fly into the air and break into arrow shaped formations. The fire we saw from a distance is gaining momentum, sending squirrels and deer running. Loud howls break out into the night. I notice a giant gate at the apex of the curve in the canyon to the left is open.

"What is going on, Nirue?" Kam is either out of breath or extremely nervous; or both. A loud scream pierces the night air. Faris. I jump off Storm and race in, not looking to see if Kam is following.

It's hard to breathe through the smoke and flames, so I follow the screams. Lost in a haze of black and grey smoke, I squint so that I don't lose the little visibility I have. I use the mask in my cloak as a filter over my mouth. Shouts from men and women drown out the loud pop and crackle of the burning, frozen wood. I continue following the screams, which are just on the other side of a twenty foot wall of flame.

I have to help. I back up, take a deep breath and sprint toward the fire. The wall of flame is unbearably hot as I approach. In the back of my mind, I want to stop. My mind screams at me to quit. That thought passes as quickly as it came. Had it been any longer, I may have succumbed to it.

The other side of flame presents immediate danger. My team is in a circle, backing up toward the wall of flame, weapons up. All of them except Sabe, who has been nailed to a tree. Four wolves the size of elk approach my team, black eyes and black teeth bearing wild. The flames behind us dance in their cold and lifeless eyes. Faris has fallen down and seems to be having a hard time getting up. Same with Dalk. They back away, not in a formal fighting position, but in pure fear, as if all they can do is deflect. Ranger and Rust stand defiant, ready to fight.

Two dead. These must be the specials.

We are in a circle of fire that is growing ever bigger. It seems that it had originated right where we are standing. Its continuous growth gives us room to back away from the wolves. There is no escaping this. I grab *Evergold* and let out a howl. Ranger and Rust look back at me. The wolves snap in my direction, drooling for my flesh. I slam an arrow into the trunk of a tree and collect sap. I put the sap end into the flames and load the arrow. A wolf charges Dalk and jumps in the air to attack him. Dalk lifts his shield and deflects the massive creature, which slips on the ground, eyes never leaving its prize.

Before it jumps back on Dalk I loose a fire arrow into its head. The creature howls and turns back toward me. Its white and grey fur catches on fire. Dalk grabs onto its tail to stop its progress. The creature digs in and pulls the now sitting Dalk toward me. I can't shoot arrows fast enough: One in the right chest area, one in its back leg. I shoot two at a time—one goes high and right. The wall of flame burns at my back. It's so hot my elbow sticks to my cloak as I shoot. Out of the corner of my eye I notice Faris helping Rust and Ranger by shooting arrows into a wolf they have funneled into a narrow passage of trees.

The creature is just feet from me now. I loose another arrow from point blank and miss. My heart is pounding out of my chest. I can no longer feel the wall of flame at my back. I forget where I am. All I hear and see is the ferocity of the beast before me. Dalk stands up and rips at the creature's tail, removing a large portion of fur from it. The creature doesn't even notice.

I shoot an arrow in the center of its chest. The beast, now free from Dalk's grip, lunges, snaps and snarls at me. I scream and raise my fists at it. As the creature is in midair, I swing my arm upward, connecting with its jaw. The head of the beast falls at my feet. Mouth open, I look to my left to see Ranger with a two-handed grip on *Darkwater*, just finished with his downswing.

Behind him, a wolf forgets about Rust and races toward Ranger. It races at him like it knew that Ranger had just killed his brother. I scream, "DUCK!" and grab *Evergold* just in time to get a double shot off. They both find their mark and the wolf yelps, snapping at the arrows lodged in its midsection. Before it can recover, Rust hops on its back and plunges two swords into its spine. The first one didn't kill it, but the second did.

Two left.

The third howls and sprints after Faris. She shoots an arrow but is way off. Kam screams, "MOVE!" and narrows his eyes. His eyes go white and he spins in an arc—the same motion he would do to hit a pinecone on the ground with a stick. His hands are together while he does it. From his hands comes an ice-lance, traveling at the speed of a bullet that tears through the wolf with ease. Kam buckles over.

One left.

The wolf that had been funneled into a narrow passage of trees is stuck. The fire is still hot, but now burns far enough away that we don't have to worry about it. We walk over to the trapped wolf. It snaps and shakes at the trees, trying to break free with every fiber of its being. It looks like it may break free, so I ask Kam to help us out. He walks over, then puts a hand on his knees to rest a moment. He touches the tree and whispers something to it. Branches begin to thicken and vines crawl around the wolf. Vines, that aren't a part of this type of tree, close tightly around the wolf's neck. It snaps and fights until it loses too much oxygen.

I look at Ranger with intent. He nods, and heads over to the trapped creature. With a single swing, the wolf loses its head.

I look around and take in what had just happened.

Blood everywhere. It's snowing. The forest around us is charred and black with soot. I calm my breathing down. A woman is whimpering behind us. It's Faris, and she looks like she is hurt—bad. Tamra pulls out a concoction of potions and bandages for the scratches and burns on her body. She begins to whisper things above Faris, and yellow light emanates from her body and pours into Faris, much like the light from the physikers realm.

For a couple of minutes, nobody says a word. Everyone else is accounted for, except for Sly and Sabe.

"Is Sly alive?" Dalk asks.

"Who knows," Kam says with disgust.

"I don't think so." Rust says while looking at the ground. He looks up, "I heard three horns today."

"True," Ranger says. "And that flashing light."

Kam shakes his head. "One of them died too."

"How?" Ranger asks.

"We don't know," says Kam.

Everyone goes quiet. I don't talk to anyone and walk over to Sabe. The sight of her makes my stomach bile rise into my throat. Holding my breath and looking away, I start taking her down, one nail at a time.

"What happened while Kam and I were looking for Dalk?" I ask to distract myself.

Nobody responds. Kam looks like he has aged twenty years.

"It was for the burial," Dalk says. We came out here to bury my brother."

"But how did you get out so quickly? We went chasing after you and got lost for hours."

Tears fill his eyes. "I just ran into a random tunnel which lead me back to my brother's body. I didn't know what to do. Sabe said she knew a good spot and that we should pay his body the respect it deserves. Said we could get there and bury him before sundown. When we got here, a few of their guys were hunting. Sabe stepped in a trap and the next thing we knew, a fire was all around us. They must have done that while we were figuring out what was going on."

No one makes eye contact with me. No one.

"Whose body is that?" Kam points at girl with an arrow through her chest.

Faris, lying down by Tamra, speaks with her eyes closed. "Shot her when the flames went up, right as they captured Sabe. Couldn't tell if it hit her or not." She coughs and Tamra urges her to lie back down.

"Then what about *our* special?" I ask. Blank faces.

I shake my head in frustration. "That's TWO dead enemies. Kam and I saw the other when we accidently stumbled on their base looking for Dalk."

I suddenly become ever cognizant of the wind, and how bone chillingly cold it is.

That, coupled with the mood itself could kill us on the spot. We bury Sabe without talking. We mark her grave and ride back to camp through the starry night. The wind freezes my tears while I ride. We come home to thousands of crows covering our base and the surrounding landscape like a shadow, reminding us of the darkness that has fallen over our camp already.

CHAPTER THIRTY-TWO

Have you ever considered changing careers? It may be
that you'll be happier with something more monotonous.

Kam's mother before he was chosen for the games

THE NEXT WEEK AND A half is quiet and laborious, time spent mostly hunting and harvesting for food. The enemy keeps to themselves for the most part. We have twice spotted them exploring the forest on high, and the few cautious scouting expeditions we have had were uneventful. They seem to be fortifying their base, expecting an assault from our end.

Most people are cordial, but everyone's spirits have been down since the day we lost Sabe and Balk. Oftentimes people go to bed without saying goodnight or even finishing food. This time has been especially hard on Dalk. The first time he tried to say something meaningful at dinner—a story about his brother, he became so overwhelmed that no audible words were produced.

A system is established. We only travel in groups of four, one group always staying at the base. We avoid what has been deemed the "upstairs forest" or the "forest on high" as I call it, because of the blue creature. The last thing we need is for someone else to die.

Sly finally came back, although, without explaining where he went or why. He looked famished and ate way more food than his slender body looked capable of handling. After sleeping for an entire day, he told us he had been doing his own scouting and knows the caves and upstairs forest like the back of his hand. He wouldn't say if he was responsible for killing the other team's fallen soldier, but it was implicit through his body language.

After being here two and a half weeks, people begin to recognize their role. The weather is getting better. It seems that spring has come early for us. The snow has melted. The trees, even some of the burnt ones, are giving back their leaves. Nobody is sure how this happened since it was autumn when we got here. We haven't completely left winter, but we are close.

The labor brings us together. I am struggling between pushing my team too hard and not giving them enough work. If I ask too much of them, they will come to resent me. If I ask too little, they won't respect me. So, I lead by example. Every single day, I am the first to rise and the last to sleep.

I am not used to manual labor like this. Plowing fields and hunting deer and picking vegetables and setting traps—these are all things that make my body strong. They respect me for being the hardest worker.

I make it a nightly ritual to gather for dinner and talk strategy. As I said in my speech before the games started, I am open to everyone's suggestions. This is fruitless initially. After another week of hunting, gardening, trapping, scouting and light-sleeping due to the ever-present fear of being attacked, the group participates.

"I thought these games lasted like a week?" Kam says before taking a gulp of wine. A cool semi-spring breeze blows through the base, flickering the fires and casting shadows across the walls surrounding us. The moon is high in the sky like a proud captain at the bow of his ship. We sit at the dinner table, which has now been moved upstairs for a better vantage while we eat.

"That's what Doctore told me," I reply, mouth half-open, exposing my dinner. I finish my food before saying, "How long have we been here exactly?"

"Roughly three weeks today," Faris says. She catches my eye and quickly looks back down, as if she is embarrassed of doing so.

"Too damn long," grunts Ranger, who stares absentmindedly out the front of our base.

"You kner—" Sly chokes on some peppered meat. He pounds on his chest ten times before he can talk again. "You know what?"

Everyone looks around waiting for a response, and none come. He smirks and begins to motion his knife and fork in circles to suggest someone should ask him the all-encompassing and necessary question.

"What?" Faris finally asks.

"Thank you, Faris. What I was going to say is that I'm actually starting to like it here. At first, I hated you guys. Na. I wouldn't say hate. But I didn't want to be a 'team' with the likes of you. I usually don't do the team thing. I do hate that you call me Sly, though."

"Better than losing your twin brother," Dalk says, eyes on his plate.

"Or having the girl you love held captive by ruthless killers," Ranger adds. The wind and clinking of silverware against plates dominate dinner conversation.

After a few minutes, Sly speaks up again. "You aren't the only ones with problems. Ever hear the story of Old Red?"

Glances are exchanged, but nobody speaks, again. Sly clears his throat.

"It goes a little something like this. A man rode into town one day and sat at the local tavern I bartended at. Now, this is a small town mind you. Your furthest neighbor is your most distant cousin's drinkin' buddy, okay? Now, Old Red really wasn't that old. But he wore all black save for a red scarf he kept wrapped around his neck and tucked into his tunic."

He clears his throat again. "Red had an all black outfit save for the scarf, which is why I called him Old Red. Seems stupid and in truth, it was. Anyway, he would come into my tavern *every* night at the same hour on the dot. Just before the sun went down, you could find Old Red sitting at the only bar in town, which, did I mention, happens to be the place where I serve? Anyway, he would come in and sit down and order the same drink. Ale—no sugar."

"Do people *normally* have sugar in their ale?" Dalk says with furrowed eyebrows.

"How am I supposed to know?"

"I don't know, because you're a *bartender* perhaps?" He rolls his fingers outward to express the drama in his point.

Sly shakes his head and continues his story. "So, six days straight, the same thing. Guy comes in, red scarf, ale no sugar, and you can hardly make out his face, did I mention that? Yeah, sorry, he's got this cloak thingy—kinda like Nirue's, yeah—just like Nirue's, actually. So this guy doesn't speak a single word to anyone for six days. Then he came in on the seventh day. Was it the seventh?" He scratches his chin and looks up, thinking. "Yes, it was the seventh, and that's when everything changed."

"What do you mean?" I ask.

"Well, he finally spoke. He said to me, 'everything is going to change. The hand moves me.' I just sort of look at him, and he grabs me by the lapel of my tunic and then I see it—Old Red is rotting away. Half of his face was decaying. The formaldehyde stench was terrible, and his teeth were yellow and broken.

"So then, I pull out my knife and slip it under his throat. I was known for being quick out there—in my town, I mean. Not like my whole country, but my town. So anyway, he lets me go and then smiles before saying, 'They are coming. Your shadow will tuck you to sleep at night. Tell *HIM* that when he meets my master, the darkness will consume him.'" The hand that moves? Where have I heard that before?

"Sooo . . . I don't get it. Was the guy dead or something?" Rust asks.

He sips his drink and nods his head downward as if to acknowledge he had forgotten the most important part of his story.

"So here's where it gets weird. He sits back down and doesn't say a word the rest of the night. Stays still till we're about to close. I suppose, now that I think on it, it was right when the last person had left. So, just before closing, he gets up and leaves. No big deal right? Wrong. I get a cook in back to close down for me and slip into the shadows to follow this guy home as no one knew who he was or where he went the rest of the night until dawn. So, I'm following this guy, sneaking behind buildings and under bridges and holding my breath through canals all the way to the edge of town.

"So, we're just outside of town and this like white mist drifts into the area, which made it very hard to see. I continue following this guy until we approach the graveyard. He doesn't know I'm following him because I keep a good distance. Then, he enters a graveyard. It's nothing *huge*, just your ordinary bury-your-dead-in-one-spot sort of collection. Anyway, he walks up to this tombstone and just stares at it. No words spoken, no hocus pocus dance—just looking. I, mind you, am totally confused at this point. The whole thing gave me the creeps I tell you, but, anyway, all of a sudden this mist covers the guy up and I can't see a lick. I move quietly to another vantage point and watch this guy lie down in a grave."

"How did he get in there?" I ask. "Wasn't there dirt?"

"That's the thing. There *was* and then there wasn't. Next thing I know, I see Old Red slip inside this grave and then more mist and BAM!" Faris drops her fork, clattering it on her plate then to the floor.

Sly continues, "Then the grave was filled up. Now, as if that wasn't weird enough . . . I walk over to the grave where Old Red decided to take a nap. On the tombstone, I can still see it to this day, the tombstone read, "Any other name. Anything besides Old Red." I didn't understand it all; couldn't understand it all. By the time I wrapped my head around everything I had just witnessed, before my eyes, the words changed and read, "Just another hand in the darkness, carrying out his command."

That's about the time I decided to go home. People think I am crazy in my town because no one else ever saw him. But I did. I know for a fact I did."

"That's unbelievable," Kam says.

"Well, turns out it was, Kam. After a while, the story of Old Red began to spread. People said, 'Old Red lives in his head, that's why he should be dead.' It never stopped. I had people attack me in the night, in the market, at work—it didn't matter where I went. It's like the very people accusing me of having a disease caught a disease themselves. A disease that compelled people to kill me. It wasn't long before I defended myself against half of the town. I never knew when I would have to pull a blade out." The room is silent, save for the moaning of the canyon walls as the wind laps up against them.

"Eventually, I realized I was cursed, cursed by Old Red. I hit the road and lived in a nearby city for some time. It was nice for a brief stint. Once a month I was visited by a different version of Old Red, what with his scarf and ordering an ale no sugar. It became insidious and absorbed my life. Everywhere I went, a so-called "hand of the darkness" followed me. Towns eventually turned on me, no matter where I was or how low profile I became. So, I just learned to live out of sight, on my own, you know? Been an orphan my whole life, so I figured I was born to live perpetually alone."

He looks down and swishes his drink in circles. Looking very weepy, he says, "Which is why I meant what I said. For the longest time I thought *I* was going to lose my mind. I would have periods where I thought I was the hand in the darkness. I would forget entire days, like I blacked-out or something. Then I met you all. You all have always been kind to me, and, more bluntly, this is the longest I have been with a group of people where a hand hasn't visited me. This is the first 'team' I have ever been a part of. Thank you."

I wrap my arm around his shoulder. "You're one of us now, Sly. We won't judge you or think you're weird. In fact, if Old Red decides to pay you a visit while we are here, I tell you what. I'll shoot an arrow between his eyes. Deal?"

He wipes his eyes and laughs. "Deal."

At that moment, one of the crowsfly onto our dinner table. It hops around and squawks at us. "Get out of here, bird," Kam slaps it away and throws a bread crumb near the edge of the base. "Here, take this and get out."

The bird eats it and lets out a shrill cry, then falls over and dies. *Don't feed the crows*. The image of Doctore races through my head. I blink once, but before I can get out of my chair, an ocean of black floods our base.

CHAPTER THIRTY-THREE

There are times that you need to play it safe, despite the hero in your head. There are times you need to be the hero in your head. Knowing when to pull the trigger is what separates real heroes from fools.

Paraphrase of an old Pantine parable

NO ONE HAS TIME TO think. The force of a thousand oversized crows are inside, pecking, clawing, tearing at our flesh. Dalk gets on a knee and uses a shield to block all of the crows away. The divergence of the continuous stream looks as if a dragon is spewing black fire at him. We grab plates, cups—*anything* we can use to defend ourselves from the birds. Ranger pulls out *Darkwater* and hacks wildly at the air.

"TO THE BEDROOMS!" I scream. "TO THE BLOODY BEDROOMS!" We scramble toward the back, knocking over chairs and furniture in the process, swatting at crows on our backs. The constant cawing, scratching, and pecking is too much. I cover my eyes and run to the back. I slip on a dead crow and crack my head against the stone floor. Birds cover my face the moment I fall. Faris hits one off with a cup and shields my face while I get up. We run to the nearest room, faces in elbows and slam the door shut. I open the door a crack to see what's going on with everyone else. Kam creates a fire barrier as him and Tamra run into the next room. Some of the birds catch on fire, shrieking and flying maniacally through the room.

Dalk throws his shield on his back and heads into another room with Ranger. Rust and Sly bang on Kam's door and slip in.

Some of the birds notice us peeking and assault our door. One wedges in and starts to peck Faris, who breaks its neck, but loses some flesh in the process. Another gets its head trapped in the crack of the door. I slam it shut, decapitating the angry creature.

We sit in silence for a minute listening to what's going on outside. The birds are still flying around trying to break into the doors of our now locked rooms. They continue to fly at full speed into the doors, seemingly unfazed. Who would have thought I would have to lock my bedroom door for fear of birds?

I turn to talk to her, but before I can speak, her face drops, "Nirue! Your face!"

"What?"

"Come here," she grabs a nearby cloth and begins to touch different areas of my face. "You're bleeding everywhere. Sit down."

We sit down on the ground a foot apart. I guess it hadn't quite hit me, but my vision is a bit red. I sit cross-legged and she on her shins. "Your pretty face is going to look choppy for a few days."

"Meh. I'll be alright I suppose."

She blots my face in silence. "Listen . . . I uh. I appreciate this," I tell her awkwardly.

She coughs and says, "You're very welcome." Nothing more.

Although I was hoping for more, her unenthusiastic response is probably a good thing. I need to be the leader, which means not falling for the pretty girl in camp.

I take a moment to reflect on my circumstances. I am in a room with a beautiful woman to whom *I* am playing hard to get. In a room that is surrounded by savage birds that want to pluck out my eyes. In a base in a canyon where kidnappers have forced me to play a game of life or death capture the flag. In a world where I have awoken a Keeper against giant man-eating trolls, in a forest where everything wanted to kill me. In the same world where I had to kill an assassin king among a city of thieves. How is that, among all the death and the pain, I am finally starting to feel alive? It must be that I am ever closer to accomplishing my goal—to get home and be with my family. Gotta get home, gotta get home I tell myself.

She runs to a water bucket and washes the cloth of blood. The birds are still going strong outside. I try to yell to Kam through the stone wall with no success.

"Sit *down* Nirue. Your wounds are serious."

I sigh. "Fine. Ow!"

"Stop being such a baby. You *are* our big leader after all." That makes me feel warm inside. I like that she sees me in a position of power. I think she likes it too.

She is focused on a wound just above my left eye. "One of them got you good here . . . can you see alright?"

"My vision is a little red and blurry, but I'm fine."

"It almost cut you to the bone."

"Those are some big crows," I submit.

She holds the cloth on my wound for seconds at a time to stop the bleeding. She counts out-loud to twenty and then checks it out. Still bleeding. She starts counting out-loud to twenty again. Her eyes drift to meet mine.

1 . . . 2 . . . 3 . . . 4

"You don't have to be so tough either," I tell her, bringing up a conversation she started a few weeks ago.

"I'm not being tough, I'm just being a good friend, okay?"

"Fine by me," I say.

5 . . . 6 . . . 7 . . . 8

Her eyes drift back down. I look at her and her perfect beauty. I would make this girl my wife in Dakota. She senses my feelings. That same kind of energy that two people sense before they both tell each other exactly how they feel. That cusp-like, cup-spilleth-over moment where emotions can no longer stay bottled up.

9 . . . 10 . . . she begins to breath heavy . . . 11 . . . the word barely escapes her narrowed lips.

I grab her by the back of her head and we kiss each other, the sensations of new beginnings long anticipated, detecting the faintest whisp of sensations. Nervous, excited, hot, lost. The combination of her perfume and sweat from a long day of work makes me desire her even stronger, as if she's granting me access to the most intimate parts of her being.

While we are kissing, images of her pop through my head. I remember first seeing her when we met the rest of our team at training. I think of her sparkling brown hair under her coat just before we went scouting. I picture her face, always so serious and mature at dinner and around the fire at night. The way the shadows hide her features make me hate them. I picture her sitting next to me at sunrise before anyone was up.

I picture the sympathy in her eyes when she nursed my wound. I open my eyes to meet hers again. They tell a story, and I know how it ends. I know she cares for me, and that kiss solidified that. We stare at each other for a few seconds before embracing again. For a few minutes, my entire world is right there in that room, and nothing else exists.

We wake from our moment when Dalk's fists hammer the wooden door. We look at each other before three more heavy fists meet the wood.

"Don't worry anymore Nirue. The black bastards have decided we can live after all. It's safe to come out," Ranger says sarcastically. Faris urges me with a "do something" face.

I quickly get up and grab the cloth she was tending to me with. I move toward the door and open it to an absolute disaster. Thankfully, no one is suspicious of Faris and me. Before us is a motley scene of dead crows, bird feathers, broken furniture, spilled drink, food and blood. Ranger puts his arm around my shoulder and looks at my face.

"Got ya pretty good did they? Eh. You'll be jus' fine."

I look back at him and say with a smile, "Just a flesh-wound."

Kam walks over and picks up a dead crow by the wing, displaying its stomach and long feet. "Should we keep these things for food?"

"Those birds look gross, man," Sly suggests. "I say we let them be."

"I second that," Rust says.

"Then it's settled," I say. "Let's get this place back in order before tomorrow."

Everyone agrees, and we spend the next few hours cleaning up the blood with cloths. When we run out, someone suggests using our cloaks to give us a more intimidating look.

Those of us with white and grey cloaks soak blood up for effect. I tell the group what Doctore had told me about feeding the birds and someone pelts me in the back of a head with a dead crow, as if to call me an idiot.

The entire time I clean I feel energy from Faris. I can feel her looking at me, and I can't stop thinking about her. I want to look over at her, but don't want to get caught by anyone else, so I avoid looking in her direction despite every part of my body telling me to. When all the work is done, the group gathers by the fire. It's an oddly cold night, so most of us share large blankets next to a bonfire.

Faris and I hold hands under the blanket while the team shares stories. We smile and laugh until a series of yawns prompt us to our rooms. Everyone is in good spirits despite what happened, everyone except Ranger and Dalk.

The next morning I wake to Dalk shouting my name. I race out of bed and sprint to the edge of the second story. Above the forest in the distance a large flock of crows circle and slowly proceed toward us. It almost looks fake.

"Been watching those damned rats with wings the whole morning. Got a torch right here in case they come looking for another fight." He lifts up a torch to show me he wasn't lying. "Anyway, about an hour ago, the things took off at once—like they were possessed or something. They flew out toward the forest and continue to circle the same damn area, slowly moving toward us. When they got to the edge of the forest, some guy on a horse road out and threw a huge stick in the ground with something draped around it. That just happened. The crows followed him out of the forest, and back in. Looks like they are heading back now."

I pause to take all of this information in. He interrupts my thoughts.

"You said we should have gotten a 'special' or something by now, right?"

"Right. At least according to Doctore. And it would make sense, since they got those huge wolves."

"Okay. So, I think those crows serve as some sort of alarm system, you know? Like an aerial bloodhound or something. I think they track the other team for us."

"Interesting thought, Dalk. Want to come with me to see what the pole is?" Dalk nods replies, "Already got our horses saddled up." I slap him on the back and head downstairs.

The ride over there is colder than I expected, probably due to the drastic fluctuations of temperature in this canyon. We get to the pole relatively quick. A large post cut from a tree branch sticks out of the ground with a bloodstained white sack. Attached to the top is another note. It reads:

Nirue:

In the sack you will find the belongings of your teammate. We have left you a few of her more inconsequential items. Open the bag and see what I mean. She provided us with a great feast. Last night, after we dug up her grave, my comrades and I told the story of how she screamed when we nailed her to the tree. You should have heard her beg for mercy! I will tell you one thing. She tastes much better than she pleads, and enemy meat always tastes better than our own. How refreshing it was.

Meet me with two of your men in the center of the forest at noon, I want to discuss some things face to face. Your beloved Atia will be there. If you don't show up, she gets the same treatment as dinner last night.

I ball the note up in my fists and clench my jaw, all the while staring at the ground. How can anyone be so sick? How could you dig up a dead woman and eat her? "Check the bag, Dalk." When he opens it up, he turns his head, only able to look in the bag with one eye.

"Teeth, tips of fingers, toes and a tongue."

"That was Sabe," I say looking into the forest. "C'mon, let's get back to the group."

"What should I do with this bag?"

"Bring it with us."

* * *

When we get back to base the rest of the team is already up. Faris had been scrambling some eggs while Sly stoked the fire.

"Where you two been?" Faris asks with a smile that she quickly puts away.

"Retrieving what's left of Sabe. Those sick bastards dug her up and ate her." Faris nearly vomits into the eggs. Sly raises his eyebrows and looks around in shock. Neither know what to say.

"They want three of us to meet them in the forest at noon."

"That's an hour from now. Let me go with you if—" I cut Faris off with a wave.

"It's going to be Dalk, me and Kam. Sly, I want you to hang out in the shadows should they have any surprises for us. Get out there now, before they come back. Listen to the crows."

Sly nods and runs into his room.

"Faris, you stay here with Ranger. Speaking of, where is he?"

"In his room sleeping," Sly yells while throwing on warm clothes. He's been sleeping a lot lately.

Faris bites her tongue and nods before removing the pan from the fire. I want to get there early to help Sly scout, but not too early to give Sly away. "Hurry up Sly, we need to get out there." No response. "Sly?" I yell. "Let's go!"

Tamra walks out of the room I was yelling toward and tells us she hasn't seen him all morning. We look around for a few minutes before agreeing he deserves the nickname.

We hop on our horses and head into the lower forest. In the distance, a flock of crows moves quickly over the center toward the frozen river. Our enemies are already there.

CHAPTER THIRTY-FOUR

In order to win, you must believe you cannot lose. You must also wait for your moment to strike.

Trip: On War and Conflicts

WE REACH THE FOREST ROUGHLY thirty minutes before noon, grey clouds forming overhead. I look up and feel the barely visible, cascading drops. It smells like wet forest. It smells good. I pull my hood over my head and enter the forest for my encounter, all too aware of the probable trap that awaits me. It smells so much better in here, as if the forest is getting a much-needed bath.

Dalk, Kam and I reach the center fairly quickly. I've got muscle, magic, range and surprise. I should be well equipped for whatever they bring. Kam sits on a fallen tree covered in moss. Dalk fixes a stare into the other side of the forest.

"SLY!" I whisper-yell toward the mountain looming overhead a hundred yards away. "Sly!" Nothing.

"Probly better we don't know where he is," Kam offers. Just before I turn to acknowledge Kam, something catches my eye. A creature lowers itself onto a branch and stares at me. It smiles ear to ear then disappears into the trees, pointed tail the last to make it up.

It begins to rain a bit harder. Kam provides us with an invisible canopy above head. Rain falls everywhere except on us. The greyness of the afternoon creates a mist both physically and psychologically. I don't know what to expect.

Through the mist I see distant torches. Crows fly above head, so we know they are close. Three people come into the square clearing. They are hooded in black, their faces unremarkable. The man in all black approaches us without words. To his right is a man slightly smaller than he, and to his left a much smaller person. I assume it to be Atia. The leader removes his hood and stares into my eyes. Still no words are spoken.

I feel Kam and Dalk's eagerness. I feel nothing but hatred for this man. I am not a killer, but I want to kill him. After minutes of silence, he begins to laugh. His teeth have been sharpened into points. They walk toward us, and us toward them. Three on three we stand in the clearing, rain pouring on everyone. I hardly notice that Kam let down his canopy.

I'm going to make him talk first. I stare at the man who murdered Dalk's brother. The man who dug up Sabe and ate her alive. There's nothing human about him. He is an animal, moved by the invisible force of instinct.

"A pleasure to meet you here, Nirue" he hisses.

"What is your name?"

"My *name* is not important. My *name* is but a word—a label. A nightmare to run about your mind, a trigger for unease and a reason to look over your shoulder. But, in the end, it is my actions that you will remember, not my name."

Our hair is matted down and our clothes soaked, adding unneeded weight.

"What do you want from me?" I ask with a stare that could freeze the ocean on a midsummer's day.

"Blood. And I want you to quit." He flicks a coin into the air, catches it, turns it over on the outside of his hand and shakes his head. He repeats this process all while pacing around our group. Dalk takes an aggressive stance and watches his every move while he continues talking.

"Even with your worthless runt here, we still out-match you tenfold. Just one of my men is worth four of yours. So, here is my offer. Give us the rest of your women, and your standard, and the rest of you will be spared."

They want Faris and Tamra? "Why our women?"

"Isn't it obvious? They taste better. We would have eaten your worthless Atia if you hadn't killed our comrade in the fire. But, no one knows what will come out of the special cave. That's a risk we cannot take."

"You've got to be out of your ever lovin' mind if you think Nirue is going to give up our teammates," Kam growls.

The leader in black looks at me, waiting for my response.

"He's right. We would rather die than do that." Atia faints. At the same time, Dalk jumps with an aerial attack. "FOR MY BROTHER!" Thunder booms in the background and lightning flashes.

Dalk is frozen in mid-air. "I thought you might try something silly. Pity you had to bring this vengeance driven goon." The cloaked man behind him has a certain yet distinct focus on Dalk. His fingers are bent with an outstretched arm. Kam slides his hand and Dalk falls from the air. He grabs his stomach, writhing in pain.

The hooded man focuses on Kam, and an explosion of fire and ice erupt in the clearing. Kam unleashes an ice spear while the other a fireball in a stalemate. Kam circles and slices a large tree with a spell. The tree falls quickly toward their group. "ATIA!" I yell as I run to save her.

In a flash, they teleport fifteen yards away, their leader holding Atia by the back of the neck. He says something to his mage. A smile grows on the pail spell-caster. He whispers to himself and moves his hands in a semi-circle. Three of the wolves we killed in the forest fire come to life. Skin and fur hang loosely from their bodies, exposing muscle and organs. Their legs are bones and sinew. Their eyes fire red. The two men laugh and disappear into the forest carrying Atia.

The biggest wolf runs headlong at Dalk. I rip *Evergold* off my back and put one through its guts. Green and brown slime ooze over its body. Dalk takes out his war-axe and uppercuts it in the face. The force sends the wolf flying about ten yards, but it returns. It appears these wolves cannot be killed. Dalk just ripped one's head open and yet manages to attack.

The storm picks up, bringing heavy rain and poor visibility with it. I can't hear Dalk or Kam. I shoot as many arrows at the wolves as I can, but they don't seem to be effective. Kam's eyes turn white and shine like a lighthouse would in a storm at sea. Wind gathers around his body, causing nearby leaves to circle upward. When the wolves are within a few yards, he slams his staff on the ground, waves growing outward then up.

The wolves are swirled into a tornado of sorts. Dalk stands there in awe while rain flies about him. I don't realize it either, but my jaw is open. Kam's arms are outstretched as he yells something inaudible toward the wolves. Lightning flashes through the trees and strike the wolves in unison. They disintegrate and their ashes are spread across the forest. Kam slowly lowers his arms and his eyes fade from white to normal.

He falls but manages to stay off the ground by holding the top of his staff. The storm has turned dangerous now. I yell for Dalk to grab Kam. As we head out of the forest, another figure appears amidst the furious rain. Ranger. He runs toward us then right past us, chasing the crows that are now nearing the opposite edge of the lower forest. I run after him, knowing exactly what he is trying to do. Three, four, five long strides and I catch him, tackling his legs from behind. He kicks at my chest.

"Don't be a fool!" I scream at him through the torrent. Still, he struggles against my grip.

Despite the rain pouring down his face, I can tell he has been crying. "She's right there, Nirue! We have to try!"

I shake my head. Thunder booms overhead, causing me to look upward. When I turn back to Ranger, lightning illuminates my face, quickly followed by more thunder. I place my hand on his shoulder, "Trust me, Ranger. I want nothing more than to get her back. And we WILL get her back, but we need to be smart, okay? I can't lose you too."

He pauses for a minute, looking her direction. "Why didn't you tell me?" I open my mouth, shaking my head trying to figure out what to say.

"I didn't want you to do anything without thinking. I knew if you saw her, you would die trying to get her back." He rubs water from his face with both hands, red eyes telling me everything I need to know. Kam hobbles over, heavily relying on his staff. With the face of a very elderly and depleted man, he says, "We need to go. Now."

I turn to Ranger, who takes one last pregnant look in the enemy's direction, then stands up and reluctantly nods his head. I turn one more time to look for Sly but see nothing. If I couldn't find him without the storm, I certainly won't now.

The wind brings different smells to mind as I walk. Dirt, pine-needles, water, wet-dirt, moss, grass, dead leaves and wet, burnt wood. I don't have time to appreciate them, I have to just get back to base. That's the only thing I keep thinking to myself.

We ride through the storm, sloshing and drudging our way through the grounds. When we get within sight of the base I notice my team on the upper level watching us approach. I don't recognize the clothing one of them is wearing. I tie off Storm and race up the stairs. Sly welcomes me with a hug. "Where the hell have you been?"

"Helping us."

"Really, because if Kam wasn't there I'm not sure we would be in front of you now."

A voice calls to me, bundled near the fire. "It's okay Nirue, he was saving me." I look over and see a pale-white apparition of the once vibrant comrade of mine. "Atia," I gasp.

CHAPTER THIRTY-FIVE

*How can you defeat your enemy without first defeating
yourself? Not literally, but hypothetically. Where are
you weak? Where are you strong? Where are you
vulnerable? Know these things before fighting, trust me.
Apply this to all areas of life, not just war.*

Trip

RANGER WARMS HER PALE HANDS in between his while kissing
her behind the ear. It's like trying to will her back to health. I walk over
and give her a big hug. Tears fill my eyes. "So good to see you again. I had
feared the worst."

"Very good to see you too, Nirue," she says with a smile. "I had wondered
if my last memory of you was going to be you getting uppercutted." We
share a laugh and she begins to cough. Ranger urges her to get closer to the
fire. I walk to Sly, whose eyes are lost in the afternoon storm.

"It makes the valley appear as though it is night," he says without
breaking gaze.

I look back out into the valley. "Sure does. Say, I was going to ask you
. . ."

"How did I get her?"

"I don't understand. I saw them grab her by the neck and take her away. Then all of a sudden, here you are with Atia."

"That was their spy—their rogue if you will. I've seen him spying in the forest from distance a few times. The real Atia was back at the edge of their side of the forest. I had a feeling there was someone else when some of the crows didn't fly over toward you all. So, I went and checked it out and sure enough, she was tied and gagged to a horse. I'm glad you sent me out when you did."

"Odd. I mean don't get me wrong, I'm very happy to see her, but I don't get why they would do that?"

He shrugs. "Maybe they figured they would need an extra guy should we begin to fight? Maybe they didn't want you to see how frail she really is? Maybe they were just going to let her die out there. Who's really to say?"

All of these things he says could be true. I'm glad she is back. I just hope we can win in time for her to survive.

* * *

Kam spends the next few days sleeping. We go back to nightly dinners which now includes our newest member. Atia fits in well with everyone. People tread lightly when talking to her, doing their best to hide that they know something is wrong with her. Most people go out of their way to accommodate her.

As I try to identify the different maladies in Atia, I cannot come to any conclusion, other than that her fire is burning very low. This means, we have to hurry these games up if we have any chance at saving her life.

I think on all of the adventures we have shared together. From being chained and being forced hallucinogens on a foreign planet, to being in an assassin city, to the man-eating Jboynei of Hardrain, to here. She deserves everything we have. Everything she has done played a part in our success, whether it's immediately obvious or not.

I gather the group and let them know the urgency of our situation. I tell everyone that we are sitting at the table until we devise a workable, thought-out plan. At first people are hesitant to voice their opinion. I start throwing out stupid ideas to get the ball rolling. "Let's create a diversion and have Sly steal their flag."

Atia shakes her head. "They will always have at least two people guarding the flag at all times. They really do fancy their warriors over ours."

"Okay. Well, why don't we stand outside their base and challenge them to a fight? Once we kill them, we can easily overpower the last two in the base," Ranger offers.

"Mmmm, I wouldn't try that either. The entire space, from their land to the beginning of the forest is booby-trapped. At least coming from the lower-level forest," Atia adds. "Your best bet is going to be coming from the top or the cave. They don't want to trap the cave because it is always shifting. And they stay as far away from the top as possible. Some guy nearly lost his mind running from some thing talking in his head."

Rust and Ranger exchange glances. "I don't mean this to be rude, but I want to be honest with you guys," she says while biting her lip. "We really are outmatched. I have seen them train. I have seen their mage, and I have at least seen Ranger and Nirue fight. These men, these . . . creatures. They are possessed by something unnatural. I can't explain it, but put it this way: Nirue, you would be the worst archer on their team, and Ranger—you the worst sword fighter."

Thunder claps outside of our base. The wind shifts, blowing a soft mist inside the base. No one knows what to say, so Rust attempts to get conversation started again. "Alright, well let's plan accordingly. At least we have narrowed it down to two areas of attack—upper level tree line and the cave," he says as enthusiastically as he can.

We throw around ideas for a few more hours but to no avail. My team looks defeated. Then, like lightning from a storm cloud, it hits me in an instant, overwhelming me with indecision. I wrestle with telling the group my plan, because I know it is our best chance, but also the riskiest ploy. My chest feels tight. How will Ranger respond?

After minutes of silence, I finally speak up. "I think I may have just figured out how to win these games. But it's going to take execution, and a little luck."

I lean into the table and begin to talk, voice low so as to not be heard. If you were an outsider on the other side of the room, you would notice a candle dancing a shadow off of my face as I offer up the plan that just might be our winning play.

CHAPTER THIRTY-SIX

*I love good anxiety. You know, the anticipation, can't
really distract yourself type of hype. That's my jam, and
that's why I love it here. I hope to make it through this next
trial, but if not, at least this was my last day—and a dang
good day it's starting to be.*

Jake Hollind, four minutes before the games begun

THE NEXT MORNING, EVERYONE RISES at the same time.
Breakfast is cooked but hardly anyone eats. The vibe is clear: This is it.
We either win, or lose today. A few words are exchanged but nothing of
importance.

The sky threatens another big storm. I can't decide if I fancy that a
good or bad thing. All I know is that this better work, or we are completely
done for. We meet at the top of our base. I urge everyone to sit down
around the bonfire. I clear my throat and begin.

"We have been here for over a month now. Who knows what is going
on outside these grounds. What I do know is that I wouldn't have it
any other way. I wouldn't be with anyone else besides this lot. We have
overcome many trials being here and we've lost comrades, but not without

retribution. Today is the day we take this game by the *throat*. Think clearly and do not be rash—for everything can go awry with one false move. Be ever the more clever."

My eyes water a little. Not because I am scared for my own life but because I fear for everyone else. I used to read about famous war heroes like Julius Caesar, Pompey, Alexander the Great and think, What bravery. Now I know that bravery personally. I know that it is not a feeling of control. Rather, it is the courage to let go and trust what you cannot control.

"Trust each other and adapt."

A somber response. Most people look down. Ranger and Atia look into each other's eyes, then hold for a long kiss. Faris looks at me anxiously. She mouths, "Be careful." She then presses two fingers to her lips, and holds those fingers toward me. I nod at her, and we descend toward the first level. The plan is in action.

As we ride, I take in the canyon one last time. It really is a site to see. A beautiful horseshoe with painted forests and ominous white walls. Illustrious colors bounce around from a hot white sun penetrating dark clouds. Birds and critters run around, apparently unaware of what's to come. We reach the edge of the forest in about an hour. We get off our horses and slowly walk them through the moss and pine needled ground. Two members scouting for the other team yell for us to stop from a distance. "Stay right where you are, or my buddy here will scorch you where you stand."

Their mage watches us quietly from a hood. It begins to rain. Kam steps forward as if to say something, gripping his staff with white knuckles. I hold a hand to his chest, preventing him from moving. Crows fly about the enemy. I hold up our standard for them to see. "We are here to accept your offer. We quit."

The two exchange wary glances at each other. Faris, Atia and Tamra feign crying, with the help of Kam, and struggle with the ropes we bound them with. They look helpless on top of their horses.

"How do we know you aren't lying?"

"Come get them if you like," I holler back.

"Stay at our edge of the forest. We will be back." The rain picks up drastically. It is pouring.

"We will wait." With cautious eyes, they ride off.

The women, especially Atia, begin to shiver. "I'm scared, Nirue," Atia says through chattering teeth. Faris appears calm but I can tell she is terrified too. Tamra is difficult to read, but then again, who wouldn't be scared?

Kam creates an invisible field around the women so that they stay dry. He mutters to me, through heavy rainfall, "You think this will work?" I nod my head. I don't really know if it will, or not. But I do know that it is our best shot. We spend the next few minutes discussing light-hearted topics, topics that make the women more at ease.

Then they appear. Five of them, just like Atia said. She lets out a whimper. Kam lowers the field and they become as wet as we are. Their leader appears at the forefront, carrying a spear. They are hard to see from far away because of the haze covering the ground. They walk in a serpentine path that I study with particular detail.

Their leader approaches us wearily, then lets out an evil grin. His teeth are sharp and bloody. "Come to your wits, have you? Surprised it took you so long."

Kam, Dalk and I remain stoic. "Take the women and our standard and be done with it. We're done with these whores anyway."

Their leader looks at his comrades, eyebrows raised. "You really are just what I expected you to be, Nirue. Weak. You are so weak that you can convince yourself to change your mind in the matter of days. Days! Let us see if you are as honest as you are weak." He hops off his horse, as does the rest of his team. He walks over to Faris and takes grip of her arm. The rest of them watch us wearily with cold grips on their weapons. We are outmatched and outnumbered.

"I'll start with this one," their leader says, eyes locked with mine. He opens his mouth and looks down at her forearm. She screams and jerks and yells, "Nirue, PLEASE!" Everything in my body wants to put an arrow through his head. I want to save her because I care for her and she is so helpless. I feel light-headed.

Then, he stops just short of her arm, saliva dripping over rope and skin. He looks up at me with black eyes and that terrible grin. I wonder if anyone else saw my unease.

"Your standard," a man the size of Dalk requests. Kam begrudgingly hands it to him. Their team exchanges smiles. Then the leader laughs. Not a human laugh. No. Something deep and dark. Something I cannot explain. It is more beast than man. He hops on his horse and turns around. Before he takes off, he asks, "By the way, where is the rest of your team? If we have your standard, why wouldn't they be here to protect you?"

I knew this would be coming. I thought of every angle to every question they would have. "A few of us had a harder time conceding than we did. Kam here had to, how do you say, *incapacitate* some of our weaker minded members. We knew they would screw it up, so we *put them to rest*, for the better of the team."

He holds up his head into the sky for a moment to think, then shrugs, and kicks the sides of his horse. "See you in another life, Nirue," he says, disappearing into the mist.

"Spit on that pig-loving, animalistic, mother bedding son of a demon!" Kam screams. Dalk breathes heavy yet slow, in and out, in and out. Dalk's breath emanates a cloud from his massive body. "Where is Sly?" he asks without the slightest jest in his voice. "Where . . . the hell . . . is Sly?"

"He'll be here. Just wait." Where is he though? Any longer and the plan will fall apart. This is the hardest rain I have ever been in, even harder than the jungle. Finally, Sly emerges from the grey with two horses.

"Were you able to track their path around the traps?" I ask.

He nods, out of breath. With hands on knees he says, "Just up until this last part. Tell me you caught it?"

"Yeah. We're good. Let's ride." I look to the sky, and notice the crows are further away than I like.

Slowly, I guide them through the first three hundred yards or so. Dalk's horse steps on a nail and lets out an ear-piercing squeal. He insists we press on. I take the lead, tracing their exact movements. I look up at the crows and notice they are nearly at the enemy base.

"We need to hurry!" I scream through the pouring rain and thunder. Sly nods and takes the lead with great pace. The rain exposes traps that would devastate any one of us.

"We thought you might be onto something," a hooded man yells. He grins and begins to move his fingers. This is it. This is where the plan fails. This is where the women—my friends get eaten. A flash blinding both Dalk and me. When my eyes adjust a few seconds later, I see a spear made of ice is sticking out of the enemy's head. Kam's eyes are ice-blue, like mine, but more than just the pupils—the entire eyeball.

"Arrogant prick. Been saving that one special for him," Kam says, eyes returning to their natural color. A flash blinds us and a loud horn bellows through the torrent.

I nod and we trample his body on our way to their base. We are within two-hundred yards. The remaining birds that were hidden in the storm are now perched at their base. When Sly gives me the okay, I ride my horse at a slow canter toward the enemy. They are gathered at the second story of their base, looking for the cause of the horn.

Their leader sees us, then runs downstairs and hops on his black horse. He rides toward me. Kam, Sly and Dalk wait in the grey rain, just outside of eyesight.

"What is this about? You're interrupting dinner."

C'mon girls, hurry up, I need to stall this guy. "I just wanted to tell you something." He raises his eyebrows, un-amused. "You're not going to eat those girls. They are my friends, and I care for them." His laugh starts slow, then like a snowball tumbling down a steep hill, gains momentum until he is in all out hysteria. He wipes his black eyes, gets off his horse and draws a sharp curved blade. I hop off my horse and draw my axe. The runes glow green. He swings at me and I block him with ease. He lunges one, two, three times. I don't handle them as well but still manage to avoid the cuts. Then he drops his head and sends a flurry of attacks as he whips and twists through the air, interrupting the flow of the rain. I dive out of the way. I can't take on many more of those.

He grins and darts toward me, creating momentum for another spinning attack. I bend my knees, ready for the attack. Then I see it. A wave of black swoops down and engulfs him, staggering his balance, causing him panic. He runs swift into the grey and out of sight toward their base.

"LET'S GO BOYS!" I yell back to Kam, Dalk and Sly. We ride our horses to the front of their base. Thousands of crows flood the area, blinding and distracting the enemy. Kam creates a fire-shield around the girls in the base. Atia runs out, throwing ropes down as she approaches. Tamra grabs our standard and Faris grabs theirs.

At the same time, Rust and Ranger emerge from the cave. It's hard to hear anyone. The girls hop on the back of our horses. A few of their members try to run out and stop us but they are overwhelmed by the constant battering of the giant birds.

"Do you know the way out of the cave?" I yell to Ranger through the torrent. He holds tight onto Atia. "It's flooded. No telling if we would make it out."

We have to move and we have to move fast. We're only gaining a half hour or so on the other team, precious time needed to get back to base and set up a defense. It's too long to go the way we came and too wet to take the caves. I make a split second decision, one that I may regret for the rest of my life. I yell for everyone to go to the forest on high. To the one place I wanted to avoid, and have avoided since day one: the realm of the blue creature.

CHAPTER THIRTY-SEVEN

They weren't chasing anything. They were running.

Shyll Baringer

WE ENTER THE FOREST. THE rain pours and lightning veins the sky with exotic flashes. We feel the rain, the ever present chill and sogginess of our clothes. We smell the pines, the wet dirt and the mustiness of damp moss. But we cannot hear, as though we've all gone deaf. We can't hear the twigs snap beneath our feet, a falling tree or even the wind whipping the deluge.

I turn back to make sure everyone is okay. Faris hops over a fallen tree and nods at me. I take the standard from her and press forward. Dalk and Kam lead the way with size and power. Ranger carries Atia, while Faris and Tamra move up the middle. I slip into the back to be with Sly. Of course, no sign of him. The rain pours on.

The world begins to get dark, a dungeon-with-no-lantern dark. My team stops and begins to look around. I curse under my breath and catch up to them. People are trying to talk but it's much too impossible for that; the rain makes it difficult to read lips. I hold up my hand as if to ask everyone to hold on. I venture on a bit deeper into the forest.

"I told you to be careful in these woods." The creature says to me telepathically, though, much stronger and louder than in our first encounter, words sending vibrations throughout my body.

I look around the forest to locate him but cannot, looking like a crazy person to everyone else. "Had no other choice. The caves are flooded and it's too stormy to make our way back through the lower forest safely." Figure I have nothing to lose being honest.

The rain has soaked all the way through my clothes. My body begins to shake. I think on how much is at stake from this conversation. My friends, in my midst, will die if I mess it up. My family may never see me again. I've got to think my way through this. The creature doesn't respond.

"I promise that if you grant us safe passage, none of us will ever come through this forest again. You have my word."

The beast cackles. Then, it appears on a large branch, hanging upside down, just feet from where I stand. Its smiles bright-yellow, then disappears. I draw *Evergold*.

"Why would I allow you passage? I see both standards. Certainly I shouldn't deprive the *dark one* his share?"

"Who is this dark one you speak of?"

"Fools. The lot of you. You were put here for one thing and one thing only. To learn suffering."

Forget the telepathy, I begin to shout at this creature. "THEN WHY DON'T YOU JUST END IT NOW, HUH? C'MON, WHERE IS THE SUFFERING? ARE YOU SCARED THAT MAYBE I WON'T JUST LIE DOWN AND DIE FOR YOU?"

He appears in another branch, in a crouched predatory position. **"The other team is making fast ground on you now. What ever will you do?"** He grins.

I move quickly toward my team with the standard and motion for them to run. Our only hope is to run. I don't know how to kill this thing and apparently I am the only one who can see it. I wait for the last of our group to pass me, ensuring that I am the barrier between us and them.

As in the aftershock of an explosion, vibrations fill the air in an instant. My team collapses to their knees, holding their ears. The pain of the sound is still present, we just can't hear it. Faris is screaming. Tamra is sobbing. Not even Ranger can cover Atia's ears for her, as he succumbs to the pain and covers his own. The vibrations overwhelm me and I fall. My teeth rattle and my ears ring. My nose bleeds fast all over my shirt. I leak blood from underneath my eyeballs. Our world goes black.

"Stop. Please stop this."

The creature appears before me, this time on the ground. It is the only thing I can see. It walks on all four legs until it gets within an arm's reach. It is much bigger than I. Its skin is like a stretched balloon—tactile yet unremarkable. Black hair covers its spine, black claws exit every appendage. A long tail whips with perfect control and accuracy, triangle fixed at the top. *I can't take any more pain.*

It comes up to me and places a claw underneath my chin, drawing blood. It raises my blood-filled eyes to meet his.

"This has only just begun," it says before flashing a mouth full of yellow knives. Then, it is gone. It is gone and we can see again, making me suddenly ever-conscious of the rain. Rust slowly pulls his hands away from his ears. The women continue to cry. Faris runs over to me and collapses into my lap. I momentarily comfort Faris, but get her up quickly. I grab the standard and motion everyone to run. At the same time, an arrow pierces Faris in the back. Her eyes bulge and her mouth opens bloody. I grab her and throw her to the ground. A flurry of arrows stick into the surrounding trees and logs, vibrating as they make their mark.

It's a strange feeling, being attacked and having to fight without sound. It must feel like being in the middle of the busiest part of the ocean, if the ocean were in space. There is so much going on and so much to take in, yet, the only think you can hear is your own thoughts.

The battle rages on. We are unorganized. Rust and Kam didn't see the arrows and are an easy target if they don't get down soon, but I can't alert them. Faris is down. Ranger is pulling Atia who nearly gets tagged herself. Dalk uses our standard and a shield to protect Tamra. I don't know where

Sly is. Their team approaches us like a wave. I fire off arrows as quick as possible.

I miss the first and fail to load the second one timely because my fingers are slippery. The storm rages on. I grab Faris and drag her backward. She gets on all fours then to her feet and hobbles toward Dalk's shield. I try to scream for Kam and Rust but it's simply pointless. Atia is as white as the snow of this place when we first got here. When everything was okay and it felt like a game. The reality of war is upon us, and there is nothing glorious about the way I feel.

We are trapped and outnumbered. A sense of panic overwhelms the group. Rust darts between trees, not sure what to do or where to fight from. Kam is focused on getting Tamra to heal Faris. Ranger is more concerned about Atia than his own life. Nobody is ready for the enemy, not even me. I grab Tamra and push her toward Faris. She rips Faris' shirt open and begins to heal where the arrow is, a rotting hole of green and red, meaning the enemy has poisoned their arrows.

I motion for Atia and Ranger to bunch up with us behind the log. He carries Atia to an adjacent tree. Ranger crawls toward Faris to take her bow, but it's a ten yard crawl. Atia looks at me with tears. Not tears of pain, but tears of sadness. She knows this is it for her. This is her last moment with me, with Ranger, in this life and the next. She pulls a glowing blue *Dicer* from her boot and slowly rises. An arrow nearly hits me in the head as I stand to protest, causing me to duck and return fire from the enemy now shooting from cover.

"NO!" I scream to her. She just shakes her head, chest rocking from overwhelming sobs. I begin to move through my team to get to her. "DON'T YOU DARE!" I scream. But of course, no one can hear me. "DON'T DO THIS!" I plead to her. Ranger pulls me down and saves me from an arrow. He reads my face and senses something is wrong. As he turns Atia looks at him, nose running, eyes blood red and barely open, hair hanging disheveled about her face. She doesn't want to, but it's clear her heart tells her she has to. She almost falls and braces herself against a tree with her pail left arm. She mouths "I love you" to Ranger, then plunges a *Dicer* into her stomach.

CHAPTER THIRTY-EIGHT

It's not just the cold that got them. It was the sorrow in their souls. Their losses were far colder than anything they experienced physically.

Shyll Baringer

A BLINDING LIGHT RACES THROUGH the grounds. Ranger sprints, forgetting about the enemy and the game and his own life. He picks up Atia and cradles her face, sobbing. He tries to stop the bleeding but it is too late. I forget about the game and begin to cry too. At the same time, two longsnouts charge up the hill from behind, darting between trees, mouths salivating for the enemy team. They pepper one with arrows, but it does nothing to deter the beast. Half of their team runs away. Their leader gives me one last look of hate, then takes off into the forest.

"TAMRA!" Ranger pleads. "Please do something. Please," he begs. Feeling that she wasn't moving fast enough, Ranger shakes his head and violently grabs Tamra toward him. Dalk moves to step in but I hold him back. Tamra rests a hand on Atia who isn't moving. Biting her lip she looks up at Ranger and simply shakes her head. Ranger flips his head back and screams into the rain, then begins cry even harder. The rain is just a light sprinkle, but it feels like more. The weight of our wet clothes, our situation, the game, and losing Atia kicks in. I haven't felt more weighed down in my life.

Ranger stands up with Atia and moves out of the forest. I pick up Faris who is also in bad shape. Dalk grabs both standards and we head down toward our base. Even when we exit the forest, and our ears work again, there is no sound. No sound other than the wind blowing my cape and heavy footsteps in the mud.

*   *   *

As we make our way to the base, the rain starts to pour again. I meet Kam, Sly and Rust at the base of the hill. "You three keep an eye out." They all nod in unison, as if they know they have messed up, but the truth is, they haven't done anything wrong. Once again, my heart feels just like the clouds over this valley.

We get to the base quickly, everyone except Ranger. A cold wind howls through the base causing my teeth to chatter. Tamra finally gets the arrow out of Faris, who looks as if she has caught the flu. Dalk places the standards in their respective places. The base lights up with a gold and green hue, emanating light into the canyon. By the time they kill the longsnouts and make it to our base, before even fighting us, it will have been well over an hour.

This should be a moment of excitement for us overcoming the odds and winning the games that we had no right to win. This should be a time of drinking and celebrating. A time to relax and let my guard down about my feelings for Faris. My guard is down, but all I feel for her is angst. Tamra has supernatural healing powers but still struggles to get her healthy.

Everyone changes into warm clothes except Ranger. He sits on the edge, looking out into the valley while holding Atia's lifeless body. I warm my hands by the fire. Sly nurses a broken arm. "What happened to you?"

"I was waiting to ambush them once they moved on you. I was off to the left, right near the cliff. I didn't see Atia die so I thought the longsnouts were coming after us. In the rain I slid off the mountain and hit some heavy branches on the way down. I'm just lucky I didn't get hurt worse. I blow into my hands and nod.

Kam says "I'm really sorry, Rue. I really am. I know how much you cared for her."

"Thank you, brother."

"You should talk to him," he nods at Ranger.

"You two have been through a lot. Not that we haven't, I mean, we've been in here over a month now. But you know what I mean." In agreement, I walk over to Ranger and place a hand on his shoulder.

"Ranger . . ." I don't know what to say

"She meant a lot to both of us. She was the glue of our team, and she gave herself so that we might live." He doesn't respond.

"I loved her and I love you, Ranger. I would die for you two, the way she died for us. I don't know what else to say other than I am sorry, and that I am here for you." He doesn't respond. I wait for a couple of minutes, hand on his back before I get up and head back to the fire. He just needs time.

Thirty minutes has already gone by, and there is no sign of the other team. A light flashes across the valley. Did another one of them die?

I check on Faris and Tamra. Faris is sleeping. "How is she?" Tamra shakes her head. "I don't know what type of poison they used, but it's nasty. It won't kill her, at least not for a few days. She needs to see the physiker right when we get back." That worries me.

Those who didn't know Atia lighten up. Rust, Kam and Dalk share a bottle of wine and some bread and cheese under warm blankets by the fire. Tamra joins them for a little. Sly is nowhere to be found. Then, in typical Sly fashion, he pops out from one of the rooms with two more bottles in his hand.

Ten minutes left until the games are over. Ranger is still sitting on the ledge in the rain. He must be freezing. He finally gets up and heads downstairs, then out into the grounds. I call to him but he doesn't respond. He gets on a horse and heads toward the center forest. Fool.

I run downstairs and race after him. Storm is faster than his horse, but he has a minute or so jump on me. By the time I catch him we are five minutes outside of the base. "RANGER!" I call to him. "RANGER STOP THIS!" Still, no answer. I race ahead of him and stop, but he avoids me and continues on. Ranger may very well lose us the game, but he is my brother, so I ride with him. Before we reach the edge of the forest, lights flash through the arena and trumpets sound.

The rain has become so unbearable that I don't even care that we won. The big gates that hold specials opens but nothing comes out. Ranger hops off his horse without tying it off and heads into the forest. The soft sound of a women singing acapella plays in the background, like an angel willing a break in the clouds. It calms me down. We get to a spot where green grass has grown over the burnt leaves and branches, near the middle of the lower level forest.

Ranger lays Atia softly in the grass and begins to dig with *Darkwater*. I pull Atia's *Dicer* from her sheath and begin to help him dig. We dig in the quietness of the trickling rain for a while. The dirt below the surface smells different. Ranger lays Atia down gently in the ground then climbs out of the grave. He stands over her and begins to sob, but doesn't say anything. I don't say anything either. He cries for a few minutes, then looks at her one last time before filling in her grave. I help him.

After we are done, we sit together on a nearby log that gives to our weight. No words are exchanged for some time, until finally, he speaks up.

"I've never been great with women. I've never had a real girl, to tell ya the truth. I once cared about a girl in what feels like a different lifetime, but all she did was cause me grief. Not Atia. Atia was different, she *understood* me Nirue. And that isn't the worst part. The worst part also isn't that I didn't save her, and that I failed her," he says through a runny nose and shortness of breath. "It's that . . ." his crying overcomes him. "It's that I *couldn't* save her. I couldn't do anything Nirue," he puts his face into his hands and lets it all out. I place a hand on his back and I cry. I cry with Ranger because that's what he needs.

Through my own tears I say, "But that's nothing to be ashamed of, Ranger. It doesn't mean that you weren't good enough. None of us could have saved her. The truth is, she was going to die anyway and she knew it. She killed herself not because she didn't want to live, but because she loved you so much, she wanted *you* to live. She wanted us to live."

He shakes his head. "Is just not right Nirue, it isn't right. Why should a girl so sweet and tender and caring and loving as her die. Die! Die at such a young age. I can't understand."

"I don't know either, Ranger. All we can do is be here for each other and hope that we can make it out of this miserable place alive. I'm here for you, brother." He looks up at me with tear filled eyes and says, "I know ya are Nirue. I know ya are," and gives me a hug.

"THERE THEY ARE!" Someone screams from behind us. "ARREST THESE CHEATERS!" I would recognize that voice anywhere.

Timbly.

CHAPTER THIRTY-NINE

Tell me the truth: Are you willing to be selfish?

Recurrent thought of a mad man

RANGER AND I STAND UP and ready *Evergold* and *Darkwater*. Timbly tip-toes his way through the forest in an attempt to avoid mud. It doesn't work. He wears a brown and red coat with an overly furry hoodie. His pointed eyebrows look more exaggerated than I remember. Soldiers in all black surround Ranger and I, threatening to loose arrows into us.

Timbly brushes some dirt off his pants and then holds his head up high. He clears his throat. "The games have been a tradition in our land since anyone can remember. And the games, themselves, are not something to be trifled with. No. The games are to be *respected* Mister Nyles and Mister, uh, whatever your name is."

"Ranger," he says through gritted teeth. Timbly waves a hand dismissively. "I gave you safe passage to Pantine, the greatest city in the world! I fed you and clothed you. I healed you when you were wounded. I did everything a good dominus could do, and *this* is how you repay me?" He motions his hand in a semicircle around him.

I can't control my tongue. "Have you lost your mind? We were stolen from our home. I was stabbed and nearly died. I was thrown into an icy maze that I barely escaped. You sold our best friend to the other team. You forced us to play a life-or-death game of capture the flag, which, might I add, we *won*. So don't give me this nonsense. We don't owe you anything."

He growls and walks toward me faster than I've ever seen him move. He stands in front of my face and begins to talk so loud that he is spitting.

"YOU CHEATED, YOU MISERABLE LITTLE CUS. YOU TARNISHED MY GOOD NAME. YOU FORCED THAT GIRL TO KILL HERSELF IN ORDER TO WIN THE GAME. WHAT KIND OF MAN DOES THAT? YOU DO OWE ME, BECAUSE THE MATCH HAS BEEN DEEMED A TIE, AND I LOST A LOT OF MONEY. YOU WILL FIGHT IN THE ARENA IN FRONT OF THE POPULUS OF PANTINE TO MAKE THIS RIGHT. AT THIS POINT, I DON'T CARE IF WE LOSE THIS GAME. I WANT YOU *DEAD*."

Ranger looks at me quizzically.

"You don't actually believe him, do you Ranger?"

He looks at him, then back at me, then back at him. "What do you mean, he made her kill herself?"

Timbly giggles. "Ever notice that he was the only one who could speak to the Nightwick?"

"What's a nightwick?"

"The blue creature. He's only showed up in one previous game, before the biggest war this world has ever seen. Anyway, he selects one person to do his bidding during the games. Someone with an evil heart but a kind mask."

Ranger's mouth stays open for a moment as he remembers. It's like watching the underside of a timepiece with clear casing. He remembers that I am the only one that can talk to it, and that I had been talking to it just before Atia died.

"You're lying. Nirue wouldn't kill Atia. There's no way."

"Don't be foolish. He spoke to the Nightwick and stalled you guys just long enough to engage in battle with the other team. He then used the Nightwick to trick Atia into killing herself to ensure that *he* gets out alive, and out of these games."

Ranger shakes his head as if he doesn't know what to think. At the same time, Timbly screams, "Arrest these men! In shackles they came, and in shackles they will go." He grins at me.

I shake my head. "Ranger. Do not listen to this fool. Don't fall—"

"Shut up, Nirue."

"Ranger, you can't possibly!"

"JUST SHUT UP, OKAY?"

I shake my head again as I am fit into my shackles and look to the sky. It's a long walk through the cold rain to the special gate. When we get there, a large wooden box with two barred windows pulls up for Ranger and me. We are thrown inside. Inside is hay covered benches. They are soaked, along with the wooden box we are in.

I'm cold and in custody. My best friend hates me and blames me for the loss of my other best friend. I am still upset about losing her. I am separated from Rust, Sly, Kam, Dalk, Tamra and Faris. Oh, Faris. There's nothing I can do to help her now. Instead of getting credit for winning the games, I am labeled a cheat and now have to fight in some sort of arena. I am only lowering my chances of making it off this world alive by extending my time here. I miss my family more with each passing day. I am trapped.

INTERLUDE 4

THE DOCTOR COMES IN TO find Celia still at Nirue's bedside. She hasn't slept in weeks. Her eyes are red, her body malnourished. *She must really love this one* the doctor thinks to himself. *I have seen mothers mourn for their children before, but most live on a distant hope that everything will be okay. Most people shut it out of their mind and practice positivity. Not this one.*

The hospital room has an air to it, the type of cold and lifeless air that a tomb does. A copy of this week's local real estate magazine sits unfinished on the table near Nirue. It is dog-eared at the countryside section.

"What news do you have for me doctor?" Celia says through sniffles.

"I'm afraid it's not good. We should wait until your husband arrives."

She waves a dismissing hand while blowing her nose. Through tear filled eyes she says, "It's no bother. He has to work to pay for all of this. It's just me today."

"Well, as advanced as modern medicine is, the truth is that . . . Well, this is hard for me to say. The truth is we know relatively nothing about comas. What we do know is that your son is as deep as they get. Even if he does come back, there's no guarantee he wouldn't be a vegetable."

Celia begins to sob through choked coughing. "So what, doctor. Do you want me to just let my son die?" Her words are almost inaudible, but he has seen this enough to understand what she meant. "Well, that also means he could wake up tonight and be perfectly fine. It just means that we don't know."

She continues to cry. She grabs for her son's hand and interlocks her fingers with his. She begins to place the back of her palm on his cheek. For a moment, it seems that she may smile. But more tears drop onto her son's arm. "Thank you, doctor. Is there anything else?"

"No ma'am. We will keep him on life support as long as you wish, and your insurance continues to pay." Celia cringes but hides it well. The doctor knows not only is she battling the emotion of possibly losing her son, she is also dealing with an adjuster on a phone thousands of miles away trying to convince her to pull the plug. *I pity this woman so*, the doctor thinks to himself.

"I will be in next week to check on you. Please do not hesitate to call me at any time. Here is my cell." She grabs the card and wipes her nose. "Thank you, doctor. I really appreciate it."

The doctor quietly slips out of the room. Celia sits on the edge of her son's bed, holding his cold hand between hers. She pets it and begins his favorite lullaby. The same one she would sing when he would climb into her bed because of nightmares. Through tears she sings:

"I know why you're crying. I know why you're blue. Someone stole your kitty-car, away. Time to go to sleep now, little one you've had a busy day."

CHAPTER FORTY

*Bright eyes and blood in the cheeks. That
one looked healthy. They all do on day one.
Something always comes up.*

Bertram after his third unsuccessful sherpa

THE RIDE DOWN THE MOUNTAIN is painfully slow. I hear one of
the drivers of our wood carriage say something about the revolt and how
it ruined part of the city. The other comments, but I cannot hear what he
says. Ranger won't talk to me no matter how many times I try.

If our friendship is that brittle then maybe I should keep him at arm's
length anyway. How could he possibly believe Timbly? I mean, Timbly,
of all people. Where does Timbly even get this information from? Is that
what the Nightwick meant when it said that it had only just begun?

Either way, I move my mind into self-preservation mode. At this point
I don't know who I can trust. I just have to get out of here alive.

The wind bites at my soaked clothes causing me to shake. I try to warm
my body with my hands but it is difficult through the shackles. The further
down the mountain we get, the warmer it becomes. I fall asleep for a few
hours.

When I wake I can smell the ocean. The air is much more humid down here. I can hear the screech of seagulls and the busyness of a crowded city. My clothes are damp and I am still cold, but no longer shivering.

We pull up to the city gates and are allowed entry. As we proceed through the town people take notice of who's in the box. I hear shouting and mass movement.

"Move out the way peasants," one of the drivers yell.

People throw fruit and rocks at our carriage. Some people even shake the box. Ranger is fully aware of the situation but still refrains from speaking to me. A man with rotted teeth grabs onto the bars and yells at me with putrid breath, "Cost me a'lot of money ya did!" He is pushed out of the way and another takes his place. "How much is the counsel payin' ya? I'll slit your throat for this!" Counsel?

City guards clear a path and beat people off of the box, but the displeasure of the crowd is gaining momentum. Shouts of "Bastards" and "Cheaters" ring through the streets.

This is getting out of control. Young boys hop off roofs and dirty women with dirty hand baskets stop to watch the procession. Finally, the carriage stops. Ranger looks out his window and adjusts himself. He looks uncomfortable.

"Move out the way!" A driver yells.

"Why don't you make us?" Someone shouts from a place ahead of our carriage.

"Guards! GUARDS!" the drivers yell. A procession of men clad in blue and white uniforms with gold helmets and long spears jog down the streets that lead to the main square in which our carriage rests.

"What's the meaning of this?" The commander yells to our drivers.

"They won't let us through. Angry at this lot for throwing the games." He gestures a thumb backward toward us. The commander takes a peek inside. "I'll be damned. If it ain't the Nightwick's puppet and the hopeless romantic."

"Yup, that'd be them."

"Where are you taking them?"

"Timbly's dungeon."

The commander raises an eyebrow to that. "And what would they be doing in there? Heard they have to fight in the arena."

The driver simply shrugs. "Just followin' ord—" before he could finish, a throwing knife hits him in the juggler. He staggers, grabbing at his neck as blood pools onto his robes.

Chaos ensues.

Market tables are overturned. Fruit and food and baked goods fly into the street. The crowd attacks the City Guard with fury, trying to get to us. Are we really responsible for all of this?

I watch as the City Guard slay the attackers with ease. They are far better trained and far better equipped. One of their spears has to be worth twenty of the citizens' broomstick handles or shovels. Only a lucky few have swords, but it is obvious they don't know what to do with them. Blood covers everything: the benches, the canopies, the outside of our wooden box, the horses in front of us, the blue and white uniforms of the guards, the cobblestone streets.

The more blood that is spilled, the more angry the mob becomes. The guards are becoming overwhelmed. They form a protective circle around our box. Ranger and I must look nervous. If they manage to kill the watch, Ranger and I don't stand a chance.

The commander yells at someone to drive the horses, and to form a spearhead in front of the carriage. Slowly, we begin to move. Pots and barrels smash into the frame. One barrel is so heavy it cracks the side of our box, revealing daylight and more bloodshed.

"MOVE!" the commander screams. Our pace hastens until finally, we break through. "Everybody on," the commander booms. We are now at a full gallop with about twenty guards hanging off the sides of the box, spearing would be pursuers as we ride.

When we reach Timbly's castle we are allowed immediate entry through the main gate, and are taken to the dungeon. We descend down cold stone steps five or six stories below sea level. I can't remember exactly because I lost count.

When we get to the bottom, we are made to sit and have our hands shackled above our heads. There are others here, though, long dead, save one. The only one alive is sleeping at the moment. The guards leave as soon as we are chained. As a rat scurries across the floor it pauses, momentarily, as if it knows me. I make eye contact with it. It holds my gaze for a moment, then wanders off, food in its tiny hands.

The only light comes from six holes of missing bricks in this narrow tower. In the center of the room is a cylinder support structure made of stone that holds up the roof. Buttresses stem from it to the surrounding circular wall. It's a cylinder within a cylinder. I cannot see much around the left and the right of it, and cannot see anything on the other side.

I am cold, hungry and helpless. My heart hasn't ached this bad in a long time. In fact, I can't remember ever feeling this sad. I thought things were going to get better once we got Atia back. I thought everything was going to be okay, and that I had finally found that lucky break I so desperately needed. It appeared all would be well. But now, everything has changed.

I no longer feel the ease of thinking positive. It's a struggle to even think. I no longer live in the moment. I live in the past, regretting things I've said and moves I've made. I live in the future—in a constant cycle of irrational thoughts that produce nothing more than angst and even more irrational emotional responses. I wish I knew that everything was going to be okay, that I could just talk to Faris again, or that Ranger would believe me. I wish I could hug my mother and tell her I'm fighting for her, and feel the warmth that only a mother's hug can give.

If something could just reassure me to hang in there and fight the good fight, I would. But right now, I struggle. I struggle to want to do anything except sleep—for sleep is my only relief. I struggle to find a hope in anything. I struggle to follow my mind and not my heart. When my heart drums at me and tears a hole in my spirit, it's the only thing on my mind. I tell myself, *"Just drop it, Nirue. Drop everything. Forget it all and move on. You have two choices: Replay things in your head, and play out scenarios that will probably never come to fruition, or forget all of it and just live."*

But that doesn't work. The more I tell myself to not think about something, the more I think about it. The more cognizant I become of that cycle, the harder it is to break, for I find myself constantly wondering if my current thoughts are nothing more than product of this loop, which circles me back to thinking of this loop itself.

I haven't felt this bad in a long time, and now I have nothing to do except sit here and dwell on it. I just want to wake up from this nightmare. I slowly fall asleep in a damp, dark and hopeless dungeon with my arms above my head, and tears running down my cheeks.

* * *

When I wake I cannot see anything. It takes my eyes thirty or so minutes to fully adjust. I pick up faint moonlight shining through a hole on the other side of the cylinder. My eyes are crusty.

There's nothing to eat and nothing to drink. I have to pee but there's no way for me to take off my pants. It smells like a bathroom. I doubt this place has been cleaned in years, if ever.

There's no sound except the soft breathing of Ranger and the scurrying of rats. The man on the other side looks emaciated. Every bone in his body is clearly defined and available for inspection.

"Ranger," I whisper. Nothing. "Ranger," I say a little louder. He looks up at me, blinks a few times, then closes his eyes.

I try to stand but the shackles will only let me get to a chair shaped position. I sit down and try to worm out of my pants to pee. I can't. I hold it as long as I can until I let it go. What a demoralizing feeling. I stay awake until my pants are dry again, then I fall back asleep.

A conversation quickly stirs me awake. Ranger and the skinny guy are talking about sheep. I guess the guy was a shepherd and spent most of his time roaming the hills on the border between the two nations. He tells a story about killing a mountain lion with a wooden staff. It's pretty hard to believe.

"How long have you been in here?" I ask.

He tells me that he's only been in here a week. He was given water the first two days and then Timbly had him cut off.

"Truth is, I will probably die in here in the next day or so." He looks up at one of the holes in the structure and takes a deep breath as sunlight shines on his face. How can one in such dire circumstances be so calm?

Ranger still won't talk to me. I get the feeling that he doesn't know what to believe. I imagine he is overcome with the grief of Atia's death. I hope that deep down, he does believe me.

*　　*　　*

Day three is worse than day two. By now, Ranger and I have relieved ourselves in every way possible. My skin hurts in places it shouldn't. The guards have brought us water, but nothing else. If my dominus were someone else, I would be wondering why he would be starving the people that are fighting for his name and his country, but I have Timbly.

I'm so hungry that I smash a rat with my heel and drag it to my body to eat. I grab it by the tail with my toes, knowing the only way I will be able to eat it is raw. When I lift my leg to my mouth all I can smell is my own excrements. I can't bring myself to eat the rat.

"Couldn't do it either," the old man says. His grey beard and deep set eyes make him look more like an emaciated philosopher than shepherd. "Figure I'll just die with dignity before stooping so low. They're gonna kill me anyway, right? So why live like an animal on my way out. That's my thinking at least." I make eye contact with him and then look down.

"Boy. Listen to me now, okay? An old man am I, and many years have I seen with these eyes. There are times in life where you must endure pain. You endure pain to learn. Learn what pleasure cannot teach. You see, pleasure does not teach us anything good. It teaches us how to relax. How to let our guard down. It teaches us how to become full of ourselves and self-centered. It teaches us how to hate. But pain—that's a different animal. The type of pain that you are feeling now, from whatever happened outside of these walls, I can relate to. I lost everything too, you know. Pain teaches us what to avoid and what to pursue. I can't begin to tell you how much I miss my daughters." He begins to cry. "I have four of them you know. But you know what bed my soul sleeps in at night?"

"I do— I don't even know what to say."

"That's okay. You're young. I believe that I must go through all of this so that they might live. That somehow, someway, I am taking a burden off of their shoulders. Surely once they hear of my death, they will cry and take comfort in their husbands. And that pain will teach them something. But, this pain—what you and I are going through, this is for the upper echelon of tough people. There's a reason we are here."

"But why me? Why you? How does that make sense—that you should rot in this cell so that someone else has an easier life?"

He shakes his head. "It's so much more than that boy. This life we live .. . This is a gift. When is it ever perfect?" He chuckles to himself. "Think on all of the ways your life could be worse, chained or not. Sure, some famous noble or prince with good looks and money might come to mind. But why compare yourself to them? There is no justice in that. Contentment is a learned trait, good man. Once you learn contentment, you realize this life is a gift, but a gift not meant for you."

He begins to cough violently. This spell lasts thirty seconds or so, then another thirty to catch his breath, before he looks up and says, "Live. Live, boy. Live like you won't walk out of that arena. If you do, live like you won't make it to wherever you're from. Live like you are on the wings of a golden eagle to unexplored lands full of insurmountable adventure. Live like you have nothing to lose. Live like you have everything to gain. Live, so that when people say your name, they tell your death story as one of resilience and honor and courage. Live, so that others might live too."

With that, he has another coughing episode and then hangs his head. Inspired, I sit quietly and watch his lifeless body hang. I know I do not have to say anything. I know that he is dead, and that I must live.

CHAPTER FORTY-ONE

Have faith, oh my soul. Just have faith.

Scratched into the wall next to Nirue

WEAKENED, I NO LONGER HAVE the strength to hold my arms up. My wrists are red and raw, purple rings where hair and strong flesh once was. I have lost all track of time. I remember talking to the old man, but I'm not sure how long ago that was.

The guard door opens. Because it is night, I cannot make out the figure. I don't hear the collision of metal on metal like I normally do when the knights come to bring us water. Ranger is in bad shape. From a beam of moonlight, I can see that he is struggling to stay alive. "Hang in there buddy," I tell him. He barely has the energy to look at me. His lips are swollen and cracked.

In the midst of fading in and out of consciousness, a hand is placed over my mouth. I shake for a moment, until I realize that it is Doctore. He has a single finger over his lips. Two of the men with Doctore begin to pull off my pants. I squirm, looking to Doctore for help.

He whispers, "This is no way to live. Let them clean you." I reluctantly oblige. It is an odd feeling, having another man wipe my own arse like my mother used to. Ranger doesn't even struggle. Doctore gives us a hot meal and fresh clothes that are disguised as rags. Ranger and I eat the entire plate and want more, but Doctore makes us to wait to eat the second serving. "Let your body adjust."

I immediately feel better. It's as if Doctore prepared a meal with all the exact nutrients my body had been lacking.

"You have been here for over a week. Did you know that?" Way off. "Timbly is an underhanded diabolical schemer. He bet all his money on the other side."

"I don't understand, doesn't he want the trade ports?"

"No, because he can bet his entire fortune on you losing and gain more than he ever would in *fifty* years of trade, let alone seven. Trust me, we have been doing our best to keep you alive. The water was provided by us. The would-be assassins sent to stab you before tomorrow morning have been . . . taken care of. Now, on to another issue. Ranger. RANGER," he says with a louder whisper.

He looks up at Doctore. "Do not be a fool. Nirue had no hand in Atia's death. Do not let your love blind you of the only friend you have in this world." Ranger begins to reply but Doctore waves a hand, "We do not have time for this! Just trust *me*, okay? Nirue is on your side, and you would be wise to realize what you have in him."

Ranger looks at me with weepy eyes. I cannot begin to explain how good that feels. Not that Ranger is sad, but that I will have him back. I don't know if it's the food, the assistance by Doctore or getting my friend back, but I am feeling a large sense of relief, as if my worries have evaporated out of my chest.

"Listen closely, for I must leave. I have arranged for your weapons to be given to you at the gate. Look for the guard with the red mask. Now, phase one is a—what do you call them? Jboynei?"

"But, I thought you can't kill them? Trust me, I have tried," I say.

"We are not in Hardrain and the Keeper is alive. That sorcerer that captured you also has something to do with it. All I know is that it *can* be killed. But it will be starving, and it will have a weapon."

Ranger and I exchange worried looks. "If you survive that phase, Timbly will be forced to put you on public display and treat you right. If the other team's players defeat whatever they face, and trust me—it won't be a Jboynei, then you will fight two on two in front of all of Pantine. With that, I leave you men. Good luck."

"Doctore," he turns and looks at me. "Thank you." He holds my gaze, nods his head, and disappears into the darkness.

Ranger and I sit in silence for some time before he says anything. Still weepy, he says, "Nirue . . . I was a fool, overcome with grief and anger—I—I didn't know what to do and when I heard what Timbly—" I cut him off.

"Ranger. You don't have to explain yourself. I forgive you, brother. I would never hold that against you. I'm just glad you came around before our bout with friendly out there tomorrow." He raises his head to the ceiling and laughs for the first time since Atia died. That makes me smile to the point of laughter myself.

We talk for a few hours about life and how blessed we are despite our circumstances. I can't tell whether Ranger just wants us to keep a positive attitude or if he really believes it. Then, as the sun peaks through the missing bricks, we turn our conversation into strategy. Ranger and I devise a plan.

CHAPTER FORTY-TWO

When things snowball bad, fix your situation. When things snowball good, do everything you can to keep the momentum. The more you do so, the more opportunities will present themselves.

Trip

"GET UP," ONE OF THE guards say while kicking me in the rib.

"The spit was that for, scramp?" He laughs while undoing my chains.

My wrists feel much better without the shackles. I rub them tenderly, pronating and supinating as if they are new attachments to my body. I can feel the blood immediately rushing to my fingers. My hands feel swollen.

I notice Ranger doing much of the same thing. We are not given food or water. That doesn't matter because Doctore left us with some provisions last night. The| walk up is tumultuous. My body feels weak and feeble. Maybe I just need to get the blood flowing.

By the time I get to the top I am tired. I must be low on energy. The sun reflecting off of the hot street causes me to shade my eyes. We are lead out of the tower door and through a city block for a few hundred yards. They gave us blankets and cloaks to wear as disguises. The crowd sees us but pays us no mind. Everyone seems to be in a rush somewhere. It's not until I see the signs that I realize they are going to watch us fight.

We continue through the city toward a square shaped arena. This thing must hold fifty-thousand people.

I begin to get a much needed rush of adrenaline. The blood in Ranger's face tells me that he did too. An old toothless man grabs me by the arm and says, "I need ya out there today! Got lots of money on you." I shake him off and continue following the guards. How did he recognize me?

When we get to the arena, thousands of people are pouring into entrances evenly placed every fifty yards or so. There is much pushing and shoving to get in and get a good seat. The building itself is five stories high.

The air smells of the ocean. A soft breeze licks my hair as I close my eyes and take in a deep breath. The flow feels good on my beard. The temperature is cool in the shadows and slightly warm in the sun. We are lead through long archways into a mountain that part of the arena is built into. We traverse through the mountain tunnels for three to five minutes, before our path turns back toward the arena. The main tunnel from the mountain to the arena is more like a covered bridge. I feel anxious yet alive, constricted yet free. My breath is quick, my senses picking up pieces of information on my journey to the arena.

The walkway is illuminated by evenly spaced holes, allowing sunlight to reflect off of the multi-colored seashells. The predominant colors are blue and coral red with a hint of green and purple with white splash. I look out one of the windows to the right. I take in another deep breath and watch the surf crash one last time. Once through the bridge, we follow a path that leads underground.

Then, we follow more tunnels lit by torches. These series of passages lead us down, then up until we are in the armory. The guards leave us with two other guards, standing at the gate that leads to the sandy arena floor. Even from where I am at, I can smell the ocean. The guard with the red mask does not turn around.

The crowd is loud and boisterous, until someone with an amplified voice begins to quiet them down.

"Citizens!" Sounds like the mage that captured me.

"Today we watch history!" The crowd cheers. "Never before have the games come down to a sudden death. What a treat for us to have the first ever sudden death match, right before our very eyes! Your representative, Lord Timbly, has been so kind to let us use his arena." Through the gate I see Timbly rotate his hand and bow to the crowd, from a box sectioned off for royalty. The crowd, surprisingly, cheers for him. They don't know who he really is.

"Now, this is your last opportunity to wager your pocket book for Nirue and Ranger, or for the dreaded Jboynei!" Hoots and hollers follow. He continues with his speech, telling them where to place wagers, to not interfere or punishment of death, among other house-keeping matters.

"Three minutes out. Go grab their weapons," the red masked guard says to the black masked guard. He nods his head and runs downstairs. Ranger's breath begins to hasten. "Stay here," the red guard commands. He disappears into a small door to the right of Ranger and me.

Ranger and I stand next to each other, looking through the spacing in the steel gate that leads to the arena. Sunlight pours onto the sand, leaving no shadows or dark areas. A hundred and fifty yards away a Jboynei's giant hands rattle the doors of his gate. I can hear his screams despite our distance and the crowd noise. This time, I do not fear, I just focus.

Ranger and I stay perfectly still—both thinking of how to execute our plan. No shaking out of our muscles or jumping up and down—just stoic faces staring at our enemy. There is no pump up speech or last words. We both know it's either us, or the Jboynei. The red guard reappears with *Evergold* and *Darkwater*. Ranger examines his blade and I my bow. Everything seems to be in working order.

Another minute or so of speech passes until the mage says, "Pantine— are you ready for *SUDDEN DEATH*?"

The crowd screams. Food and knives are thrown into the arena. Fights break out and mothers cover the eyes of their young ones. I take a deep breath and drop into my place. I look at Ranger who looks back at me. We both nod and then look forward. We must be quick. If we fail at our plan, we will surely die. I feel a bond between Ranger and me. I trust him with my life.

My eyes are fixed on the gate. The moment it drops I must move. Sweat drops drown my brow. My hands shake in anticipation. The crowd noise is drowned out by my own thoughts. All I can hear is my own breath.

DROP

A clank and the gate drops. The Jboynei bursts out of his tunnel. My first move is a left jump, directly behind Ranger. The sunlight momentarily blinds me. Ranger is in a dead sprint toward the Jboynei, the Jboynei in a dead sprint at us. I am sprinting too, just slightly bent over, hiding behind Ranger's big frame. We are a hundred yards or so from the Jboynei. "NOT YET!" Ranger screams over his shoulder.

Ranger kicks up small plumes of dust as he runs. I do the same. All I can see is Ranger, *Darkwater,* and the ground a few yards ahead of me. We continue to gain speed and momentum.

"HOOOOLD!" Ranger screams. My tunnel vision narrows and I become more laced with adrenaline. This is it. We are almost there.

"HOOOOLD!" he screams again as we kick up dust in a sprint right at our enemy. We've got to be close.

"NOOWWWW!" He bellows. In one movement, Ranger jump-stops and spreads his legs. Also in one movement, I drop into a double knee slide while loading *Evergold.* I faintly hear the creature scream. While sliding, I drop backward as far as my body will go, so that I can clear just underneath Ranger's groin. My head scrapes against the ground.

I continue my focus directly above me. I see the Jboynei's outstretched neck, open mouth and outstretched arms airborne at Ranger. I shoot an arrow through the bottom of its head so that its lower jaw sticks to its upper jaw for that crucial moment. My momentum carries me underneath the creature. In the same moment, Ranger sidesteps the creature and slices its head off, taking part of its left hand with it. The body immediately drops and begins to writhe, fingers sporadically flickering, left leg uncontrollably flopping. I look up at Ranger, who is only a shadow because of the white sun directly behind him. All of a sudden, my tunnel vision fades as the crowd erupts. I've never heard so much screaming in my lifetime. We did it. Our plan actually worked.

We wipe the blood from our faces and exchange glances. I see a smile tiptoe onto his face. I nod and we raise our weapons in triumph. The crowd sounds like a blended tidal wave of sound. Some patrons are hugging and falling down stairs, others are cheering and crying and some are filing out with their heads down. I do a full circle acknowledgement of the crowd with my weapon raised. Timbly's eyes tell me how he truly feels. He feigns happiness with a half-hearted clap, then motions a finger for me to join him in his box.

I turn my face and look into the distant ocean beyond the arena before the guards grab me by the arms.

CHAPTER FORTY-THREE

Politics are a funny thing. Outside looking in, it appears a mindless squabble. Inside looking out, you wonder how the world goes on without tracking every subtlety.

David Mandrian, the last great King of Pantine

WE ARE ESCORTED BY ARMED guards through the gate where the Jboynei entered, down a passageway, then back up to a stone staircase. Light reflects through windows onto the steps. We continue upward until we are in Timbly's three-tiered box.

He doesn't even pretend to be happy to see us. Accompanying him is the mage that captured me outside of the jumpkey, and another man I have not seen. He is garbed in a blue cloak with soft white moons. His skin is wrinkled and he smokes something foul smelling from a long wooden pipe. Another man, presumably his mage, sits next to him.

Ranger and I stand awkwardly, saying nothing and avoiding eye contact with the room. The crowd continues to cheer for us. Timbly feigns a demonstration of worship. He directs us to the edge of the box and urges us to bow for the crowd. We do. The crowd cheers again.

We are directed to two seats directly behind Timbly, the wrinkled man and the two mages. It is in that moment I notice Doctore sitting on a bench on the left side of the room. He smiles and winks at us. I smile back, but quickly hide it as I notice the pipe-smoker looking at us. To save face, I introduce myself. "The name's Nirue Nyles."

I extend my hand. He looks up at me with cold and distant eyes, then blows a puff of smoke. "I know who you are, Mister Nyles." He then returns to his pipe and stares out into the arena.

Doctore stands and says, "Nirue, that is Dorian. He is what Timbly is to the other half of the country." No response from Dorian or his mage. Doctore quickly sits down.

The spokesman who introduced us earlier walks to the center of the arena after the Jboynei's body had been cleared. "Ladies and gentleman, was that not an exciting first match!?" The crowd yells at the speaker to hurry up. More people file in to fill the space created by those who lost money on the first match. I surmise it is mostly those people trying to win their money back, but there is no way to know for sure.

"Now comes the most feared fighter in all of Pantine. He drowns would be challengers in darkness, and carries an undefeated record in the arena! Ladies and gentleman, Angor!"

The crowd cheers. The black knight from the arena steps onto the sands. He is garbed in a dark mask that looks like the clown from the picture in the healing ward of Timbly's castle, except, instead of colors on his face, all of the features are painted black on a tan base. "Because his teammates from the arena have become unexpectedly *ill*, we have brought another man to join him in this battle!" Ranger looks at me and rolls his eyes. I can't help but let out a little laugh. No one responds.

"You may have heard of this man. Some know him as '*OLD RED*'!" No rise from the crowd. The announcer looks around, arms raised, waiting for a response. He continues, "For those of you who don't know, Old Red is the greatest short-sword fighter to ever live! Indeed, he trained Angor to become the champion he is!" A man with a youthful gait jogs into the arena to meet Angor. He also dons a sinister clown helmet, although, unlike Angor, his features emphasize blood. Blood running from the ears. Blood running from the eyes. Blood from the nose and mouth. He doesn't bother waiving to the crowd.

Old Red is dead. Old Red lives only in his head. Isn't that what Sly said?

"For such fighters as these, we had no choice but to bring in the most sinister challenger we could find. I bring you, *JORRACCUS!*"

The crowd screams and jumps up and down. The spokesman runs to the side of the arena as quickly as he can. He is pulled into the crowd by two ropes and strong men.

A creature with an elongated head and six arms enters the arena. He has five long swords and a giant shield held by his upper left arm. He pounds his chest and lets out a scream of which I have never heard. He runs at the two men, who calmly separate in circled arc.

The speed, precision and fluidity of Angor and Old Red is mystifying. They dodge and parry thrusts while hardly looking at the creature. They sidestep his attacks without breaking a sweat. They toy with this thing as if this fight has been rehearsed. It actually looks fake. I hear muffled words coming from the box. The mage next to Dorian speaks underneath his hood.

Angor turns his back on the creature and parries his attacks while holding a fist to the crowd. In angst, the crowd begins to yell at him to turn around. Angry, Jorraccus begins to swing harder, then harder. He wants to cut them in half.

Then it happens. In six fluid motions, like a hummingbird darting from flower to flower, they completely disarm the creature—shield and all. Befuddled, Jorraccus walks slowly backward. Even a creature so fowl and so big looks pitiful in the moments before his death. I almost feel bad for it.

Angor and Old Red taunt the crowd and back Jorraccus up against a wall. They cut off his hands first. Jorraccus attempts a kick and has his foot sliced off by Red. They cut him open so that he can bleed without dying. Jorraccus screams in a voice not of this world. It cannot hold itself up. It cannot fight any longer, because it has lost too much blood. Angor and

Red show him no mercy. Expressionless, they watch him bleed. Only when they think he is on the verge of death do they plunge one more sword into his shoulder. The creature begins to cry as it takes its last breath.

Angor and Red cut off his head and hold it up to the crowd. They cheer, but not like they did for us. The crowd appears more disgusted than anything. Angor rips the bowels and intestine from Jorraccus. He cuts out the heart and walks to the box where we all sit.

He rips off his mask to reveal his sharp teeth and black eyes, staring at Ranger and I with purposeful hate. He takes a bite of the bleeding heart. His eyes never leave us while he devours the entire thing. Red stands stoic and never removes his mask. Grey clouds fill the sky and it begins to rain. The crowd slowly clears out.

"Phase two," Timbly says calmly, looking at Doctore. Doctore tries to not act worried, but shakes his head ever so subtly. I hope he doesn't mean phase two in the dungeon. Doctore looks at me and says, "Let's go men."

CHAPTER FORTY-FOUR

*Tell me, can anything be defeated if you have made up
in your mind that it cannot?*

Trip

DORIAN SMILES UNDER HIS HOOD. This doesn't make sense. He
is happy about their win too? That means he and Timbly are both betting
on Angor and Red. And since they won so convincingly, won't the rest of
the crowd?

"Impressive victory, I must say," Timbly says with a giggle.

"Agreed. The gods have blessed me with talented fighters. I lucked out
getting Old Red as a substitute. Who would have thought?" jests Dorian
with a rough voice through pipe smoke.

Timbly laughs. "I swear. They are so good I bet they could have won
with their eyes closed." He and Dorian both share in a laugh.

"Well, why don't we get our 'champions' to their quarters for a while.
They will need their two weeks of training before the title fight." I hate the
way he said champions with four fingers.

Doctore offers, "I'll take Nirue and Ranger to their quarters, if it suits
you Timbly." He looks at Doctore with curiosity. Doctore, feeling the need

to justify himself says, "I don't think it would be good for them to be in tight quarters with Red and Angor, especially not while their blood is still hot."

Still curious, Timbly shrugs and dismisses us with a wave. "Go. Take these mutts to their pen. It pains me that we must pretend to like them for such a long time."

"It is an investment m'Lord. If they were in the dungeons rather than the nice quarters, people would ask questions."

"Of course, of course."

"Right. I will see you in the morning, your grace." With that, Doctore bows and ushers us down the steps. Faint light shines through the clouds and into the windows of the stone staircase. It smells like a monsoon in the desert. Through one of the windows I see people using capes and blankets as umbrellas.

Once at the bottom of the stairs, we take a different route from the one we came. We make a quick left through more stone walkways and arches. The grey stone is cold. "Want the long and dry way or wet and direct route?" Doctore asks.

"Wet and direct. Let's just get there," I offer. Doctore looks to Ranger who agrees. He takes us out wooden doors and down a stone staircase. Thunder booms over the arena. The rain comes down heavy. I flip up my hood. The dirt has quickly turned to mud. We trek across an orchard of orange trees that is half grass and half mud. In the distance is a small but distinct castle, connected to a main arm of the castle by a covered walkway. I pick an orange on the way there.

We move at a fast pace as the storm intensifies. In about five minutes we reach our destination. We walk up another stone staircase to wooden doors with iron edging. Doctore fumbles with a large chain of brass keys. He opens the door for us.

Before us is a spacious common area with plush couches and nice art hanging over an unlit fireplace. To the right and left of the fireplace are two windows with a view of a private beach. Creeping vines have grown their way just inside the windows.

To the right of the common area is a kitchen with the cabinets open, showcasing stocked-full supplies. Just inside the door, two staircases frame the room.

"You two can choose rooms. Both are the same. You share a wall up top there," he says, pointing a finger at the ceiling. "Everything you need will be in here. This is a private wing Timbly saves for his most important guests. Surely the crowds will be out to watch you from the groves. It's good. Show them love. Wave to them and smile."

"How long are we here for?" Ranger asks.

"Two weeks. But you have to stay in here unless you are training. I'm sorry, but Timbly will surely insist, I can guarantee it."

Ranger and I exchange glances. "Maids will bring you hot water in the morning and evenings. If you have any questions, send a hawk to me. But *only* after your evening bath. Got it?"

We both shrug. He shows us the hawk cage and how to properly feed them and send notes without being bit.

"Listen. Whatever is going to happen . . ." his voice trails off. "I don't know what will happen. But I will do my best to ensure you have a fair shake in this." He looks out the window toward the beach, as if scanning it for a potential threat.

"Thank you, Doctore," Ranger and I say at the same time. He nods. "With that, I must leave you. I will be locking the front door behind me. Try to get some rest. I will be here early in the morning. Good work today."

Doctore steps into the rain, closes both doors behind him and locks the door. Ranger and I are left in the entry, dripping wet without the faintest idea of what's going on.

I take off my green cape and hang it from a metal hook protruding from the stone. I shake my head and fling water around like a dog. "Careful . . . you might ruin one of these nice paintings," Ranger says, coming out of a deep thought.

I laugh. "I'm serious Nirue. I know they are owned by Timbly, but it's the art I appreciate. These are originals, I can tell. Anyway, why don't we head upstairs and take that needed bath. Meet back down here for dinner in an hour?"

"Sounds good to me."

In about an hour and a half I meet Ranger downstairs. He has already sparked the fireplace. The room smells like roasted acorns. The sun struggles for attention as ashy skies fling drops of rain on the fading sunset.

"How could you possibly tell that?" I ask Ranger.

"Tell what?"

"That these paintings are original. How could you know?"

"See that one over there? The painting of the ship at sea during a storm?"

"Yeah."

"Same artist. Initials are in the top left. If you feel the ink on the blues in both pictures, they are virtually the same. This artist likes to coat it six to seven times before applying other colors. Now I didn't know that at the time I told you, but there are other clues. Look at how old these frames are. Also, it smells like oil and there are still some bristles stuck inside this canvas here. Must have been a cheap paint brush. Anyway, that's how I know."

"Dang, Ranger, you know your art. I had no idea."

Ranger shrugs it off. "What should we do for dinner?" he asks.

"Well, let's see what we got first. I'm thinking something quick and easy so we can get a full nights rest."

We spend the next hour cooking the easiest meal we could. We found dried pieces of wheat that had been shaped like fishhooks. Ranger gets a pot of water from the well outside, and hangs it over the fireplace. Once boiling, we added the wheat to the water. We drain as much water as we can fifteen minutes later, then ranger adds a quarter block of cheese. I roast bread over the fire. We barely say five words as we devour our cheese-pasta and bread.

We then lie on the sofas with our bellies protruding much larger than normal. We talk about the fight with the Jboynei. Then the fight after. We talk about what happened to Atia's soul after she passed. We concluded that it must have returned to her body before being sent somewhere else for good. Ranger teared up a bit before quickly changing the subject.

We talk until we can't keep our eyes open, then crash. It has been a long couple of months for us.

As I lie awake in my bed the moon shines through a window to the stone floor. I can't help but wonder if this happens to everyone like me. I also wonder if I will make it out of here alive. I have no idea what is to come.

*   *   *

I wake early to a man practicing violin on the private beach. After a few minutes he notices me and picks up his things in a hurry. I try to wave him back, but he moves so fast he doesn't notice.

The sun is back to shining high and white in the sky. The white reflection off of the blue waves create a myriad of colors, but the angle of your vantage point determines what color you see.

I head downstairs once I smell food. Ranger has already cooked up eggs. He dons an apron with a silly cook on the front.

I hear the jangle of keys outside the door. One is inserted and unlocks the door. I don't get the purpose of the lock. I could easily escape out the window. Sero could escape out the window. Well, in fairness, Sero is exceptional.

In walks Doctore. "You boys ready?"

"You've seen us train before Doctore. You know we are ready." He shakes his head. "This is harder than anything you have ever experienced. I have two weeks to get you into fighting shape." Ranger and I exchange glances. "And take off that ridiculous apron! For crying out loud you are going to be fighting for your life!"

I laugh. Ranger turns red and stuffs the apron into a below belly-line cabinet.

"Put on something light."

Ranger and I head outside. Doctore has taken off his shirt and closed his eyes. He is smiling at the sun. His dark skin exaggerates every muscle he has, and he is in good shape. He takes in a deep breath, and says, "follow me." So, we follow. We start off by running around the back of the house and onto the beach. We run from our private beach all the way to the public beach in front of the castle. It had to be at least three miles.

Anyone who has ever run on sand knows how difficult it is. The sand gives where it should support and holds where it should not.

Doctore does not tire—not even for a minute. When we reach solid ground outside of the castle he picks up his pace. We head out of town and down the coastline. Green hills roll into open-faced rock cliffs. After nearly six miles with no breaks, we end up on a cliff. Doctore takes a moment to catch his breath. Ranger and I bend to one knee, completely exhausted. Doctore sits on the cliff with his legs dangling.

"You know this won't be a fair fight, don't you?" Ranger asks Doctore, still gasping for air. Doctore doesn't respond and continues to look into the distance.

"I mean, what's the point of all this? We aren't running a race and those damn mages will just cast their spells on us anyway."

Doctore squints, looking at the waves some two hundred feet below us. "Look at the waves, Ranger. What do you see?"

"I dunno. Waves. In, out, in, out. S'what?"

"You are correct. In much of life there is pattern and consistency."

"So what, you telling us we're doomed? If life is about patterns, that means Timbly and Dorian will follow their same l'il pattern and make us look like fools before that berserker dude eats our hearts."

"It's possible. Might I ask, what happens to these waves if there is an earthquake somewhere out there?" He points to the ocean. Ranger shrugs. He looks to me. "Think a giant wave comes in right?"

"Right-o Nirue, right-o. A wave bigger than you can ever imagine. So big it would sink any of Timbly's ships in an eye blink. In fact, it could sink his entire fleet."

"So?" Ranger asks, finally in stride with his breath.

"What happens if the wind blows across this beach here?"

"I don't know Doctore and I don't get your point."

"His point, Ranger—if I may," I look to Doctore for approval. He nods, now sitting cross-legged. "His point is that it seems like the waves will come in an out the same way and never change, until something unexpected happens and changes them. I think what he is saying is that you never know what will happen with absolute certainty, so we ought to get into the best shape and train as hard as we can in case something falls our way.

Ranger nods his head like he understands. "Right, Doctore?" I ask.

He smiles. "More or less, yes."

We spend the next ten minutes in our own thoughts. The wind is cool up here. It dries the sweat on my body. I replay the fight in my head. So many things could have gone wrong.

Right when I start to feel lethargy kick in, Doctore pops up and yells at us to follow. By now it is mid-afternoon. We follow him through the countryside to a training facility located in the town but outside the castle. Doctore has us eat soup inside bowls made of bread. Ranger and I finish ours in under a minute. "Doctore, we have run at least ten miles by now. I don't know how much more I can take," says Ranger.

"Take? My good boy, we are just getting *started*."

I feel like I could pass out at any moment. My legs ache and stiffen up like I am dying. My eyes fight to stay open. My tiredness is only exacerbated by the food I just devoured.

"Nirue. You are quite skilled in the bow, but there is a chance it will be useless against these two. You need to improve at close combat. Come."

I am ushered into a room of roughly twenty men each holding two sticks.

"I'm going to take your axe from you and give you Atia's daggers. She would want you to have them."

"They are called *Dicers*, Doctore."

"Whatever. Before your battle, you should be able to pick up the apple at the other side of the room, and make it back unscathed. Both you and the apple.

The room is more like a rectangle, decorated like a dojo. The walls have light wood intertwined through a tan screen. The fighters wear masks. They surround me in a circle. Straight ahead are three steps leading to a stage with a cylinder shaped wood structure that holds a single red apple. The steps are as long as the stage itself.

"For now, use these." He hands me two skinny poles, like the pylons that track runners pass. They are brown and have white tape at the bottom for grip. I grab them and begin to walk toward the apple. The men hop up and move toward me. I lower myself in a fighting stance. I scare the most aggressive guy backward. Another man approaches me from the back, so I turn to fight him and block one of his hits. They get closer.

I am now turning every couple of seconds, trying to anticipate every move. One sneaks in a hit to my neck. Then another to my leg. Then another to my forehead. Before I know it, I am covering my head on the wooden floor, getting pummeled by sticks.

"Again." Doctore hollers.

Again I try, but I am worse. My fatigue is getting the better of me. "Do you think I feel sorry for you, Nirue? Do you think the heart-eater is going to feel bad for you because you are *tired*? AGAIN!"

That pisses me off. I go on the offensive. Only so many of them can hit me at once. Upper right, upper left, duck, low kick, upward spinning arc—a bludgeon to my back. I collapse to the ground. "AGAIN!"

The more I try the more I get beat up. These men are not taking it easy on me. They hit me, and they hit me hard. My arms feel like dessert contents and my vision is blurred. A hit to my face causes my upper lip to bleed and swell. A hit to my temple causes my vision to go black. The soft sound of my beating heart pulses throughout my skull.

"AGAIN!" Doctore screams.

CHAPTER FORTY-FIVE

Do something hard. Do something you don't want to do. Figure out what it is you loathe, then do it.

Doctore

WHEN I GET BACK TO my room, I close my eyes and begin to control my breathing. I spend five minutes visualizing getting the apple unscathed. I am torn from my meditation by a horn.

I hear the movement of branches in a tree outside my window. The tree is roughly fifteen feet from my window and about five feet below my story.

I quietly get up to grab *Evergold*. I nearly collapse when I try to stand. My legs have never hurt this bad before.

"Nirue," someone says in a hushed voice. "Nirue, wake up."

I load and creep toward the window, doing my best to just stay vertical. "Nirue . . . Nirue, wake up! Nirue!" The whispers are louder.

"What!" I say without whispering. "Who's out there?"

"Just look outside scramp." I know that voice. I drop my weapon and peer out my window to see the beautiful brown locks of Faris. I smile so big my lips crack. She smiles back at me from the branch. I don't know what to say. Is it wrong to have been so preoccupied that I haven't thought much about her?

"I've missed you," she says without losing her smile. She looks so beautiful. The moon cascades the perfect amount of shadows to outline the symmetrical nature of her face. It's just now that I realize I have never seen her dressed up.

"I've missed you too. I was so worried about you after the games. Especially once we became separated." Liar.

She smiles, eyes lost in distant thought. The truth is, I have missed her. I had just blocked her from my mind because I am tired of being hurt. But this is making me realize that, sometimes, you should expose yourself. Sometimes it's worth it to try and love, even if it means heartache in the end.

"Can I come in?"

"No." She stares at me blankly. "Of course you can," I laugh. "But how are you going to get in?"

"Give me a minute," she says while climbing down the tree. "Move away from the window."

A rope with an enlarged fishing hook enters my room. It hits the floor and drags until it catches on the windowsill. I peer into the hallway to see if the noise woke Ranger. No movement. "Is it secured?"

I move the hook around. The pressure applied to the stone seems appropriate, and I think the stone is strong enough to hold her weight. I place my hands near it just in case. "Good to go."

Faris bounds up the rope much faster than I would have expected, although I have always underestimated her. She drops the rope and runs to me, cuddling into my chest, head nuzzled under my chin. After a minute she senses my legs are about to give out on me. "Here, let's get you on the bed."

I sit down on the edge of the bed, back resting against the stone wall. She sits next to me. "First day of training that hard?" I nod my head.

"Harder than anything I have ever done. Training wise, that is."

"I'm sorry. It will be worth it in the end, though." She begins to rub my legs. I close my eyes, taking in every stroke. "Rumor has it the other team is practicing with live combat. I'm so worried for you Nirue."

With my eyes closed I respond, "You don't need to worry about me. Whatever happens, happens."

"But that's a coward's way out. Do you not care about being alive? Do you not care about anything in this world?"

"Of course I do. I care about you. I care about Ranger. In a very odd way, I care about Bertram too."

"Bertram?"

"Right. Bertram is err. He's this older guy." She raises her eyebrows in hesitant confusion. "You could say he's like a father figure to me."

"Oh. Okay. Well, I'm just glad I got to see you. Even if it's for a little bit." She hugs my midsection and rests her head on my shoulder. We talk for another five minutes before falling asleep in the same position.

We wake up to the clang of a large key ring. Doctore is here earlier than expected. Faris kisses me goodbye and escapes out the window. I throw the hook down to her and walk downstairs.

Doctore rests comfortably on the couch, dirty boots kicked up on the table. Ranger rubs the sleep out of his eyes on the way downstairs. "What's on the agenda today?" I ask.

Doctore smiles. "Same thing as yesterday, except you'll be carrying these." He stands up and grabs two empty sacs. He throws them to us. Noticing our confusion, he says, "You'll fill those up with sand from the beach. You have five minutes to eat. See you on the beach in five."

*   *   *

The day drags on forever. Nobody can possibly run a marathon two days in a row. Well, nobody that hasn't spent hundreds of hours training for it. We end up collapsing more times than we wish. When it becomes apparent we won't make it all the way, Doctore pushes us harder—sometimes using the whip.

The fighting is harder than yesterday. My exhaustion gets the better of me. I'm not even close to getting the apple, and truth be told, I am worried I never will be. These men are very skilled fighters and would give me a challenging time one on one. Doctore tells me that I need to train this fatigued. That I will feel like a lion in battle with the proper rest. That training when I am this tired will make me learn defenses the fastest. The idea is that because I have to protect myself and because I am tired it requires more energy and focus to properly block. If it takes more energy to block, I am more likely to memorize it in my muscle groups. The truth is, I just feel as though they are practicing on me. I do get better at fighting by day seven. I almost make it to the stage unscathed. Their moves appear more pattern-like to me, and I am learning the pattern.

The days become longer and my body more tired. After the first week of training, I feel worse than I ever have. I feel drained both mentally and physically, but I know I must stay strong. Faris continues to visit. I fall asleep within five minutes almost most every time she visits. I think she understands, but sometimes I feel like I am letting her down. I simply can't help it.

There is no weekend from our training. Ranger and I train seven days in a row, starting the day after round one. At the start of week two, Doctore arrives unnaturally early. He looks somber and tells us we are taking a different running route. We can tell something is up. I don't even try to hide Faris from him because he doesn't care. He insists that we do not go on the same path. Ranger ignores Doctore and heads up the beach.

I chase after him and Doctore after me. We make it to the castle when Ranger stops dead in his tracks, eyes upward, fists clenched. Before us, hanging from the parapets is the mutilated remains of Atia. Her flesh is blue and looks as though the skin might fall off the bones. Ranger stares.

"Come now Ranger," Doctore says to the heavy breathing Ranger. Doctore and I stand there for five minutes while Ranger stares at the only girl he's ever really loved. It really is a sad thing to look at. The once beautiful and vibrant girl on our team is now a disemboweled corpse.

"It's just her shell, Ranger. Atia is exactly where she is supposed to be now. That was just her shell," I offer. Two more minutes pass before Ranger speaks.

"Let's train. Tell us what to do, Doctore." His tone is serious. Doctore nods and heads forward. "Follow me," he says before taking off into a jog. We pass under the body of Atia. Ranger doesn't look up again.

Ranger doesn't speak much the rest of that day. A newfound energy inside him, he begins to act different. He is a dog backed into a corner, taunted with the thing he cared about most, the only girl he has ever fallen in love with. They force her memory on him to their own demise. I haven't ever seen Ranger like this, more beast than man, like a lion stalking its prey, never losing focus. I support him the only way I know how, by matching his intensity.

The pattern grows more recognizable. Not only can I anticipate where I will be hit, I can counter and send a couple of the fighters flying. "Good!" Doctore screams to me. He floats between two rooms, watching the progress of both Ranger and me. I don't know what Ranger is doing in there, and I've been too tired to engage in small talk.

I've now gotten to the apple and can get halfway back. This is encouraging because my remaining training time is only two days.

Faris continues to visit and give me massages. Ranger just seems angry, but at least it is not at me this time. Doctore informs us that our last two days will simply be fighting, and that we will have a rest day before the fight.

The second to last day, I make it back to the front with the apple unscathed. The sequence is as follows: Block up left, down right, spin and block face with right hand, back with left, release spin and block down left, and up right, uppercut up right, low kick left, then quickly spin toward the right, creating a flurry of attacks, sending three defenders reeling. Two more midsection blocks and I am on the stage. Not even close to being out of breath, I grab the apple and tuck it under my chin.

The way back I strike outwards, shoulder-height in both directions, block up left, up left, up right, kick midsection right, spin toward left and deliver two handed strike, down-right block immediately followed by a kick, leaving me a one on three. After that, it is all improvisation. The first attacker lunges at me. I block his head strike with my left arm and his stomach thrust with my right. I disable his right weapon and quickly strike his exposed face. The other two come at me at the same time. I see their hands in slow motion. In a few seconds, I block fourteen strikes: up left, up right, down right, down right, uppercut, up left, uppercut, up left, kick right, three straight blocks to my mid-chest, down right and down left. The last block broke the fighters stick which I jumped on like a wounded predator. I unleash a flurry of attacks that leaves the fighter holding his bloody mouth.

Not forgetting about the last fighter, I turn around, moving gracefully toward him. In one flash I disarm his right hand. By the time he realizes what happened, I disarm his left. He falls to his knees and raises his hands in surrender. I remove the apple from my chin.

Doctore begins to clap from an observing point I did not know existed.

"All while applying the perfect pressure on the apple, so as to not bruise it. Well done. Now, do it blindfolded." I don't even have enough time to be proud. I let out a sigh and throw on a blindfold. I hear the men in masks line up.

CHAPTER FORTY-SIX

*Be present. How many times have you walked away
from a conversation with little to no memory of what was
discussed? Why give power to tomorrow, when tomorrow
is not promised? Bring out the best in yourself by bringing it
out of someone else. Be present.*

Nirue's Grandmother

THE BLINDFOLD WENT ABOUT AS well as I had thought it would. I learned a little about sensing an imminent strike without eyesight. Although, most times, it was too late before I realized what to do.

I spend the morning of my rest day sleeping in with Faris. She comforts me and gives me one last rub. We talk of arbitrary things. She asks me where I'm from, which leads to an awkward avoidance. We talk about life and settling down and what an ideal future looks like.

To her, it looks like a spread out in the country with a strong man to protect her and help her harvest and hunt. She wants to raise children to know and understand the land. I make up a fancy tale of wanting to own a fishing business in a small town on a warm coast. She agrees to find a farm on the coast with me. I don't know how I can ever tell her.

We spend hours preparing a big dinner for the three of us. A few hours before sunset, I notice Ranger out on the beach carrying the remains of Atia.

I look at the only woman who has ever been able to read my mind. She smiles softly and nods me toward the beach. On the way out I grab a metal bucket just outside the chimney stack. The wind is blowing hard. My green cape flutters up near my head. When I reach Ranger, he had already dug a few feet. He looks up momentarily but doesn't say anything. We spend the next hour digging in silence. He places her body in the hole then pauses with his eyes closed for a moment of reflection. We fill the grave, and Ranger places a small "A" that he had crafted over the dirt. I don't figure it will last long.

We catch our breath for a few minutes. "Faris made us a big dinner. We ought'a eat, Ranger." The wind picks up and blows his dark hair about his face. He looks off into the ocean for a moment then heads back inside. I wish I knew what he was thinking. Is he angry? Is he sad?

We spend dinner mostly in silence. Faris created a beautiful spread of well-seasoned meat and bread. Our favorite dish—wheat shells and cheese was the side, and fresh milk of cow was the drink. I help Faris do the dishes. Ranger heads to the beach without saying anything.

We don't do the dishes because we have to, or even want to. It's just another way to kill time. There is nothing worse than sitting still with nothing to do, while something life altering is on your mind and in your immediate future. Time never seems so slow.

When the dishes are done I head upstairs with Faris. The sun is beginning to go down. There's not much left to say to each other. She places a hand on my face while sitting on my lap. "I'm going to let you go. I need to get back to my family and you need to be with Ranger. You guys have a big day tomorrow." I smile and nod then grab her face and kiss her goodbye. Her breath tastes like fruit. A deep inhale tells me she likes my embrace. Her eyes stay closed well after we are done.

"I'll be there. Tomorrow I mean. I will be watching. Please don't let me down." Don't let her down. What a strong woman. Most women would be crying and begging me to run away. Not Faris. Not the girl who beat me in an archery contest. Not the girl who willingly went into the enemy's base at the risk of being eaten alive. No. My girl is tough.

"I'll try."

She shakes her head. "No. You will do better than try. You hear me?"

I smile. "I won't let you down."

She kisses me one more time then hugs me tight. We hold each other for a few minutes. "I will see you soon, Nirue," she says and she begins to walk out. "Oh, just one more thing."

"Yes?"

"I love you." As though from a quake in the deep ocean, a wave of emotions flood over me. She makes me feel so alive. I don't know what to say. Do I love her back? What is love?

She stands in the doorway. Her body language begins to change. She knows I won't say it back. She knows I will only hurt her in the end. Until . . . "I love you too." Wow. I can't believe I said that. What the heaven am I doing falling so hard for a girl I won't see if I make it or not? Nirue . . . You know you are what you say. Why put yourself into such a position?

Her eyes make it all worth it. The eyes that I know will only ever see me. The eyes that you don't ever have to worry about wandering. Maybe I really do love this girl.

With that, she carries her rope and hook and leaves the grounds of our guest castle. I look out the window and see Ranger. I go downstairs, grab a bottle of red wine and make my way to the beach.

The air has calmed. The sand is cool beneath my bare feet. Remnants of ocean plant make their way to the surface of the beach. The plants are slightly cooler on my foot than the sand. I reach Ranger in a couple of minutes. He sits to the right of Atia's grave. I sit to the right of him.

The sun paints a soft array of purple and orange across the top of the waves. The sound of the waves coming in and crashing remind me of my mom emptying a large bucket of soapy water. In the distance a whale breaches the surf. I'm sure the water displacement is large but from here, it's nothing. Perspective.

The ocean smells like sea salt. The wind blows cool and calm onto my face. My body feels as good as it ever has. Even with one day off I feel like I have a never-ending supply of energy. I pull the cork out with my teeth and look at Ranger, who continues to squint into the distance.

I take a large pull from the wine. It's got a hint of wood to it, like drinking collected rain water from a tree. The warmness on my throat feels good. A sense of relaxation immediately comes over me just before an inadvertent sigh is released. Ranger doesn't move. I take another large pull and burp.

"The hell you doin', Nirue? We're fighting for our lives tomorrow." He's genuinely pissed.

"You know what, Ranger. This may be the last sunset we ever see. Look around you. Look at our environment. This beautiful view on a private beach—just for us! The wind cooling our body and soul. All three of us united again." He cringes at that last part.

"Look, man. I know it hurts, but she's out there somewhere." I point with my bottle hand to the sky above the ocean. "I can't tell you where or when, but you will see her again. Heck—could be tomorrow around noon." He laughs at that.

I smile at him and give him a "you know you want to" look. He reluctantly grabs the bottle. "Give me that," he says before taking a much larger pull than I expected.

"Take it easy, Hemingway," I jest. He doodles in the sand between his legs.

"I guess I'm not sad about 'Tia anymore. Guess I'm just . . . I don't know how to say it without sounding like a big sissy-boy."

"Ranger," I say putting my hand on his shoulder. "Don't you ever say that again. You can tell me anything in the world. I will NEVER think less of you. You've saved my life, and I have risked mine saving yours. We have been through so much together. You are, undoubtedly, my best friend. You're like a brother to me."

He smiles. "You know I think the same way 'bout you Nirue. Still don't make me feel like any less of a sissy." We share a laugh. "You know

Nirue, I guess I'm just pissed off. Ya know? I guess I'm just tired of being the underdog. I guess I'm tired of this universe stacking the cards against me. Even something so simple as peace of mind that the woman I love could be left alone in her grave, ya know?"

"I know Ranger. We have had the cards stacked against us this entire time, you're right. But what shouldn't be lost is that we have overcome every single thing thrown at us with flying colors. FLYING colors. The so-called universe you describe—it doesn't put weak people in situations like this. Nobody I have met could survive all that we have, mentally or physically. Starting with our accidents! We should be dead! But you know what? We've got another chance. Yeah, sure, it's not the easiest, and tomorrow seems a bit daunting. But like Doctore said, you never know when an earthquake or a gust of wind is around the corner."

"You're right, Nirue. Always are. I guess that Atia thing got me all worked up more than it should ha—"

"I'm going to cut you off right there. You are completely in the right to get upset by that. That's a coward move. That's an evil move. That's an unforgiveable in my book. You don't desecrate the body of your opponent's loved one. Even in the most volatile of wars, people respect the dead and give the other side the opportunity to bury their loved ones. Even Achilles gave his opponent the luxury, when he didn't want to and didn't have to. No, Ranger, you aren't wrong to get fired up about that. It has been stewing inside of me ever since I saw it."

He nods his head and takes in a deep breath of confused emotions. We share the bottle until it is gone and nearly dark. The sun falls below the waves signaling the end to this ephemeral moment. Ranger is now doodling in the sand with a stick. With purple teeth, he looks at me and asks, "Say. Got a plan for tomorruh?"

I smile at him and begin to draw a map of the arena.

INTERLUDE 5

BERTRAM APPEARS IN A RECTANGULAR chamber much too dark for his all white robe, white beard and white eyebrows. The light emanating from his body is suffocated by the darkness at the other end of the room. Pots of green glow vibrantly, reflecting dark shadows on dark walls.

"How many years has it been old friend?" The dark-being asks Bertram from a long, large, bottomless pit.

"I lost count a long time ago."

The dark being nods and studies Bertram curiously. **"It appears you are further than you have ever been, am I wrong?"**

"You are not. This group—well, minus the girl, is my best chance to make it off this planet. If they don't make it, well . . . I guess I would become you."

The dark man laughs, slowly, then insidiously, the room begins to choke on his laughter.

"You already are, old friend."

Bertram raises an unconvinced eyebrow. Silence for what feels like a year to Bertram, and Bertram knows what a long year feels like.

"I'm leaving, now. I won't be distracted from my Sherpa duties any longer, lest I do my friends and myself a disservice." Bertram picks up his robe and walks to the corner of the room to create a jumpkey.

"What if I told you I could offer you your freedom, right now." Bertram freezes, foot slowly dropping to the ground, robes falling over his hands.

"Ah. See, not so eager after all, are we?" Bertram contemplates the offer. He thinks of his life after this place. He thinks of the freedom from an eternity of guiding. But there must be a trick.

"At what cost?" Bertram snarls, knowing that the being will likely ask him to make his soul mortal again.

"Betray the two."

"Nirue and Ranger? No. Unless they get through, I am stuck here—you know that." Bertram waves a dismissive hand and picks up his robes once again. "I'm done with your madness."

"Look." The being waves an ugly hand toward the pit. Slowly, gradually, fervently, the bottom of the pit begins to glow white. Small as an orb at camp, the light grows greater and greater still, until it is a full-fledged white jumpkey to the other side. Bertram gasps and covers his mouth for the first time in centuries. His natural reaction is to sprint toward the light, everything else be damned.

Bertram runs into a force field and is knocked down. He closes his eyes, which now glow white through his eyelids as he begins to take down the force field. Once again, the being's laugh echoes through the chambers, although somewhat dampened by the force field.

"How did you—"

"Because I CAN. *I* am the most powerful on this planet. Darkness always wins. Ever looked at the sky? Notice how much more dark there is than light? Betray the two. Allow the power of darkness to grow. I'll send you to the place you've always wanted most. From here on out, no more helping them from the shadows. No more timely interventions. Just let them try to win without your hidden hand, and I will take care of the rest. You have until their last trial to decide.

Wide-eyed and lost in thought, the purifying light from the white jumpkey reflects off Bertram's face—a man looking down the hardest decision he has ever had to make in his entire existence.

CHAPTER FORTY-SEVEN

Sacrifice is the true indication of love. There is no
greater demonstration than to lay down your own life.
Nothing more heroic than choosing to not fight back,
knowing it's going to save them.

Old parable from the people of Hardrain

I'M SWEATING PROFUSELY. I DON'T know if it's the booze or my
nerves. Probably both. I can't help but think of the first time I fought that
bastard. I wanted to kill him then, but I couldn't. I wasn't skilled enough,
not even close. I shake those memories from my mind.

A trickle of sweat rides my arm from my shoulder to my wrist, I notice
while observing the new structures placed in the arena. Apparently Timbly
and Dorian spent an extravagant amount of money on it. It's still circular,
but there are lots of rocks and trees and upside down horseshoe structures
made of grey flagstone. Each is two stories, with multiple cutouts providing
good angles for protected shooting. Their side is a mirror of ours.

To the right of the shoe is a climbable boulder, to the left a hyper-dense
area of palm trees. Surrounding the outside and edging the arena is tightly

cropped palm trees. The first row of spectators had to move up so that they can see.

In the very center of the map is a triangle. The triangle moves skyward after two minutes of being on the ground. It moves upward while rotating clockwise to the height of the stadium (which has added another story of seats), then back down into place. It only rests for one minute after the initial two minutes. Of course, Ranger and I already knew all of this thanks to Doctore.

This time there are no masks. I'm in virtually the same outfit as I had on in the games, minus the furs: A brown tunic with a green cape, brown boots and *Evergold*. I added brown leather bracelets that Faris left me under my pillow, and a white belt for show.

Ranger is in all black. Black tunic, black pants and black paint. A woman painted upside down black triangles over our eyes. The speaker walks out onto the triangle, which rises to the height of the sixth row.

Ranger's breathing fast. The tops of my clenched fists are becoming increasingly sweaty. "Laaaaaadies and Gentllllleman. Welcome back!" The crowd cheers excitedly. "Comes now the four best fighters Pantine has ever seen! Behind this gate," he points to us, "is the duo that woke the Keeper in the jungle of Hardrain. The slayer of King Maji the terrible, and the winner (but-for-a-technicality) of our life or death game of capture the flag! Raaaaaaannnnggeeerrrrr and Niiiiiiiiiiirruuuuuuuuueeeeee!!!" It's hard to hear the crowd's reaction through my drumming heart. I have to extend my neck to swallow because my mouth is so dry.

Instead of jumping up and down or sticking our arms through the gate for the crowd, Ranger and I just become more still—more focused. More ready to fight for our lives than ever before.

The announcer begins to introduce our opponents. It's time for me to drop to my place. I control my breathing to six seconds in and four seconds out. I close my eyes and lower myself into a state of mindlessness. I go somewhere else. I put away all of the noise and become exclusively aware of my surroundings. The smell of the ocean just on the other side of these walls. The soft breeze blowing through the arena. The black birds blocking part of the sun's rays as they fly past. The way the palm leaves move but the rocks do not. Before I realize it, the platform is back into place and the speaker is being pulled into the stands. The crowd noise comes back to me, and I fight to stay in my place. I am much more accurate in my place, and I only have four arrows.

My heart reminds me of the drums of Hardrain. I look at Ranger who looks at me and nods, then back out into the arena. His war paint is running from sweat. I'm sure mine is too.

Six seconds in, four seconds out. The birds, the sand, the wind, my heartbeat.

DROP

I sprint to the rock to the right of the shoe. Ranger goes to the shoe. I didn't see where our opponents went. I hand signal a question to Ranger: "*where are they?*"

He holds up one finger and points to their shoe, then holds up a second finger and shrugs. "*Archer?*" I signal. He makes a shoe with his hand. *Good.*

I jump up on the rock, moving to a weathered area that gives me an angle at their structure. Old Red, still wearing his mask, moves slowly toward their thick area of trees eyeing Ranger while keeping his head on a swivel. I have a shot. I can't believe they are exposing themselves like this. I load *Evergold* as fast as possible. Right before I let loose, my body is jerked from something outside of myself. The arrow hits the trunk of a palm tree not six inches from Old Red's head.

CURSES!

I look back at the box. Timbly and Dorian are stoic, but I know one of their mages had a hand in that. I would never have missed.

Old Red rolls behind the structure and looses a risky shot at me from a hole in the shoe. I move back to Ranger at ours.

"What happened?" I shake my head. "Mage shook my arm. Had him dead to rights." He shakes his head.

"Let's mo—" an arrow nearly catches me in the face. Ranger jerks me back behind the wall just in time. "Give me a cover shot, I'll move left through the thick palms. You move right but be ready to pull out *Dicers*.

Angor is out there somewhere." Before he leaves I grab him. "Wait. I think he is hiding to get on that platform. He wants the middle for some reason. Let's not let him take that. Let's get him two on one where their archer can't shoot us. When you see the ground stirring, rush the middle through the palms. I'll shoot a cover arrow and jump onto it from the rock."

He agrees. "Let's move."

I push right, keeping a wary eye out for both players. No sign of either. I sprint to the rock. I look around the right of it. I see Old Red on the rock lining up Ranger. I shoot an arrow at him. Once again my shot is misdirected by a mage. At least it keeps Red from hitting Ranger. Two arrows left for both archers.

The ground begins to stir. We have roughly three seconds to get on the triangle before it's too late. Ranger rushes out of the forest. I shoot another arrow at Old Red. Angor jumps from one of the palms to the triangle.

With everything I have I run to the tip of the rock and jump onto the triangle. While I am on my way down, Angor kicks Ranger in the stomach, sending him reeling from the triangle before he could pull out *Darkwater*. I land, throw *Evergold* on my back and pull out *Dicers*.

Doctore was right. I feel like a lion. My blades the size of forearms glow blue like an iceberg in the sun. Angor smiles, revealing his sharpened teeth and black eyes. The crowd screams. I look down and almost faint at what I see. Ranger took an arrow to the leg.

He scrambles back behind our shoe. Angor moves toward the middle of the platform. The clockwise rotation makes me dizzy for a moment. *Focus. Focus!* I can hear Doctore screaming in my head. Or maybe I can actually hear him. Either way, I refocus.

"Did you like my present, Nirue? She didn't put up as big of a fight this time around. What a pitiful girl."

Enraged, I release a flurry of attacks: up right, gut, gut, up left, uppercut, lower kick. Angor staggers. He doesn't know I can fight this well. I see the concern fall over his face. I raise my right arm to strike him but become frozen. My body weakens and I fall to my knees. *Dicers* shake in my hands. He smiles again.

"Did you really think you had a chance, weakling?" The crowd begins to scream. Their words flood into my immediate senses. I'm losing the control of my body and my mind. I become suddenly aware of my helplessness. I feel sick.

Angor uses two short swords. He taunts the crowd. We are about one third up the stadium. "You see how he bows to me!" Some of the spectators urge him to kill me. Some scream for me to get up. I fight with everything I have to break free. He cuts the latch on my right shoulder that attaches my cape to my tunic.

"I'm going to feed on your dead body. I'm going to eat and remember nothing about you, because you are nothing. I know where you come from and what you are made of. You're not worthy to be alive in this world. The weak deserve to die."

He cuts the clip on my left shoulder. My cape falls off my back. I fight hard to move my arms but it's a losing battle. Angor raises his sword to strike me. "Goodbye weakling."

He strikes at my neck. In the same moment, a series of emotions flood over me: energy, awareness, anger. I block up left with *Dicer*. His sword starts to turn blue. His eyebrows raise in confusion and he looks over at the box. I stand up and unleash the quickest and most destructive hits I have ever attempted in my life.

Everything he said about me and Atia only worsened my hatred for him. Like a hummingbird in flight, my torso appears still, but my appendages move so fast you can hardly see them. Gut, gut, gut, uppercut, up right, down left, down right, down left, uppercut. Angor barely protects himself from the last one. I send him reeling to an edge of the triangle.

I move forward in a slow jog. I jump-step left, jump-step right and jump-spin in a downward double strike that nobody—not even a Jboynei—could have blocked. I put the force of my entire body into the strike. His weapons break under the force of *Dicers*, slicing off part of his hands, his left knee and opening up his stomach. He falls to his knees and grabs his intestines that are now pooling onto the hot granite. I cross my blades over his throat.

He looks at me as tears bead from his black eyes and says, "I used to be just like you." I pause momentarily, staring into his black eyes wondering what he could possibly mean. Slowly, as if he knows something I do not, he starts to grin. I cut his head off and kick his writhing body into the crowd below.

I think I hear the crowd screaming but I am too focused to care. I can only think of one thing now. Ranger. At the top of the stadium my head is in the clouds. I can barely see them fighting. It looks as though Ranger is without weapon. I'm going to have to shoot from here.

I load *Evergold* and wait. The triangle spins. I have stopped moving up. After a few seconds, I begin to descend. Ranger and Old Red are punching each other. Old Red kicks the arrow in Rangers leg. Ranger looks like he screamed but I can't hear him. This thing is moving too slow, but I cannot jump. I will die if I jump.

Old Red grabs *Darkwater* from nearby. Ranger crabwalks backward with only one leg and two arms. Old Red moves to strike Ranger. He pulls the arrow from his leg and tries to use it as a weapon. He nearly gets his head split open. The weight of *Darkwater* sends Old Red to the ground, just to the right of Ranger's head. Six seconds in, four seconds out. I get back to my place. My tunnel vision is on the two men fighting. They transfer possession of top through wrestling moves and punches.

While still high in the air, Old Red gets on top of Ranger. Ranger uses two forearms to block a flurry of punches but is taking a beating. Old Red pulls a dagger from his boot. My heart drops. I'm too far to get off an accurate shot. Ranger blocks one strike but I fear he cannot block another. He reaches for his pocket dagger but doesn't have the time or leverage. It's now or never. In an instant I calculate my rotation, the wind blowing the palm leaves, my distance and drop from gravity. I hold my breath and allow a heartbeat to pass and then let go.

I feel as though a lifetime has passed me before the arrow even gets close. It's like a ship floating away without sails. The arrow drops at a curved angle. It seems to pick up speed, silencing the crowd. From a distance, if time froze, one would see me on the edge of the triangle; an arrow heading toward two men; a man with a clown mask and a dagger raised sitting on the chest of a man in all black with veins pulsating from his neck—a man with black war paint leaking down his face.

Then, all at once, it happens. The arrow pierces the back of Old Red's neck and nearly hits Ranger in the face. Rangers eyes bulge, focused on the arrow point that stops just above his nose. I made the perfect shot.

The crowd is deadly silent. Not in a good way. Timbly stands up red faced and screams, KIIILLLLLLLLL THEMMMM!!!" I can see spit flying from here.

Although I'm at the lower end of the stadium, I'm still too high to jump to the ground. A group of guards enter the arena from both gates. They begin to circle Ranger who is now crab-walking toward the middle. I'm out of arrows and don't see a way out of this one.

They are moving on Ranger fast. Think, Nirue. Think!

The crowd begins to protest. Some think Timbly is wrong, and some are happy we are condemned to death. Probably those who bet against us. A small faction of people come to our aid and jump into the arena. They are without weapons and are no real threat to the guards.

More of the crowd enter the arena. We are doomed. They are screaming for our heads. I run and jump onto the rock on the enemy's side. Old Red writhes and gargles blood while holding his neck. Ranger sticks *Darkwater* in his gut from a seated position. Some of the crowd members pull Old Red by either arm toward the edge of the arena. Ranger holds up his blade in defense.

A medic takes off Old Red's mask in an effort to revive him. Dark hair falls over a young man's face. He's not elderly, he's not even old. He's a man that I know. Sly. I don't even have time to think it over. I am off the rock and help Ranger to his feet. His leg is bleeding out. The crowd moves in on us. They scream and yell but don't dare get within striking distance.

Soldiers with spears over shields move on us in unison. "This is it buddy. Let's give them everything we've got." He looks at me with desperate eyes. His skin is turning white.

I hear a scream from the crowd. A massive man with sledgehammer arms jumps into the arena. He beats his chest and begins to throw men to the side the way a teen would knock over a toddler. Arrows pick off the soldiers that are closest to us. The sun is too bright to make out where this is coming from.

"WHAT ARE YOU DOING? KILL THEM YOU FOOLS! NOW! NOW! NOW! NOW!" Timbly says while jumping up and down in the box.

Dalk fights his way to the center, clearing a path for Rust, Tamra, Kam, Faris and Bertram, who no longer has chains and wears an all-white robe. Dalk lets out a war cry and starts to fight. "Didn't think we would leave you two hangin' did ya?" Rust says with a grin and a wink.

We set in a sequence of fighting that could not have been drawn up better. Faris gives me a full quiver. We go to work keeping archers off the group. Rust moves elegantly and easily cuts up the soldiers. I guess I forgot that we are the best fighters in the world. Tamra works on Ranger. He is turning much more pale than I would like.

Dalk picks up a shield and throws it into the phalanxed unit of soldiers. When they stagger, he leaps into the air and slams down into them, crushing a man's head in the process.

Back to back, Faris and I protect the hand-to-hand fighters. Dalk is a destructive force. I cannot make out what Kam is doing, although I see flashes of blue and green from the corner of my eye.

Bertram uses a wooden club and delivers spinning attacks. He spins and releases a purple smoke into the area of the enemy. With a huge inhale, he blows a gust of wind much bigger than any man should be able to do. It bends the trees and disburses the purple smoke throughout the enemy. The effect makes them go mad and scream while holding their ears. This clears out over ninety percent of the people fighting us. The rest run with them.

Timbly screams for reinforcements. An army of soldiers marches outside of the stadium, their feet thundering the ground.

Bertram yells, "NOW KAM, NOW!" His voice carries throughout the whole stadium. Maybe even the whole city.

Kam looks as though he is dropping into his own place. His eyes turn dark and then orange. He turns his body backward, and then unleashes a giant fireball at a section of the stadium. He blows a hole in the building large enough for a group of Tempos to fit through. "MOVE!" Bertram orders. Rust and I take Ranger under our shoulder and hustle him out of the stadium. Faris and Dalk follow up the back. We get about two hundred yards from the stadium toward the beach. The skies are dark. The waves look orange and black. It's like we are inside a giant water-filled jack-o'-lantern. Faris unleashes arrows and Dalk throws his shield at the pursuing enemy.

Kam tries to lay some sort of trap but is out of energy. Nearly every single one of his veins, including the ones in his face oscillate. We make it to the beach but the army is hot on our tail.

There are two small rowboats. Bertram climbs up on a hill and eyes the enemy. "Quickly!" he yells. "You all take that one. Go to the island city of Zaragul—wait for me there! Nirue, Ranger and I must go somewhere on another matter. I will not be long."

"NO! I will not leave him again," protests Faris. Dalk begins to say something, and Rust too. Bertram does not give them the opportunity. He screams in a voice louder than anything I have ever heard. It's not human.

"THIS IS WHAT MUST BE DONE!" The sound wave pushes the incoming tide back into the ocean. They look to me to do something. They look to their leader to keep the group together. With somber eyes I hold a hand to them and say, "He's right. We'll be back shortly."

"Off with you," Bertram orders.

The sky is ominous. The four climb into their boats, and we into ours. The sea stirs with anger. I row quickly to move us out of range of enemy archers.

Faris stares at me from the bow of her boat. She doesn't even move when arrows whiz by her head. She just stares with a "I can't believe this is happening" look. I want to tell her, but I keep rowing instead. I want to tell her that I want nothing more than to be in the boat with her. That I want to go to Zaragul with her. I can't. While we are still relatively close to each other I begin to row toward them. Bertram tells me that we are going the wrong way. I drop the oars and put my face into my hands. Slowly, our boats drift away from each other. I barely notice the whizzing arrows, increasing wave size and light rainfall. I barely notice Ranger lying half dead at the end of the boat. All I see is Faris.

The boat rocks up and down, but her gaze does not. I feel the emptiness of her heart. She just risked her life to save the man she loves. The man that she has been visiting every night the last two weeks. The man that told her he loved her back. What does he do to repay her? He leaves her.

My eyes well up with tears but all I feel in my heart is anger. I'm tired of this. I'm tired of the roller coaster of emotions. I'm tired of feeling like I let someone down. I'm tired of wondering if will die. I just need to let go. I look at Faris one last time, then pick up the oars and begin to row.

"More east," Bertram hollers through the now pouring rain. I glance back to see him examining Ranger's wound. He's speaking to Ranger, but I can't make out what he is saying.

I've been rowing for almost an hour by the time I come out of my daze. The rain is torrential. It clouds my vision. Waves lift me stories above my starting point, only to drop me down in another direction even further than I started. "EAST I SAID!"

"How the hell am I supposed to know which way is east?"

"Toward the mountain with the orange and black clouds around the peak." He goes back to working on Ranger's wound. Everything looks orange and black right now.

The storm is only getting worse and we are headed right toward it. In the far distance I make out a mountain of black rock. The clouds surrounding it are indeed orange. Lightning flickers through the clouds above, and around the black mountain.

I begin to notice other boats next to us. No. Not boats. Fins.

Fish much larger than our pontoon sized boat ride the waves through the storm. They are larger than anything I have ever seen. My heart drops into my stomach as I notice that they aren't just riding the waves. They are hunting us.

"Row, NIRUE! ROW!" I pull harder than I ever have. The storm is completely blinding. The waves are insurmountable. I fear that we will perish before we get to our destination.

Then it comes. In the distance, a wave forms. A wave so big that we cannot possible hope to stay upright. Something deep and dark and ungodly. Something that doesn't even make you shiver. Something that makes you accept death.

Ranger is barely awake. He's just alive enough to spit water out of his mouth and shake rain from his face. Bertram grabs the back of my hair and moves his face right next to my ear. Water sucks into the bottom of the wave, feeding the beast like a dragon sucking in air before spewing fire. The wave gets so high it temporarily blots out the storm.

Even though Bertram is screaming, I can barely hear him. I know he is screaming because I can feel the vibrations from his voice. "Swim to the shore! You must make it! YOU are our only hope! REMEMBER, APPEARANCE IS EVERYTHING." With that, he turns backward, grabs Ranger, and capsizes the boat.

CHAPTER FORTY-EIGHT

Life is the first gift. The second gift is this chance to live again. But what does it mean to live? How could anyone on Earth understand the philosophy that goes through one's mind when entering the trials? May the sun shine on my face through this next phase, and may I advance far quicker than my Sherpa did.

*Journal entry from Bertram,
one week after completing the trials*

MY MOUTH FILLS WITH SALT water. My eyes are useless. In fact, all of my senses are useless. I am being pulled by the current down, down, down. I did not take in much air, and cannot hold my breath much longer. I swim toward what I think is the surface. I swim hard. My head becomes light. I can't tell if the pressure in my head is from going the wrong direction, or from running out of air. I swim into something sharp that draws blood.

The blow to my stomach nearly knocks out all of the wind I have left. I begin to panic. I can feel my eyes bulging out of my head. I can feel the veins in my neck bulge too as I swim the opposite direction.

The harder I kick, the more I begin to fade. I let a little air out. That provides me a moment of relief. The light plays tricks on me. Every time I think I am reaching the surface, I instead realize I have much more to go.

I kick and fade, kick and fade. I kick and fade until all I have left is one last movement upward. This is it, I think to myself as I move my arms and legs downward like a young bird learning to fly.

I move up and feel nothing. This is it. My eyes sting. Air. I gasp so loud that I can hear it through the storm. I suck in so much air that I accidently inhale seawater. I begin to gag and try to get more air but the waves throw me back under. Don't panic. I know I have at least thirty seconds. I let the currents take me, gather my bearings, and move up. I catch a clean rush of air. I am able to dog-paddle above water long enough to get ten to twelve sufficient breaths in. I no longer see the giant wave. No sign of Bertram or Ranger. No sign of fins, yet.

I look for the black mountain. I recognize lightning in the clouds far off in the distance so I begin to swim toward them. The waves push and pull me every which way but the mountain. There truly is no feeling more desolate than being in the ocean, alone, with no boat and dark skies above you. No friends, no form of travel, nothing but myself and miles of darkness below and above. The only thing keeping my stamina up is my want to get out of this water. I hate this. This is why I lived in rural Dakota. I never wanted to be near the ocean for this precise reason.

The waves pull at me and wear out my strength. I tell myself to press on. I must press on. I know it in my head and my heart. Despite the oceans productive measures of keeping me from the mountain, the rock is closer.

The storm lightens up. A bright moon shines on the calming ocean water. As the clouds break, I make out a canyon in the distance. More like a rock that has been split in two to form a very narrow passageway to the mountain.

The ocean becomes nothing more than a normal flickering of waves. White light shines on top of the darkness as I make my way to the canyon. A fin breaks the moonlit swell in front of the canyon.

My heart sinks. I take a deep breath and let it out as the waves move me. My eyes are closed. What do they say about sharks again? They attack from above? Or is it below? Has to be below. I must go below.

It's my only chance. The fin is gone. I wade water with tunnel vision on the canyon. I don't sense anything near me. Then another fin pops up, much closer this time. The canyon is a two hundred yard swim. Another fin. Then another.

C'mon, Nirue. I close my eyes and feel the water pull me left and right. I start to get a feel for the direction of the current. It's going toward the canyon, but not directly at it. If I let it take me, I calculate it would place me about thirty five yards right of the entrance. The fins dive into the darkness. I take one last look at my target, a spot on the canyon sixty five feet left of the entrance, and swim. I swim hard, then, I hold my breath and dive down. It is literally pitch black down here. The moon only offers light a foot or beneath the surface.

I go as far as I think I can before I would run out of breath on the way back up, then send myself at a curved trajectory toward my target. A shape the size of a small submarine brushes my body and stirs the water around me. I am forced to swim up for air. I take in a deep breath and go back down.

I repeat the process many more times without being attacked. I am fifty yards away now, and am positioned to take a more direct route. This time when I make my way toward the surface, four shapes move up past me with speed I did not think possible of a fish. Of any fish. They create a vortex that pulls me deeper into the dark. I close my eyes and swim as hard as I can. My lungs feel as though they will explode.

When I get to the surface, I notice the sharks swimming in a perfect circle just at the entrance. One, two, three, four, five second breath in, and I dive. I dive deeper than I ever should, and then some. I have just as good of chance as drowning as I do becoming food. I think I would rather drown. I feel the shapes move next to me, but they do not attack. It's almost as though they are protecting me, but my instincts tell me that's wrong. When I make it to the surface I realize that I swam far enough to be just inside the channel. The sharks do not follow. I swim backward to make sure that no fins are pursuing me, until they are long out of sight, then I swim as fast as I can toward the shore.

The beach is cold. Completely out of breath I close my eyes. The sand is soft and full of comfort. I breathe something close to hyperventilation until my normal rate comes back to me. I open my eyes to see an arm of the Andromeda galaxy, the same way I used to look at the Milky Way in the Dakota countryside.

I have no idea what to expect next. This must be the last stage of my trial. If I complete this, I just might be able to go home. But something doesn't feel right. My heart doesn't feel right about this place. It's the same feeling of lying in bed and knowing that something unseen is watching. Waiting. The feeling that makes little children crawl under the covers. The sixth sense.

I stand up, completely covered in sand. I dare not enter the water to wash it off. Behind me is a large black mountain. It is a couple mile walk through a barren landscape to the mountain. I perceive an uneven stone path made of some type of grey rock. I know that I must walk it.

I hear no sounds and see no lights, save for the flickering of lightning in the partially orange and black clouds surrounding the mountain. There is no sound. Not like the forest on the mountain in the games. Just the absence of life. I can hear myself breathing, and the wind blowing—that's it. I don't know what is more eerie—the fact that I cannot see more than fifty yards in front of me, the lack of sound, or the lack of life.

I think on my little brothers. How I miss them so. I would give anything to be with them again. I would love to show them how to gut a fish or load a rifle. I would love to toss the football around with them and let them know what it's like to be under those lights on a Friday night in Dakota.

I miss my family so bad it makes me sick. We were never a perfect family. Like any other, we had our ups and downs. We had our good times and our bad. But we always knew we had each other. I wouldn't make them trade places with me for the whole world. I would take their place a hundred times over. No one should ever be put through a test like this.

Months of life or death situations wear on the bones. To think I used to actually crave an adventure like this. I was so naïve.

Before I know it, the path takes me away from the mountain. At the foot of the mountain I can make out structural shapes when lightning flashes. The path takes me over hills that are without grass.

Tombstones of those long lost border the path. The names on each stone shift and change with every step. "Lisa Patelski" one reads. My fifth grade science teacher?

"Don Aribold." My Pop Warner coach. How could people I know be buried here? The names become closer to me. My grandfather, my aunt, my cousin, my dad, my sister. Andrew.

I shake my head and stop reading the stones. I won't fall victim to this curse like Sly did. I am stronger than that. Up and over I traverse nine hills before the stone path leads to a small area of dead trees. As I walk through them, I notice that not even a cricket stirs in the night.

The path turns into a small cul-de-sac. At the center of it is a stone cylinder with green gas emanating from the top. It looks like an oversized jar that an ancient indigenous person would have crafted. I walk toward it. The wind picks up and brings my hair into my eyes. I continue closer. When I reach the cylinder the wind howls so fiercely I fall to one knee to brace myself.

"Hello, Nirue." The wind stops. The voice is deep and does not sound of this earth. It sounds like the mountain itself is speaking to me. My body breaks out in gooseflesh.

On the other side of the pot, a cloaked figure stands. I cannot see a single feature on his body, if he even has one.

"Driiiiiiiiiink," the voice beckons. I am hesitant. Every time I drink something on this forsaken planet something bad happens. But it has gotten me this far. At this point, I know this is something that I just *have* to do.

I lower cupped hands into the jar and remove black liquid. Green smoke gasses off of my hand. I take a sip. Lightning flashes nearby, illuminating the presence of three other hooded and non-descript beings, looking down on us from the hill behind the cul-de-sac. I feel nothing.

All of a sudden, two giant red planets fill the sky, then quickly disappear. No. They are not planets. Two red eyes. Eyes so big they fill the entire sky. I imagine this is what the sun must look like if you were on Mercury. Better yet, if you were on a moon orbiting Mercury.

"Iiiiiii've been waiting for you, Nirue. Come, find me in the dark."

The voice comes from whatever possesses those eyes. It's so loud the trees shake and lose limbs from the vibrations. The hooded figure behind the pot looks up at the three hooded beings on the hill. They nod in unison.

I am fixated on the eyes. Never have I been so terrified in my whole life or after-life.

"I will be waaaaiting," the voice says.

The eyes disappear. The trees and the pot and the hooded spirits disappear. Instead of ending, the road now jars left, toward the structures and the mountain nearly a mile away. I begin to shake. Not from being cold, but from fear. Pure, raw fear. Then I walk. It takes fear to have courage you know.

CHAPTER FORTY-NINE

*A cold wind blew through that city. Something else,
far more cold, blew through too. Like the wind, it was
impossible to see. Unlike like the wind, it chilled me beyond
my flesh, to my inner being.*

Author unknown

MY LEGS ARE HEAVY. MY mind feels tired. The only thing keeping
me awake right now is the adrenaline coursing through my veins. The air
is thick and my clothes smell like smoke. Not the good kind of smoke, like
that of a barbeque competition. This smells of something rotten. It smells
like burned rubber, or worse.

The wind blows intermittently to remind me it's still there. The
mountain looms ominously overhead. I keep an eye on the sky to see if I
can make out a face or anything else. I also continue to look behind me—
paranoid like a schizophrenic that had just been mugged. The steps lead to
a broken arch. The closer I get to the mountain, the more my eyes adjust
to the dark. I can see a city that climbs into the mountain. I hear sound.
It's not a sound I am particularly excited about. The sound is steady and
hardly seems to fluctuate.

As I approach the broken arch, the sound gets louder. The arch is now in full view. To the right of it are broken pillars. It reminds me of the old Roman forum—dilapidated structures teasing the eyes of the once beautiful basilica or regia. The sound grows even louder as I near the threshold.

I freeze before walking through. Thousands of corpses with rotted bodies malinger without direction. Heads barely attached to bodies moan like a man passing a kidney stone. From far away I thought the sound had some sort of organization. Seeing this, I know the sound is not harmonious but consistent. What I was hearing was the constant moan of a thousand dead bodies moving in un-purposed direction, at a rate of a foot per thirty seconds.

Their clothes are filthy and torn. Skin hangs from their bodies revealing sinew and rotted internal organs. I see one man with a patch of grey hair lose three upper teeth. He does not look down to pick them up or even seem to notice they left his body. The bodies moan and trudge on in their purposeless endeavor. The moans make my hair stand up.

Well, I knew this wouldn't be easy. I must enter this city. The city of the dead.

The moment I take one step over the threshold, everything stops. The moaning stops. The dead freeze and whip their heads in my direction in perfect unison. As I am downwind, the smell of rotted flesh permeates my nostrils. Tattered clothes spiral around the dead like the tendrils of a jungle plant. My heart races. They look at me without moving. Their tattered rags and innards blow in the wind. I take another step. Nothing.

They stand and stare at me with undignified distaste. At least I think that's what they are feeling. Then again, they may not be thinking at all. Pick yourself up and go forward. I muster the courage and begin to walk. The smell becomes unbearable. Closer I get, yet, they do not move. I'll fight my way through these bastards if I have to.

When I am twenty feet away from the closest dead person, they move in unison to form a path. I wait for them to finish. A tunnel forms two minutes later. At the end of it stands a dead girl with a missing eye and a dismembered body. I can see her shins and kneecap. Skin from her thighs flap in the wind. She makes no expression and says nothing. She has the face of someone I used to know. Atia.

I approach her cautiously. Proceeding through the dead feels like giving a speech about basic chemistry to a room full of NASA scientists— no one cares about me and I know I am out of place. One man's leg snaps, forcing him to take a knee. His lifeless stare does nothing to elicit any sort of sympathy from me.

I breathe through my mouth because the stench is too bad. Formaldehyde burns my throat like bad medicine. The eeriness of this place makes me want to run. I don't belong here, and if this is what death is like, I certainly don't want to die. Maybe if I run I can escape all of this and hideout somewhere on this planet.

Atia's head gazes somewhere around my collar bone. When I reach her, she simply turns and begins to slowly walk. I follow. I hear movement behind me. The assembly had turned their heads, looking through me but not at me.

I catch up to Atia. She leads me through a dilapidated town. A broken rubble path leads to a fountain in the middle of a roundabout. Four different paths lead down streets to which end I cannot say. We take the road straight. Hanging wooden planks expose the guts of the buildings to my right. Everything is completely empty. Cobwebs and dust cover everything I can see. Oddly, one torch is lit on the outside of each building, and one on the inside. They don't move or illuminate movement.

We pass by an old thrift shop that is so worn the awning over the front porch has collapsed. We pass a tavern, a bank, a two story housing unit and a blacksmith. After following the path through the ghost town, we reach an inn off the right side of the road. This building is not as broken down as the others. It looks as though someone had restored, or at least attempted to restore parts of it. A brief gust blows dead leaves near my feet. I watch them dance down the road.

She opens the door and we enter. Four tables are lined equidistant on the right and left side of the room. Straight ahead is a bar with large barrels stocked behind it. Some of the barrels are discolored from holding whatever is inside for too long. To the right is a staircase that leads to a second story. She takes the single torch hanging on the wall dividing the bar and the staircase and walks upstairs. I can see her tendons move. There is some sort of green slime leaking from her right forearm.

She leads me upstairs to a hallway with three doors, then stands in the middle of them and doesn't move.

"Atia, what is this place?"

No response. She doesn't even move. "Atia, can you hear me?" I try touching her shoulder, then shaking her a little. She turns her head toward me. Her one eye rolls around with no purpose of locating anything, then falls out of the socket, dangling near her bottom lip. I realize this is hopeless. She walks toward the room on the right and opens the door. The room holds two beds divided by a nightstand with one drawer. A small table with chairs is in the entry to the right of the door. A window that looks to have never been opened is located at the foot of the second bed.

Hanging above the first bed is *Evergold* with a quiver holding a single golden arrow. I walk into the room and past Atia to inspect it. It certainly is my weapon, and it is in as good of condition as ever. I lost this at sea. How did it get here? I guess I should stop asking questions, because nothing has made sense from the moment I woke on this planet.

Then, in a flash, the torch is blown out and Atia runs downstairs with speed and grace. "Atia!" I call after her. I begin to chase her but the door slams in my face. It was shut by some force unknown to my eye. My world is black. I load *Evergold* and wait. I try to control my beating heart but it's hard. Slowing my breath helps.

After an hour of lying in wait, I decide to try the door. It's dead bolted. I step back and kick the knob as hard as I can. I feel like I nearly broke my leg. I try one more time. This door does not want to budge.

The hair on my neck stands up as if someone or something is watching me. My attention is drawn to a small notebook on the nightstand. My night vision has fully set in, but still, I can barely see the notebook. I walk toward it. The book flies open and the pages flip until the book has been opened halfway. The quill next to it begins to write something, but I cannot make out what. After a minute of writing the quill rests next to the notebook and the notebook shuts.

I open the book and flip through the pages until I find the page with writing. It is too dark for me to understand anything. I sit on the bed and try to read it. A light forms at the table by the door. I jump up and scramble for *Evergold*. As my eyes adjust, I notice a long rope hanging from the ceiling and around the neck of a hooded figure.

"Who are you?"

No response. The being slowly spins right, then back left, the way a dead man on a noose is supposed to. Light illuminates the hand that holds the candle. Its nails are long and skin is purple and black. "What do you want? I'll shoot if you don't answer."

As it rotates back toward me, it raises the candle closer to its face. The creature's mouth spreads an evil smile. I can see that its teeth are sharp. With its right hand, it slowly closes all fingers to make a fist. Its body moves left slowly, showing its back to me, then rotates back toward me. The ceiling creaks. It opens its thumb revealing a long and dark nail. It stops grinning and traces a line under its neck spanning from one ear to the other. I shoot my only arrow at it. A mist forms and it is gone. The candle drops to the table.

I run to the table and grab the candle before it goes out. Wax drips onto the outside of my hand. My only arrow is buried in the wall behind the table. I look around the room and make sure nothing else is in here. I check the closet and under the beds. Nothing. I hold the candle and yank on the arrow. It comes out with surprising ease. The arrow is strong—stronger than any arrow I have ever used. When I pull the arrow from the wall, I look into the hole that it made.

A piece of black cloth is in the remnants of the wood flakes and bristles. I walk over to the notebook.

"You must find me in the dark. The dark is where you came, and in the dark you shall return. Seek me in the darkest hour beneath the ruins of the cathedral. It is there your journey shall end."

CHAPTER FIFTY

Follow your heart. One foot in front of the other.
Follow your heart

Nirue's brother Andrew, in a dream,
sometime between trial three and four

I SIT IN THE BED in silence. *Evergold* stays loaded. My fingers hurt from pinching the arrow to the string for so long. What's next? Is another apparition just going to appear? Am I going to get jumped? How do I even get out of this room?

I don't dare sleep. I don't even move from my bed. By now I am so tired that I no longer feel fear. I feel anger. I know deep down that I must stay cool and calm in order to make it out of here. This place is full of tricks. From the beginning of this treacherous journey, the only constant is this: I must be bold to succeed. Period. I don't have time to become shook from beings appearing from nothing, or being thrown in an arena with all of the odds against me, or having to survive in the jungle while being hunted. I just have to move.

After a couple of hours the door unlocks and opens. The door slowly creaks as it inches toward the wall behind the table. I stand with *Evergold* loaded. It is so quiet I can hear the tension on the string. My bow creaks. Footsteps race down the staircase and into the dining hall of the inn, then out the front door. I focus my breathing and drop to my place. I sit there for another half hour or so before I feel comfortable that nothing else will attack me. I come out of my zone but stay on guard. The wood creaks beneath my feet as I make my way around the circular staircase.

Through the inn I go until I am outside. The wind is howling to the north of me. Dirt kicks into my eyes. I cover my face and turn away from the wind. In the distance, a cathedral has two torches fully ablaze. I look behind me, then back at the cathedral, to my final task.

* * *

I approach the cathedral steps. It disappears, then moves roughly a mile away. I now stand at the cusp of a lake of black glass. The glass has an intricate network of white lights coursing just under the surface.

I reach the toe of my boot toward it. The surface bends the toe of my boot. Because it feels hard, I feel confident enough to stand on it. The network of white lights under the black glass reminds me of an atrium on a cloudless night, in the middle of nowhere.

As I walk across the lake, a grey, shadowed version of myself appears and smiles at me. Then Atia appears and starts walking by my side. I try to speak to her but she won't respond. Then I see Ranger, casually flipping his pocket dagger he loves so much walking toward me. Then a chained Bertram, then Kam, then Rust and eventually, the rest of the team. One by one they appear as my own personal convoy to my last trial. I pay special attention to Faris. I miss her so much.

After twenty minutes of walking with my escort, they form a line in front of the cathedral. One by one they bow, then vanish. I nod to each one, then enter the threshold of the cathedral. It is in complete ruins. Moonlight shines through holes where buttresses once held the peaks of this building. The rubble has long disintegrated into dust and ash, with random pieces of broken stone scattered like a mountain of shale. The rubble increases upward to where the altar must have been.

I walk up the rubble. At the top of the pile, the moonlight shines through the biggest hole in the roof. The wind kicks dust around and rattles old wooden doors as though ghosts were walking into a saloon. I see a narrow passage down into the depths, and know that I must go. I know that whatever I am to face will be in the darkness that waits. I traverse downward. My footing is the largest pieces of rubble I can find, until I get to a staircase that seems unbroken. A torch is at the top of the stairs. I grab it and proceed to spiral downward.

As I travel down, my heart beats faster. I am reminded of the nightmare I had when I drank Bertram's concoction. I remember my torch being drowned by the dark, and something chasing me. I remember being grabbed around the neck.

I proceed for what feels like a lifetime. Down and down I go. The earth down here is cool and damp. Lifeless. The torch flickers in my hand, dancing shadows around me and in my mind's eye. Still, I walk.

I begin to hear a noise. It gets louder as I go down. It is the sound of a thousand monks singing a single bass chord in unison.

Aaaaaaaaaaaaaaaaaaaaaaaaaaaaaaaaaaaaaaaaaaaaaaaaaaaaaaaaaaaaaa aa aaaaaaaaahh

Then the beat of deep drums in the dark.

Aaaaaaaaaaaaaaaaaaaaaaaaaaaaaaaaaaaaaaaaaaaaaaaaaaaaaaaaaaaaaaaa aa aaaaaaaaahh

The sound sends chills down my spine. Nothing but a drawn out chord and the sounds of drums. I focus on my breathing and continue down. I continue down past the noise. I never saw where it was coming from. My torch dies when I reach the bottom of the staircase.

I enter a medium sized-rectangular room. There is a twenty foot long hole that serves as a gap between myself and the middle of the room. The middle of the room has a space about the length of the floor I stand on now, which is not much. Then there is another twenty foot gap before an altar at the other side of the room. A black chest with a golden key inserted in the lock sits in between two casks holding the same green-smoking liquid. Behind it is a large stone honeycomb built deep into the earth.

In front of the altar is a hooded man with red eyes. His wrist is attached to a chain that leads to something deep in the honeycomb. Three torches line either side of the walls in this rectangular room. A beast stirs in the comb.

The only light in the room is provided by the wall torches, the red eyes and the casks. It is hard to see detail. Shadows continue to play tricks on my mind.

The only sounds are my breathing and the rumble of a large chain being moved by an even larger beast. I sit in silence for minutes.

"You have made a grave mistake coming here, Nirue," the hooded figure says with a deep, curdling voice. His voice resonates throughout the chamber.

"I didn't come here because I wanted to. You summoned me."

He laughs to himself. *"I did no such thing. You were hallucinating. You are victim of a story that only exists in your mind."*

He's lying. "Well I'm here. So if we are going to dance, let's dance but I'm tired of waiting around. I want to go home."

A long pause. *"There is no going home, Nirue. I was hoping you would find me, but I knew you would not understand the gravity of your decision."*

"I don't understand. You're my last task."

"Not quite. You see, Nirue, I am all that is evil in this world. I am the soulless that walk the streets below the mountain. I am the darkness that drowns the light. I am the black eyes. I am the knife that hides in the shadows."

"So what does that mean for me?"

He hisses, *"I am the evil that drowns any and all hope of you going home. Thousands of years ago, I was trapped in this desolate area—forced to carry out my intentions by means unknown to your simple intellect. I have seen many of your kind come, but have not seen one go. I cannot leave this room, unless I am invited out. It has taken me many centuries to figure a way to lure that invitation to my doorstep, and here you are."*

"I haven't invited you anywhere."

"But you have. You see, you cannot leave this room." I look behind me toward the stair case. I quickly move to it. A wall is where the stairs once were.

He laughs again but this time, louder. It pierces my ear the way Bertram's did in the arena. *"You are faced with a decision, Nirue. A game of sorts. You can stay on that side of the room, where I cannot touch you until you die of natural causes. Or, you can participate in my game, but my game has consequences."*

"Go on."

"Three riddles I shall ask, and three you shall answer. If you get one right, your staircase will reappear and you can go home."

"So what happens if I get them wrong?"

He motions his handless arms open. *"Each time you are wrong, I move closer to you. If you get all three wrong, then you will fight me in the dark. I can assure you that this is not something you should find victory in."*

"And if you kill me?"

"I am released from the chains that have held me for so very long," he rattles the chains, causing the beast to stir in the comb.

"And if I decide to kill you now?"

He laughs again, *"You can't kill me until I try to kill you."*

What do I do now? This isn't my final task? It has to be, right? I mean Bertram told me to come here. *Evergold* appeared in my room. Did he betray me? What is my other option—to die? I made up my mind in the room with the Jboynei that I will fight before closing my eyes and dying. My heart sinks as I think of how it would affect the people I have come to love. Am I condemning everyone I love to die if I go forward? What will happen to the people of Hardrain? Or Rust, Dalk, Kam, Ranger . . . Faris. What will happen to the city of Rizcarth, or the innocent citizens of Pantine? But what if I kill him?

It's minutes before I realize that I have been sitting down and tracing in the grey sand. Well, if he has been trapped once, he can be trapped again. I have nothing to lose, and Bertram sent me here for a reason. I've got to give this a shot.

"Let's dance."

In that moment, giant red eyes appear from the honeycomb. I feel like prey. Almost shocked, the man says, **"Thank you for your invitation."** I can feel him smiling. He must be so confident right now—and why wouldn't he be? I have never been particularly good at riddles, and I have a single arrow.

He levitates off the ground. He is just above the chest when he lets out a shriek. A shriek so cold and loud and sinister that I cover my ears and drop to my knees. What is this thing? Stay calm.

"I wake the senses and anyone can come. The absence of souls leaves me lonely."

I drop to my place. I focus my mind and begin to forget my surroundings. Before I am completely gone, I notice the first torch begin to dwindle. As the torch dwindles, figures on nooses appear. They hang from the ceiling and appear at random. As they appear, the rope they hang from spins and audibly stretches. They are a timer. The more bodies and the less light, the less time I have.

Focus. Let's start with the first part. What wakes the senses? Spices. Pain. Pain . . . I like that, because anyone can come to pain. But then there is the part of the souls. What has no souls but is pain? An evil doctor?

The torch continues to burn out, bodies line every available space in the room. *Think*, Nirue, think! Okay, so I've got pain. Now what has pain and no souls?

"Times up." "I—I . . . an evil doctor?"

His laughter echoes around the room. **"A tomb."** This is not a good start.

My heart sinks into my chest. The torch on his end of the room goes out. The chain rattles as he laughs and levitates to the middle platform. I have a better view of him now. It looks just like the creature that was hanging in my room at the inn. His eyes change from red to black. I get a feeling that he is somehow gaining power. His hands are green and nails are grey. He clacks them against the chain, which I now see is attached to his wrist. I cannot make out the shape or size of the beast, but I do make out its silhouette emerging from the comb. It opens its red eyes for a moment, then closes them so as to stay hidden in the dark.

"Time for riddle number two. The more you answer wrong, the closer I am to you. Are you ready?"

I take a deep breath. "Ready as I'll ever be."

"Did I forget to mention they get harder?"

"Bring it, don't sing it." I drop to my place and envision every word he chants.

"My shell will not deter. In the depths of the flame I spawn. Bloody hands rip at me when tired. If I am in front of you, you would not take notice. Yet, I will not quickly go."

What has a shell that does not act as a shell? A turtle? No. A nut of some kind? Yes—a nut! Okay, but in the flames it spawns. What type of nut spawns in the flames? Isn't there a nut my grandmother used to roast to get to the good part? I think it is a chestnut, but I'm pretty sure a cashew comes in a shell too. Let's hold off on deciding that. Okay, the bloody hands. Why would bloody hands rip at it? I got it—it's saying the starving must not wait to roast it, which makes their hands bloody. The torch burns at half flame. The creaking of ropes disrupts my thoughts momentarily. My heart races and I think quicker.

Okay, so I am back to where I just was. Which nut is it? Which has a harder shell? The last part . . . I will not quickly go. So which nut has the harder shell, and is harder to eat? Both are easy to eat. Not sure which one is harder to open. I figure my odds are fifty-fifty.

"I'm ready to answer." He extends his hands as if to say "proceed."

"A chestnut." The flame goes out and his fingers clack against his shackles. The beast screams with open eyes that illuminate the low ceiling. *"The answer is bread."*

"Bread?" I scream to him. I am actually angry. What a crap answer. "How do bloody hands rip at bread? And how does bread not quickly go?"

He laughs as though heartily entertained by my utter miss. I get the feeling that he is very confident of his chances now.

"Have you not studied war, Nirue? Do you not know that bread is one of the easiest food sources to transport and keep in a time of war?" That actually makes sense to me.

He moves so that he is levitating nearly four feet away from my ledge, directly in front of me. I see him for who he truly is now. He really is all that is evil. Darkness shrouds him like the top of this mountain that I am under. His body is defiled. He's been sliced open with a blade, yet his wounds seem to only fester, not heal. His teeth are sharp and rotted. His lips are purple and his eyes are now white. The chain dragging against the ground brings me to a flashback of being in prison. He is the reason for the black eyes.

The beast leaps from the back and opens its eyes without blinking. If one truly sees a white light when going to heaven, this is what it must see before going to hell. Get it together, Nirue. This is just a tactic. They are trying to intimidate you.

"It is now time for your last riddle. What a joy it will be to kill you. How long I have been chained to this incredulous BEAST!" He rips at the chain causing the beast to howl. Again, I fall to my knees. The loudness makes my eyes water. Most of the chain now hangs in the depths of the gap. I rise to my knees one last time.

"I regret to inform you that nobody has ever heard this one before. Indeed, it is one I have crafted in the years I have suffered in this tomb. A thousand years of thinking can produce quite a complex scenario for the inexperienced mind."

I barely muster the courage to respond with a feigned confidence. "Do your worst."

Before he begins, he slashes at his throat—the same way he did in my room. *"Thank you for hanging yourself, Nirue."* He begins.

"You can trust me in a place of impossibility, for my enemies lie where you cannot see. The needy seek me for life, but the unsuspecting shall surely perish. Death follows the undeserving."

I let out a deep breath and drop to my place. Let's work backward this time. While I try to think, I am flooded with horrible memories. Memories of being chased in the darkness is the first. I grab my ears and shake my head, but I can't get rid of it—it's like a movie I'm being forced to watch. "What are you doing to me! This isn't fair!" His laughter shakes the walls.

Okay think. Who dies undeservedly? Children of a plague? Children surely never deserve to die, but what els------ah! I see my mother, lying over my carcass. She can no longer cry, because she has cried too much. I see her look at someone like she no longer wants to live. "STOP THIS! STOP!" I scream while the white and red eyes stare at me. This is exactly what they wanted. *"You haven't much time, Nirue."* Bodies appear faster than ever. People I love hang from the ceiling with blue faces and bulging eyes. Andrew's train accident replays through my mind. My hand reaching out for his. The look on his face. The realization of what he had done. My scream echoes through the chamber as he is torn away from me.

Tears stream down my face. Why must I go through this? Why must my mother? First Andrew, now me? "This is mutinous," she would tell me. I can see her now. "I told you not to be so reckless, why must you abandon my orders you fool! Look what you have done." The eyes weigh on me like the weight of a thousand worlds. They grow larger in expectation as my flame dwindles. My family begins to appear on either side of the levitating being.

One last try—wait a second. Mutinous. Death follows the undeserving—mutiny on a ship. Let's try the others. Trust in a place of impossibility—the ocean. Enemies where you cannot see—the depths of the ocean. The needy seek me for life—a shipment of goods to an army or city in need. Unsuspecting shall perish—I really think this is it. Could it be? Could his own tricks have backfired on him? Is it really a ship?

Time is nearly out. I have no other choices but a ship. There is simply not enough time to think of another answer. Then, another movie plays in my head. A friendly one. I can see him bright as day back at camp. Bertram. He looks at me with a hand on my shoulder. "Remember, Nirue" he said, *"Appearance is everything."*

If I answer this right, the world will continue to be plagued by this monster. I chose to participate because of one variable—*Evergold*. I knew that there was a reason it appeared in my room. I knew that I only had one golden arrow for a reason. But I cannot kill this creature if I answer correctly. Appearance is everything.

"Times up," the creature says as it clacks in expectation.

"I don't know, man, I just don't know!" My heart has never beat harder in my life. What a mix of emotions this is—sadness, regret, fear . . . hope.

"Is that your final answer?"

Feigning tears I reply, "No. I might as well give it a shot. But I have a proposition."

"I can almost certainly guarantee you that I will not accept."

I remove *Evergold* and unsheathe the bow, moving slightly to my left, then place them before him, bending to my knees. Through tear filled eyes I align myself so that, if he attacks straight down, I can kill both with a single shot. The fact that I only have one shot makes my mouth so dry I can hardly talk. "Clearly you know I am one of the finest warriors this world has to offer. Let me be in your service."

He laughs harder than he ever has before. The chains rattle and the building shakes, sending plumes of dust from the cracks of the walls. *"No, Nirue. We have been enemies since your arrival. It is true that you are everything I needed to be set free. But you will die today. Your answer?"*

He opens his hands revealing twelve long, black nails. Nails that are older and more hardened than any stone I have ever seen.

My instincts scream at me to answer correctly. A ship! Just say a ship and you can escape alive! I know I cannot do this. One last time, I think to myself, *appearance is everything.*

"A horse." The room is completely silent. Simultaneously, in one second, a number of actions occur. The torch goes out. I wrap my fingers at the edge of the arrow. I place its slit into the bow. The creature rolls its eyes in the back of its hear and dives with a scream. I pull the arrow back and let go.

CHAPTER FIFTY-ONE

Do it, Nirue. Do it. I love you and I believe in you.
Believe in yourself.

Andrew in a dream,
sometime between trial three and four

THE ARROW ILLUMINATES THE ROOM as it flies. First into the creature, then the beast. Like a bomb catching its fuse, the two creatures scream in unison and explode. The building begins to go down. The earth shakes and dust blinds my vision. The staircase appears. I grab *Evergold* and begin to run. I run as fast as I ever have. The earth continues to shake. Stones fall at my back. One catches me on my ankle. Not again. I am reminded of running from the Jboynei and how that turned out. The walls tremble as I run.

I brace my arms against them to avoid falling backward. This building is imploding. I run faster and faster. I am nowhere near the top, and I fear I will become stuck in this place. I think back to everything I have been through. I think about Rizcarth and sitting in Maji's chamber with Signy. I think about escaping through the stream. I think about finding flowers for the Tempo in Hardrain. I think about the bravery of young Sero—which gives me the courage to push on.

I think of being kidnapped and stabbed. I think of the torches in the cold snow. I think of the games and all that I have lost. I think on Atia. Oh beautiful and sweet Atia. How innocent and undeserving of death you are. I grit my teeth. The earth shakes even worse. The stairs behind me disappear into the abyss. I do not even notice that I am hyperventilating. At least if I run out of breath, I won't feel it when I die.

I begin to panic. There's no way I can make it to the top. The abyss closes in on me. I pick up my speed as the ground rumbles. Each step I take is slower than the rate at which the stairs disappear. "HELP!" I scream. I know there is no one out there for me, but still I try. I can now feel the stairs disintegrate beneath my feet, with just enough left in them to propel me upward.

A gap opens in the wall to my right revealing a ledge, and a way out. With the last stair I can climb, I jump and grab the ledge with one hand and I pull myself up. The roof collapses behind me. Before me is a cave of crumbled ruin. I run as fast as I can toward the light. A large stone lands on my back and knocks the wind out of me. I smash my nose on another stone on the ground. I try to push myself up but a jolt of pain weakens my arms. C'mon, Nirue. Is that all you've got? Is it? You've come this far, are you going to quit now? "NO!" I scream to nobody. If this were a different situation, someone would think me crazy. But no one can hear me. I can barely hear myself over the earthquake. I pick myself up and begin to run. I am hobbled but I run. The end of the cave is so close. Keep pushing, man, almost there.

Before I reach the end of the cave, I think I see two people standing on the beach. I sprint toward them.

* * *

Ranger and Bertram stand on the beach watching the mountain come down. Bertram lets out an audible sigh. Ranger stares with vigorous intent at the dust and rock coming down.

"If he isn't here now, he never will be. The world will be forever doomed, Ranger—but at least you won't be here to see it. Come, let's get you home before I stand corrected."

"I—I don' understand. Where is Nirue?" Bertram sheds a tear, but maintains his stoic presence. "He's gone. Come." Bertram motions him to a jumpkey stationed just off the beach. Ranger hangs his head in sadness. "I never thought it would be him. Out of all of us, I surely thought Nirue would be the one to make it. I don't deserve to be standing here."

Bertram doesn't acknowledge it. He begrudgingly moves palm fronds and boxes away from the jumpkey. "Come, Ranger. There isn't time." Bertram has the gait of a man who knows all is lost.

Ranger, after one last look toward the mountain moves toward the key. "It was a pleasure knowing you, Ranger. Congratulations. You are a fine man." Bertram begins to whisper something under his breath. "WAIT!" Ranger screams as he jumps off the platform. The jumpkey turns green just after he gets off. He grabs Bertram by the collar and whips him around, finger pointed toward the plume of dust. Through the dust a shadow appears, moving at a very slow pace. It grows larger and larger as it gets closer. It's me.

CHAPTER FIFTY-TWO

Faith. That's all this ever was. An opportunity to truly understand it, to truly capture it and to reconcile with that which you have assumed an afterthought for so long. For in the same way a little faith can proclaim the greatness of the unseen, a lot of faith can overcome even the greatest of odds.

How far will you fill your meter? Have you not noticed that when faith slipped through your hands like a wet rope, so did your chance of survival? Have you also noticed that when it is strong, the unseen works? Faith is all it ever was.

Andrew to his beloved brother, Nirue

THEY EMBRACE ME, MY ARMS under their necks, the help necessary to escape the crumbling mountain. I place my hands on my knees, then lie on my back and motion them away. It takes me a moment to catch my breath. Ranger asks me ten questions at once, "What happened? Are you okay? What is Bertram talking about? Did you figure—" I wave him off.

When I finally catch my breath, I say, "You were right."

"About what?" Ranger asks.

"We shouldn't have drank that much wine." Bertram, Ranger and I engage in deep, bellied laughter that again, probably looked insane if you didn't know the circumstances. We all shed tears, but tears of pure joy.

The sun had just come up over the horizon. We talk for a while as we head toward the jumpkey. Moored to a nearby palm is a small rowboat, pointed directly through the channel I swam not too long ago. I look around and notice that the dark haze is gone. I notice that the city of the dead looks as though it has been restored, though, I do not see any sign of life.

I spend nearly an hour reliving the riddles and experience below ground. Ranger tells me of his last quest, which, quite honestly, pales in comparison. After I complete my story, I ask Bertram if that means all evil has left the world. He chuckles and tells me that there is still much evil, but that I had done my part in ridding the world of a large part of it. I am a little disappointed, but happy nonetheless.

After another hour or so of talking, Bertram tells us that we must get into the jumpkey before it expires. He explains that we have but a few minutes left. I begin to walk toward it.

This is everything I have longed for. In every hard circumstance during my trials, I would always think of home and how I cannot wait to embrace my family again. I have literally dreamed of this exact moment for months. Sometimes I would spend hours visualizing these very steps toward the green light. As I get closer, my heart sinks into my chest.

The group has fallen silent, and our steps have gotten slower. I near the jumpkey and look back through the straight. The sun displays a beautiful purple and orange over the sea. I take in a deep breath and smell the clean ocean air. I look into the sky and at the top of the rubble behind me. I let out a deep sigh. When I look at Ranger, I notice him doing the same thing. He manipulates his pocket dagger through his fingers, eyes somewhere else.

"Say . . . Ranger. Have you ever thought about what would happen if you didn't go home?" His face lights up, and in that moment I know he is thinking exactly what I am. "What if we stay?"

He momentarily pauses. "I suppose I just worry for my family is all."

Bertram interjects, "Nirue. Surely you can't mean it. This is your chance! You're one of the few!"

"I know, I know. I just . . ."

I think about my family. I think about that image I saw below. My mother looked so dejected. I can't do this to them, can I? But let's also be realistic. What are the odds that I come out of this okay? Would that make my family resent me, if I am no longer Nirue? If I can no longer think? Is that how I want to live? A vegetable?

I can't let them down, and I never would. But, what if . . . what if this is what I have always wanted? What if I never find an adventure like this again? I am a dreamer, and have always dreamed of saving the world. And I have—for now. But, why would I leave this place, if this is what I have truly always wanted?

Ranger places a hand on my shoulder and looks into my eyes. "Like the beginning, Nirue, I put my trust in you. I know I haven't been a perfect teammate, but, you have never lead me astray. Whatever you choose, I choose too."

I look at the rising sun. I see birds circling the cliffs off the straight. I look at Bertram who does not give away any emotion. I look at the jumpkey and then at the boat. I walk toward the jumpkey and reach my hand to touch it. Don't.

I was not content with my life on earth. I hated the monotony of daily tasks, of never feeling excited. Then I came to this place and everything changed. I realized that contentment is a learned trait, that everything I have ever wanted was always right in front of me. Still, throughout these trials, all I wanted to do was get home. But now what do I want, now that I have won? Isn't *this* everything I have ever wanted? Contentment is a learned trait.

My gut hasn't lead me astray yet, and I know what I must do. I turn to Bertram and Ranger. "What do you say, Ranger? Let's have one more adventure." He grins from ear to ear, and hustles to the boat. He grabs the oars and prepares for us to row away. Bertram smiles too.

"You really are something else, Nirue." I grip forearms with him out of respect.

"You have been good to me. I knew it was you all along." He chuckles for a moment, and doesn't let me know one way or the other. I hop into the boat and grab the other set of oars.   Anxiety sets in as I wonder if I am making the right decision. I look back at the jumpkey, which is now turning white. I could still make it if I turn back now.

I turn my back to it, look at Ranger and then at the colors of the water. After a long pause, feeling whole, I let out a sigh and begin to row.

TESTIMONY

FIRST AND FOREMOST, I MUST give all glory to my King and Creator, the humble carpenter from the plains of Nazareth. I had traveled the same road many times, and every time I found myself empty.

Filled with hurt, longing for something, I sought out the things of the world to fill my void. But after time, everything left me more alone—more void and without purpose than before. Then God came into my life, and I have never been the same. He is true healing.

I know this may seem counter-intuitive due to some of the choice language in the book, or for even those who know me personally and my past mistakes. But this book is a testament of faith, of both myself and God. You see, I wish not for people to view me as a perfect person—a figure to be torn to shreds by my past, present and future actions. I want people to know that no matter what you've done, what you've been through or how you feel, God still loves you.

Forget all the debate on what you think you know. I'm here to tell you that God loves you more than you will ever comprehend—that's real. By simply accepting that love by believing that Jesus Christ is God, and that

He died on the cross for your sins, everything will start to change for the good, forever.

As an aside, I almost gave up on this book. So many times I wanted to quit or bury it in my desk and get back to playing video games or golf (which I still did, a lot). But if even one of you are out there, reading this, and it gave you some semblance of hope—if it plumed the spirit of motivation in your chest, or even helped you escape some temporary pain—then it was all worth it in the end. To God be the glory.

Forever Your Brother,

Matt

ACKNOWLEDGEMENTS

THE SUPPORT OF MY FAMILY and friends are unmatched. To my loving and supportive wife, thank you for pushing me to finish this. Thank you for believing in me when I did not believe in myself. To my beautiful baby girl—I love you, Bibi. Keep your eyes ever upward. Dream.

To my dad and mom, Bob and Priscilla, thank you for all of your love and support over the years. You stayed with me and helped shape me into the man I am today. To Anthony, Katie, Becky, Ellie, Sam, Jack and Lily: I love you all with all my heart, my siblings. You all have greatness within you. Believe and let it fly.

Shout out to Travis and Kyle—you are some great friends. To the rest of you who are close to me, I apologize for omitting your names, but you know I care for you and I look forward to our life-long friendship. You know who you are.

To all the dreamers out there: Go for it. If nothing else, this book is evidence that God can take the lowliest of us and raise us up, if but for just a moment. Chase your dreams, because, why not?

—Matt

www.ingramcontent.com/pod-product-compliance
Lightning Source LLC
Chambersburg PA
CBHW020356260626
47156CB00007B/2141